THE WAR OF WINDS

THE SEVEN ISLES

A.R. KNIGHT

CHAPTER I
THE STONE OF SOULS

Wax feared he'd never get used to the voices in his head, and now he had another.

The Tamas skar shone in its lower left spot, warmth not making it through the thick Tamas tunic Wax wore for the ceremony. The show. The performance. It was hard to gauge what the crowd thought all this was, as their expressions, sitting amid the same theater where Eujo's attempted etching had been narrowly prevented only a day ago, mixed in bemusement with boredom.

"Congratulations," said the masked man who'd handed over the skar, the same one who'd called out Eujo's fate.

He was Wax's sole partner on the otherwise empty stage, the exchange marked by a few feeble musicians in a nearby pit, plucking at their instruments. Eujo and Wax's Guardians, the bandit Torny and Wax's sister Bliss, were out front, waiting for the pomp to end so they could head to the docks and get off the damned isle.

Tamas hadn't exactly been a pleasure, and, when the masked man, his crimson robes ruffling, leaned in, Wax expected the problems to continue.

"Leave quickly," the man whispered, extending an arm to usher Wax off-stage. Unsaid apologies tainted his rueful tone. "Normally, there'd be a more grand affair for this. A play, honors, feasting, and far, far more drinking."

"But?" Wax asked when the man fell silent, answering the cue.

"It's the Najahn. They're being aggressive. That skar you carry now? It's my own. They've refused to let us gather any more."

"You're giving me your own—"

As curtains closed about them, the masked man chuckled, "I'll get another. What's important is that we hold to tradition. You performed, you deserve the reward. Now go."

Wax didn't need to ask why the man still sounded nervous. The Najahn didn't just want to keep the skars, they wanted to take the stones from anyone who had them. They'd know, now, that Wax and Eujo were present in Tamas's capital, and would probably have their purple and black thugs running right this way.

In fact, the masked man might've turfed the Tamas skar onto Wax just to avoid getting in trouble himself. Convenient.

If Wax had wanted to confront the Tamas about it, though, the time had passed: a look around backstage confirmed only workers bustling around, setting the theater for a later show, one blissfully free of Renewals, skars, and the fate of the world.

Torny, bandit and best dressed of their bunch, in svelte, fuzzy greens and blues, whistled as Wax approached and lifted his necklace. The Tamas skar did its job, glittering, even as, inside his mind, Wax heard the stone whisper alongside his friend's approval. Less in real words, more through impressions and flavored gibberish, the skars were imperfect assets. Capable of miracles, capable of mass destruction, Wax had nevertheless grown used to their constant jabbering.

Like being back home, in crowded, bubbling Kitaye.

The bandit's counterpart, Bliss, stood nearby, working on a fresh staff with a whittling blade. Every stroke cut aside stripes to replace with iron bands, a technique she'd learned on Foti, the fiery isle. Too many hard heads among their enemies, Bliss signed, and she didn't want her staff to break mid-battle.

A head far from the hardest stood near the cart's head, watching the meandering Tamas crowds going about their cool, but not cold, day. Livier, Kance assassin and one-time foe, kept a hand near his rapier and the other on the cart itself, helping to hold the man upright. Despite getting Vis skars from both Eujo and Wax, the man was taking his time recovering from a burning brawl a couple weeks back. Not that Wax minded: a Livier compromised was a Livier he didn't need to fear.

Much.

"How's it feel?" Torny asked, following her whistle, "You're tied, now."

"Tied?" Eujo, the Kance Queen and looking it as she sat on the cart's piled satchels drinking something from an earthen mug. "He's going to win. I'll never get a Tamas skar now."

"Unless I steal it for you," Torny said.

"Thought you were my Guardian?" Wax asked, coming up to the cart and slipping the necklace back beneath his shirt.

"She's a Queen, Wax. I gotta follow the power."

'She has a point,' Bliss signed, glancing up from her metal work. 'There's no Renewal anymore. Eujo is real.'

"I'm plenty real," Wax protested. "Just need Kance and Noctia, and then . . . "

He trailed off, a too-common trait when this topic came up. Torny and Bliss didn't push him on it, because they knew as well as Wax did that anything following the seven skars was murky at best. Getting a Noctia skar seemed impossible anyway: the whole isle had flipped from peaceful watcher over the isles to a marauding force, attempting to control everything through their voulges and armored soldiers.

And even if he did manage to get all seven, what then? He'd promised Pan to get the stones, and that promise had been enough to keep Wax going, but to what end?

A question he could put off answering till Wax had all the skars, perhaps, but one growing louder nonetheless.

"We should be going, my queen," Livier said, "now that the Vis is back. Your ship should be coming into port soon."

"Then let's go," Eujo replied, looking up from the short, scrawled missive next to her mug. "I hate this place anyway."

That note, urgent, was the one naming Eujo Kance's sole Queen and requesting her immediate return. She'd been staring at it for most of the last day. Wax would like to say he could understand why, but Pan's dying promise was the closest he'd come to any real destiny. Still, he climbed the cart and sat next to Eujo, hand finding hers, a grip returned.

What that was, what those intertwined fingers, hinted at was still unknown. The last night had been burned in deep conversations with Livier, the Queen catching up on what Kance was like now, what she needed to expect. Wax, soothed with ale, had slept.

The Tamas skar tried to read Eujo's mood, burbling over the other stones only for Wax to push it away. Like choosing not to listen to a conversation, or to ignore a rumbling stomach. He'd rely on old fashioned smiles, touches, and the soft crinkle around her eyes as Eujo held his look for a long moment before returning to the note, her mug—black tea—and what it meant for today, tomorrow, and beyond.

Bliss joined Livier at the cart's driving bench, the sole sun-dappled pony hitched up ready to pull them towards the dock. Torny, as she preferred, took her own seat on the cart's rear, humming some tune, tossing a stiff carrot up between bites.

The Tamas port buzzed with Winter's slow decline. Fresh ale barrels dominated, though wines and other foods added just enough variety to keep things interesting. Heavy galleons rested near the docks, recently returned to waters from dry wintering slots. Southern trading trips would be starting soon, to hear the clamber say it, and nice days like this one made for a good chance to get ahead.

What Wax didn't see amid the port's bluster was the *Storm's Edge*, Eujo's personal ship captained by the inimitable Deux. They'd last bid the vessel an aborted farewell on Whent's southern coast, dashing away under night's cover after Wax had, well, immolated an estate. Wax cringed at the memory, a reminder the skars were hardly servants ready to do his bidding. More like wild friends, willing to listen and then take matters into their own hands.

"We're early," Livier said as Bliss guided the cart to an open spot before a dockside warehouse.

"Or Deux's late," Eujo replied.

Their entourage drew mild attention, mostly from other carts and porters having to dodge around them. Otherwise, the port bustled enough to keep Wax and his friends at the bottom of anyone's concern. Anonymity sat well, and Wax stayed in the cart, watching the horizon, while Eujo and Livier bantered back and forth about Deux's timeliness.

"The Najahn could have found him," Livier said. "We ought to slip away, Eujo. Find some sailor's hole to hide in until Deux arrives."

"He'll give us away the moment he shows," Eujo countered. "If the Najahn are really hunting us, then we'll need to board as fast as possible. Drinking ale in some dark tavern won't help that."

"Don't think that's going to work anyway," Torny said, stepping off the cart's back and brandishing the dagger down the dock. "Guessing we're about to get noticed."

A galleon bearing Foti's red and orange flag slipped out to sea, shoved by dockworkers with long poles. As the massive vessel moved, its bulk revealed a purple and black frigate in the next slot down. Najahn soldiers, armed and armored, stood near keeping watch. The ship's sails were furled, provision crates sitting along its chosen pier. Reloading for a journey.

Maybe not, then, tasked with finding Wax, Eujo, and their skars.

"Then get on this side of the cart," Livier snapped. "Don't stand in the open."

Torny laughed, "What, you think they know us by sight? Got some great drawings of Wax on hand?"

The bandit's snark, though, shriveled quick as their quintet formed up near the pony. A new dockside sound approached: collective curses and the scrapes, bangs of goods on the move. Wax looked northward, the same direction their pony pointed in and opposite the Najahn ship, to see a purple and black contingent heading their way. The group held no voulges—the curved spears were hard to hide—and sported robes, not armor, looking less like soldiers and more like scholars. Stuffed packs and satchels hung heavy in the group.

"Leaving?" Eujo asked the air. "Why?"

"Noctia wants the skars," Torny answered. "Bet these are a bunch from Tamas."

The scholars walked on by, seemingly oblivious, until a pair slowed, their eyes falling not on Wax, not on Eujo, but on the Kance killer next to them both.

Livier muttered a unique curse, one that had Eujo blushing.

"Now this is a strange coincidence," said the first scholar, an older woman with more than one mark across her face. As she spoke, the rest of the scholars slowed, turned, putting almost two dozen stares on their group. "Last I saw you, you were pawing through our library on Noctia. Looking for information on Whent and its Golden Gash. Now you're here." The scholar weighed Livier, gauging his limped appearance. "Did you find what you were looking for?"

"I did," Livier said, offering up a slight bow. "Your assistance very helpful."

"So they're dead, then? The traitors?" The scholar let her look drift to Wax and the others. "You said they had a committed a grievous offense against Kance. You were so angry, and your hand . . . " The scholar nodded towards the marks on Livier's palm, brought about by Wax and his deadly dinner fork. "At least that's healed."

Livier began to answer, and Wax would've listened save

for a soft tap on his left arm. Bliss, partially hidden behind the cart. She flicked her head southward, along the dock.

Running towards them, their satchels abandoned, were two Najahn scholars. When they started shouting, Wax didn't have to guess their words.

He only hoped Deux wouldn't be too late.

CHAPTER 2
THE SKY PALACE

Kance spread below him, its many spires and their offshoots a girded web Quik had only begun to understand. An evening and now a morning, and a late one, going by the sunlight filtering all around him. Quik had to suppress a shiver, even a shout as he shifted beneath the light blanket, the small pillow.

Even in winter, he'd been advised, the nests would get hot.

Molded glass formed the enclosure, save the steps and small circular door to Quik's right. Two bronzed metal loops kept the glass container in place, holding it to the Sky Palace, a bland name that nonetheless conveyed exactly where Quik was. Guests of the two Queens, one they'd left to die and another . . . lost?

Quik rubbed his eyes, blinked at the gliders, the plant strings, the birds filling the air beneath, around, and above him. The usual needs—food, drink, somewhere to expel them both—burbled to life.

Where would his brother be right now? The last Najahn report put them on Whent, fleeing east, but that'd been some time ago. Quik hadn't had much chance to get information after that, what with Gladdring's rebellion.

Which left Quik where, exactly?

The original reason to stay on Noctia, to give Quik time to recover, to build a relationship with the purple and black, to get their support to help his brother had failed. Had collapsed so completely that Quik was now an enemy of that same organization. He'd lost his friends, family, and what little help he had came from an even bigger traitor, one manipulative and taciturn enough to all-but guarantee Quik would find himself betrayed or cut loose before long.

But without knowing where Wax was, Quik couldn't go after his brother. Not with the fiends, the fighting, the turmoil.

The isle below, though, presented something different. Kance wasn't Vis, was, with its lancing spires, mountains, and misty valleys, far from it, but the natural beauty brought with it a home Quik realized he missed, realized he might be better off returning to.

Vis, so rumor had it, was fighting the Najahn too. His parents might be laboring under a voulge's threat.

One Quik could try, at least, to fight.

Some clarity restored, Quik tossed off the blanket, pushed through the circular door into the odd round node serving as entry for at least four nests. A slim hallway, similarly sporting curving glass on top and straight clear slats below, would bring him into the palace proper. Before then, said a silver-blue Kance robe hanging from a hook next to his door, the Vis would need to get dressed.

Gladdring's voice did as much work to guide Quik as did his dim memories of the tour the night before, a walkthrough that came after so much exhaustion on the seas. Tension compounded by fears the Najahn crew would turn on him and Gladdring, leave the pair either dead or dead in the water, the Najahn cutter now holding a few more corpses. Quik had passed out hard last night, and found the late morning reprise a confusing one.

Kance, it seemed, loved portraits, and all done in a dappled style. Framed in dried filaments, soft rainbows haloing past Queens, Kance soldiers, and, according to the gilded nameplates beneath each pearl wall-hugging portrait, random citizens. What had Jonas Mylien, merchant, done to deserve his pasty visage hung in the palace? Or Paliva Veen, caretaker to the infirm?

Did Kance pick its heroes at random?

Beyond the portraits, the Sky Palace adored blues in all shades, and plastered the color on chairs, benches, hard tile at Quik's feet. Servants, soldiers, and bureaucrats bustled here and there, more than a few stopping to stare at Quik's inked face, the heavy gauntlets hanging at his waist.

Those weapons, wood-carved and now, thanks to a Najahn blacksmith, metal-tipped, would never leave Quik's side again. There'd been too many times chaos appeared with little clue, that deadly force was demanded, to err on the side of politeness.

After all, Quik was a Vis. The other isles thought him a wild man, so why not embrace it?

Gladdring held the throne room's attention, a wide chamber near the palace's summit. Quik had taken one of the many elevators—working through some elaborate pulley system he had neither the time or desire to under-stand—up from his nest, and found he was far from the first, or second person to arrive. He was not, however, too late for breakfast.

The spread, a fish-and-fruit medley, with mountain spring water, lay on a side table just inside the room, and

Quik busied himself loading a plate while Gladdring continued his overwrought tale to a crowd of killers and paper-pushers. They hooked on Gladdring's every word, the expressions ranging from sober determination on the soldiers's parts, to wide-eyed hand-wringing by the scrawny politicians. Gladdring, though he hadn't tried to claim the throne, nonetheless had the crowd circled around him, hands waving about like a conductor spinning the group to his tune.

Quik hadn't much liked those grand Noctia orchestras, and he didn't bother joining in this performance either. Instead, he ate, drank, and waited off to the side until Gladdring concluded, ending his diction with so many suggestions as to send the Kance crew off, dazed and driven. Quik then frittered more minutes away while Gladdring did one-on-one dances, the former Tenet and current Noctia traitor making sure to give Quik knowing nods here and there.

As if Quik would fall for that anymore.

He could consent to being used, but believing that Gladdring held anything more than his own success in the man's black heart . . . Not after the Noctia Renewal tipped over the cutter's edge into the water.

"We have them," Gladdring said, at last, when he came over to Quik, pulling the Vis hunter away from the big room and its twin glass thrones.

Gladdring held his tongue until he had Quik into a small side room, one that appeared meant for servants needing a break. Gladdring slid a narrow bolt across the door, shutting them in. Their only company was a single stool and tiny table, a small window near the ceiling casting just enough light to keep them from needing the tiny lantern on the right wall.

"A private room," Gladdring explained as Quik scanned the space. "It's quite normal. The Queens would use them." The Tenet crouched, causing Quik to step back, and ran his fingers along the door's bottom. Black cloth pressed down to the ground. "It deadens sound. Difficult for spies to listen in."

"Who would be spying?"

"The other Queen, obviously."

No surprise there. Quik had seen that rivalry up close, nearly died to its consequences.

"I trust you slept well?" Gladdring asked, clasping his hands, but otherwise seeming to really mean the remark. "They're a bit strange, aren't they, the nests?"

"Used to it."

Gladdring blinked, then smiled. "Of course you would be. Sleeping in the trees can't be too different, can it?"

"I meant, I'm used to being in odd places. Doesn't scare me anymore."

"Ah." Gladdring's nod came slower now. The man did like his gestures. "Then perhaps you'll be happy to know we won't be leaving this one soon. The Kance believe our story, and believe in the skars we gave them even more. I've secured our appointments as advisors."

"Our?"

"Well, me. And you as my personal guard and assistant."

Quik snorted. Gladdring frowned.

"You seem hostile this morning, my Vis friend. Have I done something to upset you?"

"Nothing," Quik replied. "But I'm not going to be your guard or your assistant. I'm going home."

Quik might've gone on into the full story, about his brother and so on, but giving Gladdring more to work with would only, well, work against Quik. Who knew what chains Gladdring could find in that story to wrap around the hunter?

"To Vis? You know the isle's lost, right?" Gladdring stuck one hand in his robe's pocket. Right where a Tamas skar would probably be waiting. "According to what I heard this morning, Kitaye's under Najahn control. Only Mottilan survives, and that's only a question of time."

"Keep your hands out," Quik said, pointing at Gladdring's pocket. "I know your tricks."

A slight smile, but Gladdring pulled the hand free. "Only some of them, my friend. The point, though, remains. Vis is falling. Kance is our best chance to stop Fassle."

"And do what?" Quik raised the jabbing finger to Gladdring's face. "You keep arguing you're saving the isles. That's what Annalyse kept saying on the beach, when you kept me in the cage, but do you even know how?"

"I'm trying, which is more than what you'll get from Fassle."

"That's not good enough anymore. I'm done waiting for you."

Gladdring looked like he was about to protest, then stopped, a puzzler's look coming over that wrinkled, jowled face.

"You know, I think there's a way we both can get what we want," Gladdring said. "Annalyse. You told her to run to Vis, right?"

Quik shrugged, "It was all we could think of."

"If anyone might have an idea of what to do with all these skars, it would be her." Gladdring smiled in earnest now. "Go home, Quik. Go back to your isle and find the scientist. Bring her back here."

"Why would we come back?"

"Because," Gladdring said, that smile growing broader, "Kance's missing Queen has been found. Alive. And she's on her way. I think you know who's traveling with her."

Wax. Bliss.

A chance to fulfill an old oath.

Gladdring had Quik again, and the manipulative bastard knew it. But what else could the Vis do?

CHAPTER 3
SPLIT SAVIOR

She'd forgotten how it felt to be alone with her own thoughts.

As if you ever were.

Her other self nestled in Maena's mind, always her company, always her companion as they stared at the dirty gray ceiling overhead. The moldering straw beneath them, beneath the worn Rana leathers Maena still put on every morning, added a rotting tinge to the room. She should change them, should clean up the box she'd claimed for herself when the Whent arrived.

A task destined for the bottom of a list that never seemed to move up.

Because we're doing more important work.

That, at least, Maena could agree with. Speaking of . . .

She lurched up, snatched her Whent-fashioned short sword, and brushed clinging straw off her leathers, from her hair. Grabbed a torn tunic and used it as a rag to rub dirt, a random beetle off her face. The bugs were a fact of life in the Dark Below, no worse or better, really, than a Rana ship. At least the rats didn't make it this far down.

Her squat room occupied a corner on the third story of what was, to any onlooker, a carved block. Half natural rock and half stone moved, mortared, and smoothed by tireless corpses, kept alive first by the Dead King and now by Svarde, the Foti barbarian, the construct mirrored more than a dozen others, with still more yet being hewn from the stone itself. What Svarde's plans were for this underground metropolis, Maena wasn't sure.

Last she'd heard, the fiends were going to get an escort up to the surface. Who'd stay down here then? The bodies? Did they even need houses?

Focus, Maena. It's a big day.

Her mirror self, a soul ripped from Maena and remade by a fiend not too many weeks ago, didn't need to remind . . . herself. The activity sang throughout the massive cavern. Carts rumbling, hammers pounding, and shouts calling for this or that to get to here or there. Every command found its following by the silent, dead masses, as they shambled, lurched, and lumbered with gear or goods in tow.

Maena watched it all from her building's doorway—her various roommates were either already working or, having come from some overnight shift, dead asleep, likely with ale's assistance. The Rana captain stifled an itch to draw her blade, cut down a passing corpse bearing a crate of what seemed like boiled mushrooms in its hands. Rations for a walking army.

Though what those firewalkers would eat, Maena wasn't sure.

Probably stragglers.

Maena half-cocked a smile at that. One that slowly fell as she made her way through the bustling city. She went through the huge front gate, its barricade coated with dusted bones from humans and monsters alike. Along a wide tunnel to another large room, this one bearing a thousand battle's scars along its natural walls, its chipped ceiling. In recent days, the space had born as many different weapons, Whent engineers churning at all hours to fortify barriers, build in artillery, and craft a fort from which the Seven Isles could hold back a fiend horde.

Now those barriers stood shunted to the side or split apart, spiked ends stacked atop one another. Ballista bolts lay in thick stacks, their launchers without strings and leaning against walls. The engineers tasked with taking care of them had their heads and hands bent to a different task: churning out thick, strange leathers masked with metals. Too large for any human, they dealt the final blow to Maena's mellow morning mood.

"Ami's talking with them right now. She thinks they understand," Svarde, man of a thousand wounds, said near the room's center.

The barbarian wore only the thinnest armor, though his real defense came from the jagged black blade always at his side. The blade's hilt glistened with opals: Noctia skars. Somehow, the sword kept the gnarled, brutalized warrior alive despite enough damage done to render any normal human to gristle. His partner in conversation had fewer scars but stood just as tall, with a beard now big enough to qualify as a nest for most Rana birds.

Jochi, Whent warlord and master of the northern isle's sweeping cavern conquest, nodded at Svarde's words. His leathers bore better thickness, metal studs, and a nasty ax pair at his waist, one that gave Maena a start every time she saw it now: they'd been Svarde's, once. A gift the barbarian made when his hands switched to favor, to need, the blade.

He'd not asked Maena to take the weapons. Svarde didn't ask Maena much these days.

Because we frighten him.

Frighten a man beyond death? That didn't seem plausible, but there it was, a flinch as Maena approached.

He doesn't understand us. He never did.

Now that, that wasn't quite true. There was a moment, maybe several, on Maena's old ship as it went north, and in the Pits, before all this, before—

"What'd you decide?" Svarde asked her. "Are you coming with us?"

You can't. You know why.

"March to a war with the Whent?" Maena snorted. "Sorry, Svarde. That's something I'll never do."

"Trying to save the Seven Isles doesn't interest you, Rana?" Jochi said, the man's voice a charred snarl after so many pipes, so long shouting orders. "Still holding to the old ways?"

"Some things aren't so easy to forget. Besides, with you all gone, might be I'll finally get something done around here."

Svarde cocked his head at that, but it was Jochi who responded first, "I'm not going either. Too much to do around here, and if I'm hearing Svarde right, it's the firewalkers and the Najahn who'll do most of the fighting. This isn't Whent's war."

"Until Fassle decides it is."

"We have a deal," Svarde said, interrupting. "Fassle and Yarvick know the terms. We bring Kance to heel, the firewalkers get their home. Once Kance sees what they're up against, they'll fold."

"I wouldn't," Maena said. "Not for anything."

Svarde laughed while Jochi glowered. "Then it's a good thing, Maena, I'm not going up against you."

Maena's lip twitched. Every so often, the barbarian showed he still had life, somehow, inside that ruined body.

Don't. It's not worth the pain.

"You won't be going up against anybody if those suits aren't done," Jochi said, looking past Svarde to the biggest working mass of engineers. "I'll hustle them along. Fassle wants you moving by tonight, and the sooner those burning bastards are out of here, the sooner we can start securing the pool."

That's what they called it, the pool. The underground lake holding those swirling gates to what Ami said were other worlds, artifacts of the gods left behind and now falling apart. The firewalkers came from one, apparently because their efforts to save their own world had failed. So now they had a chance to ruin this one.

"I should've asked you," Svarde said, turning to level his full attention on Maena. "About all of this. I don't mean to ignore you."

"But you do."

Svarde winced, but the man held his ground. "You're still not yourself, Maena. Haven't been for a long time. You say odd things, and you're gone at strange hours."

"Strange? Coming from you? A man who never sleeps, never eats, never drinks?"

A nod. "Maybe neither of us is quite what we were."

Damn right.

"If I remember, the Svarde I met wanted to destroy the fiends," Maena said, crossing her arms. "He said he would do anything to rid the world of the monsters. But here you are, fighting for them. Why?"

"Because, Maena, I'm not sure we could win. The firewalkers are numerous, they're strong, they're smart. The isles aren't united."

"A calculation. Coming from you."

Now Svarde frowned. "This is what I'm talking about, Maena. You're hostile one minute, happy the next. I don't get it."

And he never will. He's lost sight of the goal, Maena. We haven't.

"Maybe you'll understand it when you see what they do to Kance," Maena said. "When those monsters burn the sky isle to ash. Maybe you'll remember who you are."

"Maybe. But I hope you, Maena, do the same."

The Rana captain left Svarde there, wandered off into the tunnels. A person watching might assume Maena was going on a stroll, getting some air or even looking for fresh cave water. Whent scouts, soldiers, and people did the same all the time, though they went in groups under Jochi's orders. The Dark Below remained a home for fiends, remained a risk.

Maena walked alone.

As she left behind any curious eyes, ventured higher through narrow bends, a small lantern at her belt giving her light, Maena picked up her pace. Strode with purpose. She turned at notches, almost invisible, carved into the stone at intersections, making her way around the Wound's gaping chasm and up, over, and around. Nearly an hour's journey.

It ended in a bubble, a sloping chamber damp and musty. Holes dotted the floor, almost a lattice in parts. Maena didn't need to go that far, though the chamber extended deep into the dark. Far enough to do what needed doing.

A muffled groan drew her eyes, her light, to the right. Maena reached into the satchel on her back, packed slim for the short journey, and withdrew some of those mushrooms. Wrapped and ready to eat. A water skin too. She bent down, slipped the cloth gag free from the young man's mouth. His eyes were wild, skin more gaunt than the last time she'd visited.

More often, I said. He'll starve if we don't take better care. We need him still.

Maena winced as she loosened the man's bounds, kept a hand on her sword hilt as he ate and drank. At least he'd been following instructions, using those holes to void his bladder and bowels. When he finished, Maena reached back into her pouch, pulled another small box, this one marked with warnings in Whent's blocky script.

"Is this what you told me to find?" Maena asked.

The Whent nodded. Maena turned it in her hand. It seemed so small, for what it promised.

"How many?" She asked.

He gave her a number. One that would take time to for her smith to make without notice, but doable.

"Thank you," Maena said, reaching then to re-tie the man's binds.

He lurched for her, then, a desperate scrabble for her sword, and one Maena batted aside with an elbow to the man's jaw. He crumpled to the stones, a raspy moan marking an end to the struggle.

"You're lucky I need you, rockbiter," Maena said, resuming her work. "And I'll forgive you that. As will the isles, when they find out what we've done."

Yes. You'll finally fulfill your oath.

Their oath. Together. For too many lost friends, Maena would do what Svarde would not, and put an end to the fiends.

CHAPTER 4

THE LONG, DARK MARCH

Success brought Svarde exile, failure made him a king. Albeit, a king with a kingdom made of stone and corpses. Still, on the whole, a better end than the cabin on Vis's southwest corner, where his only friends were the wind, the rain, and—

Kivi snorted, just ahead, warning Svarde of a drop in the tunnel's ceiling, one that'd force a crouch. He and the ferrite walked at the rear of an amalgamated force: dead things, firewalkers, and Whent engineers—Jochi refused to spare his soldiers for the Najahn war, but gifted his scientists to ease the way for the burning fiends.

Command's raiments had grown less suffocating in the days since Svarde had first grasped the jagged blade, found himself beholden to its life-giving power. Noctia skars in the blade's hilt mingled with the blade itself, a piece of a larger dagger fashioned by Vis back when the god lived, plotted, betrayed Noctia in a brutal stab. At least that's how the legend went, and Svarde no longer put much stock in those.

Lifelong truths had been put to many tests in the last few months, and had failed most.

Up there had to be Catya's unnecessary prison, her forced aging as the skars sapped her life to create a fiend flaying net. The isles had regarded that net so necessary as to force Renewals, a world-spanning race run by the younger souls on the isles to gather all seven skars to reap the ravaging reward. Svarde had taken up the Guardian's role with solemn honor, left the woman he loved at its end to wither, and ran.

Only to learn, at Ami's—his fellow Guardian, one equally riven by Catya's fate—efforts, that the fiends weren't random tormentors but fleeing creatures. Hapless, confused, and thrust from their dying worlds into the isles. Would knowing the reason these monsters journeyed into homes, farms, and forests make much difference?

To a younger Svarde, who preferred nursing his bitterness with violence and ale, probably not.

To the older?

"Perhaps that's where you came from," Svarde said to Kivi, the rock-plated lizard, at home in the hottest places, who glinted her sapphire eyes at him. "Foti's fire-blasted ruin would be perfect for you, wouldn't it?"

As if in agreement, Kivi turned and took a bite from the wall, her stone jaws scraping away rock and leaving sparkling geode bits behind. Svarde saw all this courtesy of the lantern hanging at his belt, the swaying flame and the oil powering it giving the broad tunnel a shadowed life

The trail left by Ami and her firewalkers at the formation's head wasn't hard to follow: where the fiends walked, black burns marred. Charred mossed, singed stone, and ash littered the path.

That the firewalkers agreed to Ami's war, one requested

by the Najahn above as a price paid to give the burning fiends a home among the isles, came as a surprise. The monsters had shown, with their metal constructs and four-armed flails, a talent for destroying anything in their path. Ami, while noting she couldn't understand everything those obsidian-crowned creatures said, suggested the fiends were tired. That they'd been fighting a losing war against their dying world for so long . . .

Well, Svarde could understand that. Even if he'd chosen to watch the fight against the fiends from afar.

Now, with one more decisive strike against the windy Kance, maybe the battles could wind down. Jochi suggested barricades, wholesale slaughter against any fiends coming out that didn't show intelligence, reason. The skars backing up crossbows, spears, and swords. Eventually, those other worlds would die, and peace, or as close as the isles could get, would take root.

As motivation to march went, Svarde would take it. Beat out bitter rage, in any case.

Skars spoke, and so did the blade. While Svarde himself had never enjoyed the mental mishmash that came with a handful of the god stones, Ami relayed the impression vividly enough: like standing in the middle of an argument, unable to escape. The blade didn't speak the same way, instead touching Svarde's thoughts with connections, impressions, suggestions that the barbarian could take, leave, or twist.

Those suggestions were, invariably, dead things.

From the first, when Svarde lay at death's edge, he'd found humans the easiest to grasp. The blade took Svarde's commands—move, build, protect, assist, given in a form less verbal and more emotional, like willing himself to stand or breathe—and translated them through some

Noctia magic those bodies could understand. Humans fit those impressions best, reacted to them as Svarde wanted, though there had been mishaps. One took Svarde's demand to find food and attempted to tear apart some nearby Whent workers. Another tried to build a cooking fire by lighting its own arm to start the blaze.

Kinks to smooth out, and Svarde did, with one exception: linking to anything beyond a human.

Ami had mentioned her attempt to gather more fiend bodies for Svarde to practice on, and the barbarian could ask the blade to dig for insects, old animal bodies lingering about the caves, but his asks of those alien forms went unanswered. Perhaps Svarde wasn't pitching the command correctly, perhaps the blade didn't command dominion over inhuman souls.

Either way, the walk through the caves, as it drew Svarde away from the dead he'd been directing, had let the blade settle into a soft silence. Like someone breathing, asleep, in the same room.

Until the weapon woke.

The spark came from up ahead, like a light flaring up in Svarde's mind. He stumbled, scuffing a dusty cave floor. Kivi snorted a question.

"Something's wrong," Svarde said, shifting the blade to a two-handed grip. "Someone's died up ahead."

Kivi took the information and scurried to the side, climbed the wall and resumed her forward scuttle on the ceiling. Better for an ambush, though Svarde couldn't imagine what would be lingering in these caverns with the firewalkers moving through.

The answer came almost an hour later, after picking through a series of oblong rooms with sharp jerks around dripping pools—some smoked, still, from the firewalker's leftover heat. Two Whent engineers, their faces pale and sweat-stained, stood over a third, the blade's detected body. The figure lay blackened, burned almost beyond understanding.

"An accident," the first engineer said as Svarde caught up, her voice a dead iron. "One of the buffer vests snagged on a rock and slipped off. He tried to catch it, so did the fire-walker. His clothes caught, and that was it."

Svarde nodded at the pools, planting the blade in the stone ground before him. "He didn't try the water?"

"Stuff was boiling with all the firewalkers. Just death by a different way."

The second engineer crossed his arms, looked at Svarde. "Ami told us to wait for you, see if there was anything you could do?"

"Like?" Svarde rumbled a reply, though he already knew where this was going.

"Wake him up. Bring him back."

"There's no bringing back." The blade flickered a thought. The body wasn't so burned it couldn't stand, couldn't be used with a little Noctia effort. Svarde pushed the idea away. "Your friend is gone."

The first engineer's eyes flashed, "We're going to war, Svarde. It's not about friends. It's about another body on the line."

The day's march ended like it began, a cluster in a nameless cavern somewhere beneath the sea. The fire-walkers had split off, found a chamber several branches away to settle in. Svarde didn't know what the creatures ate, how they survived, but the fiends hadn't asked for anything yet.

"Not that I'd know if they did," Ami said, sitting with ale in hand amid the chamber's small central fire. Tents lay about the room, the Whent scouts and engineers splitting into their own conversations. "The firewalkers don't talk much to me anyway."

Ami, her red hair tied back and vanishing into her Noctia leathers, stared at the fire. The light glinted off her gold faceplate, the dual Vis skars set into the side near her cheek. A Whent blade lay nearby, a commander's horn on her belt. Insignias sat about her person, declaring Ami this and that per Jochi's demands.

"But they listen," Svarde answered, settling down across from his fellow Guardian.

Not that he needed to. Fatigue, hunger, all the natural bits about being alive didn't play into Svarde anymore. Oh, he felt things readily enough: bang his toe on a rock and it'd ache plenty, and his throat seemed to be dry at all times, but pour ale down his gut and it'd find a hole to leak from, no drunken antics, no malted pleasure to be had. Food seemed to miss the moment between hitting his tongue and tasting anything, a chalk nothing traveling to his gut and out the other side in much the same state it came in.

A creature of stasis, Svarde was, and Ami knew it.

"For now," Ami said, waving her mushroom sandwich —edible mosses squished between two large brown caps— at Svarde's sword. "For all I know, they might be scared of that blade and what it did to their leader. With you along, they'll march where we tell'em because they have no alternative."

"Is that a bad thing?"

"It is if we're meant to be sharing the isles with these monsters when we're done."

Ami didn't sling the words with much fear, though. More acceptance, even distaste. She'd stopped calling them fiends, and seemed to be searching for something beyond 'firewalker' to use. Something that'd fit in better with a curse after a few flagons.

"You heard about the engineer?" Svarde asked.

"Fried himself?"

Svarde nodded.

"He won't be the only one by the time we're done," Ami replied, though she had the grace to frown, sigh. "Been thinking about battle strategy, as if I'm some sort of general. Can't think of any except just have the firewalkers wade on in. Burn everything as they go. Wouldn't that be horrible?"

"It'd win." Svarde spoke, then stopped. "Isn't it weird, Whent and Noctia are probably the only two isles with real military commanders, save Kance, and they say they have our backs, but aren't giving us anything?"

Ami laughed, "Svarde, if I've learned anything being around Fassle, it's that he'll take any opportunity to make his allies weaker. Especially if it torches his enemies in the process."

"You're saying they're setting us up?"

"I'm saying both Fassle and Jochi would love it if Kance died destroying our firewalker friends, and us along with-'em." Ami pointed at Svarde's blade. "That's why you need to take every body that falls and put it back in line. Our power in the next war's going to hinge on how many firewalkers make it out of this one alive."

CHAPTER 5

DOCKYARD BRAWL

A scenic winter port, snowflakes blustering in as the few ships big enough to brave the ice for bigger profits went in and out. Dockworkers stuffed beneath thick leathers and furs called orders and shoved crates over cobblestones. Laughter, industry, and sunlight glinting on purple and black armor.

That last bit stuck out more to Wax as he fought off a sigh. What would've been panic a few months ago resigned itself to a new certainty now. Torny drew her daggers, Bliss her metal staff, and even Livier pulled free his rapier, the silver sword looking like it belonged in the cold. Only Eujo matched Wax's resigned frown.

"The skars, then?" the Queen said, as if pronouncing a bad deal.

"Think so."

The Najahn, Wax counted eight or so, slowed as they passed the fleeing scholars that'd sighted the Renewals. They formed into two ranks, dock workers and porters parting like some burly sea around them. The front Najahn pulled out their voulges, held them at ready, while the rear lugged off the chakram discs with their razor edges. Another few strides to bring them within range and Wax guessed those discs would aim for their heads.

It wasn't about the Renewals anymore, but the skars.

"Burn'em? Have the ground swallow them up?" Eujo said, matching Wax as they took their place behind Livier, Bliss, and Torny. "A dozen different ways to die."

"They don't have to."

"Don't think they'll be letting us walk, Wax."

"So we wash them out of our way." Wax threw Eujo a grin he knew was infuriating. "Buy me a few minutes and we'll be good."

"What're—"

Wax didn't wait, instead dashing towards the ocean and a nearby pier spiking out towards it. At the pier's end waited a small tug, currently on break from ferrying larger ships through the shrinking ice floes. The poor captain stood near the boat now, shading his eyes with a hand, watching the odd figure running towards him.

A Vis covered in warm leathers didn't look much different than anyone else on the isles, but Wax ran with a jungle lover's loping style, meant to dodge around ferns and keep footing on leaf-strewn ground. That must've drawn the inquisitive look, the wonder Wax's new skar picked up into his mind.

The Tamas skar fed possibilities, and Wax blended them, as if molding a daydream, with his own desires. The captain flinched, as if someone had slapped the man across the face, then leaned down to start untying his ship.

"We'll need to borrow you for a moment," Wax said as he came up to the captain, the Tamas skar continuing to infuse the words with fresh need, desire, want. The stone gave Wax back what it felt: the captain's boredom, search for meaning in a dull daily routine. "We're Renewals, and we need to escape the Najahn."

"Boat won't go that fast," the captain muttered, still nonetheless untying the thick ropes.

"But you can guide us through the ice. That's what matters."

A hero, that's what the captain would be, and the Tamas skar made the man believe it. Made it so true that Wax reached out, put a hand on the captain's shoulder to steady himself. He told the stone, like pushing away an itch, to ease off before Wax collapsed.

Like running a hard sprint, these skars.

Shouts drew Wax's attention back towards his friends, though his Guardians weren't watching Wax or the Najahn. Instead, Livier, Bliss, and Torny had ditched Eujo for the cart, hopping on and kicking the pony into a confused, wild charge down the pier. Eujo, off to the right and alone on the boardwalk, held a single hand out towards the Najahn.

That one hand confused the black and purple advance.

The waves ended it.

The frozen sea surged, what'd been peaceful lapping water bottoming out not far from Wax, as if a giant spoon scooped into the ocean. The hole, though, didn't fill in, but rushed towards the shore. Whitecaps ran over the stone edge, sliding over cobblestones and smashing into the Najahn soldiers. Boots once on stable footing found themselves shifting, heavy armor tipping the soldiers over into a hapless, clanking disaster.

One accompanied by more than a few pained shouts. Wax winced. Those chakrams, the voulges, would be sharp for an accidental grab.

Better, though, than death.

"Watch out, Wax!" Torny shouted, calling the Vis back to the charging cart. "She's not stopping for anyone!"

Bliss and Livier both were trying to calm the horse, but between the roiling waves, the yelling, and the morning's sheer nonsense, the pony's eyes had rolled back, her hooves pounding. Behind Wax, his tug freed, the captain cursed and jumped aboard.

Wax did no such thing. Standing straight before the oncoming pony, Wax reached towards the animal with both hands. Let the Tamas skar again take control. The stone pulsed back fear, panic, and Wax massaged those spasms into calm, into complacency. The pony shuddered, its gallop slowing, the hooves skidding as they clomped onto stiff wood more frozen than not.

Her gentle nose came to a stop at Wax's chin. Bliss's wide eyes sat behind, reins in her hands. Livier uttered a Kance curse, hopped out as Wax dashed by the horse, heading along the pier.

"Unload everything onto that boat," Wax called to his Guardians, matching Livier stride for stride along the dock back towards Eujo.

The Kance Queen—Kance's only queen now, Wax reminded himself—backpedaled away from her own flooding. The Najahn were righting themselves, a few brave ones lurching towards the Eujo, voulges striking sparks as the spearheads bounced on the ground.

"A bold idea," Livier said between breaths as the pair neared the pier's end. "Almost as creative as stabbing my hand with a fork."

"But nowhere near as satisfying."

Livier grinned, though the Tamas skar suggested the assassin wouldn't mind planting a blade between Wax's ribs at some future point. A warning to follow later, when

Livier's absolute loyalty to the Kance Queen wouldn't prevent it.

Then again, Wax had been surrounded by threats for weeks upon weeks now. At least Livier wasn't hiding it.

"Get going," Livier said as they reached Eujo, the Kance killer again drawing his rapier. "If any chase, I'll take them."

"So eager to give your life for me now," Eujo said, walking past Livier and joining Wax without a second look. "Pity that wasn't there before."

"For the Sky Palace," Livier replied.

Eujo's eyes couldn't have rolled harder, but she moved on quick with Wax, catching his point towards the tug. Torny and Bliss, now joined by the captain, tossed their satchels aboard with more concern for speed than gentleness. At least one bag broke on the tug's hard wood.

Still, among the day's possible disasters, a torn satchel didn't register.

"How'd you bribe him?" Eujo asked as they ran back, Livier following with his waving rapier, the Najahn deciding their lives were worth more than a haphazard chase. "A smile? Promise of some fresh Vis mangos?"

"Like you said, the skars."

Eujo took a stride to catch on. "The Tamas? What'd it do?"

"Let me know what he wanted."

"You read his mind?"

"Better than I can read yours."

Eujo frowned, "You'd better not use that stone on me, Wax, or I'll gut you."

Wax laughed, the Najahn and their hapless attack all-but forgotten. "You'd never."

"I'll admit, it's not top of my list right now." Eujo slowed as they neared the cart, looked back towards the dockside. The Najahn were mostly standing now, tending to their wounds. A couple looked Wax's way, but their stare said escape would be allowed, even welcome. "That was good advice, Wax. About not killing them, I mean."

"Figure, we're on this to save the isles. Not murder those living in them."

What Wax didn't say as he helped Eujo onto the tug, was that Pan would've insisted on it. They'd called Pan soft plenty of times growing up, always as a gentle jab. He'd been right, though. The wounds Wax would carry from this adventure, thanks to the Vis skar, would be more mental than anything. Nightmares. Dragging daydreams.

Best avoid adding to their count if he could.

The tug shoved away from the port, the eager captain at the tiller guiding the small, swift vessel. The pony and her attendant cart had been backslapped towards the dockyard and whomever wanted to claim her. The beast belonged to Daklin, the Tamas actor and apparent power player, but the man hadn't wanted to be seen with the Renewals.

"Reputation and rumors are all a man has," Daklin had said the night before, tipping his foppish cap one last time before disappearing.

Another soul Wax wouldn't mind never seeing again.

'So what now?' Bliss signed, joining Wax on the boat's prow.

Eujo and Livier had their heads bent together, the latter barraging the Kance Queen with information about the realm she was now ruling. Torny watched the rear, the bandit for once forgoing knife tossing to keep a sharp-eyed lookout for any pursuit. Which left Wax and his sister hunting the horizon.

"We hope Deux shows up," Wax said. "Hope the ship's all right."

'And then?'

"Kance it is, Bliss."

His sister nodded. The sun continued its shine, the sea glistened, and out there, at first a smudge on the horizon, became something bigger. Something Wax knew.

"See?" Wax said. "I knew it'd all work out okay."

Bliss could only laugh.

CHAPTER 6
THE FIRST BLOW

Leaving the Sky Palace came by several options: the steadfast and scared could use the stairs, climbing down steps for hours on end, a journey arduous enough that an inn did brisk business at the base of the palace's spire, catering to those needing Kance wine to make it up, or a bed to collapse after coming down. Braver souls could try a Kance-crafted elevator, one of two that would shoot top to bottom and vice versa through huge, interconnected pulley systems. That they broke often, leaving would-be travelers stranded for hours or days, was a risk taken for convenience.

Quik chose the third, if only for the reason it was the fastest way to get to the port, to the waiting ship, and away from Gladdring's meddling. Even with the order giving him purpose, Quik continued to feel a sticky shadow pulling his strings, something the hunter hoped distance would blunt.

Achieving that distance brought Quik to a ledge, one with a red-painted edge warning ignorant wanderers certain death lay beyond. The Sky Palace's gray walls scalloped around Quik and the ledge, blocking the hissing wind. Beautiful skies sprawled out before him, occupied by birds, by a few wispy clouds, and by the very thing waiting for him on that ledge.

The glider clung to its birth with ropes looped through metal rings. Those ropes ran up to a simple clutch along the glider's central bar, where a light tug would let them loose and send the glider into fate's own hands. Furled sails in the classic Kance blue and silver design scrunched up on the sides over the central bar, while woven baskets and straps waited below for any gear. Quik's meager possessions did little to fill them.

Especially as the hunter refused to let the gauntlets leave his person.

"So long as they don't scratch me," his soarer said, a sharp-eyed woman. "They do, we might fall."

Quik approached the ledge, looked down. The slim palace, sculpted into the rising mountain, offered options aplenty for emergency landings. Berths, all with those glaring red edges, lined the whole way down.

"You'll be fine," Quik said.

"Risk-taker, are you?"

"You have no idea."

The soarer laughed, helped Quik get strapped in. As a passenger, he rode on top, a fine silver netting serving as an almost-cozy bed between him and the soarer. His hands gripped sturdy bars. A single Vis skar, taken from Gladdring's stolen horde, muttered calm nothings in Quik's mind.

A sunny day, a gorgeous day, and with a short countdown, Quik flew into it.

If Wax could see him now.

The glider tipped off the ledge, the soarer kicking forward with her feet. Their flight angled down, and Quik's stomach made a race for his throat, only for the palace walls to disappear. With a snap, a rustle, and the roaring wind, those furled wings spread free. The glider lurched, Quik's view of approaching ground shifting to, again, that clear sky. Chilly air ran through his warm robes, thick gloves keeping his fingers from going numb, if not his face.

"A good takeoff!" the soarer cried from beneath him. "You holding on, Vis?"

"For the moment."

"Make that moment last. I've never lost a passenger, and I'd rather not start with you."

Quik grinned. Hard not to, now that the glider had leveled out, that a visit to Noctia's realm seemed not in the immediate future. Instead, they flew out over the peninsula that marked Kance's capital city—Vesphere-and the isle's western edge. Beyond the glistening sea below, Quik saw sails and ships aplenty, more even than clustered around Noctia's Ringed City.

"Are all of those Kance?"

"Ours, yes. And merchants seeking shelter."

"From the Najahn?"

"From fiends, mostly. The beasts are still thick in the water."

Right. Quik had heard the monsters weren't showing up on land so often these days. Whether the Aegis had recovered some strength to burn them away, or something else was interfering, nobody seemed sure. The aquatic beasts, though, showed no signs of slowing. They harried ships, assaulted ports, and swam up onto beaches to devour, claw, or spawn.

The soarer angled the glider into a lazy descent, narrating her choices all the while. Gliding to the base meant getting as far out from the isle itself as possible, keeping space free for gliders sticking to the middle, or coming back up.

"Back up?" Quik asked. "How?"

"Wind geysers. Kance is full of'em."

The soarer elaborated on the blowholes, launching pure air straight up into the sky. As if Kance, the god, was sighing. Gliders could set up over the geysers, take the warm air and launch high enough to get to the middle levels of most spires.

"From there, it's a hike, but not too long," the soarer concluded.

Quik let her ramble on from there, letting the conversation fade as he took in the view. Better than a Vis canopy trek, if more unstable, and a reminder of what he was fighting for, what they all were fighting for.

"See that? Out west?" the soarer asked.

Quik twisted, noted distant, dark blots far out on the sea.

"Najahn caravels," the soarer continued. "They're keeping eyes on us. We could go after them, but why waste the time?"

"Better chew them up when they come close."

"Right? They'll have numbers on us, but their ships are too slow. We'll flank'em, send those black bastards to the bottom of the sea. The Najahn are going to learn why Kance hasn't ever lost a war."

Narro greeted Quik as the Vis walked up the boarding ramp, sole satchel on his back. The Kance captain, clad in the wind isle's traditional silver-and-blue cloak, cap, and boots, looked younger than Quik, a myth the man dispelled when he caught the Vis's raised eyebrow.

"Naturally good-looking, you know," Narro quipped, stepping aside to wave Quik on. "It's a boon to me, one my family has always had. Age slides off us, it does. Readily."

"All right," Quik replied, casting his eyes instead over the Kance clipper.

The ship spread like a flat board away to Quik's left and right, white-washed boards bleeding into a sky-blue hull. A dye job, Narro explained, meant to give the ship cover at distance. All the cabins lay below deck. Even the till sat inside the prow.

"The wind, she gives us the lightest brush save where we want it most," Narro said, pointing up at the furled sails wrapping a single mast. "You'll see. When we get moving, we'll find Vis before the Najahn even know we're gone."

"And how long till we get moving?"

Narro grinned, a broad smile splitting the man's round face, mopped with thick, curled hair. "You're the one we've been waiting for. Emergency orders, you ought to know, coming in right on time this morning before we set sail. Not a big problem, you understand, just a change."

"A change from what?"

"What we're supposed to be doing."

"Which was?"

Narro picked up a different gleam now. "Hunting the purple and black, Vis, and sending their rotten skar-stealing selves to the bottom of the sea."

The likely success of Narro's original mission became obvious not long after the clipper set sail, launching free from Kance with enough speed to push Quik back against a storage chest, one of several, in what served as the ship's bridge. Set beneath the prow, Narro commanded a half-circle space flush with several sailors, crates stuffed with provisions—only enough for a few days at a time, to keep the clipper quick, and a glass-filled window at the front to see.

From Quik's few sea voyages, he figured a normal vessel would see wave after wave crash into that glass window, making it useless. The Kance clipper, though, didn't ride the waves so much as skip across them. It *bounced* as it scampered, the small touches sending light tremors through the hull. Hours sped by, the day slipping into sunset, but Narro refused to lower the sails.

They'd make Vis the next day.

Around Quik, those sailors, those soldiers not involved in managing the swirling filament canvas giving the clipper its speed spent their minutes polishing armor, sharpening rapiers, and oiling Kance crossbows.

Two, near the bridge's rear, also worked with several pots. A single black iron cauldron, with a wood funnel sitting on its top, sat between two smaller vessels. Each sailor, using high-rimmed ladles, spooned one or two scoops from their vial into the central one. As Quik watched, slight steam rose, followed by one of the sailors scooping the blend into a third container, a glass globe, and plugging the thing with a hard wood stopper.

"What's that?" Quik asked as they hit the open ocean and no answer, no explanation, presented itself.

"A surprise," Narro said, turning from the till and talking before either sailor could offer up anything. "One you'll see soon, unless I mistake my guess."

"Soon?"

"See that?" Narro pointed. The orange-lit sky, purple clouds, bled into a dark sea, one broken up by several lit points sliding across the view. "That, my friend, is a fool." Seeing Quik's confusion, Narro again adopted his feral grin. "A Najahn ship, heading north. Those lights are a signal, calling for escort. They think they're in safe waters, because Kance has been quiet. Be honored, Quik. Tonight, Kance strikes the first blow."

CHAPTER 7
WEAPONS TRADE

The Dead City, as Maena and most everyone down here called it, wasn't quite the same without its lurching dead. Ever since Svarde marched off with the firewalkers the entire city that'd hummed with those rotting corpses moved instead with the usual rhythms of a living city, the day and night cycles of industry, drunkenness, and bartering. Without the alien magic, Maena found the slate stone buildings and dreary smithies all too usual, all too sedate. The Whent were acting on their promise, to turn the Dark Below into just another home, but in the doing, they were giving up the goal, the great quest.

This place was still dangerous, still deadly, but all Maena saw as she walked towards her target was the same old routine.

Enough firewalkers remained around the chamber—with more emerging every day, now, shuttled free from their burning home in the large black iron capsules—to keep most wayward fiends at bay. Their giant flails, the ballistas, or just their burning hands squeezed the frothy life from the fiends that dared crawl up into firewalker territory. The smarter monsters swept out to sea through underwater channels, or broke for the small tunnels on the chamber's far side.

Jochi, that morning, had ordered those tunnels fortified. Those gnarled tubes pointed southward, towards Svarde's firewalker force, and the Whent commander felt like allowing surprise assaults on his friends wasn't a good idea.

Such an order meant more equipment, requisitions, and opportunity.

"What're you doing here?" snarled Maena's target as she swept inside the swat forge, its constant heat stealing the captain's breath for a moment.

Oh, he knows why.

The burly engineer, covered in more soot than Maena would consider healthy, waved tongs in her direction as if the orange-glowing utensils might scare her away.

"Helping with Jochi's latest command," Maena said. "Why else?"

The engineer would've narrowed his eyes, or maybe he did, but rusted goggles coating the black-smudged orbs prevented any perception. Instead, the man grunted, turned to his assistant, and ordered the similarly soot-smothered woman to take a break.

"I can keep—" she started for the tongs.

"I said take a break," the engineer replied. "There'll be no working of my forge without me being a part of it."

Thus cowed, the assistant slipped by Maena, muttering some useless rockbiter curse under her breath.

Don't be shy now. Ask for what we need. Really need.

"Do you have it?" Maena asked, looking around to see if the answer was evident.

Fresh shelves bolted into the walls held the engineer's

products, ranging from standard tools to heavier mining gear. The man wasn't a weapon smith, had told Maena that the first time the Rana captain had come by, but Maena already had her swords. Had a knife in her boot. What she needed, well, wasn't on these shelves.

Not out in the open, anyway.

"Going to have to be more clear, Rana," the engineer snuffed, putting down the tongs and meeting Maena at the broad working anvil in the smithy's center. "There's a lot of 'its' in here."

The man's tone suggested more than his question. He knew very well why Maena was here, knew because several consecutive nights in a simple tavern three doors down had pried the information from her.

Or so he thought.

"The plan's in motion," Maena said. "The opportunity's there."

The engineer leaned over, shoved the goggles up off his eyes. The man slipped into a shady smile, revealing several missing teeth around a gnarled, singed beard.

"Too late, by my reckoning. Most of the firewalkers are already gone." Another sniff. "Missed your chance."

"They'll die on Kance's shores. What I'm worried about is what comes next. That's what we agreed."

"You think you can do it, then?"

We're the only ones who can.

"If you help me," Maena said. "Time, though, is starting to run out. People are going to notice."

"Why's that?"

Because that scout we've tied up is going to have friends, friends who'll look harder for him every passing day. We should've killed him already.

"Better you don't know." Maena reached, pulled out a

pouch. Opening it revealed some luminescent purple moss. "This is what you wanted, right?"

The engineer nodded, swept his eyes around the small smithy. Lanterns shone in the corners, but oil to keep them lit required trade. Keeping the moss alive was easier, a splash or two of cave river water and the purple glows would keep a small room shiny. Trading, growing the mosses had become one of several lucrative businesses in Jochi's underground empire.

"I'll need more," the engineer said. "Especially if you need as much as you've said."

Maena's lip curled, "Deliver, and you'll have as much moss as you could ever want."

"Then I got your first batch, right here." The engineer turned, went to a back shelf, one little hit by lantern light. Satchels sprawled across it, most full with lumpy contents. The engineer grabbed one on the far right, pulled it off with a groan. "She's heavy. Think you can handle it?"

"I'll be fine."

The engineer didn't look quite sure he believed Maena, but his complaints stayed quiet as the two satchels changed hands. The man had it right: the satchel almost bent Maena's back, but she drew on a particular endurance, a special sort that came with sure conviction.

"It's not enough, mind," the engineer said. "Give me a few more days and you'll have the rest. With the moss."

"As I said, you'll get it."

"And no talking about this."

"Obviously," Maena replied. "I wouldn't want either of us fed to the fiends. Such a terrible way to go."

The engineer scowled, said nothing more as Maena left the smithy.

The prisoner had a pallid cast when Maena dropped off

the satchel, the day—if you wanted to call it that—having dwindled without the man getting a meal. An unintentional torture, but remembering, much less acting on the Whent scout's well-being ranked low on Maena's concerns. She was, after all, bent on stopping the fiends, on keeping anyone else from suffering what she'd suffered.

Compared to that, a little thirst, a little hunger . . . did it even register?

"Please," the scout said, "I've shown you everything you wanted. Let me go, and I'll never say a word."

Maena had the satchel on the rocky ground, her belt lantern scattering orange about the small stone patch before the natural lattice hanging over the chamber below. The drawstring pulled away, revealing clumped boxes. All metal, with two divided halves. A thin twine tied them all together, looping through a small ring at the top. If Maena pulled on that twine, a divider within the little boxes would shift, allowing the contents inside to mix.

From there, light the twine on fire, and as the flame reached each container in succession, the cavern would explode. The stones would crumble. The gates, the pool, would be buried beyond all saving.

No more fiends, no more terror, no more like us.

"It's not that I don't believe you," Maena said to the scout, the man's hands tied, the gag lying on the floor between them. She'd already given him water, more mushroom paste on thin bread. "It's that I still need you."

"What for?"

"I'm working out the specifics, but don't worry, it won't be long."

"I don't feel well, Maena—"

"Don't call me that, rockbiter. I'm nothing to you,

nobody." She stood, put a hand on the scout's trembling, thin shoulder. "You should sleep. Dream of something better than this."

The scout continued to beg until Maena slipped the gag back in place. She sighed at the sight, turning away quick. It wasn't that she wanted to hurt the man, even if he was a Whent. That the scout would go blabbing right to Jochi upon the man's release, though, was a given. A waste, seeing as the scout still had some use.

The most important part to play.

True. Maena would let the man end his suffering soon enough, but to do that, she needed more moss to trade. More devices to cover the lattice. She stretched, felt out her legs, her arms. Fit, ready to go, and still a few hours yet before she ought to get back to the Dead City.

Time to forage.

Jochi's scouts—the ones not trapped in Maena's secret alcove, anyway—kept good maps. The originals sprawled across broad tables in the Whent camp, watched by guards and often perused by Jochi himself. Those maps outlined patrolled paths back to the surface, dotted growing camps along the way. Maena tracked one of those paths now, heading up and veering off here and there to tread deeper.

Always deeper, now that the mosses were so valued. The caverns were getting scraped clean. Maena's lantern drew shadows as it shuddered with her steps, spiked shoes giving grip, if not the most comfortable walk. Still, as you left the larger tunnels behind, sudden drops and climbs made good gear a necessity.

And, if the spitting growls she heard were any indication, a good weapon helped too.

The noises suggested conflict, so Maena hooded her

lantern beneath her Whent cloak as she approached. Narrow cave walls forced the Rana into a tight squeeze, spitting her out onto a thin lip. Beneath lay a small pool, filled by water dripping from a ceiling almost in line with Maena's platform. At its edge, haloed not by their lanterns but by harvested blue and purple mosses, stood several Whent. Their burly outfits were too clean to suggest a long time in the Dark Below, and they didn't wear Jochi's colors.

Traders, then. Or layabouts hoping to find fortune beneath the earth. That they'd come across a slithering, spitting fiend was a poor play. The snake-like creature, with a narrow blue body jutting with legs and spiny ridges, staked its own spot a few strides back of the Whent. Twin tongues jutted from a slit mouth with every hiss, bumpy orbs on its feet suggesting a home far different from where it now found itself.

Both sides, then, unlucky.

But not us.

No. Maena slid her legs beneath her, settled in as the traders brandished blades and clubs towards the fiend. The monster didn't seem intimidated, the reason coming clear as it reared back, opening that slit and spitting some foul-smelling gunk at the trader trio. The Whent howled as it hit, the gunk sticking, stinking, and . . . steaming?

The Rana leaned forward, stared as the fiend tried to take advantage. The beast darted in, knobby legs keeping it unsteady. The monster barreled into the lead Whent, the burliest man, and knocked him back into the pool, one deeper than Maena first thought. The Whent disappeared, sucked down by his heavy clothes, a disaster that nonetheless left the fiend open for a brutal strike by the trader's allies. Club and blade hit, digging deep, and sending the fiend into a blue-blooded frenzy.

Wounds traded, and as the fight grew more desperate, a joint, fatal defeat seemed more certain.

Maena watched, smiled, and thanked Rana for the foolish rockbiters. Today was a good day.

CHAPTER 8
SURFACING

Daylight.

Two weeks in the dark, eating mushrooms and wondering, wondering when Svarde would crack the surface, at last feel air untainted with the firewalker's scorched scent. The Whent scouts delivered that hope through a seaside cave on Kance's northern end, one blocked by landslides and cleared, now, by the firewalkers themselves and their blunt strength.

"We could've blown it up," Olgata, the Whent scout and Jochi's chosen speaker on the march, said to Svarde as they stood well back from the firewalker pair hacking aside the rock. "That's what we brought the explosives for."

"And risked the caves collapsing on us?" Ami asked, wearing her full Noctia armor, pink moss light turning it an ethereal violet.

"We're not morons. We would have planned it right, as we have a thousand times before."

"Then consider it a benefit to the firewalkers," Svarde said, calming Olgata's frown with a dead man's ease. Drama seemed so far away when life had disappeared. "We give them a task, let them complete it, bind them to us ever so slightly."

Olgata sniffed, "If you think they care one whit about us, you're reading them wrong." At furrowed looks from both Svarde and Ami, the scout continued. "They're desperate, is all. They want to survive. They'll do what it takes for that."

What Olgata meant, that the firewalkers might decide, at any point, that working with Ami, Svarde, and Noctia wasn't the most important key to their continued existence, went unsaid. It was an eventuality that couldn't be confirmed, planned for, plotted. Instead, Svarde figured they'd keep the firewalkers busy and rewarded.

Enmity kept at bay through bribery.

The sun and fresh sea breeze sank into the cave as the hole expanded, the firewalkers coming to their conclusion when the opening was large enough to handle a pair of the hulking, burning beasts two abreast. Those fiends wouldn't be the first ones out, though, necessitating the minor dance needed to get the scalding creatures around Svarde, Ami, and Olgata without charring the humans. A trick in the caves, but one that, by now, everyone was used to.

Though, for all his time, Svarde still couldn't understand the firewalkers and their motes. Ami seemed to have some idea, and that was enough for him.

Not like Svarde would be living among the monsters for that much longer. One torched wind isle and he'd be free of the burning fiends, would have time to . . .

Svarde stopped that dire line by leaving the cave, setting foot on real sand, albeit sand crusted with melting ice and driftwood. Scraggly winter bushes and thin trees lined the beach's end to the south, Kance's spires rising right behind them up, up, and up some more. Birds swooped and swirled, a few diving down to investigate the new creatures emerging into their midst. Any land-bound animals stayed well hidden and away.

Smart.

"I'll take a look," Olgata said, breaking away to the south. "What's our first objective?"

"To get a surrender without a fight," Ami replied, shading her eyes as she looked around. Her gold faceplate glimmered, itself almost as blinding as the sun above. "Failing that, we signal Noctia and start a bloody march south."

Olgata nodded and stepped off, loping over the trees and stones marring the otherwise pleasant tan sand.

"A bloody march?" Svarde asked, glancing back at the cave. Kivi lurked at the entrance, nibbling on some gray wet stone. "Guessing it's not our blood you're talking about."

"Do the firewalkers bleed?" Ami asked, sounding more tired than excited. "I don't think so."

By the time Olgata returned, the firewalkers and their Whent followers sprawled out across the sand. The firewalkers had to adjust their footing quick, their heat melting the sand into glistening glass with every step. Soon the beach became a glinting mirror, a slate both searing in its heat—despite the cool temperature—and slippery to walk on.

Svarde had the Whent climb back into the trees, await Olgata's promised word.

"There's a town less than an hour's walk south and west," Olgata said, meeting with Svarde and Ami beneath leafless branches. "Small enough I wouldn't expect a fight."

"Perfect, then, for the signal, and an easy opening." Ami nodded, slid her eyes to Svarde. "You agree?"

"Perfect to let Noctia know we're here, sure. Easy?" Svarde chuckled. "Nothing in our lives has come easy, Ami."

"The ale used to."

Olgata looked between them both, her weathered face not the least amused.

"The scout doesn't seem to appreciate our humor," Svarde said, stretching his gray face into a wider grin. "You're too serious, Olgata."

"We've an army of burning fiends at our backs," Ami added. "The Kance will either fold like a weak breeze or burn like soft paper."

"How can you know that?" Olgata asked, turning to look back towards the noted town. "They've fought raiders, they have strong armor, and—"

"They've never fought anything like this before. Everyone's a coward when the unknown comes to call. Kance will be too."

Ami wrangled the firewalkers forward with simple words and gestures. A point down the beach, a walking motion, and off they went. The firewalkers, their diamond-shaped obsidian heads sparking, set off after the Guardian. Most carried two heavy flailed, the chains and spiked balls dragging through the dirt. The big constructs so noted in their assaults hadn't made the journey, the tunnels too tight for those massive treads to travel through.

In that, at least, Svarde found a certain relief: the firewalkers would be alien enough. Bring in the creaking, crunching metal machines and even their Noctia allies might find it hard to accept. It was one thing to invite military aid, another to play a part in your own destruction.

Then again, here Svarde walked, now up next to Ami, with Kivi in tow. An undying man with a jagged blade, who at once was and was not like the woman he matched stride for stride. Food, drink, even air to breathe were as distant to him now as death had once seemed during those heady days marching the isles with Catya.

A strange force, but one with noble ends. The dream would carry them.

Olgata's target, the small town, lay nestled between several towering silver-gray monoliths. The spires framed the clustered buildings and the central spike, a stair-wrapped cylinder with glider launch points at its top. A skilled flyer could use Kance winds to get halfway across the isle from a spike like this, and Svarde had to wonder if one had already launched, carrying warning across the wind.

Deep afternoon brought an orange glow and shadows to match, the firewalkers themselves blending in to the sizzling air following their marching ranks. Black and burned lines followed their steps, glassy sand marking their prints. The beasts marched in silence, though Svarde saw their skulls sparking every time he turned around: golds, blues, greens dancing against the obsidian.

Battle strategy, he hoped.

Ami whistled a halt outside the town, in a muddy field meant for spring planting. Spindly trees and the monolith edges bordered their formation, which had Svarde and Ami in front—Kivi snorted between them—and the firewalkers well behind. Olgata and the other Whent stayed beyond sight back on the beach, holding to their role as if-necessary reserves. The town, with curling smoke rising from reddish chimneys, its shock-white buildings standing firm, didn't notice.

"Wait for it," Ami muttered.

"Oh, I know what's coming."

Ami curled a smile, "Do you, Svarde? You ever invade an isle before?"

"The last time, I wound up helping Whent fight off some fiends. Don't imagine it'll be the same now."

"No, probably not."

That answer found its truth when a single glider launched off the town's spike. It made a long, lazy turn in the cloudless sky, sweeping over the firewalkers before soaring down to a soft landing some strides before Ami and Svarde. Its pilot, a wiry Kance man, ran to a stop, pulling on a wire to collapse the glider's wings into a narrow line. The man shrugged off the contraption, catching it and settling the glider into a gentle rest amid the muddy lumps. With his wrist, he nudged the flight goggles up and off his eyes, blinking at Svarde and Ami. A lone rapier rested in a sheathe at his side, his gear otherwise made for flying, not for fighting.

"Hello, invaders!" the man said, walking up, a slim mustache and brave grin lighting on his face. "Welcome to our blustery isle!"

Ami frowned, glanced at Svarde, who laughed.

"Welcome indeed," Svarde replied. "I'm Svarde, this is Ami, and behind us are our friends, the firewalkers, who come to fight for their right to live in our world."

The man stuck out his lower lip, nodded, "An unusual request, but then, when one marches with fiends, I suppose the usual has already left. My name's Veloc, and I'm here to say that Kance has no war with you or your fiends. In fact, I'd say we don't have a war with anyone save those damned purple and black." Veloc nodded at Ami, wearing her Noctia armor. "Guardian, I'm surprised to see you wearing their colors. Last I heard, you and the Circle weren't on friendly terms."

Another glance between Svarde and Ami, though this time the flame-haired Guardian took the lead.

"You're well-informed, Veloc, for being so remote," Ami started.

"You make it sound like I shouldn't be." Veloc crossed his arms. "It's not like Whent's been keeping their mouths shut. Winter's thawing and rumors travel fast. What matters now, though, is the truth. What're you planning, and what're you expecting us to do?"

"Surrender, and tell the other towns on Kance to do the same. We're not interested in destruction."

"Then what are you interested in?"

"A home for the firewalkers. And more fiends besides, if we find them."

Veloc strode past Ami and Svarde, drawing a curious snort from Kivi. The man peered at the firewalkers, standing in calm formation, their obsidian flashing. He watched them for a long moment, before scratching at his chin.

"So they are smart, then. Civilized?" Veloc asked.

"Enough," Svarde replied. "They deserve a life."

"I'd ask why, but the day's drawing down and I fear we're at an impasse," Veloc said, and for the first time, his voice tilted away from a scoundrel's snappy verve. "I've no desire to see my home obliterated, and I know my ale-swilling friends stand no chance against those monsters you've got over there. I can't, though, promise you the isle." Veloc walked back, planted himself again between Ami, Svarde, and his town. "Give me one day. I'll send a messenger, explain our dire position, and advocate for peace. Then, if Kance says no, you can march on with no fear from us. And if they say yes, well, we can put this fight to bed without a single life lost. How does that sound?"

"Like a fool's promise," Ami said.

"But one we can try," Svarde cut in. "Ami, if the first stories of the firewalkers are about how they destroyed a town, they'll lose any chance of acceptance. We need to try."

"The man, the, err, very ill-looking man has it," Veloc agreed. "With the gliders, our news travels fast. A day, my friends, and then you can have all the violence you desire. Make your camp here if you wish, I shall return on the morrow."

With a sharp bow, Veloc turned, began his walk towards the town. As he went, the man held up a single hand, a white cloth pulled from a pocket and waving. At the sight, two gliders launched from the spike, their dark forms surfing the twilight winds around the monolith, curling south, death or deliverance on their wings.

CHAPTER 9
ON THE SEA

If asked to compare his treehouse on Kitaye with the accommodations aboard the *Storm's Edge*, Eujo's decadent ship, Wax would have to admit the fine bedsheets, the dinner spreads, and general luxury made a striking impression. Spiders didn't crawl along his legs at night, and the fresh sea breeze countered the jungle's oft-oppressive humidity.

And it was hard to deny the delight in a crew preparing every meal, delivering coffee or tea upon request.

'I know,' Bliss signed when Wax, sighing, relayed these thoughts to his sister as they sat on the ship's uppermost deck.

The silver-white roof over the expansive dining room served as a sun-catching layabout during the fine sunny day after their departure from Tamas. Wax and Bliss each had a thin canvas chair, clean Kance robes replacing their tattered adventuring gear. Neither wore a weapon, both had faces and feet cleaned with seawater showers, and they clinked steaming mugs as shimmering Kance sails fluttered above.

While ice floes bobbed here and there amid the deep sea waves, Deux no longer considered them a concern, and the *Storm's Edge* simply bludgeoned them aside. Not every ship could say the same, however, so otherwise the ocean sat deserted, not a shadow on the horizon or anywhere else. No clouds either, a sunny, beautiful day.

Almost enough to make one forget why he was out here at all.

'I can't believe we've made it this far,' Bliss continued, signing with her left hand while sipping with her right. 'Nobody's really hurt either.'

"Thanks to the skars," Wax replied.

And that's only the physical wounds, though Wax kept that part quiet. Eujo's ultimatum back on Noctia arose every time his thoughts trended in that direction: push away the trauma, the terror, the lasting damage and focus on saving the isles, being the Renewal, so on and so forth. A litany, almost a mantra, that Wax had taken to muttering to himself at the start and end of every day.

Whether Noctia believed it or not, the isles needed him, or so Wax would tell himself.

'What do they say?' Bliss asked. 'When we're sitting here like this, do they talk to you?'

"All the time. Constantly."

'You understand them?'

"It's like talking to an animal. You can tell what they want, and they might listen to me if I urge them to do something, but it's not perfect."

'Right now, what do they want?'

Wax chuckled, "Well, Vis is focused on a toe I stubbed this morning. Foti's quiet now. Rana keeps telling me to get the ocean to shove us along, while Whent seems to want the ship broken up into tiny rafts."

'What?'

Wax raised the tea mug up in a shrug. "Like I said, they're not smart. They're mindless and strange."

'What about Tamas?'

Wax glanced at his sister. The Tamas skar ran different than the others, less focused on the natural world and more the life around him. Right now, it snatched honest curiosity from his sister, mingled with worry and a little desire.

"You want to try it?" Wax said, reaching beneath his robe to pull the necklace free. With a little pressure on either side of the Tamas skar slot, he squeezed the topaz out. "It's not going to hurt you. Just, you know, don't drop it."

'As if.' Bliss held out her hand, took the stone. Closed her eyes for a moment, then shook her head. 'You're not very interesting, Wax.'

"Don't I know it," came a new voice, Eujo, climbing onto the upper deck.

"Hey," Wax said, turning in his chair to throw the Queen a hurt frown, "I'm plenty interesting. You know I've been to all but one of the isles?"

Eujo took the third and final chair on Wax's left, her silver-blue robes rippling in the wind. "Have you? See anything interesting?"

"Well," Wax said, putting his arms behind his head, leaning back against the chair's canvas. "I met this crazy lady who keeps insisting she's royalty. But she's such a bad actor, she nearly got us killed, and—"

"Hey, they weren't going to kill us. Just give me a nice tattoo."

"Is that what that was? Should I have let them, then?"

"You?" Eujo laughed. "If I recall, it was Livier that did the saving."

Wax denied, deflected, joked, and jabbered with the Queen, the two trading barbs and banter, stories and silly ideas until the tea ran dry. About as perfect a morning as Wax could imagine, until Eujo lifted herself off the chair, mentioned she, Deux, and Livier had to discuss what would happen when they reached Kance.

When the Queen would become the isle's sole ruler.

As Eujo left, Wax looked over at his sister, who'd napped some of the time, but now had her eyes open, wore a wide grin.

"What?" Wax asked.

Bliss held out her hand, the Tamas stone sparkling in her palm. 'Know what this told me?'

"That I'm the best?"

A slight head shake, still smiling. 'That you love her, Wax.'

Torny's surprised curse at the news Fassle and Yarvick were working together made the bandit blush, drew Deux's raised eyebrow from across the long dinner table as the foursome, plus Livier and the ship's captain, shared a late meal.

"I'm saying," the bandit continued, "that these two have been fighting in the dark for, like, as long as I've been alive. We're talking throats cut, stolen treasure, bribes and blackmail. There's no way."

"Apparently, a way has been found," Livier said. The assassin still looked a bit pallid from his wounds back on Tamas, but nights spent clutching a Vis skar did work. "Necessity and all that."

"Necessity?" Wax asked. "What necessity? What's the threat?"

Eujo raised her hand and tapped her bracelet. "These. The skars are why Fassle cut off the Renewal, and I guess

Kance stole a bunch from Noctia. Fassle wants them back, and so does Yarvick."

"An alliance like that lasts only till the skars are recovered," Deux said. "After, I suspect, they'll go back to their old ways."

"Grand. Not something we'll see," Torny said. "So they're sending all the Najahn after Kance?"

"Not all. Vis is fighting as well, though that struggle appears to be all but over. Mottilan holds out, Kitaye has fallen."

Wax gulped, shared a drawn look with his sister. Would his mother, father have taken part in any fighting? Unlikely. Still, they might have lost friends. Bliss's Lira would've been in the thick of any rebellion. A younger Wax might've jumped up at Deux's words, demanded to head right back home, but instead he held silent.

There wasn't anything Wax could do for Vis, not back home anyway.

"Wax?" Eujo asked. "You don't have anything to say?"

"What can I say? We made our decision a long time ago. It's the skars, it's the Aegis, or nothing."

"You agree, Bliss?"

Wax's sister nodded. 'I'm his Guardian. I go where Wax goes.'

"Thank Noctia," Torny said. "I do not need to go to that plant-infested isle."

They were, however, going to Kance. Deux, with Livier and Eujo sprinkling in details, delivered a fresh briefing to Wax, Bliss, and Torny. The latest word, before Deux had left for Tamas, detailed those stolen skars and the Najahn in pursuit. That Fassle and Yarvick would wage wholesale war on Kance seemed inevitable, that Kance would eventually fall seemed similarly destined. Foti, Rana, Whent, and

Tamas supported Noctia, and with those resources, a conclusion was already defined.

"Except we have the skars," Eujo said at the end. "With those, we can turn back any army."

"Yeah, except Noctia has 'em too," Torny countered. "You want to save your isle, Eujo, you'll need something different."

"What's that, Torny?" Eujo's familiar steel back in her voice.

"Get rid of Fassle's support. Yarvick's too," Torny said. "They're talking about stopping the fiends, saving the isles? We do it first, they have no reason to fight. The other isles won't give themselves up for nothing."

Livier laughed, "You make it sound so easy, bandit."

"That's because it is. We get Wax here to Kance, toss him a couple skars from that stolen stash, and bam. That's a set of seven."

"And then what?" Livier asked. "The Aegis's throne sits in Noctia's center. They'll not let you near it, and even if you somehow make it there, who cares? They won't stop."

"We'll show the isles there's a different way," Wax said, drawing the looks to him. "I'm not trying to become the next Aegis. I don't want to use the skars to kill or hurt anyone. But, I believe, I have to believe, we can use them to stop the fiends. Like Fassle and Yarvick, but without their armies, without their control. We can be better, because we have to be."

A speech, a small one, and Wax would've liked to see support on the faces staring back at him, but instead he found concern, doubt, and more than one sigh. Eujo noted their food was getting cold, and the conversation melted, without any obvious solution, to other things.

"You tried," Eujo said, after, when she and Wax stood at

the ship's aft. Sichi shone bright, her pink light turning the sea into a frothing summer flower.

"I am trying," Wax replied. "I just don't know, yet, how we're going to do this."

"Stop the fiends? Save the isles?"

"Two hard questions."

Eujo leaned over the aft rail. She bore a serious look, her hair flying in the breeze. Always so driven, so set on conquering the next challenge. So different from himself, from those days swinging through the jungle.

From Sawi too.

"We can't rest, Wax. We can't give up. I'm not going to let my isle fall." Eujo didn't look at Wax as she spoke, as if the ocean held some answer out there. "But I don't want my people to die either. Do you think it's worth it? Fighting for the skars?"

"Or what?"

"We give Fassle and Yarvick the stones, that's what. Make them promise to back off."

"The other Queen didn't. She must have had a reason," Wax said. "I think we get to Kance, we find out what that was, and see. Who knows, if we're lucky, the answer will be waiting."

"If it's not?"

"We'll find one, Eujo. That's what we've been doing this whole time. We can't stop now."

"Guess not." Eujo smiled, straightened. "We'll see Kance tomorrow. First time in months I'll be home. The first time you'll see the spires, the gliders. It's amazing, Wax."

"You'll give me the tour?"

Eujo put a hand on Wax's arm, turned him back towards the cabins. "Everything, Wax. I'll show you everything. And for once, we won't have any knives at our backs."

"Sounds boring."

The Queen's eyes shone as she chuckled, "Wax, I guarantee you, nothing about this is going to be boring." She started walking, giving Wax a light tug, a laughing wink. "Including tonight."

Eujo turned, stepping backward, her hand in his, looking every bit the mischievous, the mighty, the magnificent . . .

Wax shook his head, followed that bright smile, that determined hope.

The Tamas skar hummed its truth, and Wax could only agree.

CHAPTER 10

BOARDING CLAWS

The Kance embraced terror. As Narro put it, hiding a ship on the open sea, even at twilight wasn't something easily done, so why not embrace the attack, become your enemy's end? The Kance soldiers, those not maintaining the sails or steering the clipper, clambered up on the slim deck in a cloudy twilight, thick robes and rapiers at the ready.

No plate, not for these swordsmen.

Instead, they pounded hilts on the ship's rail as the two vessels closed. Their voices rose in a thundering song Quik didn't know but soon learned, a simple recitation calling for the wind god's aid and their foe's downfall. Quik watched, sang, took part in all this from the clipper's prow, his own Kance robes light in the chilling twilight. He wore no sword but instead his wood gauntlets, carved on Vis and now metal-tipped thanks to some enterprising Noctia blacksmiths.

Ironic, perhaps, that effort would now cause harm to their own forces.

The Najahn didn't ignore the approach. Like the Kance,

the caravel didn't seem meant for soldiers. Sailors in Najahn black and purple tunics and leathers gathered on the top deck, some passing crossbows to a front line for the first fire.

Quik was about to call out the imminent quarrel rain when the Kance clipper jolted, slicing hard to starboard and away from their straight-on slam towards the Najahn vessel. The move cut the ship into the water, lowering its profile just as the Najahn fired. Quik had to grab the prow's railing to keep from falling over, heard whistles as quarrels meant for him, for the Kance, whistled overhead.

A ridiculous maneuver, a wild pull, and one reversed in the next second: sails snapped and the Kance ship swung to port, closing the gap quick to the Najahn caravel. The enemy ship had size, the Najahn sailors leaning over the rail to angle their next salvos down, only to find grapples flung into their faces.

"For Kance!" Narro shouted.

Some of the three-pronged iron hooks bounced off their targets to fall into the sea. Others bit into the caravel with hard chunks, wood splintering. Their tossers shifted aside, and Quik saw Kance runners waiting to leap, robes fluttering, onto the ropes. With careful steps, the Kance planted one foot along another to rush the Najahn. Behind them, other Kance fighters opened up with their own crossbows, aiming for Najahn archers trying to reload amidst the chaos.

And hitting.

Quik heard the first screams as he made his own leap, eschewing the Kance ropes—he wasn't so confident to think he had the balance for those—for a strike into the caravel's side. Quik's gauntlets bit in, his booted feet scrabbling for footholds. Finding none, the wet hull a poor climber's aid, the Vis hunter relied on his arms. One lurch at a time, yanking himself up the caravel's side near the vessel's prow.

In the twilight, not a soul saw him. Or perhaps they did, and assumed Quik's strength would fail him long before he could make the railing.

A poor thought.

As Kance and Najahn engaged in old fashioned swordplay, rapiers meeting more traditional Rana cutlasses and a couple drawn voulges, Quik kept up his climb. Narro had given the Vis a different objective, one he would meet.

With wood chips sprinkling his hair and his arms beginning to burn from the effort, Quik hit the prow's top railing, pulled himself over with a clumsy roll. He came up to a kneel to see a whirling Najahn, crossbow rising to find Quik's face.

The hunter sprang forward, his boots at last finding traction on the flatter, dryer deck. Quik tackled the man, used the hit as leverage to stand himself up and, lurching to his left, tossed the Najahn over the ship's side. The sailor bounced once off the hull before disappearing into the waves, a wordless scream the last sound he'd ever make.

The Najahn caravel matched the same design Quik had rode on Foti, which meant the hunter was on the wrong side. To his right, the caravel's prow curled up, a sail linking it to the main mast in the ship's center. A smaller mast and sail lurked at the vessel's aft, glinting orange in daylight's last embers. That smaller mast and the tiller near it, the cabins beneath, were his goal. To get there, Quik would have to wade through a bloody morass.

Narro's confidence in the Kance seemed, at first glance, to be misplaced. Their rapiers gouged the sailors, drove the Najahn back, but the small blades didn't have the reach to close with the voulges. The curled spears came to the fore, the Najahn dropping their cutlasses as more voulges came from the lower decks, handed up by servants, prisoners, or other sailors. Even as Quik looked, tried to plan a way across, the Kance fell into a desperate stand.

The Vis hunter had never fought in a war before—the closest he'd come had been the Najahn beach raid against the bandits—and what to do seemed an utter mystery. Barrel in? Try to sneak around the starboard side? Shirk off the Kance cloak and try to claim he was a Najahn spy all along?

"Vis!"

The word carried, hard and panicked over the slapping waves, the screams, grunts, and curses. Narro, scaling the ropes and looking at his pressed, losing band. The Kance had one hand and both feet on the rope, the rapier raised, and a pleading look aimed Quik's way. One more than a couple Najahn followed.

Well, there went the stealth option.

Whooping, Quik juked towards the wide steps at his left. Two voulge-wielding Najahn reacted, breaking away from the Kance attack to aim those curved spears towards the stairs. A normal soldier might've run right into those sharp ends, betting on his abilities with blade or shield to knock the voulges away.

Quik was no normal soldier, and while that might mean he had no idea how to fight in formation, no idea how to counter and thrust, it meant he had something else: unpredictability.

Kicking from his juke, Quik leapt off the second step, bouncing off the prow's higher deck to his right. Like launching off a jungle tree, Quik felt his foot plant and pressed down, flying higher than those raising voulges reacted and landing in a flailing, tackling sprawl. The Vis drove both Najahn to the ground, those gauntlets piercing the poor protection offered by the Najahn's robes. Hot wet splattered Quik's own robe as he bore the pair to the ground, the momentum spurring his next move.

When hunting hanoko, always assume the cats came in packs. Never make yourself an easy target.

Quik rolled off the Najahn bodies, bringing his gauntlets and the bone, the skin, the fabric caught in their tips up across his chest. The expected strike from a third, surprised Najahn came, slashing down with wild intent. The blade cracked into Quik's right gauntlet, lodging into the wood plate. The Najahn sailer stared at it, attempting to withdraw the edge and failed.

The Vis snarled, the Najahn flicked his eyes from weapon to warrior. He had but one blade. The warrior had two, and the second gauntlet had no difficulties. Surging up, Quik pushed the stuck sword and its wielder into a fumbling retreat, one ended with a hard forward jab from his left gauntlet. Its victim coughed, shuddered, and collapsed.

But the guttural howl didn't come from the sailor, nor did the cutting blade nicking Quik's arm. The hunter whirled, saw another Najahn collapse to the deck, Narro's rapier withdrawing from the man's side.

"Keep your eyes about you, Vis," Narro said, giving Quik a nod. "We have the opening. Back to it."

Narro's spare words told the truth. While Quik had only cut down three, the chaos in his charge split the Najahn defense, letting the Kance raiders break through. The rope lines secured, more Kance fighters sprinted up, while the Najahn struggled to form a defensive line along the top deck. Those voulges still held a murderous advantage, not one Quik cared to brave.

Instead, Quik broke right, calling for Narro to come with. The Najahn spread to follow, chasing the Kance pair across the caravel's top deck. The motion thinned the purple and black's line, an effect Quik caught more in shadow as the sun descended past the horizon. Nobody had time for torches, for lanterns, the battle sinking into dark.

Sichi had yet to rise, and in her tardiness, Quik found advantage.

Narro countered the first arrival, using his rapier to knock the voulge thrust aside. Quik, staying to Narro's right, ducked the deflection and cut in close. His gauntlets pushed the voulge haft high, opening the sailor for Narro's follow-up stab. The purple and black robes fluttered as Quik continued his charge, staying in the body's cover as he pushed the poor soul into following friends.

Barely visible in plain view, Quik darted right, giving the body one more shove into a sword and spear gaggle. The Najahn cursed, missed the Vis as Quik broke towards the original goal: the Najahn captain's cabin and the secrets that hopefully waited inside.

Behind Quik, Narro hollered, drawing attention. The Kance pressed their attack, and Quik, listening for pursuit, heard none. A fighter fleeing the scene brought less worry than the blade already at your neck.

Or perhaps they couldn't even see him anymore.

Quik almost ran dead into the cabin, the wood door and wall appearing more as a feeling than an object seen. His gauntlet tips scratched, found the door's line. Quik pulled on the handle—an awkward move with the huge gauntlets, but the Vis dared not disarm with the fight still roiling at his back. The handle shook.

Locked.

Quik stepped back. Aimed, and snapped his left gauntlet forward. The metal tips shattered the door's upper hinge, bending it inward. A second, crunching blow knocked out the lower hinge, the bent metal creaking. One shove now would—

Steps, running his way. Quik whirled, thrusting with his right gauntlet. The incoming voulge, spearing straight towards Quik's neck per Najahn training, slid a deep furrow into Quik's right gauntlet, lined a burning cut through Quik's right shoulder. The Najahn followed the miss with a shoulder charge, one that might've worked against a weaker opponent, a slighter build.

Quik met it with a left shoulder thrust, the impact punching through the Najahn's robes. Ribs cracked, the man gasped for breath, and Quik snapped a kick after the stumbling fool. The blow struck the man's groin, dropped him and his voulge to the deck.

There'd be no more fighting from that one.

Ignoring the gash on his shoulder, Quik turned back to the ruined door, delivered a second kick. The lock did its job, wheeling the door in to the right, where it slapped against the cabin wall and hung there, a ruined thing, and one Quik could finally see, thanks to the candlelight coming within.

There, waiting, stood a single armored form. The Najahn captain, with his crossbow raised. The weapon clicked, the bolt flew, and Quik felt a stinging pain in his chest. The hunter faltered, the captain bent to reload, to crank the crossbow.

For Vis. For his friends. For his brother.

Quik snarled a hunter's prayer, fell into a bull rush. One, two, three strides and the captain dropped his crossbow.

Didn't reach for the sword at his waist, but instead the lit candles beside the table at his back. One covered with thick papers, lines blurring as the crossbow bolt tore at Quik's lungs, heart, something important.

The captain reached, knocked the candle over as Quik drove his gauntlet into the narrow seam at the man's arm. The candle hit the table, the flames finding their lick. Quik's claws found their own grip, biting through the softer rings beneath that Najahn plate, hooking into skin and what lay beneath. The Najahn screamed. Quik pulled, kicking at the same time, yanking the captain into a bloody tumble back to the floor.

Smoke's first tendrils, a burn's first scent, hit Quik's nose, and he spied an answer: a jug of wine. Quik reached for it, found his fingers numbing, his gauntlet too clumsy, his vision too blurred. So he swung instead, smashed the jug onto the small flame threatening to devour the maps. A deep purple washed across the table, swallowing the orange, two colors dancing, until they became one, single dark.

CHAPTER II

CHARITY

The setting was beautiful for a murder: a cave pool, water lapping at moist stones and stalagmites around the edges, the drip-drop as more leaked in from above. Dead air picking up some life as a far-off gust made its way through. And, of course, the snarling, twitching demise of the fiends who'd ambushed the Whent party, had fallen victim to their swords and axes, though of course, not without taking their own bites in exchange.

Ones Maena was about to finish off.

Two rockbiters made it out of the right alive, one sorely wounded and trying to bandage himself up while the other checked the bodies of their comrades. A grim effort, marked by claws, offal, and curses. One that also kept him from checking on his friend, a check no longer necessary as Maena dropped from her vantage point. The cutlass led the dive, angling down and delivering its mortal blow with only a shocked sigh's sound. She rode the crumpling body to the rocky path, stepping off into a striking crouch, each foot nestling into the grit without a crunch. The cutlass, ever sharp, withdrew at a tug from

Maena's hand, her left serving to balance the Rana into her next move.

The narrow path to the pool lit up with the target: pink-glowing moss. Clumped here and there, the moss coated the space in a rose glow, the blood and bits scattered about picking up shadows, a more crimson hue. Her target bent over the last of his friends, axe back on his belt and another curse on his lips.

Finish it.

The man put a hand on the body's shoulder, an affectionate squeeze. A harsh rebuttal to the voice in Maena's head, and one that prompted a question, a shift, a gasp of something she'd thought was long gone.

"What happened?" she asked, her voice a stiff whisper.

The man whirled, hand going for his axe before hesitating, confused. He bore a Whent's typical trappings: thick clothes , a beard, scars mingling with broken noses past. Bulky, wary. A crushed pine scent rolled her way. A furred cap covered his head tight, its once pristine silvers and browns now clotted with battle's leavings.

"Who're you?"

"I was looking for this," Maena said, gesturing at the moss with her cutlass. "Heard the sounds and came to see if I could help."

"You're too damn late." The man started to say something else, then noticed the slumped form near Maena. "Dammit, no."

He shuffled forward, brushed past Maena. The Rana sidestepped, watched as the rockbiter bent over his friend's form.

You burned your first chance. Don't blow this one.

Maena wanted to sigh, to curse, to lament the follies that'd led this man and his friends to their miserable ends.

Instead, she raised the cutlass, aligned for a simple, neck-severing stroke. The rockbiter, his hands on his friend, shivered to a stop. Those fingers would've found the new wound, would be realizing its clean cut didn't come from any fiend claws.

She swung.

He dove to his right, rolling off the cave's side in a twist. The cutlass didn't miss: it cut a red line along the man's arm, slicing through Whent leathers like they were little more than paper. Whent's own sharpening at work, there. Jochi's efforts going against his own people. Fitting.

"What're you—" the man started, tugging his axe free as Maena pressed, whipping the cutlass in another cross-cut.

The Whent didn't have time to draw his axe, had nowhere to dodge, and took the cutlass swing on his arm. The blade bit deep, the bracers and coat doing little to deter the swing. But it bought the man a second, one he used to bellow out a wild challenge, swing the axe in an upper-cutting swath.

Such wild swings had their downsides: predictable, inaccurate, and Maena ducked this one, letting the axe cut the air over her head as she yanked the cutlass free. In a crouch, she sprang forward, aiming for a fight-ending gut shot. The opening should've been there, should've been an easy take, but the Whent didn't withdraw his swing, instead dropping his elbow as he continued sliding along the cavern wall. The hit struck Maena's unprotected head, dashed her towards the ground. The cutlass skittered off the rock wall, blade striking sparks and missing flesh.

Maena tasted gravel as she hit dirt, her hands and knees pressing to keep her moving, keep her—

The axe bit into the wall above her head, a consequence

less of luck and more of the Whent's dodge. His sidesteps had him splashing into the pool, his footing sliding ever-so-slightly to put the swing up. Maena dropped her cutlass, instead popping up to grapple the Whent's wrist, bend it down with all her weight as he tried to keep hold of his weapon. The tension, the torque made something crack, the man howled and let the axe go, pulled his hand free, and stumbled back, falling into the pool with a chill splash.

Maena let the hand go, rising slow and adopting the lost weapon. She retrieved the cutlass too, wielding both ax and blade as she turned to the wounded Whent, the pool losing its pristine clarity as blood and dirt fouled the waters.

"What do you want?" the Whent snarled, kicking back into the pool, the deeper water.

"As I said, the moss," Maena replied. "All of it."

"Then take it!" The Whent broke into a half-sob. "It's not worth dying for, none of this is."

"That's where you're wrong. What this moss will get, what I can do . . . " Maena shook her head, approached the pool's edge. "Do you know me?"

"What? Know you?"

You can't, Maena. If he goes to Jochi's camp, he'll identify us. We'll be trapped.

"Who I am," Maena asked the Whent. "Do you know me?"

"Never seen you before in my life."

"But you'll remember me."

The Whent seemed to grasp the import as he held his broken wrist, sitting three strides deep in the pool. "Nah, I can barely see you. In fact, never saw you at all. Fiends. Fiends attacked us. Took everything we had. I had to play dead, see." The man was gibbering now, pleading. Tears. Snot. "Should've died, I should've."

Make it so.

Maena watched the sad show for a long moment. So far from the rockbiters she'd fought on the decks of a hundred ships. So far from Jochi's own warriors, ready to take on the firewalkers and other fiends down below. Finishing the man now would be almost a mercy, delivering a gift.

But.

We're killers, Maena. Because we have to be. Because of what needs to be done.

But not heartless. Not yet.

"Stay there," Maena said. "Don't move from the pool until I leave. Then count to one hundred, and do it slow. Once that's done, you're on your own."

Her other half, her split soul, raged as Maena packed up the moss. As much as she could carry, stuffed into pouches, satchels, and the parts of her it could stick to. The Whent whimpered at first, then fell to a stoney silence, watching Maena as she moved. Yet he held to her threat, made no motion to leave the pool. She steeled herself to potential insults, but they never came. No foolish bravado that would force Maena to deliver a killing stroke.

The Whent stayed quiet, and only after she'd disappeared around the bend, after she'd stopped to listen, did she hear him talk again.

Numbers, one after another, counting up.

The smith was asleep when Maena returned. The Dead City never quite fell quiet, the dark and depth proving ample encouragement for ale swilling and drunken debauchery, so Maena's hard knocks came with a singsong calamity behind her. Brawls and buffoonery. It took three sets, the final one conducted with her cutlass hilt, to get the man to open the door. He took the packs without a word, opened them once, and nodded at her.

"Two days," the smith said. "You'll have'em in two days."

Maena returned, then, to her own bed. The flat straw mat. She cleaned her cutlass with a tattered rag. Refreshed herself, and settled onto the hard bed.

That was stupid. He will tell others.

So what if he did? A strange woman appears, defeats him in a fight, all for some moss?

Maena laughed to herself, then stopped, glanced around. Nobody was there to listen, her housemates now all doing their best to obliterate yesterday before tomorrow could begin.

It's a risk, and we cannot afford to take anymore. We're saving the isles, Maena. This is worth too much.

The Rana captain frowned. She'd done terrible things. Rationalized them against a greater good, a better future. One that seemed to never arrive, until now. They were so closed.

Two days. Two days until she'd have enough. Then, the earth would shake, the chamber would collapse, and the fiends, all of them, would be destroyed.

Which is why you cannot play these games.

True. Not anymore. Though, what did it matter? A single wounded, weaponless Whent lost in the Dark Below? Maena patted the stolen axe haft, the rest of the weapon buried beneath her satchels, leathers, and other gear. The weapon had good quality, could be traded for something better. Its former owner certainly wouldn't need it anymore.

The man would never survive.

CHAPTER 12

GLIDERS AND GLORY

Because sleep was no more necessary for Svarde than breathing, the barbarian, along with a few Whent scouts keeping watch, caught the Kance attack. It didn't come via the ground, some mashing army marauding across the roughed-up fields towards the firewalkers and their friends. Instead, the glimmers arrived with the early dawn, Sichi's rose colliding with the sun's first oranges to highlight those Kance filaments like waving blades just pulled from the forge.

A swarm, that's what Svarde first thought as the array swooped around the mountains to the south and east. At first nothing, then bright dashes all lining up in a tight formation. High and steady, they came in towards the sleepy encampment—the firewalkers, while Svarde wasn't sure if they slept, did settle into a calm, crackling doze overnight—just now being roused by alarmed Whent whistles. Some tundra drum banged, a rapid beat overpowering the constant Kance bird calls and the soft waves.

"Kivi, best we find cover," Svarde said, lurching up from

the stone he'd selected at the field's edge. Part of a marking line and good enough for a seat, one he'd lurched up from every so often to take a walk around the nighttime camp. "Whatever these wind riders are planning, we won't be able to do much to stop it."

Ami, closer towards the field's center, didn't share Svarde's fatalistic view. She'd bounced up at the first Whent call and started running around, barking at firewalker and Whent alike to rise, grab arms, and prepare for an attack.

As if they had the time.

The gliders moved faster than any marching army, and they swooped in like diving birds. From beneath a palm's broad fronds, Svarde watched as the first gliders dove in. At first, he couldn't make out their weapons, those golden dashes seeming to have nothing, but puffs from the ground suggested otherwise. Whent scouts and soldiers too slow to leave the field began calling out in pain, a few stumbling into the sand and not rising again. The firewalkers had no bellows, no war cries, crossing their arms to deflect any incoming missiles.

Svarde saw not a single one of the burning fiends go down, even suffer an injury. No ash white patches, no sparking fury.

He did see their counter.

As the gliders leveled out their dive to soar overhead, the firewalkers leaned down, ditching their flails for rocks, for dirt clumps hardened by the fiend's heat to molten glass missiles. With four arms, the fiends launched their replies at the passing gliders. One took a strike in its gentle wing, the craft spinning hard into a circle before plunging straight into the ground. Another lost its pilot, the flailing, struck form falling to a final landing. The gliders didn't take the deadly fire without action, the smooth assault breaking as gliders twitched this way and that, a spastic dodging that held its own consequences.

Svarde winced as one glider pair flew into each other, as another, ducking a thrown stone turned too sharp, slammed into a nearby mountainside. The first wave broke up, most turning their gliders back towards the town.

As if they'd be safe there.

"C'mon, Kivi," Svarde said to the loyal ferrite. "I know how we can be useful."

The barbarian broke into a loping jog towards the town, the great black jagged blade resting on his left shoulder. No axes at his waist, no shield in his right hand. The Noctia and Vis skars, or the blade fashioned from them, joined their whispers in his mind, a constant hum both feeding Svarde life and removing it, rendering him a tasteless void. Albeit a capable one.

Kance had some tricks left, the results visible as Svarde kept his glances going back to his army. A second glider wave came in higher, their bolts—shot, Svarde noted from the first wave, from rail-mounted crossbows—less accurate but merely an opening for their next weapon: small bombs dropped by hand.

The tiny things screamed down, striking the earth and erupting in popped explosions. A bright idea stolen from Foti and Najahn craftsmen, now deployed against the scattering Whent soldiers. They dropped, too, amid the fire-walkers, who soaked in the heat, the pressure, with indifference. The fiends proved they could throw higher as well, the dirt clumps, the stones, soaring so far into the purple-blue dawn they seemed like shooting stars.

Gliders fell. Pilots died. The Kance assault withered, retreated.

No third wave rounded the mountains.

Svarde ran on, alone.

The Kance town had a small stone wall around its outskirts, less a defense than a pleasant border. Murals coated the white-washed bricks. Names too, calling out the town's notable citizens, its leaders. Names Svarde would soon render into ash.

Yet the barbarian sighed as he clomped closer, leaving the fields for the hard dirt roads leading in. There'd been such slight hope yesterday, a chance at peace, and now that hope was gone. Too stubborn, this stupid isle, and now they'd die for it.

Well, Svarde would pick his targets. Those who didn't fight would be spared his sword. Whether the firewalkers would adopt the same mantra, he couldn't say.

Better, then, that he had first crack at the enemy. Break them, and in the doing, save them.

Three soldiers in Kance's glassy armor stood at the town's gate, really just a gap in the wall. Behind them, as Svarde approached, chaos reigned. Crashed and landing gliders, those who hadn't kept enough momentum to vanish into one of the mountain passes, lay strewn about the square, smashed into rooftops, or caught on chimneys. Townspeople ran this way and that, many with stuffed satchels on their backs.

Fleeing, then. Smart.

"Morning," Svarde said, Kivi snorting at his side, as he approached. "Don't suppose you'd like to surrender now, seeing as your attack's only provoked us."

One guard stepped forward, and Svarde recognized the face between the helmet, shadowed across half as the rising sun shot its orange-purple rays across the land.

"Wars aren't won in a single skirmish," Veloc said,

drawing his rapier and holding it level towards Svarde. "Today we learn. Tomorrow we win."

"Those gliders that got away, maybe. You, definitely not." Svarde kept his big blade on his shoulders, nodded at the rapier. "That little poker's only going to get you killed. Put it away."

Veloc flushed. The other two guards stepped up at his sides.

"We'll buy our families and friends the time they need," Veloc said. "For that, the rapiers will be enough."

Svarde tilted his head, "Surrender will give you all the time you want, your lives as well. We're not here to kill you."

"And we're not here to lay down and let the rockbiters and their fiends walk all over us."

The barbarian lifted the jagged black blade off his shoulder, gripped it with both hands. The Noctia voices surged, hungry, demanding Svarde strike. Behind them, beneath them, the Vis stayed quiet.

"Your choice, your consequences," Svarde said, then gave a low whistle.

Kivi darted forward and left, angling towards the guard on that side. The man, seemingly startled at a ferrite's speed, jabbed at the rock lizard. The strike came in wild, the rapier hitting Kivi's stone skin and shattering. Kivi didn't stop her charge, barreling into the guard and carrying him to the ground.

"Help him," Veloc snapped to the other guard, before taking a step towards Svarde. "If I kill you, will your army break?"

"That's the thing," Svarde said. "You can't."

Veloc's puzzled look turned horrified as the man's stride turned into a straight-on stab, one Svarde let puncture his right side. The rapier slid in, and Svarde felt the pain, albeit so distant, so vague, as to resemble a dream. No blood came forth, no wince, no agonized shout. Instead, Svarde cut across with the jagged blade, battered the rapier from Veloc's hands to the dirt.

The Kance soldier backed away a step, head shaking. "You're not real. This isn't real. It can't—"

"It is."

Svarde kicked the rapier towards Veloc, the blade's hilt bouncing off the man's armored boots.

"Pick it up and die, or leave it, and surrender."

Behind Veloc, his two guards didn't make the choice to fight any easier. Kivi, having head-butted her first target into unconsciousness, had the second guard's leg in her mouth. The ferrite's jaws crunched, shattering the Kance armor and causing the woman to scream. The noise found its echo in the town, those scrambling people realizing the war had arrived, and sooner than expected.

Veloc gulped, found enough bravery to pick up the sword. Again he leveled it at Svarde, though the barbarian saw the tip shake.

"Bold, and stupid," Svarde said.

"I am no coward."

"Didn't say you were."

Svarde moved as he spoke, driving into a broad two-handed sweep, one that would've knocked Veloc's head from his shoulders. The Kance fighter ducked, dropping to one knee as Svarde's blade whistled overhead. Veloc took the opening, again dashed forward, stabbed Svarde in what should've been a fatal blow to the barbarian's gut.

Again the distant pain, the Vis murmurs. No blood, no heat, no dimming of his dead vision.

Svarde reversed the swing. Veloc, his rapier catching on

Svarde's leathers, couldn't retreat fast enough. The barbarian's strike caught the Kance mid-chest, the blade breaking Kance armor and flinging Veloc to the dirt, wet red following. The rapier lay beside its owner.

Veloc, groaning, put his palms to the ground, started to rise, only for Svarde to get a booted foot on the man's back. Pressed him to the dirt.

"Last chance, Veloc," Svarde rumbled. "Stop, or I grind your skull into dust."

"You're a bastard," Veloc spat through gravel and grit.

"A point I won't argue, but my offer stands."

Veloc cursed, a weak, sad thing, then fell limp. Svarde nodded to nobody, then stepped off the man's back to kick the rapier away. As he did, Svarde whistled again, calling Kivi off the moaning guard and to his side.

"Nice work, girl," Svarde said to the ferrite, kneeling down to pat the rock lizard on her head. "Proud of you."

Kivi flashed her sapphire eyes, a particular glint. Svarde laughed.

"True, they weren't much," Svarde muttered, rising and looking at the town.

People continued to stream away, towards what Svarde assumed was a rear exit, a passage through the mountains. One their army would follow soon enough.

"Content with three?" Ami asked not long after, the Kance guard trio left sitting against the wall. Only Veloc had a serious wound, and Svarde had helped the man patch it up with cloth from his satchel. "I saw you leave and expected the whole city to be burning by now."

"If you invite those firewalkers in, it will," Svarde said, looking at the blazing ranks formed up behind Ami.

"They're what's left. I sent the Whent back below. They're at risk here, and we don't need their bodies."

"No?"

Ami, flame hair and golden faceplate blazing as morning erupted in full, held a grim smile. "You're immortal, and the firewalkers might as well be. Kance is doomed, Svarde. The only question is how many of them need to die before they realize it."

CHAPTER 13

SEA AND STONES

The Najahn came at the *Storm's Edge* with impossible efforts. Deux's first call to the deck came soon after dawn, with Kance soon to appear on the horizon. Already visible to the east and closing quick were several Najahn clippers. Behind them, bloated Foti galleons conscripted by the purple and black emerged.

"An early thaw's made this harder than expected," Deux said to Wax and Eujo as they made it to the deck.

Both Queen and Vis wore a pleasant exhaustion, one partially shed after a rinse from a seawater shower. Any lingering good mood from the utterly amazing night before dissipated fast at those closing flags and the soldiers they represented. Wax put his hand on his necklace, felt the warm stones waiting beneath his shirt, the Kance robe.

That he'd be calling on their power before long wasn't a question anymore. That Wax would have to control the god stones again and again was now his life's pattern, as inexorable as eating, drinking, and . . . his attention drifted to Eujo, who'd fallen right into a straight tactics talk with her captain.

"Can we outrun them?" Deux replied to the Queen's question. "The galleons haven't a chance at catching us, and in a fair race, I'd say we might beat those clippers too. But here they're cutting us off, going half our distance with fair weather besides. I'll call the crew to arms."

"You don't sound confident," Eujo said, sharing the railing with Deux and matching his stare to the enemy ships.

"We're sailors, not soldiers, my queen. Livier is the only true fighter we have aboard, save your Guardians, perhaps. Every one of those clippers will have a squad or more Najahn soldiers, armed and trained in killing. We'll be hard-pressed against one, much less three."

"Then we won't fight them," Wax said, getting both stares his way. "We don't have to." He tapped the necklace. "Use your Kance skar, Eujo. Give us the same boost you did on the way to Whent."

Eujo nodded, reached for her bracelet, then stopped. "Deux, the Najahn are fighting us, right?"

"They are?"

"Then every one of their ships we sink, helps us, right?"

"It would?"

"Eujo?" Wax asked. "What?"

"We're not running," Eujo declared. "Kance's Queen won't arrive back home running. I want to inspire my isle, not give them more reason to be afraid."

Deux's brow furrowed, loosened as Eujo held up her wrist. "You want to use the skars?"

"Not want, but will. I will, Deux. For my isle, my people, and to win this damn war."

Wax stayed quiet as Eujo and Deux planned the defense, the first clipper nearing the *Storm's Edge*. Bliss and Torny had their robes on, leathers beneath. Staff and daggers ready. The Kance sailors had armed up too, though Eujo had them focused on keeping the *Storm's Edge* sailing at high speed. Just because she wanted to use the skars to annihilate the Najahn, didn't mean she wanted to make a lucky boarding easy.

And that, there, was the thought Wax kept coming back to. Eujo bristled with a cold fury. The Tamas skar hanging from Wax's neck told him as much. The Kance Queen wanted to bring fear and ruin, destruction and death to the purple and black attacking her home. She was ready, and though she hadn't asked, Wax knew what was expected: when the skars sapped Eujo's energy, he would need to take her place and complete the massacre.

Accidents and desperation had driven Wax's skar disasters before: the Rana bubble fiend, the estate in Whent's coastal city, the swirling fire and rippling earth at the Najahn outpost near the Golden Gash.

Eujo could've fled. Instead, she wanted to use the skars as weapons.

'Shouldn't you be up there?' Bliss signed, moving before Wax with a frown on her face.

They both stood strides back from the *Storm's Edge*'s prow, where Eujo and two Kance sailors holding stiff wood shields waited. Those sailors would catch any incoming missiles, give Eujo time to focus her onslaught. The clipper was moments away now, its narrow deck coated with armored soldiers. Chakrams, voulges, and crossbows bristled.

An old way of killing about to meet the new.

"Pan wouldn't have wanted this," Wax said.

'Pan wouldn't want you to die either.'

"So that's the choice? Use the skars to kill, or die?"

Bliss didn't give Wax a frown, a hand, any support. Just

a straight look. 'Might not be your fault, but that's where we're at, Wax.' She flicked a glance towards the clipper, closing fast. 'Only kids get to pretend otherwise.'

"That's not—"

'Find a way, brother.' Bliss nodded at Torny, the bandit oblivious, watching the approaching Najahn. 'I didn't come all this way, find her, to lose her now.'

The Najahn didn't offer a preamble. No negotiation, no terms, no calls to surrender. The collection on the prow raised their crossbows. Wax didn't hear the clicks, but the bolts flew, darts soaring into the air towards the *Storm's Edge*.

They never made it.

Eujo took the first volley. The wind picked up as the Queen extended a hand towards the clipper. The bolts slowed, tilted and splashed into the waves. Not a one reaching the Kance ship. Wax kept his eyes on the Najahn, saw surprise pour over some faces.

Some, not all.

"They know," Wax said, hands on the prow beside Eujo, the two ships coming near each other. "They're expecting the skars."

"So?" Eujo replied, breathless. "They can't stop us. Your turn."

Wax looked towards the waves. The Rana skar leapt up in his mind, fresh inspiration, bright and ready. Wax let it loose, and the stone lurched. Wax himself leaned forward, pressing into the rail, the water pulling at him as much as the skar lunged for it. Below, the waves shifted, a rush billowing away from the *Storm's Edge* and rising towards the clipper. Against any current, against the other waves, an unnatural wall.

The clipper slammed into the wave, the force shoving

up the ship until it stood vertical, toppling over. Soldiers fell into the cold ocean, splashes and screams riding up as the clipper vanished with its crew. Wax saw it in a haze, like watching a party after too much peach wine. The Rana skar snatched, stole, and devoured him, and the Renewal would've fallen over if his sister, if Torny hadn't grabbed his arms and held him up.

The single broken wave began to swirl, twisting around the ruined ship, the swimming soldiers, frothing into a whirlpool. The *Storm's Edge* passed by as those purple and black souls vanished forever. The skar wanted them deeper, buried into the bottom of the sea. It reached for more, urging Wax in wordless pressure.

"Wax," Torny's voice a distant noise.

He couldn't let the Najahn come back. Couldn't let them swim away. The skar wouldn't let them either. Together, they could—

Wax hit the deck hard. What little breath he had flew out, the Rana skar dissipating in a confused cacophony as the other stones around his neck urged their own reprisals. Eujo's glare pushed them away, the Queen's drained, icy look paired with the concerned eyes from his sister and Torny.

"It's done," Eujo said. "Let it go, Wax. Let it go."

No sooner had Eujo spoke than one of the Kance soldiers pulled her away. Deux's voice rose, calling for Eujo to head back to the bridge. Bliss reached out a hand, grabbed Wax's own, but the Vis didn't move. His legs were lodestones.

"Not yet," Wax said.

"Sorry," Torny replied, matching his sister's grip and, together, the two pulled Wax up. Bliss snuck her shoulder beneath Wax's right arm, steadied him. Torny nodded further starboard, past the dying whirlpool. "That's one down, but those other two are closing quick. You better get some spice fast, Wax."

Spice? If Wax managed to stay awake another few minutes, he'd consider that a victory. Eujo, at least, seemed to have her color back. He caught her iron eyes for an all-too-brief moment as the Kance sailors swept her aft, where the other two clippers closed.

"Go," Wax said. "Go with her."

"You can barely stand," Torny replied. "Kinda hard to—"

"You can fight. That's what matters."

The bandit, ever ready with a cocky retort, only frowned and looked across Wax to Bliss. The Vis hunter gave Torny a slight nod and they pulled Wax back, leaned him against the dining room's forward wall, a slanted slat of bleached white wood. As a resting place, it'd do well enough, and with his Guardians dashing away, Wax didn't have much choice.

The *Storm's Edge* sailed on, a smudge on the horizon growing more and more clear with every passing minute. As calls for counters, for shields, for boarding, rang out behind him, Wax found it hard to keep his eyes open, to do anything save listen to the skar's ever-present mutterings. Their wordless rumbles offered no solutions, no destructive demands, and in that, at least, the Vis found some small comfort.

CHAPTER 14
WAR-TORN REUNIONS

The pain, sharp and snappy, popped Quik from an unknown darkness and into a soft, sandy, sunlit world. Standing over him, a chill concern on her face, was someone Quik had given up seeing again. It'd only been a few weeks since their hurried escape from Noctia, but the isles had flown so far into chaos during that time, anything earlier seemed a blurred dream.

Annalyse, right here, right now, in a Vis weave, with a growing tan declaring she'd spent more time outside than Noctia ever allowed, crashed that dream right into reality.

"You're awake?" Annalyse said.

Quik tried to nod, felt the aches, heard a Vis skar's thunderous rumblings as it thrashed against his wounds. The skar explained why he couldn't muster the energy to move, to even shake his head. The damn stones took as much as they gave, though, as the moments in the Najahn caravel's cabin came back to him, Quik figured he once again owed his life to the skars.

What would linger, the memories, the trauma . . . that he could deal with later.

"I'm sure you're tired," Annalyse said, apparently judging Quik's open eyes as an adequate answer to her question. "We're going to need you to get past this fast."

The blunt line led to more. The Kance ship, with a wounded Narro still captaining, had careened into port hours before. They'd put the torch to the Najahn caravel, dragged the wounded and the prisoners with them, and sailed for the closer Vis. A decision made in equal parts to get faster aid, and because of what Quik had preserved in the Najahn captain's cabin.

"Crude maps, but maps nonetheless," Annalyse said, settling into a sit next to Quik. The pair weren't alone—the Kance ship swayed at a nearby pier, Mottilan porters working with Kance sailors to unload the vessel, its slim cargo, and its fresh prisoners. "That caravel had been crossing our coast, noting likely landing spots. Where we did and didn't have defenses. There were also plans outlining an overland attack."

The Najahn would be pressing from the West, apparently ignoring or overwhelming Kitaye's remaining resistance. When the soldiers crossed the mountains, the Najahn navy would come in from the sea, smashing Mottilan between two hammers to force a quick surrender. A plan that'd be a risk so long as Kance held any control over the ocean between the two isles, something Narro said the wind isle was committed to.

"Which leaves us with a puzzle," Annalyse said. "The Najahn have to know Kance wouldn't let Vis, their only ally in this fight, to struggle alone. What would get Kance to withdraw its own ships? What would keep them away?" Annalyse glanced down at Quik, still too tired to lift his own head. "You don't know anything, do you? Narro didn't."

Quik forced the slightest head shake.

"Thought so." Annalyse swept a look out beyond the waves, as if the answer might be lurking there beneath the midday clouds. "Then we have to plan for what the Najahn might do. And that's attack."

"When?" Quik's throat scratched, a faded iron taste lingered on his tongue.

"The scouts say a few days," Annalyse said, pulling a water skin from her waist and pouring the cool nourishment down Quik's throat. "They're moving fast." She pulled back the water, as grim a look as Quik had ever seen coming over her. "They must think Mottilan won't fight back. Fassle doesn't know how wrong he is."

By sunset, after sleeping away the afternoon, Quik sat in a stiff chair around a large stone table bearing a map of Vis's eastern side. Deshiva, somehow alive, somehow as vibrant and dangerous as ever, presided over the first real war council Quik had ever seen. She dished out commands and took advice from elders, hunters, Narro, and Annalyse alike. Quik himself kept quiet, letting the orders and their recipients come and go.

Deshiva delivered the edicts with force, without Gladdring's silver tongue. A command to double up scouts on the mountain passes came with clear warnings about how many lives would be lost if the Najahn came unexpected. A plea to Kance to send more naval support dashed out the door to fishermen with boats so small, pilots so skilled as to make discovery on the open ocean next to impossible. That those tiny boats might wreck in open sea was a risk rewarded with Deshiva's open admiration, a trust that their bravery would be remembered.

If Gladdring pulled people with strings, with knives at backs and skars shifting souls, then here was a real leader.

When Deshiva, at long last, turned to Quik, he stood. His knees almost buckled, the hunter planting his massive palms on the stone table, but Quik didn't return to the chair. He wouldn't, couldn't show weakness here, not among his peers, especially the Mottilan hunters. Annalyse twitched at his right, but Quik shrugged off her attempted support.

Deshiva gave him a solemn nod, "Quik, I can say it's a true lift to see you standing here with us. Those gauntlets at your waist are ready to find fresh Najahn blood?"

"They are, hunt master."

"He nearly died, Deshiva," Annalyse spoke up. "The Vis skar is doing its best, but he needs more time. He—"

"We all need more rest, Annalyse. If Quik says he is ready, I believe him." Deshiva tapped a spot on the map. The Great Sana. "We'll win this war by outlasting the Najahn. To do that, we need every one of our hunters to count for a dozen of theirs. The only way that works is with more Vis skars." Deshiva again put her hard eyes on Quik. "Go up the path. You'll find a group on the third house on the left. They leave in an hour. Join them. Take the Sana."

"Take the Sana?" Annalyse asked. "But the Najahn are everywhere—"

"They expect us to hide, to cower," Deshiva snapped. "We will do neither. Quik, do you understand?"

The hunter did.

Quik caught the group, a scattered mix of Mottilan, Kitaye, and Lira hunters. Inked skin called out each, the tattoos rising up off their skin in Sichi's rose light. Quik knew not a face among them, save one.

"How?" He asked when Sawi ran up, wrapped the hunter in a tight hug. "How are you here?"

"Turns out those caves go a long way," Sawi said, stepping back, folding her arms. "Annalyse thought you'd need more time. I knew better."

"So did Deshiva."

A whistle drew them both to the group's leader, a grumpy hunter named Reth. The man hefted a spear, a Mottilan blowgun hanging from a thread around his neck. Every other hunter wore the same, and Sawi handed Quik his own shooter to go with his gauntlets, promising to teach him on the run, after they'd swapped stories.

Without another word, with satchels on their backs, pouches tied to their thighs, the fifteen hunters broke along the cliffside path leading up and away from Mottilan. As they loped, Quik noted covered spike pits, platforms nestled in branches where archers could shoot from cover, and stacked logs and rocks ready to be loosed for devastating slides. Some Mottilan builders still worked even now, digging out trenches for more traps.

"Surprising, right?" Sawi said as they jogged near the group's back. Quik's legs were heavy, but the feel of Vis dirt beneath his feet, the tropical scents, jungle sounds, brought with it invigorating memories. "Mottilan isn't the lazy disaster we thought."

"Didn't they try to kill you last time you were here?"

"The man who did that's dead. The Najahn killed him."

"I would've done it if they hadn't."

Sawi laughed, "You would've been too late."

The words forced a different look from Quik. That Sawi, once the mild-mannered gatherer, would talk so casually about winning a fight against a noted hunter? That she would throw out vengeance as a certainty rather than a wish?

They were so far from where they'd been. So far.

"It's never coming back, is it?" Quik asked as they

reached the cliff's top, curling west now into the mountain passes. "The life we used to have?"

"Never. Do you even think we'll see Wax again? Bliss?"

"I promised I'd help him, Sawi. I haven't given that oath up."

Another laugh, a crass one. Sawi started to say something, then broke it off.

"Quik, I hope you keep that one. I really do."

"But you don't believe I will?"

"I came home, Quik, because I wanted to be here." Sawi's voice dropped, almost to a whisper. "But, no matter who wins this war, the isles are never going to be the same."

Ahead, the trees thickened. Treehouses that, in better days, would've held Mottilan families sat dark and abandoned, their owners huddled in makeshift shelters on the beaches below. The dirt road bore little evidence of traffic, the usual trade dead. An alien feel, and one removed only minutes later as Reth directed their group off the road, into the undergrowth.

They'd be approaching the Great Sana from the jungle, using the Najahn's ill abilities in the wilderness against them. A good plan, one Quik didn't think much about as they hiked the night away.

Because as Sawi described the Dark Below, the coming fiends, and the undying barbarian at their head, the journey back to the life Quik loved seemed impossible.

CHAPTER 15

THE MISSING MAN

The morning started well. A late wake-up after her long night followed by fresh eggs and bread, brought into the Dead City from the first of many Najahn supply drops. The Wound rang with hammers and squeaking wheels now, as Whent engineers worked from the bottom while their Noctia counterparts came down from the top to string ropes and elevators along the massive length. As Maena heard tell, larger ledges were being converted to way stations, where posted soldiers would transfer satchels from one slat to the next, making a days-long journey from the surface in hours.

Even in its earliest incarnation, the deliveries brought relief from mushrooms and moss, and Maena devoured her portion amid the crowded tables set up along the Dead City's central square. The ancient, gnarled stone played host to frenzied meal times decreed by Jochi and his quartermasters, declared by ringing bells every few hours. Anything beyond those intervals required bartering, but if you were willing to accept whatever slop Jochi provided, you could eat for free.

For now, anyway.

Maena, always alone, cast her eyes about the people eating around her. They were cleaner now, less an explorer rabble and more a civilized—as much as any rockbiter could be—group. Color-dyed leathers and furs denoted positions, ranging from brown and black engineers to deep crimson for the scouts. Fresh water basins kept faces cleaner, functioning smithies meant knives and blades were sharp. Smiles and laughter had replaced the mordant fear that'd dominated when the firewalkers were still force to be dreaded instead of friended.

Dupes, all of them. The fiends will turn, and Jochi will lose everything.

If Pennifer or Rasslebeck had still been here, instead of ditched back to Rana, they would've agreed. Jochi saw peace and profit, untapped glory. Maena stopped a rising chuckle. She'd give him that, though he didn't deserve it. Closing off those gates would hand the Dark Below to Whent and Noctia, and Maena knew she'd receive no credit for it.

The true heroes never get their due.

"Waiting for anyone?"

The question, asked by a stretched and toneless voice, snapped Maena's look up from her remaining scrambled eggs, salted and delicious. The speaker had a Whent scout's body, thin and meant for ranging, but wore no weapons, no battle-ready leathers. Instead light furs, a bone tooth necklace, and a bland tunic gave cover to ashen skin, a face that looked like it hadn't seen sunlight as long as he'd been alive. He smelled like campfire, a scent growing more and more rare as the Dead City established better braziers to combat the depth's constant chill.

A newer arrival, then.

And not an accident.

True. That someone would randomly approach Maena, a person whose reputation seemed to spread instantly to anyone arriving this far down, was ridiculous. She bought into that aura too: no need to have rockbiters harassing her few moments of peace.

"Going to answer, or am I that interesting to stare at?"

Maena set down her fork, nodded to the stone stool at the small square table's opposite side.

"There's room."

The man slouched onto the stool, his elbows splaying to either corner, hands steepling in the table's middle. No food or drink, putting to rest any innocent reasons for the sit down.

"You're Maena, the Rana captain, right?" The man asked, knowing full well she was exactly that.

"Who're you?"

"Haggerth. I'm here on Jochi's account." The man stayed rigid as he talked, not a muscle moving, not an eye blinking. "Going to ask you a few questions, if that's all right?"

"Questions about what? And what do you mean, on Jochi's account?"

"You're Rana, so you might not know, but Whent's not all brawlers and boors. The Pits are for criminals, and I'm one who catches them."

He disappears people who aren't wanted.

"Justice is a malleable thing on Whent, from my experience," Maena said.

"It's that way everywhere. Including down here."

Maena twitched her fingers in a tossed off agreement. Threw a look around, saw not a soul interested in their conversation. No watching reinforcements, no onlookers curious. Meaning either they didn't know Haggerth, or knew well to stay out of it.

"There's a scout that's been missing a few days now," Haggerth said, keeping those slate eyes on her, letting the words dangle.

"People go missing every day down here. Up there, too."

"It's my job to find them, Maena."

"Gathered that."

Haggerth delivered the scout's description, one so matching Maena wondered where he'd picked up the information until Haggerth revealed his source: the scout's partner.

Of course, we wind up with the one scout who loves something other than being alone in the dark.

"Our missing man's been a scout for a long time," Haggerth continued. "Not like him to disappear without a word, without a sign. You catch what I'm saying?"

"Maybe that's how it is up on the surface, but that's not where we are, Haggerth. Fiends crawl these tunnels and they don't like to leave evidence."

Haggerth nodded, "Except he wasn't on ranging duty this month. His lead and his partner both say he'd been tasked with detail mapping. Sites for camps, mining, and so on. Well inside the shell."

The protected range, where Whent troops kept tunnels clean and clear. At least, the ones they knew about.

Don't give him anything.

As if Maena would. She matched Haggerth's stare.

"You're telling me all this why?" Maena asked.

"Because I've been talking to more than one person who says they saw you with him last. Talking, leaving by the southern tunnels. You and him, alone."

He's done the work.

"That's the man you're talking about?" Maena asked.

"It is."

"He showed me a faster way to the shell's edge. We parted ways. That's it."

Haggerth moved not a muscle.

Not buying it.

"Why him?" Haggerth asked. "Of all the scouts, why him?"

Because Inglan hadn't recoiled at the tavern the night before, hadn't edged away when Maena started talking. Had nodded when she whispered the truth about the swirling gates and how they could be stopped.

Too bad his faith broke.

"He was going that way. That's where I was heading, and I needed help."

"Help with what?"

"You haven't been down here long, have you Haggerth?" Maena said, spooning the last bits of her eggs into her mouth.

Never let a good meal go to waste.

"Long enough to know you've been here longer than most," Haggerth replied. "You're a Rana captain, means you have experience navigating unfamiliar places. Means you don't hold a healthy opinion of us."

"Whent?"

Haggerth gave her a nod.

"None of that matters," Maena said. "What does, is what's in that chamber, below those waters."

Haggerth tilted his head, "Which is?"

"The reason we're here, and the reason I've stayed."

"I'm listening."

Maena stood, lifted her ceramic, gray plate. Haggerth matched her.

"Listening won't help you much, Haggerth. This, you have to see to understand."

Haggerth plunged his hands into the light coat. Drew it in close around him. As if the idea of going anywhere gave the man a chill. Which, looking at his thin frame, wasn't surprising. For all his talk, Maena would bet the man hadn't been on the rougher side of the outdoors for long.

An opportunity, then.

"You'll show me?" Haggerth asked.

"Depends." Maena ditched the plate into a washing basin. "Do you want to know what's really happening here?"

"It's my job."

Maena laughed, "Then come along, Haggerth. I don't know anything about your missing scout, but I can show you something much more important."

CHAPTER 16

INVASION

Victory under a leader's guide wasn't satisfying. Svarde watched the Whent move into the Kance town, claiming buildings and forming the few remaining residents into groups to be watched, ordered, occupied. Beyond the walls and back to the dirty, fallow fields, the firewalkers clustered into their usual camps. Ami was out there somewhere, talking with the one fiend she trusted, the one she aptly named Spark.

Doing a general's work while he sat on a drained fountain's rim and stared. Kivi munched on the same, gouging out a grainy stone snack.

"How's that taste?" Svarde muttered to the ferrite and Kivi snorted in response. "That good, eh?"

Another snort, the ferrite not breaking from her meal. High quality stone indeed.

For a day marked by battle, the night's only issue seemed to be the clouds on the horizon. Thick and heading their way. What might've been snow a week or two earlier would likely spit rain now, and not the nice drizzle. The Whent around Svarde were shuttling their gear inside homes, using Kance stoves instead of open fires. Windows shuttered, the streets clearing. What victory songs and celebrations there were stayed within closed doors.

Then again, the Whent had done little but watch the gliders go by. What did they have to celebrate?

"Going to get wet out here," Olgata said, the Whent scout and the main link between Ami, Svarde, and the rock-biters. Svarde winced at the term, an old habit he'd need to kill. "Storm's coming."

"See that." Svarde nodded down at the jagged blade, its great line resting on his gray thighs, the battered leathers over them. "Just might ride it out."

"Don't feel the wet either?"

"Feel it plenty, but I'm curious." Svarde looked towards the town walls, the burning groups beyond.

"I'm worried."

Svarde chuckled. "My guess, a lotta steam. That's what happens when you get water too close to heat. Real foggy tomorrow."

Olgata didn't join in the laughter. "You've seen that? The rain on these firewalkers?"

"Surely they've dealt with it."

Olgata scratched at her nose, "You think Foti, the god of fire, puts rain in his home?"

The scout's damn premonition came true. Svarde wasn't asleep when the storm struck—he was never asleep—but he'd gone deep enough down a what-if rabbit hole re-running Catya's Renewal that the first drops came without notice.

The firewalkers' panic, though, was hard to miss.

Steam did bellow up into the dark, the burning forms out in those fields like beacons in the night. Orange mist rose like clouds. Svarde started to stand when the tremors began, a mystery to his feet answered by his eyes: the fire-walkers were running, as one, towards the town.

"Kivi," Svarde said, standing. As ever, despite sitting for hours on end, his legs obeyed with nary a complaint. What he'd give for a little needle, a little twinge. "I don't think the firewalkers like the rain."

The Whent had posted watches, cowled wanderers patrolling the town in pairs, and they responded to the approaching maelstrom of steam and fire with curiosity. Svarde, with Kivi at his heels, ran past gawking groups.

"Spread the alarm!" the barbarian shouted, the words breaking the rainy night's spell.

"Alarm?" one called back. "Aren't they on our side?"

"Right now they're on nobody's side but their own!"

Svarde passed houses, inns, dark shops and stables. His feet slid and stomped on wet stone. The walls sat in shadow, haloed against the oncoming rumble. The fire-walkers clumped together as they ran, the glows merging into a single bright ball heading right for the town. They'd arrive in moments.

The Whent guarding the gate fled by Svarde, heading the opposite direction, a choice the barbarian encouraged with another bellow.

"Tell the others to leave the buildings! Stay in the open!" Svarde called after them, making a guess.

To keep a forge hot, you kept it covered. If the fire-walkers hadn't lost their minds entirely, they'd be seeking the same. Those Kance roofs were the closest things this inlet had to shelter, and anyone stuck inside would be ...

Svarde snarled, stuck a battle stance in the gate's middle. Wide enough for large carts and little more, Svarde's bulk made an imposition, one added to with Kivi's snorting assistance. He held the jagged blade out before him, hoping for a little remembered menace.

Hoping for a different sort of fear.

The firewalkers swarmed, a churning mass of hissing white and gray broken here and there by orange and red flashes. Those obsidian triangles floated too, hovering on the mist, their surfaces a wild light surfeit. No clarity rested there, only panic. The charge ran wider than the gate, stood taller than the walls on Svarde's either side, and paid no mind to what they approached.

"Stop!" Svarde shouted into the storm, the blitzing wind and rain making a mockery of his call, one the fire-walkers heeded not in the slightest.

They would have to heed his blade.

The firewalkers crashed towards him, no weapons trailing their forms, no metal gear. Only pure flame, and Svarde met it with his sword. Roaring out another plea to stop, Svarde stepped into his first swing, aiming it low toward's the leader's legs. Like attempting to hit the sun, and Svarde's attack slowed as the heat washed over him, seared his dead eyes and burned what remained of his crackled beard.

The blade swept into something, into that raging inferno, and found a mark.

The firewalkers did not slow. They trampled.

The inferno wrapped around Svarde as panicked, burning, massive bodies buffeted him. There was nothing to see save fire, nothing to feel save stifling heat, and nothing Svarde could do save hold onto the blade with blistering skin. Something heavy and hot fell on Svarde, smothering him in dancing fire.

For yet another time, a deserved death was stolen from him.

A dull agony remained. Not pain, exactly, but the thudding drain as limbs shuddered, as his eyes, mouth, lips, vanished. As Svarde became little more than bone, as he—

His back moved, scraped along steaming stone. Something hard gripped his shoulder, and Svarde turned, saw with eyes that shouldn't exist, Kivi pulling at his charred skin. The blade shivered along to Svarde's right, and he didn't have to look that way to feel his skin, body, and broken bones knitting themselves back together. He could see it plain enough as his legs, nothing more than ash-blasted bone rattling free from the firewalker, began to sprout dead gray skin anew.

The skars echoed their infernal triumph in Svarde's mind. With their cries came a different sound: stone crunching, shifting, the earth shaking as the firewalkers found their reprieve. If any Whent or Kance died in the rush, Svarde wouldn't know: the rampage drowned everything else.

Svarde sat up some hours later. His body's knitting continued, a slow growth done muscle by muscle, or at least that's what Svarde told himself. That no organs would be replaced, regrown, was a fact he refused to consider.

What was impossible, though, to acknowledge were the smoldering ruins out in the fields and, of a different sort, in the town. Amid the muddy tracts lay great ashen bodies, a sight that would've stolen Svarde's breath had he any to lose. At a measured glance, Svarde counted more than half the burning fiends had died out in the storm.

A massacre by nature's hand, by their own ignorance.

The town had suffered too, though its losses came in buildings knocked asunder. Displaced roofs became makeshift shelters, steaming as their heated slates caught the rain. The firewalkers beneath, visible as Svarde looked over the wall, cowered. The mighty burning warriors curled into balls, embraced each other in sputtering candles. Many bore telltale ash patches, wounds suffered far from any battle.

"What've we done, Kivi?" Svarde asked the ferrite, steadying himself on the gate's singed remnants. His left hand rubbed the stone, more bone still than dead flesh. "We brought the monsters to their slaughter."

Worse, Svarde could see Jochi, Fassle, and Yarvick declaring this a double victory: The firewalkers laid low by the simplest weapon the isles could command, while at the same time devastating a Kance town. The first day in the Kance invasion had proved ill for both sides.

"So what now?" Svarde said, the ferrite still his only audience.

Beyond the clustered firewalkers, the water-logged streets were empty. The Whent must've heeded Svarde's advice, fled for the spires, the canyons beyond. Ami would be with them, trying to find some order, some strategy.

Svarde watched his left thumb, saw skin sprout like a small plant from the bone. It wrapped up and around his fingertip, disparate parts melding together. He'd been trampled by the firewalkers, burned to nearly nothing, yet here he was, nearly whole. If those fiends couldn't destroy him, then what could?

They'd brought an army to Kance, but perhaps the isle needed something both less and more to lay it low. Perhaps Svarde ought to do what he did best, and do it how he liked it.

"Kivi," Svarde said, "I think it's time we put an end to this ourselves."

The ferrite snorted a question, one Svarde answered as he started a halting walk into the town. The narrow pass lay on the far side, and through it, after a long march, waited the Sky Palace. Waited the Wind Isle's leaders. Svarde would break them, one by one, until they surrendered.

And once they did, the barbarian would escort the fire-walkers through the deep tunnels, safe and secure until, at last, they found their new home.

CHAPTER 17
SHIP TO SHIP

Up until this moment, Wax had never felt trapped on the sea. The waves and the ocean beyond were an inscrutable mass, one to be ignored like clouds or the vast jungle. The boat would see him through to the other side, so long as he trusted in the sailors. Even when they'd boarded the Rana merchant intent on rescuing Bliss and Torny, the whole craft sinking slow beneath them, Wax still felt able to escape. To blow, burn, or float his way free.

The Najahn assault put up walls Wax couldn't bring down. Not by himself.

The seafaring soldiers eschewed thicker plate for warm, maneuverable robes and leather helms, and they swarmed the *Storm's Edge* from the two clippers who'd caught her. Grapples bit into the wood railings, tugged the vessels tight enough for boarding ramps to plunge across the decks. Deux's own sailors, packing rapiers, clubs, and whatever seemed handy hollered their way into combat, but they weren't fighters.

Kance hadn't been in a real war for years upon years, and the Queen's ship wasn't meant for this sort of fray.

Wax saw the first stabs, the voulges and Najahn short swords cutting into Eujo's crew in a deadly first blow. The Vis Renewal leaned on the railing near the *Storm's Edge*'s aft, Bliss standing nearby with worry writ across her face. Wax couldn't see Eujo herself, though sudden shouts and loud splashes from the opposite side, where the second clipper attacked, suggested the Kance Queen wielded the skars now.

Going by his own stretched breath, his heavy arms, Wax figured Eujo's troop-tossing tactics wouldn't last long. Then it'd be—

'Here,' Bliss signed, handing Wax his own sword, one she'd pulled free after his collapse. 'Didn't want you to cut yourself, but you might want it.'

His sister planted her staff before her, watched Wax hold his sword with eyes that doubted he'd be able to.

"I'll be okay," Wax replied. "At least for the moment."

'One of those at a time.'

Neither, though, charged towards the boarding ramps. Instead, Wax glanced back beyond the prow. A distant smudge suggested Kance, confirmed any escape to the isle would be hard-pressed.

"No choice," Wax said. "I'm sorry, Bliss."

'For what?'

"Dragging you into this."

'This is the Najahn's fault, not yours. Let's make them pay.'

Bliss's confidence might've matched a duel against a hanoko, the jungle cats back home, but neither she nor Wax had real experience matching trained soldiers or knew what to do in a pitched battle. That worry nagged his first steps as they broke towards the fighting, towards a faltering Kance resistance.

The voulges had range, and the Najahn knew it. The curved spears jabbed forward, cutting and grabbing Deux's sailors. Wax saw one knife under a rapier's guard, slice through the blue-white robe, and pull its target, screaming, over the railing into the frigid ocean. The voulge's wielder stood side by side with two other Najahn on the boarding ramps, the trio taking their patient time slashing the defending sailors.

An easy task, with the rapiers short reach. Wax noticed, too, other Najahn on the clipper loading and firing crossbows. The jolting ships and wave action made targeting difficult, but every quarrel striking home sent a sailor to the deck or stumbling away.

Four hapless Kance remained when Wax and Bliss reached the assault, bloody, sweating, and cursing.

Bliss saw the obvious and took the lead, dancing to the rail to the boarding ramp's left. She planted her foot on the railing. Wax pushed past the Kance sailor on that side, swiping his flat blade in a wild swing, one that drew the two nearer voulges in for a block. Metal struck metal, and Bliss had her chance.

The Vis hunter flew, swinging her staff as she jumped. The metal-barred end beat the leftmost Najahn's rising voulge to strike the man's helm. The black gear crunched as its owner fell to his left, into the next guard. Bliss stuck her toes on the boarding ramp's edge, cutting her swing short to draw the staff back into a follow-up jab.

"Charge now!" Wax cried, lunging into the distracted gap Bliss created.

The Najahn trio found themselves barraged by rapier points, the small blades slipping through the soft robes and light leather beneath. Bliss's staff struck again, going for weak knees and sending the farthest Najahn slipping off the boards. The other two followed quick, a victory tempered by the last, in a desperate hooking flail, snaring a sailor and dragging the poor soul with him into the abyss.

For a brief moment the ramps were clear.

The crossbows filled the gap.

Wax stuck out his hand, pressed the Kance skar, and felt its wind rise. The dozen quarrels bent, smacking the boards themselves or flying off into the sea. Wax's own knees buckled, a fall staved off as Bliss, letting her staff linger in her left hand, pulled Wax back onto the *Storm's Edge*. The three remaining sailors lifted off the first ramp, threw it into the sea. By the time they reached the second, more Najahn soldiers charged in.

The reckless Najahn approach gave Bliss an opportunity as she pushed Wax onto the *Storm's Edge*'s deck. Keeping her staff low, Bliss stepped past the sailors and washed her weapon across the ramp. The first Najahn brought his voulge low to counter the blow, a smart play that stopped Bliss's cross-swing, a dumb one as his momentum carried the Najahn forward. He tripped over his own block, fell to his right, where the tossed ramp had been, and plunged into the dark waters.

Bliss shook off the blocking voulge, threw up her staff to block the next strike, a jumping attack from the next Najahn. The soldier's brave vault brought him off the ramp onto the *Storm's Edge*, a collision earning him rapier stabs, but driving Bliss and the sailors back from their boarding ramp barricade.

More Najahn sprinted across.

No more slow, measured assault.

Wax pushed himself up as a Najahn came for him, the

leading voulge making a gutting stab the Vis deflected with a frantic slap. The soldier darted the voulge in a second time, scooping it away as Wax went for the block, sending the weapon's butt end to crack against Wax's chest. Fresh pain, both a dull ache and a sharp pierce, rattled Wax as he stumbled back. The soldier brought the voulge home, sent it in for another straight stab. Again Wax flung the sword in a wild block, the curled spear's end snagging on Wax's thigh, drawing a burning line.

The Vis yelped. The soldier went to hook the voulge up, extend that line through Wax's stomach, chest, and all that lay inside.

Wax charged his would-be killer, half falling and half attacking, his sword taking advantage of the voulge's low position. Wax struck the Najahn's shoulder, the strike sliding through with only a grunt. The move, though, had closed the distance, freed Wax's leg from the voulge.

And put the Vis's head in the wrong spot. The Najahn snapped his own armored skull forward, delivered a crack that sent Wax's vision blurring, his sword tumbling from his hand. The Najahn, though, reached out, caught Wax as he fell back. Pulled the Vis up by his shirt, the Najahn's hard eyes locking on Wax's neck, and what lay clasped around it.

"We have them!" The soldier barked, wheeling Wax around towards the ramps.

With blood streaming from his nose, Wax started to swing at the soldier. His fist struck the man's robes, drew no reaction. At his sides, Wax saw more Najahn streaming by, the Kance sailors driven back or dead. Beneath him, the ship's deck gave way to the boarding ramp, bordered by frothing surf and the last gasps of drowning fighters.

"Bliss!" Wax tried, the shout going nowhere, getting nothing.

Amid the purple and black robes, the battle cries and clashes, Wax couldn't see his sister, Eujo, or Torny. The skars burbled in his mind, but when Wax reached for one, felt Foti's fire ready to burn, the soldier noticed. As the man jumped down to his own deck, he put a hand to Wax's throat, pressed in his thumb.

"Call to the stones, boy, and you'll die before they answer," the man snarled.

That's what he thought. The Foti skar would show otherwise.

As Wax felt the first heat build in his palm, the Najahn soldier's glare flicked up past Wax's shoulder. Those hard eyes widened.

And the skars fell silent.

CHAPTER 18

TOP OF THE WORLD

Quik waited out the day with Sawi and the other hunters beneath a warming canopy. Spring's first whispers came on the wind, fresh buds and birds building nests. The heavy loam as nature woke. Back in a weave, his marred Kance robes left in Mottilan, Quik spent much of the day just *being*. Naming songs and scents, stalking through the ferns, feeling bark too long absent from his touch.

"It comes back fast, doesn't it?" Sawi asked, joining him in the afternoon along a woody hillside. She'd brought fruit and some salted fish, a water skin filled and ready. Like Quik, she walked, talked without youth's vigor now. She wore scars inside. "You leave Vis and it feels like you're lost, but home doesn't hold a grudge."

"I didn't realize how much I missed it," Quik said. "It's like coming alive again, after all those buildings, the ocean, the fighting."

"That last isn't going away."

"True, but at least I know I'm on the right side now."

"Why, because we're trying to kick the Najahn off our isle?"

"That's the obvious reason."

"Ever think about what happens when we win?"

"When?" Quik snorted. "Sawi, I'm not going to dream."

"You don't think we'll do it?"

Quik shook his head while munching on the fish. He had to give it to Mottilan: the town did know how to season their seafood. Kitaye loved the ocean's bounty just as much, but his home preferred a simpler spicing. More fruits and leaves, less salts and peppers.

"I think Fassle and Yarvick won't stop," Quik said. "I think they both want to hold on to power, and the easiest way to do that is to conquer the isles or keep them at war."

Sawi laughed. At Quik's questioning look, she pointed her own sandwich at him like a point. "Listen to you. A few months ago, you were all gruff and bluster. Punch first, talk later. Now you're going on about the fate of the world."

Quik drowned a little blush with a smile. "I've been around Gladdring long enough, I guess."

"What happened there? I mean, not why you're here, but with Gladdring? Getting away from Noctia?"

He told the story, starting from the top. When a note had been left in his barracks bunk—continuing his Najahn rotation, Quik had been spinning time on port side patrols —asking him to show up outside a bar late that night. Gladdring, somehow still alive, had made an offer Quik couldn't ignore: get back into the action, help his brother, and stop wasting time.

"From there it was one fight after another," Quik said. "We fled with the Kance Queen, stole a bunch of the skars on the way. You should've seen what they'd done to the lab,

Sawi. A mess, but they were dumping new skars there anyway."

"Guess that's what happens when you lose the best scientist you've got."

"Maybe," Quik said. "We sailed to Kance . . . And the Najahn declared war. I didn't want to sit on the sidelines, and now I'm here."

Why didn't he want to talk about the Kance Queen? About leaving her to die in the ocean, or what Quik suspected happened to the Noctia Renewal?

Dark thoughts like that demanded darker times, and the afternoon was too pretty to ruin. That, and Sawi might not understand. Might not—

"I'm glad you are," Sawi said. "I mean, Annalyse is nice, but she's not one of us. Not, you know, our group."

"You mean, the morons who wanted to play in the trees all day?"

"Hey." Sawi gave Quik a little shove. "You liked it too, before you decided to be all hunter or nothing. So serious all the time."

"It's what Kitaye wanted."

"Funny how it's always what everyone else wants that pulls us around, isn't it?"

To that, Quik had no answer.

Night brought with it a long run. Reth had them gearing up and going as soon as the sun slipped beneath the trees. Sichi was stuck somewhere behind the eastern mountains, making their dash through the jungle a dangerous trek. Ankles twisted, feet caught on branches, and Quik himself earned more than a couple scratches from thorn bushes impossible to notice in the utter black. Any sane attack would've been called off or delayed.

But Mottilan was desperate, and if the Najahn wouldn't expect an assault, so much the better.

The Great Sana claimed a midpoint on the slow rise from jungle floor to the mountains on Vis's eastern side. Quik had once thought those mountains large, but compared to the spires on Kance, and even parts of Noctia's jagged craters, Vis failed to impress. Not that he minded now, the crossing and its descent to the giant flower taking only a day at swift speeds rather than several.

A longer journey would've only given the Najahn more time, and the hunters' alacrity found its reward as they approached the Great Sana's base from its backside, where trees, ferns, and other foliage grew thick.

The near-total black broke with blurred oranges from the Great Sana's far side, Najahn torches giving Reth enough shadows by which to direct his forces. Quik and Sawi would break right with one group, while Reth and the others would sweep left. Further responsibilities had been laid out earlier.

Not ones to Quik's liking, but he knew what it was to be a soldier within the ranks.

A Mottilan hunter took their group's lead, pulling their soft-shoed footsteps across chilled grass to the Sana's barked base. The flower itself lay inside a massive shell, ribbed and thick from centuries of slow spread. Quik put his left hand on the outer bark, felt its solid texture with his palm. His gauntlet's tips nicked the surface, drawing a glare and a silent admonition from their leader.

Not that the warning mattered. Before Quik's group made it near the entry, those torch halos flickered. Grunts and a single gasp leaked into the chirping night. No alarms, no screams. A good start. Their Mottilan leader, apparently following some intuition, beckoned the group around their side.

Three Najahn lay on the ground, tugged beyond the torchlight to sit, bound and gagged with cloth in the grass. None wore real armor, only robes. The voulges splayed on the ground.

"Blow darts did their work," Reth said as Quik and the others formed up. "Get to the top, fast, and take every skar you can. We'll hold the base until you return."

"Hold against what?" Their Mottilan leader said. "Three Najahn? And no other guards on the trail?"

The Mottilan had it right, an odd fact Quik struggled to reckon with. The Great Sana had to be the most important place on the whole isle, yet the Najahn only secured it with a trio of slipshod soldiers? A look down the hill, towards the damaged outpost, showed some late night activity, but no patrol heading this way. No watch wondering why a whole host of shadows now stood before the giant flower.

For so long Quik had held the Najahn as the greatest force on the isles, yet here they were, letting the Mottilan walk right into victory.

"Vis favors us tonight," Reth replied. "Don't question fortune. Use it."

While they might've dared to run through the jungle in the dark, nobody cared to attempt the same inside the Great Sana. Quik, Sawi, and the other hunters lit new torches and started the long climb, making their way up the mushroom-like platforms, the odd ladders, and the bug infested webs. Along the way, Quik and Sawi stuck together, both knowing they were the only Kitaye Vis in the group.

A pair among rivals. Quik felt the stares, the scowls here and there. Sawi had mentioned the failed attack on the

Najahn outpost not long before, one where Kitaye and Mottilan fought each other and wound up giving the base right back to the Najahn. Their desperate circumstances now would hopefully preclude the same outcome, but there wasn't any harm in being cautious, right?

"Wax and Pan would've climbed all this," Sawi said as they scaled another mushroom ladder. "Think they were afraid?"

Wax had told that tale, another Mottilan and Kitaye clash. Another one best put aside.

"Knowing my brother, he would've been dragging Pan along," Quik replied.

"I'm not so sure."

Quik smiled. "What do you think, then?"

"I think, for all his talk, Wax was happy enough with the way things were."

"Because he could spend all day with you."

Quik, his hands—those gauntlets had reclaimed their ties against his legs—mid-hold said the words without thinking, with jest. Sawi, just ahead and crawling over the next lip, turned, met Quik with a fierce glare.

"We were perfect for a moment," Sawi said. "That moment's gone. Wax killed it when he chose to go to Foti."

"When he kept his promise to Pan, you mean."

"When he left me."

Sawi spun on her heel, bounded towards the final stretch.

His brother had made a bad choice there, Quik had to admit. Sawi had fire. Spirit. More adventure than a bunch of god-possessed gemstones would ever offer.

That thought, the potential life his brother would've had with Sawi, dissipated as Quik climbed up onto the Great Sana's flower petals. Rather than celebration, the scraping of life-saving Vis skars from the flower's center, Quik joined Sawi and the other hunters in mute shock. He'd never seen the Great Sana's top before, but Quik knew ash and fire well enough now, knew the barren slag in the flower's center wasn't what belonged.

"There's not a single one left," Reth said, voice dead and drained. "Not a damn one."

The words ended with a whoop, though one that came from the ground far below, not from their group. Quik, closest to a petal's edge, turned and saw, crawling like embers, a torchlit swarm rolling towards the Great Sana's base.

The Najahn hadn't just taken and torched the Vis skars. They'd set a trap.

CHAPTER 19
THE HARD TRUTH

Murder morphed into something more as Haggerth proved willing to play along. At first, leaving their morning meal, Maena offered the journey as an opportunity to find answers, expecting to knife Haggerth as soon as they'd traded the Dead City and any watching eyes for the caves and their secrets. Instead, Haggerth agreed to grab satchels, food, water, and Whent lanterns to carry on their belts.

"If this will help me find the man, I'll go along," Haggerth said when Maena tossed out the offer.

A day's journey, there and back. Maena wouldn't say where, dangling the idea. Haggerth took it, because what choice did he have?

He's already sure you're the cause.

That was clear enough. But Haggerth kept his aloof tone, his open questions. The man wasn't calling for Jochi's guards or drawing some weapon from his crowded jacket. They formed up, supplies gathered, on the Dead City's southern side, ready to venture.

Every exit from the Dead City had living guards now.

With Svarde's departure, the corpses had fallen to nothing, their bones and bodies lying in the dust and forcing living replacements. With the firewalkers still holding their place, though, the fiend incursions were minimal. The guards joked, sharpened axes, and stared at nothing for hours. Maena suspected more than a few filled their water skins with ale, going by the glassy eyes and grunted goodbyes.

Whomever came after Haggerth wouldn't be getting good information from these bums.

"You're either lucky or very, very skilled," Haggerth said several hours into their walk, after listening to Maena tell the long, winding story of how she'd wound up here.

"Both."

Haggerth huffed a laugh, as if the man didn't want to admit he found it funny. "The best way to be, I'd say."

"Which are you, Haggerth?"

Maena led the pair, now long past outer lanterns. The tunnels were darker now, with mosses scraped away by enterprising scouts and searchers. Her own light cast shadows amid the twisting rock, the occasional stream, the jutting formations cutting up and down. Haggerth tailed, keeping several strides behind.

Too far to stab without warning.

All her other half wanted was another body. Haggerth kept thwarting that idea. Not just because of the range or Haggerth's obvious suspicions, but because the man didn't seem blindly against her. He listened, he asked questions, he—

It's a ploy, Maena. You know this. He'll wait to be sure, until you're questioning yourself, and then that'll be it. You can't risk it.

"What're you thinking about up there?" Haggerth asked.

"Watching my steps," Maena tossed off.

"Tunnel's easy enough."

Maena stopped. Haggerth stopped too, keeping his distance. She looked at him, her cheeks feeling the fur lining on her thick coat. Her hand lingered at her waist, right near her blade's hilt. Three motions: a draw, a step, a lunge. As many heartbeats to pull off. Haggerth couldn't move left or right, could only retreat.

He'll stumble and fall. An easy kill.

"I've looked into a lot of bad eyes," Haggerth said, breaking the soft silence. "Yours aren't like those."

Maena blinked. Left her hand off the hilt. "What?"

"Why I'm here. I've seen heartless bastards. The ones who've done terrible things and belonged in the Pits, belonged in the fights that nobody was getting out of." Haggerth spoke with both hands lazy at his sides, not in any defensive stance. "That's not you Maena. Maybe you're stuck in something bad, maybe you pulled my missing scout into it, but you're not evil."

Maena laughed once, gave a quick head shake. "You don't know what you're saying."

"That's just it, Maena. I do. I really, really do."

Now Maena squinted, studied the man. "Who *are* you?"

"That's not the question here." Haggerth nodded ahead. "Think we should keep going, if this place is as far away as you said."

Plan scrambled, Maena did as Haggerth suggested, her steps again advancing. This time, she stopped measuring Haggerth's distance.

They arrived and took a late lunch at Maena's target, a slim opening onto a broad slope rolling down into the vast pool. The one swirling with colors and, in the distance, reaching the firewalker's encampment. Ami had told

Maena about this place—indirectly, the Guardian had been talking with Svarde and Jochi, ignoring the Rana captain—and Maena had come here several times since, hunting for options.

She found one now, as Maena often did coming this way: with great, slimed wings, a snub-nosed fiend scrabbled on the slope's watery edge. It emerged with sputtering fanfare, breaking through the surface with harsh breaths from holes peppered along its sides. Three eyes, each a narrow diamond, glistened green as the creature fought for purchase in a world very much at odds with its home.

"A fiend," Haggerth stated the obvious as they looked down, their wrapped mushroom breads and dried carrots strewn on set satchels near their feet. "Is that what you were hoping for?"

"I wanted you to see," Maena said, starting down the stones towards the struggling creature. "All these monsters you know, the ones you've seen tearing apart your homes, ravaging the isles. That's not all. Not even most."

Haggerth didn't follow, folding his arms and watching as Maena closed with the beast. Those diamond eyes centered on Maena, the creature's struggles slowing. The heavy wings weren't meant for a windless place like the cave. Perhaps it'd come from Kance's silver swirls, a land likely blowing in a constant rush.

What a cruel surprise, to escape death and find something worse.

Maena drew her blade, turned back to Haggerth. "These fiends don't belong here, Haggerth. Their worlds may be dying, but that doesn't mean ours is where they ought to go."

"Nowhere, then, is what you're suggesting?"

"When a Rana reaches their final journey, we don't drag

them on," Maena said. "We give them a dignified end. We don't let this happen." She pointed the blade at the exhausted fiend, resting its head now on the pebbles. Breath no more than a whistle. "It's cruel, it's pointless."

"And the ones that can survive? Like the firewalkers?" Haggerth asked, his voice as toneless as ever. "What would you say to those?"

"I'd say we gave them a chance and look." Maena lifted the blade, waved it at the glow across the pool. "They've barely moved. The ones that have, they're just a weapon."

"I thought a deal was made, that—"

"A lie, and Svarde knows it. The firewalkers will be used or destroyed. Nothing in between."

"And you would give them mercy instead?"

The fiend lurched, a sudden push up the stones. Its left wing swung up towards Maena, ready to knock her away, only for its webbing to catch on a sharper rock. A mouth flush with serrated teeth gnashed from beneath the fiend's eye trio, well shy of the Rana captain. She turned and, with a single thrust, ended the pitiful creature's short time in her world.

"Mercy, dignity," Maena said, withdrawing her sword slow. "Call it what you will, Haggerth, but the end's the same: the gods made this world for us, and us alone."

"All this, then," Haggerth said when Maena returned to his side at the slope's top, "has something to do with my missing scout?"

"All this has to do with a choice," Maena replied. She still held her blade, dripping with water after a cleansing dip in the pool. It rested on her shoulder, Maena's other hand tapping her lantern's top. Haggerth, as ever, kept his hands loose. He leaned against a rough gray rock wall, his lantern at his feet. "I've told you what's going to happen. You can either help me, or not."

What that 'or not' meant was clear to both of them. What Haggerth would choose . . .

"I think you're making a choice that belongs to more than just you," Haggerth said. "I think you're declaring yourself the arbiter of too many fates, Maena. If what you're saying is true, if the fiends are destined for nothing more than death, then why is it your responsibility to give it to them?"

"Because I'm the only one who will."

Haggerth sighed. "Maena, I said your eyes didn't mark you as a monster. I still hold to that. But I'm seeing something else instead, something altogether more dangerous."

The sword came off her shoulder, leveled at Haggerth.

"Your next words could mean your life," Maena replied, low.

"You're a zealot, Rana. You've been alone with your own thoughts for too long." Haggerth spat to the side. "Thing is, though, you can have those thoughts. What I care about now is my scout. You tell me where he is, and you can deliver mercy killings to these fiends all you want."

I told you. I TOLD you that he wouldn't see things the right way.

Yes, she had. And Maena couldn't deny it any longer.

She started forward and Haggerth kicked his lantern. The burning globe struck Maena's leading blade, shattering and sending burning oil splashing over her clothes. Cursing, Maena swung anyway, her sword hitting air as she threw off her coat, let its burning bits smolder on the stones below.

By the time she straightened, Haggerth had disappeared.

If he makes it back before you and says what he thinks, we're dead.

Ever a speaker of the obvious, but her other self missed the same just as often. Haggerth had no lamp, had only walked the confusing tunnels to get here once. She had hours, knowledge, and light on her side.

This would be a hunt, yes, but Haggerth wouldn't get far.

CHAPTER 20
A STAND

The miserable day turned into night turned into day again and Svarde did not stop. His feet, in boots so far burned and crumbled, trod upon the cobbled road, bearing every pinch and rock in stride. Svarde felt the pain, but like any pointless thing, he pushed it so far away until it was as distant as the memories of home, of their journey, of Catya.

Much closer was the ferrite. The stone lizard kept Svarde tethered, as much as he could be, to reality. She snorted as they walked, pointing out roosting blue birds and their golden chicks, hanging from the crystalline bushes poking from the rising gray spires all around them. Those same bushes let loose the shimmering webs when the wind picked up, tinsel that somehow had the grace never to fall in Svarde's hand, hair, eyes.

As if Kance itself refused to countenance such rudeness.

A poor thing, then, for a barbarian to tromp through her wilds.

After the rainstorm, the air weighed heavy with humidity, spring's early grasp thwarted by winter's remaining chill. Those gusts snapped and writhed between the thin trees and rocks, as alive as the Foti lava rivers or those Vis jungles. Svarde's hair and beard had burned away in the firewalker assault, their lack making Svarde shiver as Kance held its windy conversation.

Not that he could freeze.

Svarde spent his steps taking in the scenery, running and re-running the proclamation he would give to anyone who dared stand in his way: a protest against taking life, a dream for the firewalkers. When his audience, hopefully those fools up high in the Sky Palace, turned him down, Svarde would persuade them in a different way.

The jagged blade didn't feel heavy, though Svarde figured the slice broken from Vis's dagger wasn't for those who preferred lithe weapons. His arms helped the sword rest against his shoulder as Svarde went, striding forward at a comfortable pace. Maybe Svarde could've jogged, held an outright sprint with his unflagging energy, but that would've meant ditching Kivi, putting his precarious bare-foot balance at risk.

Then again, the speed might've slipped him past the array now clotting the path before him.

Seven Kance soldiers, skipping the robes for the glassy armor the isle's more serious fighters sported. They stood in a line across the road, and Svarde didn't have to search the trees, the cliffs on either side to guess there were archers hidden too.

"Hold, invader!" called the center one, a woman stocky enough to defy Kance's windy reputation. She still had a rapier at her side, though the blade looked tiny next to her mail's ridges and sharp angles. "Your march ends here."

"Does it now?" Svarde asked, slowing to a stop ten strides away. Next to him, Kivi snorted and released her vents, steam puffs floating up around them. "Who're you to stop me?"

"Tyfate," the woman replied. "Commander of the north Kance guard. You are Svarde, are you not? Barbarian of the West?"

"Barbarian of the West? Is that what they call me?"

"You're no longer a Guardian, in spirit and in action, so we needed something new." Tyfate made a show of looking to Svarde's sides. "You walk alone?"

"Kivi's here." Svarde nodded down at the ferrite. "Otherwise, I walk alone to save lives."

"By giving up your own?"

The conversation had gone on too long already. Ami and the Whent would be getting the firewalkers moving, assuming the burning giants could be brought down from their panic. Once on their way, Svarde's whole purpose would be ruined if the army caught up to him. As would Tyfate's life, her soldiers, and any Kance standing between the firewalkers and Najahn victory.

"I have a message for your rulers," Svarde said. "One that gives them a chance to keep their isle from being destroyed."

"If it involves giving in to the purple and black, you can take that message with you to the grave."

Svarde brought the black blade off his shoulder, let its wicked point rest in the dirt near his feet. Let the Kance take a long look at its malevolence and decide if they really wanted a taste of its dark iron.

"There are forces at play here, Tyfate, that go beyond anything you could hope to defeat," Svarde said, even and slow. "Your isle faces an impossible war. To wage it will be to lose everything. Take my offer and escape, damn you."

"Threats will get you nowhere. One more time, Barbarian. Turn around and leave, or stay and let your corpse fertilize the spring grasses."

A small part of Svarde had hoped for something different. Had hoped this time, the enemy would see reason. But the Barbarian did stand alone, and while Svarde's gray pallor might seem odd, and his giant sword might make a bar fighter or single adversary pause, a force with numbers and surprise might think they could win.

They were, of course, mistaken.

"Then persuade me," Svarde muttered, before breaking into an old roar, a feral cry, and one that felt as good as anything Svarde had done since grasping the black blade.

Tyfate didn't play the hero leader's game. Nor did any of her soldiers. At Svarde's first move, crossbows sang from the thickets. Quarrels broke into Svarde's skin from the left and right, biting, tearing, and leaving a hot fire lacing the barbarian.

A hot fire Svarde quenched with another charging step, another—

The next quarrel struck Svarde's neck, singing in and robbing the warrior of his voice. Svarde had seen enough men choked, robbed of their breath to know he should've been collapsing, should've been grasping at his throat. Yet he stepped on, and while an aching weight pulled at his chin, no desperate need arose.

The black blade did as its curse demanded.

Svarde saw the first fear alight in the Kance soldiers. Their determined courage depended on a world they thought they understood, and now that world was breaking. Tyfate called for her soldiers to stand for their Queen, a well-timed inspiration, and four rapiers leapt to meet Svarde's riddled advance.

The barbarian greeted them with a sweep, rumbling

forward with abandon so heedless as to guarantee death by any normal man. The rapiers to his left and right snuck under and over Svarde's attack, taking a leg and a shoulder. The blows proved worse for the attackers, as Svarde's reply cleaved their plate like smooth silk. The armor parted, lattice fractures spreading, followed soon by the dark red bloom. The two soldiers in the middle tried to parry, a pointless attempt that saw their rapiers cut off just above the hilt, the metal snapping and flying far away.

As Svarde finished the blow, the four soldiers stumbled back, fell, and Svarde kept on charging. Off to his left, someone in the bushes screamed. Kivi, no longer on the path, finding a victim. He hoped the ferrite would restrain herself, knock out the poor archer. If the man hadn't tried to shoot the ferrite first, he'd have a chance.

Otherwise, well, Kivi might find the Kance armor a tasty snack.

Three more remained before Svarde, Tyfate in their middle. All had their rapiers drawn, though their steps came in a backward retreat. Terror lit all their looks, so absolute Svarde wondered at it till he looked at himself, at the bleeding cuts closing up, the quarrels once lodged in bone being pressed away by the Vis power roaring in Svarde's thoughts.

"There is no victory here," Svarde said, stepping over a fallen Kance soldier. "You lose yourselves and gain nothing."

The words made Svarde grin. He didn't talk much like his old ale-swilling self either, now. Weeks with Jochi, the burden of leadership, and perhaps the Dead King's fate had turned Svarde towards fancier speech, to the sort of words that build legends.

That would be respected by kings.

"What are you?" Tyfate stammered, again matching Svarde's advance with her own retreat.

Another archer hollered. A breaking crossbow's stock snapped. From the other side a quarrel, again, found Svarde's side, stopping the barbarian not in the slightest.

"What am I?" Svarde asked. "I am exactly what I said. A bringer of peace, if you wish it."

Tyfate shook her head, "This is no peace I can understand."

"Then best you learn, or you'll match your men."

The Kance commander again looked at her two fellow soldiers. In their frightened eyes, she found some courage. Some spine that had her slowing, stopping.

"We stand for Kance," Tyfate said, her voice trembling at the first, steady at the last. "We will not yield her."

Her soldiers, to their credit, found their resolve at their commander's words. Formed alongside her. Their rapiers gleamed in the mid morning's dewey sunlight. Svarde measured up, raised the black blade with both hands, the last fight's results still dripping from its edge.

"The old me," Svarde said, "would've praised your courage. I won't, because this fight is already decided."

"We will see about that."

"Soon," the barbarian said, not a trace of victory in his words, "you won't be seeing anything at all."

<h1 style="text-align:center">CHAPTER 21</h1>

LIVES ARE LIVES

Wax woke up when he hit the floor, shoulder popping as he rolled off the swinging hammock onto wet wood, then a cold metal grate draining splashing water deeper. Lanterns creaked, the noise splitting yells from crew, the rolling lash of thunder. All that didn't hide the aching roil in Wax's head, his bruised bones, and the strange echoing silence in his thoughts.

Not a single skar spoke to him.

On his back, Wax reached for his neck, felt skin where the metal clasp ought to be. His clothes remained the same: Kance linens, fine woven, though Wax's robe was gone, and in its absence he shivered. Grey light filtering through an opening to the upper deck suggested daytime, but the deep shadows, the rain, told of clouds. A worry, given where he was.

Where he . . .

The Najahn clipper. A small ship. They'd bashed Wax, knocked him out and stuffed him down here. That he was

141

still aboard meant Eujo, Torny, Bliss hadn't been able to rescue him. If they lived at all—

No. That was a trail he wouldn't walk down. not yet. Not ever.

Instead Wax reached for a post and used the drenched wood to pull himself up. They'd left him the boots he'd worn since Whent, and the sturdy things gripped the lower deck well enough. The hammocks around him suggested a couple dozen beds, though they all swung empty now, twisting as the clipper lurched with wave after wave. Crates and personal effects stuffed into small lockboxes sat roped into the corners, along with spare gear. Voulges stood tied to a rack near the stairs to the upper deck, and their gleaming points gave Wax an objective.

The Najahn might've taken him captive, but they'd made a mistake leaving Wax untied.

He took measured steps towards the rack, listening to the shouts up above. The Najahn calls were anything but calm: a leader's voice, a hard woman's tone screaming to cut the sails, to toss ballast, to get a rope after some poor soul who'd gone overboard. Her shouts were met with a mix of ayes and panic. The clipper rolled. A wave splashed over, streaming down the deck stairs as Wax neared the first step.

The Renewal hesitated.

Grabbing a voulge and emerging a violent threat would get Wax what, exactly? He couldn't take on the whole ship, and if they were truly out at distant sea, then Wax would ensure his own dismal fate by trying to slay more of what must've been a skimpy, wounded crew. The bandit encounter back on Foti slashed through, a forced cooperation that let Wax live, carry on, because he'd been patient.

Maybe the same would work again.

Wax fell onto the deck ladder, held its sides with both hands, and pulled himself up, one short step at a time, to the top deck. As he neared, the cutting rain began smacking his cheeks in cold gobs. His fingers went numb quick, teeth starting to chatter. Without the Kance robe, Wax might just freeze to death before he made it far.

The skars, though, could help with that. They'd keep him warm.

They could, too, save the ship.

Wax lunged up the last rung to flail onto the top deck, the storm's rage revealed in its full terror. As the Vis slipped onto soaked, half-frozen wood, he saw waves towering over the clipper as the small ship seemed to spin in fraught circles. Before him, the clipper's single main mast and the sail stretching from its bulk to the prow split the gray horizon in two. Sailors, soldiers scrambled across the ship, some falling, others dancing along the deck as if the turmoil was as normal a thing as could be.

"Get those ropes tied!"

The captain's voice again, behind and above Wax. She focused on a couple lines near the prow that'd become unmoored, casting about like snakes looking for mice. Two soaked crew broke from the rigging to dive on the things, wrestle them back together, a fight that seemed to go their way until a wave crashed over the bow, tumbling the pair against the boat's starboard side. The ropes resumed their wild snapping, Wax getting to his feet—and pressing his back against the captain's cabin for support—in time to see one, highlighted by lightning, whip across and knock one of the two sailors all the way off.

The body splashed into the raging sea, deep blue and

white froth disappearing the poor soul in a second's snap. Nevertheless, more sailors dashed to the side, hauling ropes and ringed buoys to chuck in after the man.

As if the clipper would stay close for more than a moment.

Though, perhaps, Wax could help with that.

Nobody had noticed his arrival yet, a fact Wax put to use as he looked at the captain's door at his elbow. He reached for the handle, pushed, and found it locked. Found it swinging open a moment later, a man with sword drawn, dry Najahn robes waiting behind it.

"You?" the man asked.

"Me," Wax replied, and swung a fist.

A desperate offense beat a perplexed defense, or something.

Wax's swing, wet and numb, made contact with the man's cheek. The Najahn—was this guy the captain? Hiding in his cabin?—stumbled back and Wax followed, the door whacking closed behind him as the clipper rolled again.

The Najahn tried to steady himself against the pitching ship, in a cabin dominated with a table, a side bunk, and several crates. Low ceilings, a lantern hanging on a hinge, and a smell of vomit coming from the appropriate pot completed the picture, one Wax sought to disrupt by running at the blade-wielding man.

The man, still back-pedaling against the table, swung the blade in a broad arc. Wax slowed just enough to let the sword slash by before darting forward. The Vis's right hand snatched out, took the Najahn's sword-arm by the wrist and pinned it across the man's body. With his left, Wax drew back, was about to deliver a throttle to the man's harried face, when Wax noticed his missing necklace, right there on the table.

"A deal," Wax rasped, throat parched despite all the cold rain he'd swallowed. "A deal to save the ship."

"What could you possibly do?" the Najahn snarled, tried to wrest his blade free.

Wax drove his knee into the man's gut, drawing a gasp.

"I'm a Renewal. Trust me."

"You're a traitor." The man's words came hollow, died in another crack, more screams and frenzied orders from outside. "I can't—"

"We'll all die if you don't."

Wax felt something sharp against his abdomen, glanced down to see the Najahn had pulled a dagger with his off-hand, had the point pressed where it could flay Wax in a moment. The Najahn, red-faced, wheezing off Wax's hit, held what should've been the final blow.

"You destroy this ship, you destroy us, you'll drown at sea," the Najahn said.

"Gathered that," Wax replied. "Now either get out of the way or kill me, because you're losing more sailors every second."

The man swept aside, a move smooth enough to make Wax wonder if the Najahn could've killed him earlier. If, maybe, the Najahn wasn't as dumb as Wax figured. That, though, was a worry for later.

Now, Wax reached, grabbed, and pulled on the skar necklace. The stones and their reassuring nonsense flooded his mind. The Vis skar attacked his cold hands, the bruises on his back and head. The Foti skar drew upon its warmth, drying Wax's soaked clothes. And the Tamas skar confirmed the killer sharing the room with Wax was more cautiously curious than murderous.

The stone that mattered, though, was the silver glint and the water it called.

"Come with me," Wax said, spinning back to the door. "I'll need you."

"For what?"

"To hold me up."

The Najahn asked something else, but the words died amid the tumult as Wax barreled through the door. The rain continued, the sea swirled, and sailors ranged the clipper's sides, holding on for their lives while trying to throw ropes to those who failed. The captain seemed to have given up trying to steer the clipper, instead calling out where souls had gone overboard and how to find them.

Wax had a better idea, the better tool.

The Rana skar roared as Wax let it loose. A giant wave surging towards the clipper swung away, delivering the ship only a glancing blow rather than crashing over its deck. The Rana skar found, in the nearby waters, struggling sailors and pushed them to the surface. Cold threatened to take their lives, and Wax, feeling the sailors less as people and more as distant intuitions, gave direction to the Foti stone.

Behind Wax, the Najahn stiffened, as did Wax, while the Foti skar stole their own heat and shoved it out towards those swimming souls. Enough to give their fingers strength to grip, their legs feeling to kick.

"Help," Wax said, a murmur the Najahn, trembling behind him, caught.

Arms slipped beneath Wax's own, keeping the Vis aloft. The Najahn called for assistance, though Wax didn't see if anyone heeded it. He fell into the Rana skar's efforts, let the stone's will cleave one wave after another, whisk away the icy wet from the deck, and push the clipper forward, a surge the captain felt and used.

To save the isles. To try. That's what he'd promised Pan, no matter what, no matter how, no matter if Wax went so deep into the god stones that he never came back.

CHAPTER 22
A FAR FALL

Attacked by bandits, river monsters, another Renewal, and a master assassin. As Quik saw the Najahn soldiers rushing the few Mottilan hunters at the Great Sana's base, he almost dove off the giant flower. This had to be a dream, right? The sheer cascade of crazy conflicts that'd pursued his footsteps over the last few months beggared belief, broke reality, sent the idyllic life of a Vis hunter swirling away into fantasy.

What was he doing here? How had everything gone so wrong?

"We jump," Sawi said next to Quik, the other Mottilan hunters with them jabbering in the background, everyone trying to find their own way out. "We catch a vine, swing away."

"Have you lost your mind?" Quik said, only just covering his own. "The nearest tree is a long way down."

"What other choice is there?"

"Fight our way out?"

Some of the Mottilan had already decided that, jumping down the hole near Quik to bring reinforcements to Reth and the others at the Great Sana's base. The move made little sense unless the goal was to die with some false sense of honor. Or maybe hope the Najahn would be interested in taking prisoners. There would be no slashing their way through the attackers.

"That won't work, and you know it," Sawi muttered, making no move to stop the other Mottilan from leaving.

One asked what Quik and Sawi were going to do, and when neither answered, the hunter bared his teeth, declared he'd take a couple Najahn heads before joining Vis, and disappeared.

"That's a choice," Quik said, approaching the grand petal's edge and looking down. If anything, more torches glimmered now, sprawling well away from the Great Sana and back towards the mountain road. "Look. This isn't even all of them."

"Surprise," Sawi said. "Someone must've seen us coming. The Najahn get a whole bunch of hunters trapped out here, send in a surprise attack while we're all gone. Mottilan goes down easy."

"Annalyse has the skars. She'll fight. So will Deshiva."

That they'd both die quick against those numbers, even with the skars, went unsaid. Instead, Quik went back to Sawi's earlier idea. A jump was true suicide, sure. No tree sat close enough to the Great Sana to make a leap viable, much less tall enough to catch them. But . . .

"I might have an idea," Quik said, standing and walking to the flower's opposite side, the one facing the dark mountains. "Can you hold onto my back?"

"Like when we were little?"

"Just the same."

Quik slipped the gauntlets onto his hands. Took a deep breath. He'd not recovered all the way from the boat stabbings, and it'd been a long day trekking through the jungle, climbing the Great Sana. What he was planning to do now . . . well, a true Vis had to be ready to meet any challenge.

"What're you doing, Quik?"

"Just watch."

Quik walked onto the petal, its smooth filaments soft against his shoes. Kneeling, then sliding his feet to the edge, Quik moved himself as near the Great Sana's bark as he could. With his gauntleted left hand, Quik reached down and jabbed the metal tips into the massive plant's bark. The ancient wood split, a satisfying crunch proving Quik's weapon had teeth.

That he wasn't all insane.

"Get on," Quik said, and Sawi didn't hesitate.

She understood, then. Both what Quik would try to do, and the end that'd come if he fell.

Sawi gripped Quik's weave, slipping her fingers through the dried plant ropes, and held tight. Quik tensed his muscles, muttered a prayer to Vis, and dangled off the petal. Those filaments bent with his weight, and Quik used the flexibility to swing himself, and Sawi, into a hard strike at the Sana's bark. The knotted, wrinkled chips broke at the impact, the gauntlet sliding, scraping off the bits as Quik, and Sawi, slid down. He swung his right arm, jammed it into the Sana's shell, and together the two grips slowed, stopped the pair. Quik's feet scrabbled for purchase, found tiny cracks.

Muscles burned. Breath came fast. Sawi's weight on his back did more to knock off Quik's balance than drag him down, and the hunter leaned into the Sana's side.

"We're in this now," Sawi said. "Keep going, Quik."

Quik wanted to snap a reply, but being clever demanded energy better spent on priorities like staying alive, and figuring out his next handhold. Down beneath the flower petals, they had no light, only the slightest glimmer from Sichi. The Great Sana's side seemed a black wall and only that, stretching down to a blank nothing far, far below. The trees they might leap to flashed here and there as a breeze brought stray branches, leaves into the little light. A climb where he couldn't see the next move?

Why not, given everything else?

Quik found himself grinning as he slid the left gauntlet free, let those sharp claws drag down, twisting his hand as it came to his waist. They hung by a single gauntlet, the small support from Quik's shoed toes. His right wrist burned as he jammed his left into the Sana's side, once more burying the tips into the flower's trunk.

Now the right. He eased it free, the sudden drop scraping the gauntlet along the bark. Sawi yelped, Quik jammed the gauntlet in, catching them fast. His left arm sat well above his shoulder now, aching, and they'd barely dropped. This wasn't going to work.

"Sawi," Quik said. "We're going to slide, and you're going to jump."

"I'm going to what?"

"Jump. On three."

The hunter started counting.

"Jump where, Quik?"

He took one more breath.

"I don't under—"

Quik slid the gauntlets out together, going to their barest tips. The purchase gave, the bark splintered, and they dropped. Quik fought to keep the gauntlets close, pushing in even as bits smacked, scratched, stuck into his face, pushed through his weave into his chest, mauled his legs. His shoes broke open, and Quik flipped up his feet, letting the battered soles bounce off the bark as their speed picked up.

Sawi started to yell, then stopped, coming to the right conclusion that any escape would be hard to keep secret with her screaming. Not that the descent came quiet: the snapping bark announced their fall plenty loud, but Quik couldn't worry about that. Not now. He wanted to turn his head aside, watch for the trees, for the right distance, but they fell too fast, had too much speed, had—

She leapt without warning. Bunched up her legs on Quik's back and kicked, soaring off. Without her weight, Quik tried to jam his gauntlets in, slow the fall. The tips broke, metal bits flying off with their bark brethren. The hunter tried his toes, angling for any foothold. Plastered his broken hands against the bark, and found nothing big enough amid those ridges to grab hold. He'd strike the bottom in moments, and there would be no surviving that impact.

So Quik, instinct, panic, pure desperation driving him, pressed his knees up to his chest, put his burning palms against the bark as he went into free fall, and launched, flying into the dark a bloody, battered thing.

CHAPTER 23
PURSUIT

Running through the Dark Below came with risks: a wrong turn might toss you down a slope, bashing your head on a sharp rock. A slip on gravel or years-old dust could spin you into a snagging wall, leaving you bleeding, a smell that might attract the wrong fiends. Or you might simply lose your light, the oil running out, ditching you in the wandering dark until you starved, gasping and crawling for help that would never arrive.

Haggerth might suffer any one of those fates, should Maena not find him, and her search was growing ever more frustrating. She'd gone down one side tunnel after another, ducked through small opening, splashed through shallow pools and climbed around deeper ones, but the Whent rascal hadn't left any traces.

Or you're a terrible tracker.

A possibility. Rana didn't teach its children to hunt like the Vis and Whent did. Why, when the river isle offered so much more to someone who could cast a line, throw a spear, rather than track a wild beast?

As it was, Maena relied on what her eyes told her,

what her nose could smell, what her ears could hear, and right now that whole collection offered precisely zero hints.

Then go where you know he'll be.

She'd already been doing that, keeping her routes in pursuit of Haggerth to the ways that'd bring her back towards the Dead City. Every jagging twist slanted Maena across the likely lines Haggerth would take to get home, and not once did she cross his path.

Which left one likely conclusion: in his lantern less flight, the man had turned the wrong way. A fatal mistake, and one Maena could let claim him.

And if he shows up, a knife then will do the trick just as well.

Maena sniffed in the dim glow of her own lantern, feet finding the automatic trail back to where she'd come from, to the corpse-addled town now crawling with Whent explorers, engineers, and greedy hopefuls wanting to exploit the Dark Below for something better. The impression stuck with the Rana captain as she walked, the distaste moldering in her mind.

What, it's the truth. You hate them. We hate them. They deserve what's coming.

What Maena did know, what she'd been helpless to prevent, was the growing homicidal bent from her split soul. The part that'd been rifted free by a shadowed fiend and wouldn't go away, wouldn't stay silent, would poison Maena's thoughts every moment until she had no other option than to obey.

Obey? That's a convenient excuse. You want this as much as I do. It's what you told Rasslebeck and Pennifer.

Had she? Back on the surface, when Jochi barred the Rana's friends from joining his deep-diving expedition?

Yes. You told them you'd carry on the fight, fulfill their oaths to destroy the fiends. Don't forget your promise, Maena. Your promise, not mine.

But promises made in ignorance—

No. Not this. Not now. We've had this discussion a thousand times. The plan is in place. By the time we get back to town, the explosives we need will be ready. Then, we'll bury all those monsters once and for all.

The idea had a certain appeal, and what else was Maena going to do? Stay amid a bunch of rockbiters, without responsibility? With Svarde gone, Jochi didn't give one damn what Maena said or did. Returning to the surface was a choice, one that'd see her going back to Rana and . . .

That's a question for another time, Maena. When our work is done, and you come back a hero for saving the isles.

Ah. Right. A hero. Maena laughed to herself as she stalked the tunnels heading back towards the Dead City. Celebrated, writ into legend, a life worthy of remembrance, and her oaths to those Rana slaughtered by the fiends fulfilled.

Her other self might be murderous, might think in terms of blood as benefit, but she did have one thing right: what choice did Maena really have?

The Dead City greeted Maena's return without remark. A different guard waited at the southern tunnel exit, but he gave Maena the same bland nod she'd received when they left. The fur-clad, axe-carrying boulder of a man didn't question her about Haggerth, meaning the previous shift hadn't passed anything along. A lucky break.

Luck? You assume people care about you and your doings, Maena. Only one did, and he's lost back there in the dark. They will, though, after.

Maena bundled her anonymity about her and walked through the expanding Dead City towards its center, where her chosen room and the nearby smithy waited. The hour, marked by lantern silhouettes on carved notches in cavern walls, suggested Maena's return came late. Loud, drunken noise from various carts, taverns, and streetside gatherings seconded the impression. Whent did love to celebrate after a day, any day, ended with them alive.

Of all the things, I have to agree with them on this.

Maena could share that feeling, though she didn't stop at any of the revelries passed along the way. Nor did she spare a glance at the miserable corpses, shoved along and sat up against walls. Garlic and other herbs had been spread along the rotting bodies to cover the smell. Svarde hadn't wanted the bones buried so he could use them upon his return. Until then, the Dead City stank like a distorted springtime festival, with a too-deep breath bringing with it offal's lingering acid.

One more reason to detonate our play and be done with this awful place.

The smithy's doors were locked when Maena arrived, the windows dark. She knocked once, received no answer, making it likely her blacksmith had joined one of the evening's parties. Looking for the man floated as an idea, one Maena dismissed. She'd wandered a long way, and her legs made it known they wouldn't mind a rest. Perhaps she could take one, return in the morning, and commence her heroic devastation fresh.

The idea brought her to her room's building, off the Dead City's central square. Rounding the last corner, though, Maena pulled up short. Standing near her door were two more Whent, just as armed and armored as the tunnel guard. They held no ale mugs, and their eyes searched the street with purpose. The Rana captain curled back around, leaned against a building's wall, and breathed.

Haggerth might not have made it back, but the man had friends.

A trick and a trap.

But Maena hadn't fallen in yet.

You can't go back.

No, but she could go forward. If Jochi or some other Whent forces were after her, then Maena couldn't depend on the engineer either. At least, not waiting till morning. She had to get those explosives and use them now, this very night.

The walk back to the smithy took her on different routes, narrow paths between buildings rather than the broader streets and their drunk crowds. Maena whipped her head around, watching for, well, the watchers. She tripped over an herb-wrapped body, caught herself on a wall. Took a breath, inhaled the garlic, and retched.

You're bad at this.

She was a Rana captain. Not a spy. Maena led raids, clashed blades. Skulking around wasn't her life.

It is now.

Tears threatened. Their arrival sudden and unexpected, and Maena matched her back to the rough stone wall. Overhead, the cave's dark ceiling dripped spikes. No stars, no clouds, no horizon. You could only ignore freedom for so long before its absence encroached upon your every feeling. She was trapped, so trapped here.

Until you bury the fiends. Then you can leave.

Right. Journey back to the surface, either in a dashing, secretive escape, or as a celebrated hero. Maena wiped her eyes on her dirty sleeve. She couldn't control that part. Only the trigger, the collapse. That was hers.

The focus helped. Maena made her way with unflinching strides to the dark smithy. Nobody came after her, no drunken Whent bothered to ask what she was doing. The barred door loomed. Windows around the building were narrow, too narrow to squeeze through.

Even if you could?

Jochi put a swift end to thieves, preventing crime with blood.

The smithy pressed back against another building, with no alley on either side, limiting other options. How could she get in?

Wait.

Yes. Her apartment might be watched, but the Dead City hummed tonight. Maena might be exhausted, but an ale or two, a light meal, could all be had nearby. She could mix, could mingle, and when the engineer returned to his store . . .

CHAPTER 24
ONE MAN, ONE ISLE

The attacks didn't end and Svarde didn't stop. The bodies marked his progress, as Kance bands struck from trees, cliffs, caves, and simply striding down the road, astonished to see the barbarian and ferrite, both coated in the results of their brutal labors, in their way. Every confrontation went the same, a question, a threat, a conclusion wrought by Svarde's jagged blade or Kivi's stone jaws.

They left no survivors. If a Kance tried to run, Kivi chased them down, the ferrite's stamina greater than any soldier.

Did Svarde mean to be so final, so absolute? The question vanished as the hours, the two whole days passed and no sign of Ami and the firewalkers appeared at his heels. Their army, which had been an all-conquering force mere days ago, had been halted by a storm, or at least slowed to irrelevance. Which put the weight of success, of securing the firewalkers a home among the isles, on Svarde and his ferrite friend.

Being undying wasn't a free ticket to domination.

Svarde only had his body and its many scars. A prepared force could overwhelm, destroy, or trap him. Surprise remained his best chance, and one Svarde realized he couldn't relinquish.

So Kance fell, soul by soul, along the muddy road south.

Svarde took no side paths, would slip off beneath neighboring, skimpy trees if a glider appeared on the horizons. When a pool presented itself, the barbarian would bathe, but those were the only diversions on his otherwise relentless press. The rain, at least, kept the worst of it from his eyes, but by the time Svarde crested a hilltop and looked down upon Kance's capitol, the gleaming spires and sky filled with gliders, he wore little more than scraps, drenched in dried blood and spit.

Kance's great city held the same enchanting look it had the first time Svarde had traveled here. Admittedly, back then, Svarde had been alive and with true friends on an exhilarating adventure. This was . . . different.

How much of the city would he need to carve through to reach the Sky Palace? To convince the lords therein to give up their pointless war?

"I don't know, Kivi," Svarde said to the ferrite, "but if I don't try, then every single one of the firewalkers dies."

"Is that why you're charging ahead like a homicidal hero?"

Svarde whirled at the words, though he knew the voice well enough to keep the blade low. Olgata, a lead Whent scout and the woman who'd been near Svarde since they first reached the Dead City, watched him from several strides away. She sat on a rock, a guide stone etched with the hours to the small towns Svarde had passed along the roadway. Slim pouches lined her thick scout's cloak, shirt, and trousers. A hatchet on one thigh and a blade on another. Deep green face paint cloaked her face.

A setup for a long time alone.

"Someone has to finish this before it gets started," Svarde answered. "From what I can see out there, the Najahn haven't assaulted the isle. You being here means Ami and the firewalkers aren't close either. Which means I have time."

"To do what, slaughter everyone in that city?"

"Only takes the leaders losing their heads to change minds."

"To surrender? Kance?" Olgata slid off the rock, gave Kivi a pet as the ferrite ran up to greet her. "The Wind Isle isn't going to give in. They'll fight to the last."

"People say that, but you know what I found on Whent? As proud an isle as this one? A town in flight because a few fiends came to visit. When you're faced with impossible odds, you take your family and run."

Olgata seemed to concede the point, matched Svarde in his look towards the Kance capital. "And you are those odds?"

"I have to be."

The scout's bluster faded as they watched the swirling gliders, the sparkling sails in the harbor.

"The firewalkers are in crisis," Olgata admitted. "Ami hasn't been able to leave the town and the roofs they've turned into shelters. The rain is too frequent, too dangerous for them."

"Then it's over. The next clear day, they should return to the caves."

"That'd leave you alone. All alone."

"I already am."

Olgata nodded, "Svarde, why are you doing this? Why

not come back with me, leave Fassle and Yarvick to their blood. The firewalkers can argue for their place. Foti won't refuse their heat for their forges, and Whent could use them too." The scout grinned. "Plenty of inns wouldn't mind a fiend like that keeping their common rooms warm all winter."

Svarde almost bought into the scout's idea and its wider meaning: let the fiends in, those that weren't all blood and teeth, and each would find its place among the isles. Sure, it would take time, it wouldn't always be easy, but there were homes to be had, needs to be met. Svarde could sit in the Dead City and watch the gates until all the worlds beyond collapsed into nothing.

A pleasant thought, of a sort.

All it would cost is thousands of Najahn and Kance lives as their armies and navies slaughtered one another across the seasons.

"If I can end it fast," Svarde said, "then we can accomplish both. The fiends can have their homes, and this city can be saved, its people spared."

"A noble conqueror, then."

"No, a warrior looking for a path."

The wind continued to blow—it always blew here—and the clouds wafted away from the massive mountain spike at the city's western end. The crag's green-and-gray surface was dimpled with Svarde's objective: the Sky Palace, shining as its diamond multitudes caught the sun. Gliders darted off as sight lines opened, like birds alighting from their perches. The spire's winding stair shimmered, groups walking along its many, many steps. Others would be on the inside lifts.

Either way, an option.

And an idea.

"Could you stay?" Svarde asked Olgata.

The scout didn't seem surprised by the ask. She flicked up a small smile, "Are you suggesting, Svarde, that a monster like you might have a hard time getting all the way up there?"

"Not without a mountain of bodies to match that spire."

"So you want me to find a path, then?"

"So I don't have to carve one, yes."

Olgata squared up to Svarde, looked him up and down. That small smile faded into a straight nothing, work going on behind her stare.

"I'm a wild scout, Svarde. I don't infiltrate cities," Olgata trailed off, "but we need you alive. Well, at least as much as you can be."

"Then you're coming?"

"On one condition," Olgata said, then pinched her nose. "There's a cave pool twenty minutes back. We're going to get you cleaned up, and then, Svarde, then we can see how to keep you and that giant sword out of sight."

Even Kivi snorted at that idea.

CHAPTER 25

ARRIVAL

The Ringed City answered the call of the crisis. The Najahn war engine and the efforts required had the huge port bustling as Wax had never seen it before, with winter's lingering touches doing little to keep ships flowing in and out, smithies humming, and trade booming. Najahn soldiers crowded the docks, overseeing crates loaded onto vast Foti galleons, conscripted from their usual service hauling ore into arms transport. Smaller clippers like the one bringing Wax into port abounded too, with new ballistae from Rana getting fastened onto their railings, ready to target speedy Kance ships. New weapons, barbed ropes, lay in clumps to go with those ballistae, designed to shred Kance sails and founder their vessels.

A military litany continued, one Wax drowned out as his escort marched the former Renewal through wet streets and chill air towards the Najahn quarter. The familiar stepped and stoned avenues danced back not so distant memories, nights with Eujo going from one feted dinner to the next, a far more pleasant diversion than hearing yet more bluster about how his home, Vis, and Kance would soon be crushed by Najahn might. The skars helped Wax, their murmurings a convenient diversion: the Whent skar found all the rock and stone around them appealing, suggesting in wordless urges that Wax let the skar crumble a building here and there. The Rana stone sniffed out the rain barrels lodged beneath the sharp rooftops, hinting that it could wash away the quarter escorting Wax, leaving him free to . . . burn it all down, if the Foti skar had any say. Start a massive inferno that'd leap from home to home and turn the Ringed City to ash.

Tamas offered a different idea: Wax's Najahn escorts were curious about the Vis Renewal, even inspired by the young man walking with them. Wax could, with a nudge, turn that inspiration into rebellion, that Wax alone, with the skars, could stop the fiends and put the world into its prior peace. A rosy idea discounted by all the weapons around them, by the fact they were taking Wax to meet with Fassle himself, leader of the Najahn's guiding Circle and the same man who'd ordered the isles to war in the first place.

That Fassle would let Wax simply become the next Aegis and call everything off, buying a few years of relative calm, seemed absurd. Wax himself didn't even want the honor, or the debilitating curse that came with it, a curse Wax was realizing didn't come just from the Wound and its throne.

He'd used the skars to see the clipper through the storm, to speed it past lazy currents and opposite winds to bring the boat to Noctia's port faster than anyone would've expected. The effort had Wax lying down at all hours, getting food and drink handed to him bit by bit from an appreciative crew, diminished by battle and drownings. The episode hadn't left Wax wondering about the possibilities, but more about the drain still afflicting him: heavy steps, slow breaths, eyes half-lidded even amid the bright, early spring afternoon around him.

The skars had some power all their own, a burst exhausted quick with any real effort, and the god stones wouldn't hesitate to take more from their host. Not just a day's will either, but a week's, a year's, a lifetime's. How much had Wax already lost with these skars?

"So you see," the Najahn captain's voice broke through as they passed the Najahn quarter's gates, "this is all a foregone conclusion. Kance and Vis are brave isles, nobody is discounting that, but the sooner this fighting ends, the more lives are saved. You recognize that, don't you?"

Wax turned a bleary eye the man's way, "You think I have any power here?"

The Najahn captain, ensconced in his helmet, took the question with a frown, then a laugh. "Suppose you don't. Forgot you Renewals aren't what you used to be."

That sentiment stuck with Wax all the way through to the Circle's meeting chamber, a literal circle with a sunken platform in the middle from which visitors would address Fassle, the two Adepts, and any other people deemed necessary to decide one way or another. Wax, now bundled up in Najahn purple and black robes, walked into the room beneath lanterns and their warm glow. The room itself had a smoky heat bubbling up through furnaces far below. Fassle, the only one sharing the space, seemed to indulge in the manufactured climate: his robes looked as thin as the man's face, as bony as his steepled fingers.

"The rogue Renewal," Fassle said by way of greeting, once Wax had found the golden, ridged ring marker in the room's center and stood on it. "I can't say I ever wanted to see you face to face, but I'm not disappointed you're here."

The Najahn escort hadn't given Wax much on the walk up save for two things, requests Wax made as the Najahn turrets and their dire flags grew near. Coffee, fresh brewed from Vis beans, and the thick, formal robes he wore now. The ones that would've made Wax sweat if the Vis skar wasn't doing its level best to keep Wax's body in perfect alignment. As it was, the Renewal that stood before Fassle took the man's light insult without a hitch, throwing back Wax's classic broad grin.

"You're lucky you found me," Wax said, enjoying the thrill sent along by the Tamas skar, detecting Fassle's surprise.

"Lucky?"

"Sure. You're about to throw all these people, all those beautiful boats out there to waste, but now that I'm here, you don't have to."

"And let Kance and Vis keep their skars?" Fassle leaned forward, studying Wax from his higher perch. "I think you misunderstand, Vis. We cannot risk the future of the isles on benevolent trade."

"That's my point. You don't need anymore skars."

More confusion. Crinkled eyebrows, a scrunched nose.

"Let me elaborate," Wax said. "Over the last season, I've been across most of the isles. I've seen the skars in action up close. I know the power they have. I know, too, that a single set of seven can keep the fiends at bay for a long, long time."

"Shorter now than ever before. The whole reason we're here."

"Right, but that's because you haven't tried anything new."

"Anything new?"

The look of a leader befuddled. Was there anything more precious?

"Look," Wax said, reaching up and tapping the necklace. "The Aegis has, as long as we've been around, burned these skars to keep the fiends away, right? All that power, doing one thing. But what if we did something else?"

"That is what we're doing. We're going to train our soldiers to use the skars to take the fight to the fiends and eradicate them." Fassle seemed to realize he was explaining himself to his prisoner. "Now, what—"

"I'm telling you, there's a better way," Wax said. "Give me seven skars and a chance, and we can put an end to the war before it really gets going." The Vis pointed at Fassle. "Think about it this way, right now, your legacy is destroying how the isles have worked for a long, long time. With my help, we can twist it further. You can be the savior. The one who broke the chain."

"With your help." Fassle flattened those steepled hands. "I must say, Wax, this was not how I expected this audience to go."

"I try to defy expectations."

"Apparently. But I find your idea intriguing enough to give it one chance, though you're too late to stop the war. Kance has already been invaded, and the final assault on Vis is commencing as we speak." Fassle tapped his fingers. "Still, if you work fast, you might spare a few lives. Two days, Wax. Two days to prove your idea has merit. If it doesn't, I'll sit you on the Wound with your seven skars. You'll be our new Aegis while the Najahn take the isles and ready our forces to rid the world of the fiends once and for all.

If all goes well, you shouldn't bear the skars' curse for

long. A few gray hairs on that youthful head of yours. Agreed?"

Eujo was probably already on Kance, possibly under assault that very second. Same with Wax's family, friends on Vis. Already late, possibly too late. Still . . .

"Done. Two days," Wax said. "I'll need a Kance and Noctia skar, though."

"Oh, I know just where you can find those," Fassle said. "And I think you'll be very interested to meet her."

As Fassle signaled to a watching guard that the meeting was at its end, Wax turned his attention inward, to an imagination that hadn't failed him yet.

Because the Renewal had promised a miracle, and Wax hadn't the faintest damn clue what that would be.

CHAPTER 26

FALL AND FIGHT

Sichi saved the hunter, as the moon so often did. The rose light gave Quik a shadow to strike, a lingering branch at his reach's edge as the Vis plummeted towards grassy ground at the Great Sana's base. His hands, still wearing those gauntlets, snatched up and found the thin stick, wrapping it in a double grip. Quik's stomach lurched, the branch swinging down with his weight before finding some hidden strength and looping him towards its trunk.

A jungle revealed in silhouette, a hundred options and traps emerging as Quik flew, as the branch . . . snapped. A fall arrested became a fall resumed, but Quik had his goal, had his changed momentum, and he swung his body forward. The fern leaf caught Quick's chest, bending, holding as the hunter slid down its chilly length to smash through the other side, rolling, battering into bushes, leaves, and dirt. Thorns and stones tore at his weave, gashed Quik's skin, and his right shoulder snapped with enough sudden pain to make Quik want to scream.

He held his tongue. Bit his teeth. Lay there, instead,

amid the cold ground. Beyond, the battle around the Sana's base began to die. Mottilan hunters weren't whooping war cries anymore. Najahn orders to surrender floated over instead. Quik forced away the implications, all thoughts of the bigger struggle at hand. What mattered now was standing, was breathing, was making it out alive.

The first goal came with pain's litany, aches stabbing and throbbing in equal measure from his ankles, knees, and waist. Quik's shoulder had vanished into a numbing void, the arm hanging limp, leaving the effort to rise to Quik's left. The gauntlets, toothless, weren't much help here, but removing those would wait until Quik made it to his feet, to a point where more trivial matters could—

Noise, and not blade on blade, or blade on body. Crunching leaves, shifting grass, and spoken questions. Armor's telltale clanks and clinks.

Shoving into a crouch was easier than a stand, and Quik's bloodied legs seemed more eager to take the halfway approach, accepting his left-handed push to a squat. Turning on his heels in the dirt—his shoes, already scraped to scraps by the Sana, had broken off in the landing—Quik once again thanked Sichi for her benevolence.

Three Najahn approached, voulges at the ready, across the narrow green span between the Great Sana and the jungle. They moved slow, cautious. Well-trained, then, and not cocky. Bad luck.

Most of the Najahn Quik had met on Noctia had been all too eager to share their seeming invincibility, their disdain for the other isles. A few of those cocky fighters here, and Quik might've been able to teach them a lesson. A fatal one.

Instead, the hunter stayed low, kept on the front of his feet. He took a measure of his weapons: one working arm, a toothless gauntlet, and legs that might buckle after much use. Not great, but the damaged gauntlet could still block a swing, and the Najahn wouldn't know Quik's right arm, his legs were near useless. Surprise, too, was his.

And this was Quik's home.

The hunter sidestepped left as the Najahn trio found the broken branch, caught in the spindly arms of smaller trees. One asked if an animal might be the cause, his partner slapped that idea away, suggesting any coincidence tonight was an enemy until proven otherwise. The third kept moving forward, using their voulge to push aside bushes, the fern's first leaves.

Quik waited till the Najahn hit the fern's middle, till the voulge swept wide to clear the way, leaving a gap in the man's defenses. Najahn helms kept the sides and tops protected, but left the face clear, an opening Quik exploited with a palm-sized stone. The hunter whipped it, rising to a stand as he threw, and the rock crushed the Najahn's nose, sending the soldier stumbling, tripping over the undergrowth.

Heavy armor had its advantages, getting up from going down wasn't one of them. The Najahn would be on the ground for a few moments, gaps Quik would, must, use.

The hunter kicked right, angling for the sprawling tree whose branch had been his savior. The other two Najahn shouted, and Quik had a fleeting hope the pair might retreat, look for reinforcements, and give the hunter an opening. Instead, they forged on, ignoring their downed friend to split. One followed the fern path opened by their bashed ally, while the other, showing their ears worked better than their reflexes, cut left, right towards Quik's chosen cover.

A necessary mistake, separating, and one Quik would use.

He broke towards the leftward cutter, putting a few strides between that Najahn and the other two. Quik didn't have another stone, but a dirt and leaf wad in his left hand worked almost as well. His legs burned, the hot blood trickling down, but they worked well enough to scramble the hunter around the trunk's side. The Najahn angled the voulge Quik's way, opened her mouth to call for help, and caught the dirt right on her lips. The shout turned into a cough. The voulge wavered, and Quik hit it away, the gauntlet's backside knocking the voulge's curling spearhead towards the ground.

If Quik had a working right hand, a simple jab would've ended the fight then and there. The Najahn expected it, her panicked stare matching the dirt spewing from a retching mouth. The hunter had no such option, but he did have a skull, and the dirt made an easy target to aim for. His forehead struck the Najahn's face hard, her eyes crossing as she collapsed. The armor clanked as her body bunched up, as clear an alarm as any shout.

Quik turned to face the oncoming pair, the purple plate catching Sichi's pink streaks to make the Najahn appear like harrowing phantoms as they charged. The simple turn taxed Quik's tortured legs one step too far, and Quik's right ankle gave out, collapsing like his right arm to send the hunter into a one-kneed defense. He raised the gauntlet, then dropped it, matching the weapon to its limp pair.

The Najahn duo stopped, voulges leveled at Quik's heart.

"Surrendering, Vis?" asked the one Najahn as yet unscathed.

"Don't let him," said the second, a blubbery, burbling

voice. "He deserves what he's about to get. Pavarde can eat her orders. She's not on her ship now."

Pavarde? The name itched, something for later, if Quik lived that long.

The first Najahn glanced at the second, an opening granted by some small moral smudge. Quik used it. Like with his second ambush, Quik scooped dirt with his left hand and flung it at the Najahn, rising with the swing's momentum into an uppercut follow-through, one that should've tracked right into the Najahn's chin.

One that glanced off an armored forearm as the two soldiers blocked the spray with voulges and metal. The first Najahn twitched the butt of his voulge, catching Quik's shoulder and sending him sprawling into the soil. The second pressed the spear point against Quik's neck.

"Like I said," the bloodied Najahn growled.

"Do it, then," said the first.

Quik didn't have a chance to reminisce, to say any last words. His body flagged, overwhelmed with the fall, the bash, the fighting. The voulge, at least, would put an end to all that, and to do it while Quik lay in the cold comfort of his home isle?

A certain justice.

Except the strike didn't fall. A surprised grunt, a curse, and a loud, metal thump. Scattered dirt brushed Quik's cheek and he turned, looked to see Sawi facing off against the first Najahn. The woman's Whent blade flashed, batting aside the Najahn's voulge in a narrow counter. She tried to close, but the Najahn wasn't a rookie, and he canceled the advance with a retreat.

One that brought his knees right near Quik's prone body. As Sawi, blade double-gripped before her, waited, the

Najahn took his chance. The soldier slid his left foot forward, going into a straight thrust.

Quik swept his gauntlet in a backhand, a blow lacking power, but doing enough to stumble the Najahn. The voulge strike went left and low, impaling a bush. A bad miss, and one Sawi didn't match.

"C'mon," Sawi said, a heartbeat later, with the Whent blade shoved in her back strap. "They'll come looking soon."

"Can't move fast," Quik replied, accepting her assistance to get his weary legs under him. "I'm not outrunning anything."

"We'll hide when we have to." Sawi threw Quik's arm over her shoulder, started them off in a shambling walk into the jungle. "This is our isle, Quik. We're not done fighting for her yet."

CHAPTER 27

DRINKING WITH THE DEAD

A single ale didn't make it much easier to party with the enemy. Maena drifted through the Dead City's streets, the nightly revelry flush with flagons, bad drum music, and the roaring challenge of one Whent arm wrestle, race, or drinking contest on her periphery. She watched for any searching eyes while trying to fit in, always ensuring Maena had a drink in her hand, a ready laugh at whatever stupid thing was happening nearby.

The Whent, however, didn't want to let Maena play her game. A reputation Maena herself had cultivated by avoiding their raging parties in the past meant the burly warriors, scouts, and traders found the Rana a curiosity, and not one to be indulged. One friendly brawl came to a halt as Maena slithered to the inner ring, stares going to the Rana captain until one Whent, bruised and bloodied from the previous bout, demanded to know what Maena thought she was doing there.

"No gutter lovers here," the man growled. "Don't care if Jochi says we're not supposed to punch ya, doesn't mean I need a Rana rat spoiling my good time."

"As if you knew how to find one of those," Maena snapped back, but she dashed off quick enough as too many other fists rose to press the issue.

Maena found similar treatment at drinking contests, while grabbing a snack from a table overflowing with mushroom pastries, and even just walking the streets. The hostility wasn't all new—Maena wouldn't lie to herself that she'd stolen a Whent scout for her deeds in part to assuage the old, ever-present urge to deal some damage to her isle's ancestral foe—but with Svarde gone and the corpses quiet, rusty tensions shook off their paralysis.

Don't pretend you're surprised. It's always been this way.

Had it? Back on the surface, after Maena and her team had defeated those first firewalkers, Jochi gave her a rousing welcome. Invited her into the long march into the Dark Below. She'd ate at his table, gave her opinions and had them heard.

Until they stopped listening. You know why.

Svarde's fault. The barbarian left, played vanguard with those axes and the ferrite and left her alone, he—

You don't need him, and that's not why. Don't lie to us, Maena.

No. The invitations stopped coming because Maena stopped making sense. At least, that's what Jochi said. Too bloodthirsty, too wild, too dangerous, and her being a Rana didn't help things. Stay quiet for a while, the warlord said, and so she had. She'd chased Svarde and . . .

We grew close in the dark, didn't we?

The ale's last drop woke Maena from her memories. She'd wandered away from the music, the bravado, and found herself in the silent cathedral Svarde used to dominate. Now, sitting on the plain, huge stone chair—it was too bland to be a throne—was the Dead City's former owner. Bereft of power after Svarde left, the Dead King hunched forward, massive, dented armor settling on itself.

Was his body decomposing in there, or did the blade's enchantment, once gifted, keep the man preserved? The other corpses sure seemed to be stinking up the place, but then, Maena hadn't yet seen any crumble to dust either.

At least, not by natural means. More than a few had lost limbs or been destroyed by wanton Whent.

"I'd think you'd approve," Maena said to the towering figure. "All these years holding the line against the monsters, waiting for an end, and here I am to give it to you."

The Dead King offered no reply, so Maena chucked her empty flagon at the First Guardian. It shattered amid his marred and mottled plating, marking no move.

"But they won't sing any songs about me," Maena continued. "They'll never remember the Rana pirate who closed the gates, who saw the truth."

You didn't either, until I showed it to you.

"Showed it? You wouldn't let me forget it!"

Maena's voice echoed around the cathedral. Without a living occupant, nobody had replaced much of the moss. Instead, small rose light leaked through from far above. A tiny gift from Sichi, all the way through Noctia, down the Wound, to right here.

Because you needed to accept the truth. The fiends are the gods' mistakes. They must be destroyed, not forgiven.

"Don't I know it . . . " Maena muttered, turning back to the Dead King. "You could've saved us all so much time." A low laugh, because how absurd was all this, really? "How much effort would it have been to swamp the chamber? Shovel dirt with your corpse-driven army into the pool until you buried it?"

Once started, the accusations poured out, one road not taken after another, all laid at the Dead King's feet. Maena crossed back and forth before that throne, finding catharsis in the solemn Guardian's silent attention. Sure, the Dead King didn't answer, didn't offer up suggestions, but Maena found them nonetheless.

The messy, winding path that'd brought her to this precipice couldn't be changed, no, but Maena could deliver others from the same fate, and even if not a soul knew her name, no statues rose to proclaim her brilliance, the effort would be worth it.

Not all legends needed to be told.

"I'm having a hard time finding you so noble," Haggerth announced, appearing flanked by axe-wielding Whent guards at the cathedral's entrance.

Maena, who'd just wrapped up her declaration of purpose, wondered if Haggerth picked his timing to avoid interrupting her.

"Were you listening?" Maena said, putting her back to the Dead King and counting the five soldiers, Haggerth included, before her. None had drink's glassy eyes, all had hands on weapons. "Judging me?"

Bad odds, Maena. Is there another way out?

Not that the Rana captain knew. Not that Haggerth seemed prepared to offer, either.

"When a Whent warlord falters," Haggerth said, keeping his spot in the center of his guard, who began fanning out around the cathedral's broad, blank chamber, "it's often because they overstep their abilities. Delusions of grandeur, some call it. Too obsessed with becoming something they can't, that they lose who they are. Sound familiar, Rana?"

Sounds like Haggerth has no sense of purpose.

"There's a difference," Maena countered, backing up closer still to the Dead King, as if the armored, giant corpse would offer her an answer. "I'm not in this for myself. I'm trying to save the isles."

Haggerth, who, now that Maena took a sharper look, did indeed appear like he'd stumbled through rough caves for hours. His furred Whent cloak held rips, the man himself bore dirt stains and cuts along legs, arms, and head where a blind whack had taken its price.

Good.

"Then why be so secretive? Why kidnap one of our scouts and lie about it?" Haggerth asked. "Why press one of our smiths to make explosives without even asking Jochi about your plan?"

"You are thorough, aren't you?"

"Didn't think I'd find all that?" Haggerth, ever loose, stood his straight ground between Maena and the cathedral's exit. Four guards flanked her now, on all sides. "Didn't think anyone would notice? Or that the smith hadn't told Jochi what you'd asked for from the first?"

"He knew?"

"Some. The vanished scout was my sleuthing, and now the only missing piece is where, Maena. Where are you planning to put the bombs? Is that where we'll find our scout?"

"Jochi knew, and never asked me?"

Haggerth frowned, "My question first."

He won't kill you until he gets the scout. You have leverage.

As if Maena hadn't ever been in negotiations before. Admittedly, most of the time, Maena had been pressing hapless sea captains to give up loot to save their own lives, but the reverse wasn't so alien to leave her floundering.

All that mattered was finding the advantage, and pressing it.

"A deal, then, Haggerth," Maena said. "Together we'll go find the scout. I'll show you how to save the isles. If you don't like it, you can kill me there."

Haggerth considered, then nodded at the sword on her belt. "No weapons, no tricks. From this moment, Maena, captain of Rana, you are a Whent prisoner." At his words, the four guards approached. "Resist, and I'll have you sent straight to the Pits. Few survive them once. You won't make it out a second time."

CHAPTER 28

RISING REUNION

S varde, much as he hated to admit it, owed Tamas his continued un-death. The damn isle, back when he'd been Catya's Guardian, had insisted he perform a background role in Catya's performed scene. He'd needed to move with music, act light on his feet while carrying a white-painted lid meant to be the sun. Ami had mocked him for it, and even Catya couldn't quite hide her grin, but Svarde had done his job, flouncing across the stage as the lines called for it.

Now he flounced on soft feet through Kance avenues. Clouds obscured Sichi, sprawling shadows cast from corner lamps wicked with Noctia oil. A supply Kance was rationing already, going by how many winding blocks lay cloaked in darkness. Olgata figured Kance had put in a curfew too, as too many taverns sat quiet, too many streets lay empty. Soldiers wandered here and there, robed and wearing rapiers in the cool air. The bird calls, Kance's natural symphony, shifted with nightfall, changing to low hoots and trills from creatures Svarde couldn't see.

The great blade sat on his back, cloaked in the stained raiments stolen from several Kance soldiers who wouldn't need them anymore. The robes weren't Svarde's size and fit tight, the pants chaffing against thighs that couldn't feel it anymore. At least death granted Svarde that minor blessing: the aches and pains of travel, of war, were gone.

For a wartime city, though, Kance kept its security lax. The patrols didn't come thick. Svarde didn't feel eyes watching him, spies from a populace intent on remaining vigilant. Perhaps because Noctia hadn't brought the fighting this far, perhaps because Kance believed its victory would come easy. Or its defeat inevitable.

"If we're going to get to the top of the Sky Palace," Olgata said as they scampered to a stop between two dark houses, the Kance bungalows squat and dotted with windows, thin woods. "Then we have two options: the stairs, or the elevators."

"Stairs."

"Wrong. The stairs wrap the spire's exterior. They'll see us coming and trap us. You might survive that, but I won't."

Svarde huffed, patted Kivi, the ferrite scrabbling at his side. "You don't need to come with us."

Olgata nodded at the blade's hilt rising over Svarde's shoulder, where it kept in constant contact with the gray skin along his upper back. A concession to the skars in the weapon, what they demanded to keep Svarde alive.

"That blade cannot fall into anyone's hands," Olgata said. "If you drop it, I need to take it and bring it back to Jochi."

"That's the reason you're here? The blade?"

"One of them."

Svarde would have to re-evaluate the Whent scout.

Slippery, skilled, and always ready to ditch the moment for a bigger, more distant objective. Olgata had dashed away from Svarde and Maena when the Dead King's corpses made their first approach, and she'd taken the lead in mapping the tunnels south from the Dead City to Kance, to Vis.

"Why're you so loyal, Olgata?" Svarde asked. "What does this get you?"

The scout shook her head, "Not now. We live through all this and you get me very drunk, maybe I'll tell you. Until then, let's focus on the elevators. If we get this right, you'll be ruling Kance by breakfast."

They lurked near the main avenue heading towards the Sky Palace and the giant, jutting spire it topped. Kance's love of flowing, silver style dominated the view, even in very early morning's darkness. Sky diamonds lined the broad avenue, splitting sculpted hedgerows and flag posts billowing various Kance insignias. Lanterns burned here, guards patrolled, and Olgata wasn't thrilled.

"It's beautiful in the daytime," Svarde said. "One of the few places in the isles that was really worth it."

"Quiet," Olgata said.

They had their backs pressed to a stone building, one several stories tall and that looked designated for official business. Kivi clung to the wall above Svarde's head, the occasional chip from her claws speckling his robe.

"Stealth's got us this far, scout," Svarde said, moving his hand up to his blade. "Might be time to change tactics."

"I said they'll cut the elevator cables if they see us get in," Olgata snapped, her voice a hard whisper. "Weren't you listening?"

"Just have to move fast, then."

Olgata seemed ready to bat that idea aside too when an approaching rustle, many feet on stone, cut her off. The pair, well in shadow, looked away from the Sky Palace, saw yet more guards. Marching in formation. For a second, Svarde wondered if they'd been discovered, if Kance was finally fortifying its most important place. For only a second, then that thought vanished with a single face.

The Vis wore fresh years in the seasons since Svarde had seen her last. The staff she carried, too, had changed, from flexible but breakable Vis bamboo to hardened wood and metal. She wore Kance robes, too, and walked like someone who'd spent time with civilization instead of the jungle's jaunty ways. Svarde took all that in with a glance, but spent the rest of the march by studying her other features, the downcast eyes and frustrated mouth, the tight fists at her sides. The way she kept throwing looks back towards the sea.

The way she walked without any of those others with her.

Bliss, that'd been her name. The girl the only one willing to share some pipeweed on his cabin's deck that night. A brave one, but how'd she come here? And alone?

"That's the queen," Olgata said, almost awed. "Kance's only one now. She was their Renewal too." The scout put a hand on Svarde's wrist, nodded towards the defiant-seeming woman in the soldier's midst as they walked past. "Her bracelet. There's skars on it."

"The stones are everywhere, Olgata. What matters is whether the queen knows how to use them."

"No, what matters is we have our opening."

"What?"

"The Regent, or whomever is leading Kance now, is

about to lose their station. The Queen will take over, and now, you can take her." Olgata nodded after the royal entourage. "Kance will lose its will to fight with her at risk. Your stupid plan might just work out."

"Wait, stupid plan?"

Olgata sniffed, "Obviously. Now's our chance. Let's go."

Before Svarde could inquire further into what, exactly, made his plan so stupid, Olgata curled along the building's side, into the broad avenue, but keeping to the shadows. If the guards in view weren't distracted watching the Queen, the move would've been caught. Instead, Svarde lumbered after Olgata, and Kivi after him, all staying low.

Kance helped its invaders here too, with its ornate, yet flat architecture. No fences, odd rises to entries, or other barriers forced Svarde into difficult jumps or noisy twists. Instead, they kept at a crouching slow jog, using the hedges and budding gardens. Olgata said no words and Svarde made no mistakes, bringing them to the avenue's end without incident, just as the Queen's group split into several parties. The Queen herself headed towards the spire's center, the elevators waiting inside. Most of the guards broke off to rest their legs at ground-level barracks, Svarde assumed.

"Now we wait, then make our own break," Olgata said. "We'll take the second elevator, and—"

"No," Svarde muttered. The barbarian's intuition had given him a new idea. "I'm changing the plan. Cover me."

"Cover? What—"

Svarde broke out in a straight line dash across the courtyard. Kivi, ever loyal, matched him stride for stride, breaking through the hedges in a crackling burst of leaves and twigs. The Kance guards at last took notice, turned and shouted. Some thought to draw rapiers or crossbows.

"Distract them, Kivi," Svarde said as his feet pounded the diamond-touched stone courtyard. "Don't get yourself killed."

The ferrite did as Svarde asked, breaking hard at the nearest guard and tackling the poor man. Kivi didn't stop to maim the soul, but kicked off at the next, one steadying his aim to shoot Svarde. The crossbow didn't get its bolt off before the ferrite shattered it, driving its owner to a hard whack on the ground.

Svarde used those seconds, made it to the flowing arch marking the spire's entrance. Silver-touched lines swirled right and left, as if the spire's mouth was blowing wind. Instead, the man-made cave welcomed Svarde in with nary a gust. Inside, soft lanterns haloed the twin elevators and their massive doors. The Queen and her party, Svarde took a quick count of ten, were boarding the elevator to the left.

Two, guards, these in the ornate Kance armor, with those pretty gilded rapiers, abandoned the elevator effort to stand in Svarde's way.

Poor souls.

Svarde didn't stop running as he reached up, swept the great blade free. As he did, Svarde's robe split, fragments on his sleeves billowing out like some strange creature's fins. The odd appearance didn't stop his swing, amid the shouts, the curses, the calls to get the damn elevator moving.

One rapier struck Svarde's left shoulder. The other never made it, its owner cleaved to the left and, with the swing, barreled into the second guard. Svarde continued on towards the elevator, the rapier still sticking from his skin. The remaining group with the Queen must've been a bunch of sniveling advisors, worthless politicians, as they shrank to the elevator's back.

All save for two. A scrawny young woman with a dagger

in each hand, and Bliss, her staff drawn and ready. A battle stance that faltered as she saw Svarde, recognized the lines in his dead face, as she heard his demand, delivered as Svarde set his undying feet upon the elevator.

Peace, not for Kance, not for Noctia, but for the fiends.

CHAPTER 29
AMONG THE FLOWERS

For all the ferns, flowers, and vines Wax had touched on Vis, he'd never felt anything quite like the lelune in Noctia's vast Wound crater. A few flowers bloomed, Sichi sneaking through clouds to kiss the nighttime show with her rose red light. A crisp wind raced around, shivering the budding plants and reminding Wax that he hadn't worn the warmest robe Noctia had provided. The armoire in his room had been stuffed, really, with so many garments Wax had to assume they'd been leftover from someone else.

Yet, all had fit.

"These are my favorite," Catya, the former Aegis, said as she led him through the flower fields. She stepped slow and careful, a cane always in her hand, but she spoke sharp and clear. "Every night I could, I'd leave the Wound and watch them bloom."

"They're beautiful."

"A reminder of what I was trying to defend, I think. Moreso than the Najahn, anyway."

"They didn't treat you well?"

"They used me," Catya glanced back at Wax, gave a rueful grin. "Well, we used each other. These skars might've stolen much of my life, but I never had to barter for a meal, worry about keeping warm, or if a fiend was going to bite my toes off."

Wax laughed, "I know more than a few people who'd make that trade."

"Would you?"

Ah. The sudden tone switch again. Catya liked to do that, a habit Wax had picked up as their evening had gone on. The Aegis would laugh about this, joke about that, or seem lost in a pleasant anecdote only to twist it on Wax like some sneak attack. A test, maybe? Or just a quirk developed over a decade with little to live for?

"No," Wax said. "I made a promise to go this far. But I'm not sitting on that throne."

"Because Fassle put an end to it?"

"Because I think it's a mistake."

They reached a sparse patch. Catya sat on the soft stone, patted the space next to her and told Wax to break out the wineskin, the tarts baked for them.

"Strawberry," Catya said, smiling as she lifted the pastry free. "A season ago, I wouldn't have been able to eat this. Not without having it smashed to a paste."

"Guess it's a relief, then, to be off that throne?"

"That's just a chair, you know. There's nothing special about it."

"But—"

Catya set the tart aside, reached into her robe's pocket and pulled out a necklace. One that looked an awful lot like the one Wax now wore upon his neck. All the skars were there save one, the Vis stone Wax knew so well.

"They let me keep them all, but I've not put the necklace on since I took it off," Catya said. "The one skar that I still hold?" Her free hand went to her neck, where a simple brooch hung. Wax could guess what sat inside it. "Vis has given me back what the other stones took. At least a little more time." She turned to look towards the tented center, its guard relaxed since the Whent force had staunched the fiend flow. "The chair was a symbol to everyone else. It didn't, it doesn't matter to the skars. Fassle, of course, likes that he can control it."

"Then how do you, er, did you do it? The Aegis?"

A small smile, "They call the Renewal while the Aegis is still alive for the transition, which is more than just sitting your young butt on that chair. As I understand it, Demion told the one after, and her words have been passed down from one to the next, all the way to me."

"Words?"

"After. Before it gets cold."

Catya held up a finger, then proceeded to dig into the tart. Wax took the cue, loaded up two small wooden cups with red Tamas wine—a good southern vintage, so stated the Najahn who'd appeared at his door with the late night assembly and orders to meet Catya at the Wound—and tasted his own pastry. Still warm, still gooey, and delicious in a way nothing Wax ate on Vis could be. Artificial, almost. Crafted without nature's thorny hand.

They ate in silence. Catya took an easy time of it, a pace Wax decided to match once he realized haste wouldn't get him answers faster. That'd been the way of it since the meeting with Fassle. A Najahn stuck to Wax's side, ready to answer his questions—to a point—and direct him to meals, to parts of the Najahn quarter he hadn't seen in his first stint at the Ringed City with Eujo, and to avoid telling him what would happen later except to warn against slamming one ale after another.

Which Wax wanted to do, because that might blur the nightmares threatening assaults every moment. Visions of Bliss and Eujo wrecked in the sea or stabbed by some Najahn voulge. Torny, riddled with crossbow bolts. Or, almost worse, carrying on without Wax, assuming him dead and lost.

The Vis couldn't commandeer a ship, couldn't swim to Kance. He'd asked his Najahn minder whether he could send a message, and that answer would come in the morning.

"You're struggling," Catya said, in between licks of strawberry filling off her fingers.

"That obvious?"

"You're here without friends. No Guardians, though Fassle said you were a Renewal." Again, Catya put up a palm, then lowered it to hold Wax's wrist. "I don't need your story, Wax. Don't have time enough for it anyway." She laughed, turned her look up to the moon. "These walks aren't easy."

"Then why take one with me?"

"Two reasons. First, because Fassle ordered it, and he'll take away my skars and all I have if I don't do what he wants. Second, because you have a real chance to change everything."

Wax emptied his cup, refilled it. "Too many people say that."

"The difference is, I know what I'm talking about." Catya pulled the skar necklace back out. She reached towards the glimmering diamond in one slot and, with nimble, stretched fingers, popped it free. "This is yours, I don't need it anymore."

"Kance?"

Catya nodded as Wax took the skar, blended its curious whispers with the others. "More than any other, this one tried to get me to run away. It sang of freedom, always."

"Sang?"

"That's what the stones are doing, Wax. Singing."

"I always thought they were talking in a language I couldn't understand. The gods speech, or something. Then the emotions, right? The urges pushing me to let them go, do this or that? You're saying it's a song?"

"A part of one," Catya said. "Like a band, every skar is its own instrument, playing its lines. When you give it a solo, that's when it's abilities shine and you get your fire, your wind, your shaking earth."

Wax blinked, turned to his wine. Hoped Catya wouldn't see the skepticism on his face.

"The Aegis before me? He was a musician, so perhaps its his interpretation, but it fits," Catya continued, no hint of offense in her ever-polite tone. "The gods united their powers to create the isles and the world we live on. That we know. And making the shield to circle them requires shifting the skars to be in sync, to play in harmony."

That, at least, Wax could buy. The stones wanting to get a starring solo turn? Eh.

"How do we do that?" Wax asked. "Or, how did you do it?"

"First, you have to listen. Not to one, but to them all. Then when you have their songs playing together, you conduct. Tell Foti to slow down, Vis to speed up." Catya waved a finger in the air as she spoke. "For all the time I sat on that chair, Wax, I wasn't doing nothing. Rather, I was keeping the skars in harmony. Day in and day out, catching sleep where I could, for years and years while the skars drained me for their song."

Wax had started to listen to the stones, stopped when Catya finished, with the implication.

"I don't want that," Wax said, dropping his hand from the necklace where he'd slotted the Kance skar. "I'm not trying to be you."

"Then don't." Catya rose to a shaking stand. "Wax, you need to get yourself a Noctia skar. Then, then, you ought to do something different, something I didn't consider until I saw all these skars being used in new ways."

"Which is?"

"All the Aegises before me had the skars play a single tune, the one that kept the fiends out. Wax, I'm telling you, there has to be more." Catya reached, put a steadying hand on Wax's shoulder while she planted her cane on the crater's pebbled floor. "Maybe you can find the song the gods meant for us to play, the one that can set this cursed world right again."

CHAPTER 30
BUGGED

Limping through the jungle on a dark night after an exhausting day took much of the joy from Quik's home. Every fern, vine, and gnarled root became an obstacle, every slick patch made so by melted mountaintop snow became a chance to twist a sore ankle. There weren't many bugs yet, but what ones were out seemed to find him and Sawi and harass their slow forms without remorse: itchy bites soon speckled their battered selves.

Quik figured it'd been at least two hours by the time Sawi gave up, by the time they stumbled into a relative clearing on the upward climb towards the mountains and Mottilan. She set Quik down, leaned him against a tree before collapsing herself. Leaves and needles provided a bed, albeit a cool one. The blood from their wounds clotted with dirt. Quik's mouth ached for water, and he suspected Sawi wasn't any better.

The early spring season meant Vis didn't yet have its verdant fruit. Their stomachs grumbled without an easy solution, so Quik fell back on the old ways.

"We have to be hunters," he rasped to Sawi, visible as a

rose-tinted shadow. "Live like the hunters did on long journeys."

"How?"

"Eat what we can."

"I don't understand?"

Quik felt a curious bug land on his thigh. His right arm didn't work, but his left moved just fine. Sawi had taken off his gauntlets, left them lying in the dirt, so when Quik snapped his hand over to the bug, when he cupped the winged creature in his palm, the wooden weapons didn't get in his way.

The swallow didn't come easy, but the bug went down all the same.

"They won't make you sick," Quik said. "Enough, and you'll survive."

The silence answering him made Quik wonder if Sawi's disgust had stricken her quiet. Then he heard the soft slaps, the swipe from hand to mouth. He grinned, let his head loll against the soft bark while he snatched another bug. Sawi hadn't forgotten what it meant to be a Vis after all.

The isle, the god, would provide.

Sawi, in fact, took the idea further. She began running her hands through the decomposing leaves, finding juicier worms, beetles, and grubs. Every bite pushed back at Quik's life, what he'd learned to accept, to aim for, but savagery was survival, and before all that long their stomachs were full. Their thirst nourished by warmer things than water.

"I think I've had worse," Sawi said, sitting next to Quik now, both leaning against the same tree. "Noctia could learn a thing or two from these bugs."

"You don't mean that."

Sawi croaked a laugh, "Maybe not, but their fish was always so tough."

"It was, wasn't it? I'd chew it for an hour."

Now they both laughed. It pushed the pain away. They slumped together, swatting idly at those few insects still braving the pair for a bite, and let the night wear on, swapping one story after another.

"We should sleep at some point," Quik muttered, later. "It'll be dawn in not too long, then we'll have to walk again."

"Or we could just wait here, eat bugs until the isles settle down."

"I swore an oath to Wax, Sawi. I can't quit."

"I think he'd understand, given the circumstances."

Quik shifted, looked at Sawi's shaded, filthy, bug-spattered face with its matted hair, bloody clothes. He must've appeared no better, and yet, he saw there a certain sense, a considering that just lying beneath the leaves telling tales might be as good as it could get, so long as it was the two of them.

Except Quik was half dead, and Sawi had been his brother's partner.

"I'm not sure that he would," Quik said, pulling his focus away, settling on some dark trees across the clearing.

"How well did you know your brother?" Sawi asked, not giving Quik any distance.

"He was my brother? What kind of question is that?"

"You were always hunting, Quik. Acting important, only to show up here and there and tell us to grow up."

"Because you all were getting into trouble all the time."

"It wasn't because you were lonely?"

"I . . . " Quik swallowed, blinked. The life of a Vis hunter meant days in the jungle, alone, tracking prey and returning with it in hand, or at least a location for a party to raid. That's what was expected, what was done. "Maybe. No more than anyone else."

"If you'd spent more time with us, then you'd know Wax isn't the kind to dwell on the past, on failure. He keeps going. Tries again and again, sometimes just for fun." Sawi chuckled. "He'd get us into trouble because he wouldn't say no to an idea. He always wanted you to come too. He missed you, when you grew up."

"I miss him now."

"Me too," Sawi said. "He'd have some dumb idea to get us out of this. Something we wouldn't think of."

That Wax would. Quik stared off into the trees. What would his brother do now? He'd have the skars, which would change things. A Vis skar, for example, would help quite a bit right now. Quik should've taken one from Annalyse.

Wait.

Quik looked at Sawi, saw the girl had indeed fallen asleep. Her head lay on his shoulder, but at her waist was the Whent blade. One that could, used right, maybe . . .

"Give me your sword," Quik said, reaching towards the blade.

"Why?" Sawi asked without opening her eyes.

"I have an idea. Like Wax."

That roused Sawi further, and she drew the blade, handed it to Quik. "What're you going to do?"

"Help me find a rock."

That search, on a forested mountainside, didn't take long. A stone about twice as large as Quik's fist, dragged over by Sawi. They set leaves in a pile on one side, Sawi muttering about the chance they were taking.

"Mottilan has people watching, they'll see it," Quik said, measuring the stroke, the moment's hope doing its best to push away the aches and heavy eyes. "They'll come find us."

"Or maybe the Najahn will do it instead. A voulge apiece. Wouldn't that be nice?"

"Wouldn't have to worry about all this anymore."

Quik slid the sword across the stone. A shriek, no sparks.

"Have to get that blade in there," Sawi said, and Quik ran it again. Still nothing. "Here, let me try."

Easy enough to hand the sword over. Quik only had one working arm anyway. He slumped back to the tree, watched Sawi sight her angle.

"Think Annalyse is wondering where you are?" Sawi asked.

The question threw Quik far enough that he didn't notice as Sawi made a measured stroke, sent the first sparks flying into the leaves. She drew the sword back, repeated the slide. More sparks, more shrill metal-on-stone shrieks.

"Maybe?" Quik replied.

"Guarantee she is. Did you not pay attention to how she looked at you?"

Of course he did. Of course he noticed. Of course Quik had wanted to find some time with Annalyse, to pick up what they'd left on the pier back on Noctia.

"How was that?" Quik asked, and Sawi laughed, slid the blade.

This time, the sparks left some smoke. The next time, they left an ember, one that grew.

"I'm just saying, Quik, we make it out of this, I don't think you need to be alone."

Quik chuckled, watched the flames build. Dawn neared too, the sky overhead losing its clouds and gaining light. Mottilan might not see the fire's glow, but they'd definitely notice the smoke. They'd come, beat any armored Najahn trying to navigate the jungle. Quik and Sawi would live, would get to fight again.

Or not. Slip away to some quiet beach on the isle's southern edge . . . without Wax, Quik would've held to that idea.

"What about you, Sawi?" Quik asked. "Who's waiting for you?"

"My family. My isle." Sawi stood over the flame, blade held at her side. "I came back to fight, Quik. Looks like I'm going to get that chance."

CHAPTER 31

BECOMING LEGEND

Years and years at sea, starting as a simple runner, a deckhand, a waif aboard Rana cargo haulers. Once she could hold a cutlass, fire a crossbow without hitting an ally, Maena graduated to the clippers and cutters, dashing the waters between Noctia and Whent hunting for easy prey. Through all that time, all those raids on coastal towns and clunky Whent craft, Maena had never found herself a prisoner.

That'd changed with Svarde and his dive into the Dark Below. Brought to the Pits once, and now, again after following that reckless barbarian, she walked with Whent rockbiters at her back, ropes tied tight around her wrists. Haggerth paced closest, his breath near enough to tickle her neck. That he held a blade with a point aimed right at Maena's waist wasn't easy to ignore either: he made sure to nick her leathers any time Maena slowed up.

They'd left the Dead City well behind, trekking through the slanted, thin tunnels upwards and around the vast chamber whose waters held those dire gateways to other worlds, to the gods' first mistakes. Maena had at first tried to think of a clever trap for the Whent trio following her. Maybe a side passage to a cavern where fiends might live, or a quick dash to disappear ahead of their lantern lights.

Both of those options ended in the same way: Maena lost in the dark, without weapons and with bound hands, food for the same fiends hopefully eating the Whent.

Those fiends, too, couldn't be counted on anymore. The monsters, with the firewalkers proving a bulwark and Jochi expanding Whent territory as more and more people arrived seeking fortune or freedom from a more miserable existence, had largely disappeared. Scouts, watching the chamber, reported water-friendly fiends still slipping out through the deeper tunnels leaking into the oceans, but land-loving monsters found themselves under assault the moment they swam free.

So Maena walked to her chosen hideaway, said nothing. Listened, instead, to her rambling other self, a personality always on aggression's edge in the happiest times, tilting now towards full derangement.

I'm only trying to help you, since you seem unwilling to do so yourself.

Yes, Maena turning and trying to headbutt Haggerth into submission was a definite strategy. One that'd result in her painful death, but a strategy.

I don't hear you making any suggestions.

True. Maena had her focus on something different, something she was going to have to deal with in about another minute or two.

"Nearly there?" Haggerth asked. "We've been walking awhile. Been a long night."

"Your choice."

"Actually, yours. If you hadn't done any of this, I'd still be back up on the surface. Asleep in a cozy bed."

"Still your choice."

Haggerth snarled, but let the sniping die. The man's cool demeanor had been fraying the whole walk over here, like a costume peeling off. Whether it was exhaustion, or the fact that Maena hadn't yet folded, the slick guise slipped.

A possible weakness?

If so, exposing it would have to wait, as they'd arrived. Maena tromped up, with Haggerth having to help her with his free hand, the last few strides into the broad cavern spanning the pool. The group walked in, and the scout, Maena's prisoner, gave a pathetic whimper at the sight. The man, thin, drawn, and dry, stretched his head towards the Whent trio, and Haggerth ordered one of the guards to untie him.

"Stand over here," Haggerth said, directing Maena to the left wall.

The man unclipped the lantern from the hook on his belt and set it on the ground, told the guard not tasked with helping the prisoner to keep tabs on Maena, then Haggerth walked forward, taking in the chamber. The gaps in the rock floor gave clear evidence what lay beneath their feet, and the dark boxes, tied together with fuse cords, offered a puzzle that had Haggerth crouching, poking at one of the cubes with his blade.

"What're these?" Haggerth asked.

Maena eyed the guard watching her. The man seemed as tired as the rest of them, but had a hand on his axe hilt. A bold beard, thick leathers, and a face coated with dirt. Someone who worked the stone by day, then. Not a hand-picked Jochi expert. Was it Haggerth's hubris, or had Jochi too many higher priorities, like the war with Kance, to spare his best soldiers for this little side mission?

"Maena?" Haggerth asked again. "What was your plan here?"

"To solve a problem Jochi and Svarde aren't willing to."

"That's not an answer."

The former prisoner was on his shaky feet. The scout tottered, the Whent lifting him almost losing his footing. Maena's own guard shifted, held out an arm to steady the man.

Now.

For once, Maena and her other self had the same idea. The Rana stepped forward, swung her leg and kicked Haggerth's lantern. The globe spun through the air, struck a rock slat and burst, scattering burning oil. More than one drop landed where it needed to, igniting the fuses at several points. Hissing filled the cavern as Maena's guard cuffed her, knocking the Rana sprawling back to the side, against the rock wall.

"Run, dammit!" Haggerth shouted.

The Whents' experience hacking stone showed its worth, as they understood what the burning fuses meant and moved fast. Dragging the scout, leaving Maena, the trio scurried down the tunnel. Haggerth followed, stopping to pull at Maena's shoulder, lift her up.

"C'mon," Haggerth growled, those fuses glowing brighter. "I'm not going to let you escape this easily."

Maena twisted away from him, put on the manic smile that came so naturally now, "I already have."

Haggerth reached for her again, and the cavern blew apart.

The pressure came first. A wind so hard and strong shooting Maena right into Haggerth, barreling them both into the wall near their entry. Fire followed, a brief lick giving way to more blasts as the other explosives took their turns. The earth rattled. Dirt and stone smashed Maena's back, sliced her every exposed skin. Her breath shoved out in an instant gasp.

Through it all, the force pushed her against Haggerth, and she saw his eyes roll back, consciousness leave as his head bashed hard on the cave wall. For a second, escape seemed a tantalizing possibility.

In the next, the cavern's remaining floor collapsed, sucking Maena and Haggerth back with it. Falling came as a vague sensation, Maena's connection with reality rendered tenuous by the repeated shockwaves. The engineer had done his job, and while Maena hadn't finished the full mapping, what'd been there was enough to send her, ears ringing, head aching, and body half-broken, plummeting with rock and stone towards her goal.

Haggerth, a shadowed smudge lit from above as the lingering bits of burning moss and fuse spent their final moments, fell near enough to Maena, close enough that when they struck the pool's cool waters, she could reach out and—

Swim, you moron.

Her hands. Burned and battered, but free. The rope split in the blasts. Maena couldn't feel her fingers, but her arms churned in the murky water, her legs kicked. She reached out to Haggerth as boulders, as pointed stalagmites plunged around them. Their clothes, the thick Whent leathers, dragged them both deeper, a certain death.

And Maena wanted Haggerth to see, to understand who it was that'd brought him here. The man hadn't won, hadn't succeeded, and as her lungs burned, Maena's scarred touch found Haggerth's coat. She pulled him near and almost despaired, the water too dark to see. Haggerth, too, seemed limp. Possibly dead already.

Enough of a final victory.

Was it? Maena looked up at the surface, but saw no light, no ripples. Only stone after stone, rubble and dust crashing down. Perhaps she'd succeeded anyway, perhaps the caverns were fragile enough.

Maybe, maybe she'd saved the isles after all.

Yet Maena's descent into darkness didn't continue. What'd been black found sudden light, a hazel glow, amber motes rising up around her. Maena, still holding Haggerth with one numbed hand, kicked herself in a circle as the motes grew ever more crowded. Kicked, until her feet weren't swimming any longer, until they felt a weight, and pulled her, and Haggerth, through to a place no Rana, no human, had ever been.

CHAPTER 32
CHANGING MINDS

The slow grinding of gears became Svarde's ally in the Kance elevator. The pulleys creaked with grinding motion, pulling the thin wood construct upwards while its occupants shot curious glares back and forth.

"You're here because you trust Fassle to keep his word?" Eujo, the Kance Queen, asked. She stood flanked by her two Guardians, a name she used despite Noctia's discarding of the Renewal.

A word Svarde still used to describe himself, though his run at the Renewal had ended more than ten years ago.

"I trust them because I don't have a choice," Svarde said. He kept the great black blade, held before him with both hands. Not that he intended to strike, but surprises could come from anywhere, and both Guardians still held their weapons. "The fiends are fleeing dying worlds. They need a place to go."

"Do they?" Asked the smaller Guardian, a spunky, slasher woman who held a dagger in each hand. "Do they need a refuge? Because by my reckoning, they've killed a lot of us. Why should monsters be getting free land when there's plenty of us who could use it."

"We're not having policy discussions in this elevator," Eujo said, resting a hand on the Guardian's shoulder. A hand, Svarde noticed, leading to a wrist with a particular bracelet on it. He could recognize the skars anywhere now, those magic stones seeming to be both the blessing and curse of his life. "What matters is what we're going to do right here, in this moment."

'Give up,' Bliss signed, pulling one hand away from her staff todo so. A risk, and perhaps a signifier she thought Svarde wasn't quite the enemy he looked to be. 'We can find a different way if you put the blade down.'

"There's no alternative," Eujo agreed as Svarde flicked his glance back to her. "I don't know what's keeping you alive with all those wounds, and you look dead already, but at the top of this elevator there'll be too many guards even for you." She jiggled the bracelet. "And I can use these. You know what that means."

"I do." Svarde, though didn't move the blade. "Killing you would bring chaos, Queen of Kance. Noctia would exploit it. They would take your isle and give my fiend friends the home they deserve—"

"Again with that trust. I'm telling you, Fassle's not going to do a damn thing," The dagger Guardian cracked. "Once he has the skars, he'll have his power. That's it. Everything else is either useful or tossed out."

"You talk like you know Fassle?"

"I know Yarvick, and Yarvick knows Fassle damn well," the Guardian snapped back.

The elevator crept onward, upward. On either side climbed close rock walls. No rails, the gaps between wood floor and the rough stone slim enough to stop an accidental fall. Nevertheless, Svarde almost stepped back at the Guardian's words. Instead, he shook his head, glanced at the Queen.

"You found quite the Guardian collection."

"They're not mine," the Queen replied. "But Torny's right. I can't trust Fassle, which means I can't trust you."

'You can,' Bliss signed. 'Svarde helped us, back at the beginning. On Vis. Wax and Sawi would be dead without him.'

"I did kill that fiend, though I regret it now," Svarde grumbled. "That beast was probably trying to understand where it wound up, just running from—"

"Stop," Eujo said, then nodded up at the elevator's tan ceiling. "We'll be at the top soon. If you're going to live, Svarde, then we need a plan."

"Negotiate," Torny, the Guardian, answered. "Fassle might not be trustworthy, but he's a power-hungry bastard. He's gotta know any invasion here's going to cost a lot of lives. Won't make him any friends. We talk, stall for time, and then take him out."

If there'd been a better way to draw everyone's attention, Svarde wasn't sure of it.

"Repeat that last part?" Eujo asked.

"Sure. Seems obvious this guy's part of the problem," Torny said. "Yarvick always said Fassle was Noctia's biggest mistake. We get him out of the way, maybe the next Najahn leader's willing to play. In the meantime, big ugly here can get all those fiends into the Dark Below. Build up pressure. When there's too many of the monsters to hide, we force the isles to pick places for'em. Easy."

"Did you come up with all that right now?" Svarde asked.

"Been noodling on it for a while, actually. Spent a lot of

nights staring at the stars, contemplating the fate of us all." Torny rolled her eyes. "Of course right now, moron. I think fast. Any good thief needs to know the way out of a jam."

"Then we send a ceasefire to Fassle," Eujo said. Svarde opened his mouth and she stopped it with a wave of her hand. "With an offering. We'll return the skars I'm hearing were stolen from Noctia. They won't get their outpost on our isle, but they'll get their stones back." She leveled a straight look at Svarde. "Will he accept that?"

The barbarian nodded, "He'll have to, or I'll cleave him in half myself."

The elevator deposited the group into a white stone, lantern-lit great hall. Eujo put herself in front, Svarde at the back, though Bliss kept herself between the two. A cool breeze welcomed them, along with a smooth, wandering flute, whose airy music guided the group rightward. Or, it would have, if at least twenty armed and armored Kance soldiers weren't standing with blades drawn and pointed Svarde's way.

"Put your arms aside," Eujo announced, and while Svarde judged her young yet, her voice held a forged commander's steel. "We've reached an agreement."

The Kance soldiers hesitated. Eyes and looks dashed around under those ornate, glassy helmets.

"I said, return your swords to their sheaths," Eujo said. "Or are you intent on ignoring your Queen?"

Again the looks, the utter lack of movement.

"Now, now," came a new voice, arrogant and familiar. "You heard your Queen. Put up your swords." Several soldiers parted, revealed a large man clad in silver-blue Kance robes. Despite the late hour, Gladdring—Svarde picked the name from a general Noctia fog, the man had always been memorable—appeared boisterous and bright.

He spread his arms before Eujo and dropped into a deep bow. "I'm so happy you've survived your dangerous way here, my Queen. And an attack at your palace's entrance?" Gladdring slipped a look to Svarde. "If we hadn't been keeping a watch, we wouldn't have been ready at all."

At Gladdring's words, the soldiers did put up their swords, but those hard eyes didn't change. Most found Svarde, but the barbarian noted more than a few followed Bliss and Torny too. Trust, it seemed, was not in high supply on Kance. Nevertheless, on this isle, the Queens were paramount.

Eujo would, hopefully, be getting word quick below to keep Kivi and Olgata out of danger too. Ami and the fire-walker force would come next, a clean escort back below the earth and out of the rain's way.

For a ruler, Svarde had found Eujo reasonable. Eager, even, to clean things up. Maybe age hadn't quite calcified her as it had so many of Svarde's own peers.

"Naive and reckless," said the man who would be regent, the man Svarde had last known as the Najahn's trade Tenet. Gladdring welcomed them into the Sky Palace's grand throne room—the two thrones occupied one side, resting on a silver dais with broad windows behind them giving view to the ocean. "You cannot negotiate with a brute who has you within a blade's reach."

"And yet, I did," Eujo said, striding right past Gladdring for her throne. Despite wearing sea-going robes and leathers beneath, the Queen kept her noble aura as she alighted on the stiff stone-and-sky-diamond construct. She fluffed the robes beneath her, clasped her hands, and glared at the Regent. "Your role here is over, Gladdring. I thank you for your service, but you can leave now."

The Kance force that'd greeted them at the elevator's

exit had followed the quartet to the throne room and now watched the conversation. They arrayed in a curving line, cutting off any easy exit, a detail Svarde noted only because the movements had been deliberate. Not a general settling of soldiers wondering the next move, but a step in an ongoing plan. That they didn't mutter among themselves, held their focus, was either the result of admirable training or something far worse.

"My Queen, you've only just arrived," Gladdring said, keeping his position in the room's center. "Take some time to acquaint yourself with Kance, with our situation—"

"Our?" Eujo interrupted. "There is no 'our', Gladdring. This is my isle, these are my people, and you are neither. Leave. The elevator can take you down, and I'm sure you have enough valuable trinkets in that robe to barter passage to somewhere else."

Svarde chuckled as Gladdring's face went red. "She's got you there. Queen's orders, Gladdring. Get moving."

"You stay quiet," Gladdring snarled, before whipping his narrowed eyes back to Eujo. "I'm sorry, it seems you don't plan to be reasonable?"

"Plan to be reasonable?" Eujo stood up from her throne. "My isle is under attack, and just now, I've received an offer to put an end to it. To find peace. What could be more reasonable?"

"You would turn Kance into Noctia's pawn," Gladdring said, his voice picking up a new tone, one that carried with it a particular weight. The man's hands had disappeared into the pockets of his robe, giving him a calm advisor's appearance. "You would give up your people to Fassle. To the Najahn. The very people who murdered our elder Queen. You have spent too much time away, Eujo."

As he spoke, Svarde's mocking doubt shivered, broke.

Gladdring had a point. Fassle would take Kance. Peace would just be opening a door to disaster, not when Kance had all those skars, could hold its own. Eujo was so young, so naive. Gladdring had the right of it, had—

The drawing blades snared Svarde's attention. The Kance soldiers had their rapier's free, had them pointing towards the Queen. A Queen who, herself, looked pale, afraid, and doubting. Torny and Bliss, her two Guardians, seemed confused. Bliss's staff hit the stone floor with a hard thunk, dropped from nerveless fingers.

The sight gave Svarde his answer, brought the strange brew messing with his thoughts into fresh clarity, even as Gladdring gave the order.

"Take the Queen to her chambers. Kill the others."

CHAPTER 33
THE LAST HOPE

Wine and wonders had a way of making the night disappear, and Catya had no shortage of stories. Once Wax had his goal out of the way—ask Fassle about getting his own Noctia skar—the impossibility of doing that this late at night left the pair with a bottle, beautiful flowers, and a Sichi-lit sky to enjoy.

The last day's tension, the lingering frustration over not being near Bliss, Eujo, and Torny didn't quite bleed away, but was kept at a distance as Catya reminisced over experiences they both had shared: realizing they'd never see home again, understanding what the skars would do to them, and how there was no other option than to keep pressing forward.

"All so my friends could keep gambling their ores away in Smythe's casinos," Catya said, smiling, with wine-flushed cheeks. "How's that for a noble cause?"

"At least they're having fun," Wax replied, draining the bottle's last drops into his glass. "Vis is getting torn apart, and nothing I do's going to stop it."

"That's not your fault."

"Well yeah, I know that. Doesn't mean I'm not frustrated."

Catya nodded, the both of them looking down the crater towards the Wound and its cover, patrolled by Najahn soldiers. Without an imminent guard changing, the lanterns were low, little noise drifted up their way. As peaceful as the site of a divine murder could be.

"Well, my Vis friend, I believe the wine is out and the night is long," Catya said, putting weight on her cane and rising. "Care to walk me back?"

"Of course." Wax grinned. "Too bad Noctia doesn't have any trees and vines. It'd be so much faster to swing."

"As if this old bones could handle that."

"There are plenty of Vis elders still loping through the jungle, Catya. We could teach you."

The Aegis put her hand on Wax's shoulder as they took the first steps along the pebbled ground back towards the path and the tunnel back to the Ringed City. "I'd like that, Wax."

Catya's second step didn't land. As she said Wax's name, the ground lurched, a sudden sliding towards the Wound. Catya's cane slipped and she fell as Wax twisted, grabbing for her even as his own feet slid underneath him. Together they tumbled into the lelune flowers, the earth trembling for several brief seconds, until, using Catya's cane and jamming it into the tumbled rock, Wax pulled them both to a stop. Catya's boney fingers clutched Wax's robe, but the Aegis had no fear in her features, only determination.

Looking at Catya, below Wax, gave the Vis a glimpse of the Wound, and where it'd been. The gash grew, swallowing tumbling rock as if it were some great mouth devouring Noctia. The canvas covering snapped and fell, the first screams echoing their way. The ground continued to shake, tremors growing more violent.

The cane rattled in Wax's grip.

"Let me go!" Catya called, her tired voice barely rising over the grinding roar. "Save yourself! The Isles need you!"

The isles didn't need Wax, they needed the skars, and at Catya's words, the stones leapt to life in Wax's mind. Kance, newly acquired, urged a gust to shove him and the Aegis up the crater's side. Vis mumbled its way through the new cuts and bruises already scored on Wax's legs and hands. Foti, Rana, and Tamas were nonsensical, a barrage of useless impressions battered aside by the one skar that made any sense.

Wax let the Whent stone free, the god's power surging around him and Catya to catch the tumbling rocks. Rather than chaos, the Whent skar kept the landslide in line, letting Wax give up the cane and coast down towards the crater's center, with Catya lying below him, on a stable stone bed. Their momentum petered out near the Wound's new border, a jagged circle with fresh gashes darting out into the ruined lelune fields. More landslides spawned as the tremors subsided, and each time, Wax let the Whent skar redirect the rubble to pile up around them in harmless lumps.

"Help!"

The shout came as the landslides lapsed, and more followed. Calls from inside the Wound. Wax checked himself, Catya, found the Aegis wincing but alive. The Vis also seemed to have escaped serious injury, and the imperative therein spurred him to the Wound's edge.

Sichi's rose light splashed into the hole, one now covering almost all the crater's floor. The expansion hadn't come evenly, with cliffs and crevasses jutting out amid the fractured ground. Najahn soldiers, the canvas overhang, and all their gear lay scattered amid the outcroppings. Wax counted eight Najahn calling for help, their armor catching Sichi's light to stand out amid the dark rock.

How many had there been before the quake?

Wax shook his head. Help the ones he could, mourn the ones he couldn't later.

That help, though, would have to come by clever means. The hole had swallowed all the Najahn gear, leaving Wax with little more than broken flowers, rocks, and his own hands to draw the soldiers free. And, of course, the skars.

Kance came to the fore this time, those gusts offered as a possibility. When Wax focused on the nearest soldier, a woman coated in dented black-gold mail slumped over a curled, cracking stone, the skar suggested in feelings over words that weight wouldn't matter. The stone could effect the rescue, could save them, if only Wax would let it sing.

Okay. Wax relaxed, let the Kance skar flood his arms and legs with a breeze's cool touch. Air shunted away from him, an invisible hand swooping below the soldier, whose eyes went wide, whose mouth issued a panicked yelp as she lifted from the rock, flew up and over the Wound's edge to land with a heavy crunch amid the rocks.

"Ouch," Wax muttered, wincing at the groaning body. "Gentler next time?"

The Kance skar didn't respond save to push Wax to let it free again, this time targeting a scribe, dressed only in Najahn robes, who'd managed to find hand- and footholds on the crater's far side. Wax let the skar loose, felt the rush again, and saw the scribe lifted out. The poor man flailed as he flew, but this time the skar didn't drop its prize in the dirt, but set the man smooth on a crumbled clearing.

"Much better," Wax said, his throat scratching as he spoke. His legs trembled, the first sign the Kance skar was taking its power more from Wax than the god's remnant energy. Wax sat, looked, and found the next soldier to save. "That one next."

Three more flew out in quick succession, leaving another trio remaining in the pit. These three were deeper, and while Wax wouldn't admit it out loud, he'd left them for last because the effort would be that much greater.

"Let me," Catya said, walking step by slow step to Wax's side. She'd recovered her cane, looked to be bleeding from her side, but maintained a ferocious life all the same. "You're about done, aren't you?"

"I think I can do one more."

"And if your spirit fails? They'll fall. No. Give me the skar."

The Aegis had it right. With the Vis skar still knitting his cuts and salving his bruises, with the effort burned by the Whent stone to secure their landslide ride, and at the end of a long day, Wax's reserves dwindled. How Catya could have much more, Wax didn't know, but one didn't say no to the Aegis.

Not when the skars were involved.

Wax popped the Kance stone free, handed it to Catya. Around them, the rescued Najahn picked themselves up, came to the crater's edge and called encouragement to their friends. Several others began the struggling climb upwards on the ruined path, angling for home and help. Ropes and rescue from those means wouldn't be coming soon, though, and waiting risked failing grips, slipping feet, and . . .

"All this time, I only used the skars for one thing," Catya whispered, slotting the god's stone into her necklace. "Now, I get to see what we could've done."

"Just let the skar guide you, Catya," Wax said. "It will—"

"That's where you're wrong, Vis. Look what the gods did when left to their own devices." Catya smiled as she closed her eyes, held out her free hand towards the pit. "They're calling out for guidance."

Wax expected the wind to rush around him, but the air stayed still. Instead, alarmed cries came from the three—all armored Najahn soldiers—in the pit. Wax leaned forward, saw their clutch outcroppings shiver. The rock itself, then, began moving around their hands, shoving the three upwards in a single motion. The air, now, blew, but not from Catya herself. Instead, it rose from below, billowing up in a broad rush, coupling with the moving earth to send all three soldiers flowing to the crater's edge, up and over. The soldiers found help waiting, hands and relieved hugs.

"Combining two skars," Wax said. "Never tried that before."

Catya said nothing, and when Wax looked over, she'd taken a seat next to him. Her skin drew tighter than before, and while her eyes were open, the lids lay heavy. Her breathing light.

"You have to go," Catya whispered, her hands reaching for her skar necklace.

"Go?"

"The Wound. What caused this is waiting down there." Catya slumped forward and Wax caught her. The Aegis continued to fumble with her skar necklace. "I watched and waited for ten years. We can't anymore, Wax. The isles are breaking, and you're the only one."

"I'm the only one?" Wax followed her fingers, the stones they worked free. Noctia, Kance. "The only one for what?"

"Bring the gods together. Undo their mistakes. Save us."

The words came halting, barely more than whispers. Catya's eyes found Wax's for a single, slow heartbeat, before closing one last time. A gentle sigh escaped her lips, and the Aegis was no more.

Just like Pan.

Wax pressed his lips together, turned a tear-stricken look up to Sichi, but the moon held no answers. Those would only come from down there, deep in that pit, into the Dark Below. Catya had tried to give him two skars, but Wax knew something she didn't.

He lay Catya's head down as the first Najahn soldiers noticed their Aegis wasn't standing any longer. Their metal boots clomped Wax's way, their first curious calls came over the cold air. Wax didn't answer them as he found the clasp, undid Catya's necklace and pulled it free.

Tired, torn, but with duty dropped on his shoulders, Wax tied the second necklace around his neck. The first soldier reached his side, asked a question Wax didn't hear over the new skars buzzing in his mind. Possibilities, power, and hope, if he could only grasp it.

The Vis Renewal, the next Aegis, took one step forward, then, and jumped into the dark.

CHAPTER 34
JUNGLE'S BITE

Climbing a tree in the waning night, with a busted body fed with little more than bugs and dew, wasn't an experience Quik wanted to repeat. He and Sawi had crawled from branch to branch, handing the torch between them, and sometimes lighting new ones if the handoff seemed too hard. Yet now they sat amid the uppermost leaves, the burning branch lodged high enough for its flames to clear the canopy. Dawn emerged, banishing the stars and the fire's bright mark.

"It'll still be enough," Quik said as Sawi murmured a worry. "Any hunter worth the name could pick this out from those mountains."

"Or that outpost."

"If the Najahn surround us, Sawi, we'll at least get to take a few of them with us."

Quik bared his teeth as he spoke, meaning to inject a little courage with the grin, and Sawi gave him a quiet laugh for his efforts.

"Stabbed by a voulge. Not how I thought I'd go," Sawi said.

"I doubt you're alone there."

Another laugh. Despite their parched throats, the pair resumed trading stories, swapping out the burning branch for another as it burned low, as the morning grew long and the clouds retreated into a sunny day, one bearing the first real warmth of deepening spring.

The first sign their perch had found some attention came with rustling to the south, cracking branches and breaking leaves. An ill omen, and one that had Quik frowning as he watched the treetops, the green below for telltale signs of what he already knew. Yet, the coming death was confirmed by called Najahn orders, confident in their victory.

"Surround the tree," came the shout as the clomps and clanks, mail that must've been hot and heavy in the jungle still coating sweating, tired soldiers.

They did, though, hold their voulges up. Others kept chakrams ready, loaded crossbows mingling with the sharp discs on their backs. A concession to the jungle's many barriers to a large circle making it through to any target. Quik would've smirked at the Najahn bending to his isle's will any other time, but he found the spirit lacking there, as he and Sawi watched the purple and black encircle their selected tree.

The Najahn hadn't come entirely unprepared: woodcutting axes, doubtless taken from the outpost, hung off several Najahn backs, and those soldiers unlimbered the tools as their commander, a willowy woman who'd seen far more seasons than Quik, issued the orders. First, in breezy hacks, the trio sliced away ferns and saplings from the tree's base, buying space with time and energy. The other soldiers, any threat from the Vis pair apparently not worth worrying over, took seats on stones and moss around the clearing. Helmets came off of hot heads and side conversations rose, angry bursts complaining about a familiar friend hidden in the jungle: the Lira. Stinging nighttime ambushes, death delivered and disappeared before the Najahn could gather a counterattack.

As her squad complained, the commander called up to the pair with questions, all of which Quik and Sawi refused to answer.

"Should we drop some branches on them?" Sawi asked. "I think a heavy one could—"

"That'll only get us shot," Quik said. "Those crossbows could kill us now, but they're holding off. I want to know why."

"You aren't asking?"

"You think the Najahn will tell us?"

Sawi shrugged, her back against the bark. "Couldn't hurt."

Gatherers. Always with the strange ideas.

"Najahn," Quik called as the ax wielders finished their demolition, "what do you want?"

"Information," came the reply, hard and eager.

"What would we have to give you?" Sawi answered. "We're only a pair of lost hunters."

The Najahn glared, a funny look from so far down. As if Quik was being insulted by a sparrow.

"We know who you are. Your trail wasn't hard to find, even if that fire gave your destination away." The captain reached out, touched their tree. "There were several Najahn injured by the Great Sana last night, who swore their assailants were a young man and woman, a pair who match your description. Your lives should be forfeit, but for a proper price, you can have them back."

"And go where?" Quik asked. "To live under your boots in Kitaye?"

"Better that than the dirt."

"So you say," Quik said, only for Sawi to jump on his words.

"You'll let us down, if we give you what you want?" the Vis gatherer asked.

That glare switched to a serene smile too swiftly for Quik's liking, but the hunter spared his shock for his friend. Sawi, though, ignored him. When the commander agreed to those terms, she started the slow, aching trek down.

"And you?" the Najahn captain asked Quik. "Join her, or my crossbows will have their target practice."

Not leaving Quik much of a choice. He took the captain's offer, began his descent. Left the torch burning up above—the wet leaves and living branches would guarantee a burnout without much damage, but every second those flames flickered meant . . . hope? Would Quik go so far as to say he still had any?

The grim reality hardened as he followed Sawi down from one branch to the next. The Najahn seemed content enough to watch their climb, more than a few of the fourteen or fifteen breaking out water skins and bread. Quik measured the distance with every drop down, trying to find what height would work best to make a leap and land on one of those soldiers. He had no weapon, what with his toothless gauntlets sitting on the forest floor below them, but Quik had weight, and landing on an unprepared head could—

A whistle mingled with the jungle's morning birdsong, sharp and light enough for the Najahn to miss it. For Sawi and Quik to understand. The gatherer, several branches beneath Quik and within reach of a voulge's point, stopped her climb. Wavered, with her bare feet balanced on bark. The Najahn captain frowned.

"Keep going. We're returning to the outpost before dark, with you or without your bodies." The captain punctuated the words with a slight wave to a soldier near her, and the man raised his voulge. "You won't like what these can do to a Vis."

Sawi, in answer, glanced up at Quik, opened her mouth, and gave a whoop. The loud, classic shout would be known across the isle, along with the story it told: the Vis giving its cry was not defeated, was still standing for her god.

Quik answered with a call of his own, the sounds causing the Najahn to put down their water skins, their bread and fruit. They reached for their weapons when the whoops continued, now coming from the trees, ferns, jungle all around the Najahn.

Not that the voulges, chakrams, and crossbows mattered now.

Darts zipped in, the slightest sound in their wake, discovered only when missed shots bounced off helmets of the few Najahn still wearing them. Other soldiers slapped hands to necks, to cheeks sporting the narrow needles. Najahn scrambled for their gear, to stand only to see their fellow soldiers, poisoned, wobble and fall. The captain tried shouting an order, her call cutting off as Quik, breaking a branch, threw the stick at the Najahn's helmet.

The captain stumbled, cursed, and stuck a finger up towards Quik, a damning gesture rendered moot by the Vis emerging from the jungle. Feathered spears in hand, blowguns still on some lips sending second waves, the Vis strode into the Najahn with ruthless efficiency. At their head, as she always seemed to be, was Deshiva, and her spear found poisoned and standing victims alike. The Najahn, with more than half their numbered down from darts in seconds, found no cohesion, discovered bloody death. Armor proved little use against combined thrusts from all sides, and by the time Quik snapped off a second branch to throw, the skirmish had already concluded.

The Najahn captain remained alive, though a broken nose and blood leaking from pierced armor suggested that status might be fleeting. Deshiva stood over her prize, the other hunters clearing space around the tree for Sawi and Quik to descend. Only as he reached the bottom, did Quik hear Deshiva's second order.

"No prisoners," the huntress snapped. "What they did to us, we do to them. Honor Vis with Najahn blood."

Sawi started to protest, but Quik stopped the gatherer with a hard hand on Sawi's arm. When she glared in return, Quik nodded at their rescuers, at the Vis who'd done this ambush so well. At the gnarled hands and tired bodies using hunting knives to effect a final end to the remaining Najahn.

These weren't Mottilan or Kitaye hunters, young and vibrant. These were elders, ones whose fighting days were far behind them. Without the darts, the panic, the Najahn would've taken those wrinkles and weak arms and massacred the Vis.

"If the Najahn know this is all we have left," Quik muttered, "then we have no chance."

Deshiva delivered the Najahn captain from her life, then regarded the pair. "I hate how right you are, Quik. We saw your flame as soon as it was lit, and it took us so long because these brave ones are all we have left." She looked them both up and down. "You can walk? Run?"

"Slowly," Quik said.

"Then slowly we will go." Deshiva waved the hunters

back into the woods, towards the mountains and Mottilan. "The Najahn are advancing. We've lost scouts, more hunters. You and Sawi are the only ones back from the raid." As they slipped around ferns, ducked beneath branches, Deshiva continued to speak in dead lines. "The end is coming fast for Vis now. We will die, my friends, but in doing so, we will create a legend."

CHAPTER 35
ELYSIUM

Death welcomed her with golden flowers.

Except you're not dead.

Maena absorbed her other self's declaration with ready refusal, for where else could she be except the same great beyond every soul went to when shuffled free of its physical confines? The air, if there was any, sat still. On her back, Maena felt little beneath her and saw only those honeyed flowers stretching above her head, curling over to mask a burnt, cloudless sky. No birdsong, no distant weather, no buzzing insects.

I wouldn't be here if you'd died, Maena. I would be free.

That, at least, had logic's touch. Unless not even death could heal the cursed split that'd haunted Maena's every moment since . . .

A moan further cracked her delusion, and Maena turned, a roll onto her right shoulder that carried such a spastic, painful cascade with it that Maena's eyes flashed, her breath snapped. On her side, the rippling burns continuing, Maena saw a bloodied, sopping wreck on the wet mud around them: Haggerth.

The Whent looked flayed, his leathers shredded and laying in strips about his person. What skin Maena could see bubbled in white and red, burns Maena herself had only seen during raids gone wrong, when a tossed torch found fuel and sent a seaward vessel into a raging inferno.

Burns Maena, going by the icy agony racing around her body, no doubt shared.

We were too close to the detonations. The cavern too small. We paid the price for victory.

Did they? Achieve victory?

Ami, the former Guardian and the only one to traverse the motes and return, had mentioned going to another world. Twice. Ami had seen the windswept disaster of Kance's god, and the silver seas of Foti's realm. She'd described a vast otherness, where expectations bent in unpredictable ways, yet not so far as to kill her outright.

This, this felt the same.

But which god's home? And what does it mean?

Maena couldn't answer either question, and with her legs a mutilated disaster—Maena glanced down at herself and just as quickly looked away, unwilling to face the devastation that was her body—she didn't think she'd be moving anywhere soon.

What then, we lay here and die?

Haggerth moaned again. The man's eyes were closed. Consciousness a distant thing, and likely a mercy, given the pain he must've been feeling. Maena could sense it herself, a vacuum not out of reach. She could close her eyes, fade into the torment, succumb to it. A release she'd earned, one she could—

No. No you will not. I've come too far to die here.

But that'd been the plan. Detonate the mines, collapse the chamber, bury these gates in so much stone as to keep the fiends from ever crossing again. Death had been an accepted price, had been the deal.

A price for success, maybe. How do we know we've achieved anything at all? Our mission remains unfinished.

Or perhaps her other self no longer wanted to wander off into the beyond.

Those deliberations ended when the soft, wet ground beneath her trembled, when a chill wave washed over Maena's shoulder, head. She sputtered, hot skin afire anew with water's touch, and looked towards the shower to see a lagoon, a pool, not too different from the one they'd fallen into. Broad, blue, and coated in golden flower petals from the bordering plants, the water rippled with new arrivals: rocks, stones, and rubble.

It's coming in. All of it.

The stones bubbled, rocks that'd known nothing but damp cave for untold centuries thrusting through the god's gateway into a new world. Cracks and clacks echoed as the first stones found themselves shoved by more coming behind, a mound growing at the pool's center, pushing the water out and away. A wave rushed over Haggerth, turning another moan into a sputtering cough, the Whent's eyes flickering open.

He screamed.

Maena wanted to, but clamped her mouth shut, took the pain and set it aside. A commander's lesson, compartmentalize smaller problems to focus on the larger one, like the water rushing around them now as rock and dirt continued to roll up from the pool's bottom, from the gate.

The Rana captain returned to her legs, now laying in swampy, roiling water. She tried, found them alive, attentive, and weak. Nevertheless, they kicked when she asked, and with her arms, Maena pulled herself around, made a lunge towards the golden flowers at the pool's edge.

Haggerth screamed again.

Maena spared a look at the Whent, his body sinking into the spreading waters. The man's eyes rolled, his burnt, beaten face twitching in a mix of terror, agony.

You can't help him.

As if Maena wanted to. Haggerth had put them both here, had thrown her plans into disarray, and he was a rockbiter too. Everything she should despise, and yet, he was the only other person here. Potentially, other than the brutal voice in her mind, the only other human in this strange flower world.

Facing the unknown alone was a greater fear.

Maena lunged back into the water towards Haggerth. She splashed, slid, kicked, and half-swam as rising earth pushed dirty waves across her face, into her mouth, ears, eyes. What was more pain, more irritation to what she'd already earned?

She found Haggerth's legs first, grabbed them with scarred, tight hands, and pulled. The next wave helped Maena sit up, its push letting her rise on her thighs and tug harder. Haggerth, sputtering between shouts, slid her way, but his head dipped below the surface as the wave passed.

"Sit up," Maena said, her voice not even a rasp, not a whisper, but a discordant growl.

Like everything else, her throat too was burned.

You're dooming us both.

Maena pulled again, Haggerth's legs sliding past her. She moved her grip to his chest, bent to lever her shoulder against the man, and timed the pull to the next wave. The passing water helped enough to get Haggerth's chin near

Maena's tilted shoulder, and she slipped her arm behind his neck, pulled the Whent free.

He coughed this time, those rolling whites settling on her as Haggerth hacked water from his lungs. Waves battered them, though their power, their height had passed some zenith as the thrusting earth spread the pool too far into the flowers. The rubble hill flowing forth was becoming its own risk, boulders and broken rocks tumbling away as fresh cave chunks followed.

"We have to move," Maena said. "I can't move you alone."

Haggerth didn't try to talk, but nodded, rolled forward and free from the Rana's hold. Lying on his chest in the shallowing water, Haggerth swam, flopped, pulled his way forward. A dismal display, and one Maena mimicked, slopping through mud and muck until they reached the golden flower fields. Still sopping, there, but far enough away from drowning, from the tumbling rocks.

Safe, alive, barely.

"Where are we?" Haggerth asked later.

They lay on crumpled flowers, broken into a stiff bed by flailing bodies. An effort that had left them exhausted. Maena thought they'd slept, but the sky looked the same as it had before, a dim yellow, without clouds, sun, or Sichi. The only marker of time she saw was the continuing tumult growing ever closer: the Dark Below seeping into this world.

Would it keep going? Could all the Seven Isles fall through the motes into this strange place? Or had the gods made their new world so much larger than the old as to ensure this one's crushing demise? Had Maena simply assured this realm would die a different death than the one already prescribed to it?

"Maena?" Haggerth asked. "Do you know?"

She shifted her head, looked at Haggerth. "I'm as lost as you are."

The man hacked what seemed like a laugh. "Then we're dead."

"Not yet."

That earned a sharper look, though one etched with pain. "Why? Why save me? Save yourself? We're ruined, lost." Haggerth's eyes closed. "I hurt everywhere."

"Because we don't know."

"Don't know?"

"What we can do, yet."

Another hacked laugh. Haggerth shuddered, fell silent. Maena turned back to the sky, those golden flowers. Agony lashed again, and she slipped away.

The touch woke her with euphoria. All the pain, all the fear, the wonder, disappeared at an instant, replaced with blissful happiness. Maena cracked a wide grin, the scarring lines along her face spitting and giving her no pain whatsoever. And why should it? The flowers were so beautiful, shinier than the cleanest coins. The air and sky as pure as the cleanest river. That she was here was a miracle, was—

She choked, gasped. The touch withdrew and with its absence returned the worst. The smile vanished, the ache of its effort remaining. Maena sat up, rage and confusion mingling with pain's comeback.

The source. The source of that happiness, where?

She found it on her right, staring at her, though not with anything Maena could call eyes. Milky white, like a cloud in its fluffy lumps, the creature lingered at her side. Almost as tall as the flowers, larger twice again as Maena herself. As Maena stared, that purity found cracks, amber lines racing around the bumps and oblong balls making up the thing, splitting and coming back together here and there.

A fiend.

Yes, but what kind? As Maena stared, a tendril emerged from the fluffy body and reached for her. Maena tried to jerk away, but a withered, starved, and exhausted body proved incapable, the tendril touching her cheek.

Again the ecstasy, the absence of all ills. Even Maena's split mind fell into silence.

Until that tendril slipped away.

"Again," Maena said, soft, the barest tears forming at her eyes. "Again, please."

The fiend, whether it understood her or not, granted her wish. Again and again and again. For how long, Maena didn't know, but the fiend rescued her from despair, and when she surfaced, the flowers had disappeared, hidden behind more of the fluffy miracles. They crowded in every direction save one, where the ever-rising rocks tumbled, broke, and fell.

Even so, Maena would have accepted such an end, would have given into a death delivered with pure happiness and love. She would have, save for what began to mar the sky, appearing first in ones and two, then in swarms too large to ignore, even with her every hurt held at bliss's bay.

A fiend had split her soul, a fiend made of gusting wind and darkness. Maena had never seen its like before, or since, until right then, until they blanketed her glorious grave.

CHAPTER 36

IMMORTAL SWORD

Gladdring's order should've landed like a hammer blow among the Kance soldiers. The glistening armor should have turned as one and skewered the former Najahn leader for advising the capture of their queen. That they didn't, that stares at once vapid and vicious locked on Eujo, told Svarde forces of a different nature were at play.

Not too long ago, the barbarian would've stood mystified. Even among the adventures with Catya, the most magic he witnessed came from the odd fiend, or when Catya, distracted, let a skar's whim escape. Now, now Svarde understood the Seven Isles were far from a sensible place, that the gods hadn't made a miraculous home but instead built a fraught, random cage for their frail creations.

Surviving the divine mistake depended on good people, and, based on the elevator ride up, Eujo and her Guardians were good people.

Gladdring, Svarde knew with dead certainty, was a power-hungry Najahn who ought to be stopped.

So the barbarian did just that: letting the big, black blade that'd once pierced a goddess's heart fall off his shoulder into a steady grip. The Kance soldiers began to close with Eujo and her Guardians, a sweep meant to pin the trio at the Kance throne, with nothing but those glass windows and an infinite night sky beyond.

Svarde lowered his dead shoulder, the gray skin matted with scars that no longer mattered, no longer panged with battled long over, and charged. He came in from the left, making first contact with an oblivious Kance soldier and driving him—or her, Svarde couldn't tell and couldn't care less— into the next warrior in the line. The armor cracked, a startled yelp jumped high as the soldier's right arm smashed into his partner's side. Rapiers fell, soldiers stumbled, and Svarde pushed on, trampling his first hit and mashing into the second.

The blade had yet to swing.

The second soldier, off-balance, didn't have time to react to Svarde and fell much like the first. Svarde's right foot landed on the guard's helmet, crunching nose and bone beneath as he barreled on to the third. The ranks thickened here, with a fourth approaching from Svarde's right, angling the rapier to gouge Svarde's back. The barbarian accepted the scrape to keep up his momentum, bashing into the twisting third soldier and sending them flying into the Kance crowd. With two broken bodies behind them, a rapier's blade withdrawing from his right shoulder, Svarde's charge at last faced a force with some understanding.

With weapons far too thin.

The jagged blade swept across Svarde's chest, a two-handed, slaying strike that split rapiers, Kance armor, and the skin beneath without pause. Red flared, glimmering light sparkled as glorious Kance metals flew into the lantern-lit air, and as Svarde completed his swing, the dying before him had doubled.

More rapiers rushed to fill the gap. Over their clanks, Gladdring redirected the rush, splitting his force in half. One man against a dozen ought to be a quick decision, despite the surprise attack.

How wrong Gladdring was.

Svarde had no picture of Eujo, Bliss, and Torny. His whole world was a bright, lethal battle. Rapiers sliced in, some followed by swinging gauntlets, all backed by those vapid stares. Svarde met them all, laying about with his blade less with a swordsman's skill and more with a raging animal's bloody abandon.

Gladdring's hold on the soldier's mind frayed with fresh wounds, screams and panic restoring the soldiers Svarde struck to some semblance of their former selves, an added cruelty for too many final moments. Those same calls fell into the pit that was Svarde's concern, his thoughts, his emotions save a complete focus on the slaughter before him and those saved by the carnage.

One after another the soldiers fell. Sweeps, stabs, slashes, stomps, all found easy targets and took them. Svarde earned replies in turn, though Svarde shrugged off the strikes as he had so many times before. Until, covered in the results of his handiwork, Svarde stood alone in the Kance throne room. Five or six Kance soldiers remained standing, ringing him. Of Eujo, Bliss, and Torny, there was no sign, though a shattered window behind the throne marked one possibility.

"Guardian," Gladdring said, the Tenet standing with a heavy hand on a soldier's arm. "How do you still stand?"

Svarde, red dripping into his eyes, wiped unknowable offal from his lips. Angled the blade at Gladdring.

"What matters is that you do," Svarde replied. "Throughout all the isles, Gladdring, one law is constant: traitors go to their gods for judgment."

Gladdring huffed a laugh, "And who names the traitors, Svarde? You? That Queen, as like as not dead and broken far below?" Gladdring straightened. "I am trying to save the Isles. To bring them together and defeat the fiends with the only weapon we have. You being here, you doing all of this, only dooms us all."

"Spare me your fancy words. If the Queen's dead, then someone else will take the throne after I've lopped the head from your body."

Gladdring sighed, seemed about to start talking again, but Svarde had heard enough. The blade sat heavy in his hands. The Vis and Noctia skars raged about his head, their peculiar blend working to keep Svarde's immortal bones whole, a skill sorely tested by the wounds he'd taken. Svarde didn't feel those blows as pain, but as sore stretches, as fingers unable to hold the blade so tight, as a left leg lacking the burst to charge forward.

The barbarian limped over one body, over another, closing with Gladdring. A rapier found his back, followed by another. A third soldier sought to stand in Svarde's way and the barbarian cut the man down with a single crossing slash, the Kance rapier little more than a blade of grass in Svarde's way. Gladdring waited, watching with glazed eyes and a sweat-drenched forehead.

"I've been close to death so many times," Gladdring said, pushing his support-soldier away to stand alone before Svarde. "I will not go to Noctia at your hand."

"Say what you want."

Svarde started to swing the blade, and found his will to do so disappear. The determined rage died, as Gladdring's earlier words found new purchase. The Tenet did have a point: the isles were fracturing. Someone had to unite them, if not to destroy the fiends, then to accept them. Gladdring would understand better than Fassle, than the young and inexperienced Eujo, how to bring the firewalkers into a world not ready for them. Gladdring might be stained by a hard past, but so was Svarde.

That did not make him unfit to be the hero the isles needed.

"Drop the blade," Gladdring said, his voice thin, exhausted. The soldier he'd pushed away came back now as Gladdring's knees buckled. The Tenet, though, didn't grab onto the soldier's arms, but kept both hands in his robe pockets. "Give up this foolish assault."

"I cannot let go of it," Svarde answered, though he lowered the sword's point to the floor. "My life is tied to the blade."

"Is it?" Gladdring asked, his eyes fluttering. "Then you can both serve the isles one last time. Follow the Queen, Svarde. Ensure she doesn't fall alone."

Svarde hesitated, looked to the shattered glass. The order didn't make much sense, but then, Svarde had never been known for his intellectual aptitude. If Gladdring was the isles' best hope, then Svarde ought to do as he said.

That flat acceptance carried Svarde across the throne room to the broken window. He limped to its edge, looked out into the vast night. Below, Kance shimmered, lanterns and torches marking a city and an isle alert. Sichi coated ships in her rose glow. A cold wind dried the blood on Svarde's cheeks, legs, chest.

"Jump, Guardian," Gladdring called, a rasp and little more.

What the hero demanded, Svarde must do. Somewhere down there was the Queen, and Svarde would find her.

She would not fall alone.

CHAPTER 37

DESCENT

Across the span of his life, Wax liked to think most of his ideas had been better than this one: jumping into the Wound was a mistake.

The deep dark enveloped him as Wax's stomach leaped into his throat. Rushing air belied the many killer overhangs and jutting rocks now whirling past, a sure death only moments away. One delayed by a panicked call to the Kance skar, to its sudden winds slowing Wax's fall. Whent helped too, molding a soft landing from a hard rock along one side, letting Wax touch down without fatal complications, just exhaustion. Sheer, brutal exhaustion.

The Vis Renewal had no food, no water, just some lingering buzz from the wine Wax had shared with Catya and the dying savior's spark that'd prompted the jump in the first place. All that won him was a lonely perch deep in the pit, with Sichi's glow far above. A few curious Najahn called down, but Wax didn't bother answering.

He wasn't going back.

Nor was he going to dive off this refuge and risk the skars again. Not for a while, anyway. The stones had burned through their small supplies, and their blunt urges suggested they'd steal what they needed from Wax at the next opportunity, rendering shaking legs into pure jelly, tired arms into limp noodles. Not something Wax could afford, not if he . . .

What, not if he what?

Wax sat on the hard stone, gathered his ragged Noctia robes around him, and stared at the glittering geodes and stiff, brown earth around him. Yet again a dying friend— Wax decided then and there Catya numbered among those —had given him a dream without a clue how to realize it. Stop the fiends, save the isles. Wax had the skars now, had multiples of most, so it should be simple, right?

All the Renewals through the isles' history, going back to Demion, hadn't found a way to stop the terror, to change up the cycle. Why would Wax, a young man not even granted adult status on Vis, be able to change the course? What was he even doing here, when Fassle waited up above? Wax could've given that man the stones, let the Najahn have the responsibility, and returned home to the mangos and Sana he loved.

Or find Eujo. The Queen's face, hard and determined, drifted over one of the dark stone walls nearby. She'd pulled Wax into this race as much as anyone, given it hard purpose after Wax's own lackadaisical drive. She'd be fighting back on Kance now, struggling to save her people. Like Wax, and she sure wouldn't be doubting herself. Even if Eujo didn't know the way, or how, she would try whatever she could until Kance was safe.

Bliss would be by her side too. Wax's sister, always up for a fight. She'd braved the fiends alone, had already saved Wax's life too many times. Never a question in her eyes. If she'd been at the Wound's edge with Wax, she probably would have jumped in after him, found some way to scale those rocks and keep up.

Torny, of course, would be right with Bliss. The bandit as unlikely a hero as Wax himself, yet she'd come with them through fights and perils no thief could've expected, and still sharpened her daggers for the next. She had stolen those Tamas souls, all because Torny had given an oath, all because the bandit so clearly loved Wax's sister.

His brother, too, had given up his hunter's slot on Vis. Abandoned everyone he knew to try and get the Najahn to help Wax. That effort must've failed, as Wax had checked, hadn't found Quik anywhere on Noctia in the days between his arrival and this, but still, wherever he was, Quik would be striving to make the isles better. He wouldn't give up.

"Guess that answers that," Wax muttered to himself. "No ditching out now."

Determination was all well and good, but intentions didn't offer up a path forward on their own. Catya had suggested a dive to the Wound's end, to the fiend's apparent source. How would Wax get there?

A plunge, blind, down the pit would end with Wax bashed and broken on some rock. But maybe there was another way?

The Vis crawled to his outcropping's edge, used Sichi's glinting glow to look around. Found elation, a little chagrin, and a whole lot of hope: rope ladders and spikes to hold them stretched up and down the Wound's length. Many were frayed, scattered, or looked to be barely holding on after the quakes, but they offered possibility for a dexterous descent.

At least for someone crazy enough to try.

Noctia had been buzzing with the Whent mission to the Dark Below, and Catya had mentioned the camp waiting deep down. Wax's path lay open before him, all thanks to that effort, kicked off, so rumor had it, by the same barbarian Wax had found back on Vis. Svarde? Had that been the man's name?

A long chain. Almost too long to be anything save fate.

Wax nodded to himself on the outcropping, gauged the first jump, the ladder he'd grab. With a little skar support, he could move fast. Foti might spring up a flame to grant Wax enough light to make the leaps . . .

The jumps came fast and easy, the handholds firm, the ropes strong. Sure, some of the spikes snapped loose, but Wax kept the Kance skar burbling close and clear, helping him swing from a sudden drop to safety. Foti sparked up flashes as needed, and Wax left smoldering mossy patches in his wake. Noctia and Whent's trading network proved more than just rope ladders too, with provisioned camps bridging the distance every few hours. Water, food waited there, along with bed rolls. The quakes had wrecked pieces of them all, but Wax was able to salvage enough to survive.

Sunlight gave him day and night, visible in slight shafts in the Wound's center, and Wax used the glow to travel faster, leaping and bouncing like he would from fern to fern back home. His ravaged shoes blunted the landings just enough to keep Wax going, the Vis skar tending to any rough scraps, to broken fingernails and the occasional smack of head, elbow, or knee upon unyielding stone.

Here and there Wax came across the reasons for those camps, and perhaps a victim from Noctia's surface. Crumpled gear and more than one broken body lay among the rock, any rescue both impossible and unnecessary. Wax did, though, offer up a prayer to Vis for every one he passed, those brave souls making a dangerous journey at an unlucky time.

Worse than those awful sights, though, were the quakes. They continued at random, waking Wax from his short naps or threatening to fling him from a perch. He'd cling to the rock when they struck, sometimes using the Whent skar to keep himself steady, to draw out stone above to shield himself from falling debris.

Whatever was causing the tremors had to be Wax's first goal. Stop that chaos, then see about the fiends. Assuming he even could.

The Whent skar rose at that thought, surging with clear confidence as Wax clung to a narrow ladder between two sharp bends in the Wound. No matter what, the skar seemed to say, Whent could alter the earth to suit Wax's needs.

Boundless confidence was the order of the day, and Wax embraced it.

The Wound's conclusion came in ripples, with more lips bearing evidence of Whent craftsmanship. Dropping off points for gear, food, and traded goods lingered, with carts and crude rails serving as quick transport. All unmanned now, and some crumbled with the endless tremors. The deserted posts, which Wax alighted on and then kept going down—the Wound provided a straight path, who knew where those offshoot tunnels might go—were curious enough, but more concerning were the sounds echoing up from below.

Metal clashes, shouts, and the occasional unnatural rumble. Wax, his energy flagging from the day's drop, decided he couldn't try to make one last camp. Hard to sleep when a battle raged nearby, even if continuing meant he might find a fight he couldn't finish.

The Wound's end came in a narrowed point, a hole not much larger than Wax himself. He settled on the dusty floor at the hole's border, looked down into a sweeping, smoothed dome. Nothing natural about it, including what he saw inside: a hulking, silent figure clad in strange armor sat upon a giant throne. Around him moved bodies of monsters and men, some rolling in red agony, others making swings with axe or claw at one another.

Fiends and Whent fighters, and the latter looked hard pressed.

Wax counted two of the leathered, bearded, and bloody Whent on their feet, maneuvering back to back to hold a trio of snarling, dog-like fiends at bay. Crimson manes flowed off the hound-like creatures, their long snouts holding longer, snapping fangs. The fiends herded the Whent pair towards the dome's back end, where a wall would mark a final stand.

Catya had sent Wax down here to save the isles. What better way to start than with a rescue?

Muttering a quick prayer to Vis, Wax gave the Kance skar its leeway, and dropped into the fight.

CHAPTER 38

FIGHT OR FLEE

Becoming a legend, as Deshiva put it, would happen faster than expected.

Quik and Sawi had returned, courtesy of a slow climb through the jungle and mountains—the Najahn crowded the main road and its overpass—less than a day before the clanking, marching, indomitable black and purple force. Mottilan scouts, only children by the usual Vis standards, found Deshiva as their band stumbled down the verdant, dewy mountainside towards the steep cliff paths above the town and forced her to abandon the pair, along with those elders most proficient with their blow darts.

Which left Quik and Sawi to make their haphazard way past fortified homes with archers young and old, but few in between, in the windows. Spike pits covered with leaves dotted the sole descending road, while side trails had been littered with sharp stones, poisoned branches, and so many nasty concoctions Quik felt darn glad no open war ever broke out between Vis's two cities.

Kitaye might have the numbers and an advantage in a

running jungle fight, but he'd have nightmares about all these clever traps.

Seeing Annalyse again dispelled those torments, at least for the moment. She continued working on makeshift arms and armor for the Mottilan defenders, despite having long since run out of skars to slot into her creations. Instead, she applied Whent science to stiffen bracers, insulate weaves with scrap plates to blunt a blade's edge, and add a sharper tip to arrowheads so they'd have a better chance at piercing Najahn defenses.

"Not that it'll matter," Annalyse said as she walked with Quik and Sawi to the beach, where simple thatched shelters served as wards for any Mottilan needing medical attention. Thin blankets sat on sand, many occupied by scouts, hunters, and those hurt crafting Mottilan's resistance. A bleak picture, drawn faces without Deshiva's eternal determination. "This is as doomed a fight as any I've seen."

Neither Sawi nor Quik responded to the words, because what could they say? Instead, rather than wallow in despair like so many around them, Quik took a different direction, one clued in by Annalyse's words.

"Then why are we staying?" the hunter asked.

"Because we're on a beach with nowhere else to go," Annalyse replied. "Or is that not obvious to you?"

Quik nodded at Sawi as they settled onto a blanket pair. A young girl brought over two coconuts filled with sweet milk, a wonderful antidote to their parched throats and bug-filled bellies. Just a sip, coupled with the fresh ocean breeze, the rejuvenating waves, let Quik ignore the groaning wounded around him and focus on the idea beginning to grow.

"Sawi," Quik asked, "you came by tunnels, right? The Dark Below?"

"Guided by Whent scouts, yes. It wasn't easy." Sawi started shaking her head as Quik held his look, the woman parsing his idea. "If you're thinking we tell this whole town to run into the caves, then—"

"Not the whole town," Quik said, turning now to the ships out in Mottilan's harbor. Fishing boats and a few trading vessels, too few to carry everyone here and thus dismissed as an option. "Just the ones who can't flee on those. We can take the elders, the really young, to Kance. Gladdring's there, he'll accept them."

"Will he?" Annalyse asked. "Gladdring never does anything that won't give him an advantage."

"He'll embrace it. Older islanders and children? Gladdring can tell the isles the Najahn are trying to murder them. Let Fassle convince Whent, Tamas, and Foti that they should send their soldiers and ships to fight for that."

Sawi squinted, "Betting a lot on that idea, Quik."

"Did you see those traps, Sawi? How many Najahn will they stop before everyone here gets spitted on a voulge's edge?" Quik sloshed the coconut milk as he swung the bowl towards the town. "Deshiva can say what she likes about dying a legend. I prefer being alive."

Quik hadn't been the first to suggest fleeing by ship, but adding Sawi's flight through the tunnels made it an idea Deshiva could accept. Annalyse helped Quik, buttressed by the scientist's personal Vis skar and its rejuvenating energies, pitch the plan to what remained of Mottilan's ruling council that evening, the last night before the Najahn were expected to start their assault in earnest. Cookfires had been spotted not far from the cliff road, and several scouts had come back marred with crossbow quarrels fletched in black.

"We're out of time," Deshiva said, glaring around the

broad stone table, the room crowded with people, smoking pipes. She existed as constant fury, every word delivered with simmering fire. Whether this was her moment, or Deshiva had simply decided to make it hers, Quik couldn't help but be swept up in her aura. "Quik's plan offers us the best chance of making it out of here alive, at least some of us. Those of us most able will stay and fight as long as we can to buy time. Once the ships have left, we'll slip away to the caves. Sawi, that's where you'll be, waiting to guide us."

"Guide us where?" Sawi asked. "Even if—"

"Anywhere, Sawi. If the Dark Below stretches between all the isles, then we make for Kance. North, as best we can."

Sawi seemed about to protest further, but Quik stilled her with a hand. There were too many doubting, nervous faces in the room. Too many people who needed spines stiffened, not made soft.

"It's a risk," said one older woman, "but I see no other chance. I vote we go." She curled one lip. "Besides, if we keep the fighting free of the city, there's a chance we may even have homes to return to."

Mutters rose there, more than one suggestion crawled out to burn Mottilan, spare the Najahn any victorious looting. That idea dropped when Deshiva repeated the evacuation's urgency. Anything that didn't get supplies and people on those boats wasn't worth doing, and with that order and a stamp of Deshiva's spear, the meeting ended.

And Vis's first retreat began.

Quik waited in the bushes. His gauntlets, restored to working order, rested on his wrists. Across the way sat a two-story house built of dried mud and stacked stone. Sawi, in one of her stories from their night in the tree, had mentioned fleeing a house just like it once. She and

Annalyse waited at the entry to the Dark Below, far along the beach's northern reaches. Behind him, sail after sail unfurled and broke to the north at all speed. Najahn cutters would likely be coming in to intercept what they could, though their prizes wouldn't be warriors or treasure, but people deserving, hopefully, of pity.

The Najahn weren't heartless. Not all of them were Masayo.

Yet the ones marching on Mottilan now were determined. Quik heard their clanking boots, heard a Noctia anthem rise on the morning wind. The birds, perhaps understanding the moment, had fallen silent. The waves, a few curious buzzing bugs, provided the harmony to a solemn melody of slow breaths from the fighters around him. Old, young, willing.

Deshiva lurked across the way, invisible with her face-painting and camouflage. The first line, the starting ambush. Every minute counted as a success, a victory for his home.

The first armored line came into view. Eight across, spears and shields in hand. Quik couldn't tell the depth, but as the Najahn came onto the cliffside path, they slowed. Someone whistled, and a loud voice carried out a threat, a command, a declaration. Surrender, the man said, and join Noctia in bringing peace to the isles.

Surrender.

Quik snapped looks at the warriors, the hunters, the valiant waiting to fight for their home alongside him and saw no fear, no doubt.

Surrender.

Vis would never.

CHAPTER 39
THE BALANCE

Vengeance, again, proved all the motivation Maena needed.

Seeing those shredded fiends drifting through the sky overhead brought clarity through the caustic static flushing Maena's body. One of those things had split her asunder, brought this fragile ruin upon her, and if she couldn't find that specific fiend to ravage, this group would have to do.

Enacting that vengeance, though, became a difficult question. Beyond the golden flowers, Haggerth's useless presence, and the odd fluffy cloud creatures, weapons were scarce. The continual shaking earth offered options from behind, tumbling stones that could be picked up, wielded, but Maena's arms seemed no more capable of throwing a pebble than slinging a sharp rock.

Then we'll have to get clever.

To that end, Maena reached out and touched the closest fluffy creature. Those cloud-like forms, split here and there with amber cracks that flashed and vanished, continued to swarm Maena and Haggerth, as if the pair were some sort of rare treasure. Only, after a light touch, the cloud creatures seemed content to wait nearby in silent observation. Was proximity enough?

Why?

The cloud creature didn't recoil from Maena's reach, and the ecstasy coming with the contact pulsed as strong as ever, drawing Maena into a sharp breath, a pain-free moment. In that blissful paradise, Maena's thoughts ran wild, dashing without distraction from one idea to the next while her eyes centered on the grim ghosts above.

Seven gods. Ami had gone to a wind-swept ruin, declared it Kance. Had visited Foti with the firewalkers, described its blasted stones and silver sea in detail. Neither matched the realm Maena stood in now, which left the Rana captain with five options. Noctia could be ruled out by the light and flowers alone: what goddess of death would craft a pleasant place like this, filled with emotionally charged fiends?

It is close enough to a nightmare, though. Perhaps Noctia would—

No. Svarde, Jochi, Ami and Maena had debated this long enough in the Dead King's shadow back in the Dark Below. The motes swam in a pool deep in Noctia's heart. That the goddess, mortally wounded by Vis, had nevertheless preserved something from each of the other gods suggested she wasn't some demonic monster. Her isle, too, offered beautiful lelune flowers. Noctia was not a terror, but neither was she a golden goddess.

Rana didn't match either: aside from the pool now banished by the trembling rocky rise, Maena found no familiar elements of the river goddess. Whent, ever a master of crags and boulders, seemed equally absent from the flat, golden expanse. The horizon stretched on forever, only those golden petals visible.

Which narrowed it down to two, and Vis was not a god of golden fields, but jungle.

So you think this is Tamas's home? What then?

The cloud creature retreated from Maena's touch and the Rana captain lurched after it, almost falling to preserve the transcendent escape. She couldn't go back to the agony, not now, not yet. The creature bumped into another of its puffy friends, bounced into Maena's hand, and, trapped by its encircling fellows, gave up its retreat. Again, Maena sank her hand into its squishy, light body and found her worries disappear.

If this was Tamas, then the fiends would bear the god's aspects: soul, emotion, the mind. It would explain the soul-splitting monsters continuing to cluster above, and, perhaps, give Maena a way to deal with their disaster.

What, curse them out? Tell them they're being mean? Hurt their feelings?

In a sense.

Maena turned to the creature she touched, caught more amber lightning spreading across its body. The jagged arcs ran near her hand, and Maena shifted her palm to run over the shimmering split.

Serenity disappeared. Cold enveloped her, a shuddering despair shut Maena down only to whiplash away as the lightning dissolved. Fled her touch and disappeared, while on the other creatures near her, the hazel lines lingered.

What was that?

An answer. An explanation. Maena eyed the soul-sucking fiends overhead. They'd stuffed the sky, seemed to be descending now in wafting whirls. The cloud creatures around Maena didn't seem to react, though, and Maena couldn't be sure, those amber cracks flared faster and faster. The cloud creatures were breaking apart.

Tamas. God of soul. Emotion. The inner being. The sort of thing Maena used to dismiss with a flagon of ale and a well-sharpened saber. Here, without physical weapons, what did they have?

You're thinking in riddles, Maena.

Back in the cave, when the wind-swept fiend had cornered her, the monster hadn't ripped off her arms or clawed away her face. The fiend had siphoned her spirit, her happiness, her dreams, the very essence of her. Later, to hear Svarde tell it, they'd knocked words, experiences, whole memories free from the fiend with every strike.

Maena fell to her right, wincing, gasping as the second free from contact ushered in her broken body's reality. Somewhere near her feet, Haggerth continued his slow death, rasping curses into the quiet. The Rana captain reached her target, another cloud creature crossed in lightning scars. Her hand fell onto the fluff, the euphoria rising, only for Maena to banish it by wandering her palm over the lightning. As she did, as the numbing harrow rose within her, the scar faded away to the pure gray-white fluff.

You're healing them, how?

By doing what she'd done all her life. Second nature to any Rana, to any fighter who wouldn't accept a loss. Maena kept going, and with that effort, she pushed away the despair. Took it in and destroyed it with defiance.

Nonsense. You can't heal a wound by imagining it away.

In a realm made by Tamas?

Maena smiled as she ran her hands along the cloud

creature's lightning scars, their lines disappearing even as their chilly sorrow failed to find a home in Maena's resolute soul. Strange, yes, but no more so than what she'd encountered ever since setting foot in the Dark Below.

Now what, you touch them all? How many will you get before those things reach us?

Two was the answer. Two among too many to count. The ghoulish creatures, little more than formless voids shrouded in dark rags—not for a second did Maena think those ripped cloaks were real cloth—descended on the cloudy creatures and devoured them. The still air found life, sucked in towards the fiends, and with its pull, the cloud creatures went too, stretching, vanishing into those monsters. Riddled with lightning scars, amber flashes zapping across their bodies in constant flares now, the cloud creatures didn't fight back.

They simply shook, shrank, and vanished into the soul-sucking fiends.

All save the three near Maena, in a conquest so fast Maena didn't have time to lurch to any others. Instead she leaned on the duo, each hand on their pristine, puffy forms. Behind her, the only gap in the dark throngs, lay the growing spire, its tumbling edges collapsing onto the golden flowers. A slow burial.

Everywhere else Maena looked, she saw the faceless voids. They encircled her and the two cloud creatures. Haggerth made one last, desperate noise, before all he was vanished into one of the fiends. Any sadness Maena might have felt at being left alone, the sadness she'd tried to stop by saving Haggerth from the flooding pool, never pierced the ecstatic veil.

The rage, the loss, the confusion did. Those blank fiends tried to tear away the cloud creatures, tried to feast on their joy, and found their meal stymied by Maena, who in turn found the wallowing despair thwarted by the pure happiness at her fingertips. A balance, for a moment, between overwhelming melancholy and beautiful contentment.

The duel at Tamas's heart.

Do we stay like this forever? On this edge?

No.

A sundering of herself, a mirroring of two parts: Maena's soul split again, the fiends and their despair flooding through to Maena's angry self, the pit that'd driven her to attack Whent, to fight the fiends for their assaults on the Isles and all those friends those battles had cost her. Shove that aside, bundle it up and throw it away. A task she would have found impossible without the reward already there, those cloud creatures showing her what could be Maena's, if she could free herself, if she could cast it all away.

The fiends took it all. Those monsters sucked and sapped Maena, drawing away all of her anger, her fear, her loss, and once that was done, when the Rana captain should have been empty, they found only joy instead. Ecstasy, bliss, and nothing else. They came for that too, and changed.

Fill a well with poison, and the sickness spreads. Purify it instead, and the village will return to health. An old, easy saying and one Maena saw proved true yet again around her: the ghastly creatures changed, their shredded shapeless forms rounding out, becoming whole, reaching towards Maena not in hate, not to feed, but to share, to embrace, to become what Tamas must have wanted, must have broken with the god's disappearance and death.

Time had little meaning in that place, but when Maena fluttered her eyes open, when her body again became hers, its aches and pains repairing her to reality, the Rana captain saw the clouded creatures drifting through the golden flowers beneath a burnt sky, happy and clear.

And in her mind, there echoed only her thoughts, and her thoughts alone.

CHAPTER 40
FACTIONS

A ferrite's nuzzle was neither soft nor gentle, but Svarde found his dead lips grinning at the familiar touch. That those lips could move at all was a testament to the Vis power buzzing about his soul, stringing together a body that would not, could not die.

The fall echoed in flashes as Svarde lay in a new ditch amid an otherwise pleasant field dotted with trees. Svarde suspected they grew fruit of some kind, but as he couldn't move his arms, his legs, his head, he couldn't confirm that suspicion. All he could do was hold tight to the blade, the tension the only thing he'd done in the long hours remaining in the night, one that had crossed into day, back to night, and now approached dawn again.

Kivi had found him not long ago, the ferrite appearing as if by magic over Svarde. At first, Kivi didn't understand, and Svarde, whose throat must've been crushed in the collapse, couldn't summon any words to explain. The ferrite did its own discovery, though, feeling about Svarde's smashed body, snorting her sorrow as she learned the brutal extent of his injuries.

At least the blade's curse, its blessing, kept pain at a distant remove. Thirst and hunger held no sway, and other bodily needs that might have made lying in the dirt for days a disaster had long since disappeared from Svarde's existence. He'd lain there, felt the twitches as bones reformed, as muscles repaired their connections, and watched the sky.

There were memories to traverse, of course. Ideas to consider. Plans to plot. All those withered away after the first few hours, leaving Svarde in a comfortable, numb, void amid the dirt. Aside from Kivi, his visitors included a few curious birds, three beetles, and an ant swarm that attempted to nibble on his eyes but found their efforts thwarted by the Vis power in the blade. All had since moved on, and so Svarde drifted, until Kivi's latest nuzzle announced something new.

"You're alive?" came the snappy, disbelieving sarcasm as Eujo's bandit, Torny, appeared in his view.

The bandit offered much with a first look: her last day had been spent in bloody battle, going by the cuts and sweat along her brow. Her hair had taken a cut too, a chunk missing near a gash along her forehead. At least her eyes seemed bright.

Not that Svarde could answer.

Kivi snorted on his behalf. Torny glanced at the creature, then squinted at Svarde.

"You look like crap," Torny said. "Like you should be dead. Your ferrite seems to think otherwise, and your eyes are moving, so I guess that means you're still with us?"

Svarde blinked.

"I'll take that as a yes." Torny looked up and away, off towards the ocean. Svarde's feet pointed towards the spire and the Sky Palace at its top. "Look. It's not good. Gladdring's claiming Eujo slaughtered a lot of Kance soldiers.

That she's trying to sell us out to the Najahn. Not everyone believes him, but there's a lot of people unhappy with her right now.

"Thankfully, I'm amazing. I kept these letters, kinda moldy now but good enough, that said the old Queensguard was ordered to kill Eujo. I was keeping them for blackmail, but hey, circumstances change. That's bought us enough sympathy to split the city, but Noctia's on the move again. Which is why I'm here." Torny frowned again. "Well, we were hoping you'd be more, you know, mobile. But we need you to convince those Noctia fiends to join us."

Svarde blinked again. An interesting notion.

"The deal we discussed, remember? Eujo can make a peace with Noctia, but we need Gladdring off the throne to do it. That's where your fiends come in. They'll break the soldiers still loyal to Gladdring, and poof. We win. Easy."

Nothing was easy with the firewalkers, but Torny wouldn't know that. The bandit didn't dwell on that issue long, breaking fast to a tale of their escape from the throne room, on how Eujo used the Kance skar to swing the trio to the level beneath, shattering another window. From there, a mad dash to the stairs, outrunning Gladdring's command to escape into the city, where open war reigned, one Svarde could end.

"So what do you think? Can you do it?"

At the rate his muscles were healing, Svarde wasn't sure he'd be able to stand—

"Here. I'm borrowing this from Eujo. Don't lose it."

The rush came fast. The Vis mutterings in his mind turning into a conversation, wordless and fantastic. Bones began filling in like ale poured into a flagon, rather than a slow knitting. His hands and feet twitched, responding to Svarde's reach. He dared to take a breath, and the wild joy at his throat making moves was at once alien and astounding.

"Seems to be working, then?" Torny asked. "We thought another Vis skar might help. But, you know, Eujo's vulnerable while that's here, so . . . "

By lunch, Svarde could stand, though he leaned on Torny with so much weight the bandit strained with every step. With Kivi leading, the pair took a slow meander through the trees to the orchard's border, a slim wood fence leading to a large stone building, one Svarde figured must've been where the produce was handled before rolling out to the isle's cities. How that process all worked was a mystery the barbarian had no desire to investigate.

One he did was how he and Torny would deal with the Kance soldiers marching towards them. A full squad, armed with rapiers and glittering glass mail, the soldiers didn't seem surprised to see a broken barbarian leaning on the lithe bandit. Torny's daggers sat in waist holsters, Svarde's blade dragged on the ground, neither ready to counter an attack. Only the ferrite, snorting and opening her steam vents, made any display.

Yet Torny didn't stop pulling Svarde along, only slowing when the soldiers were several strides away, their ranks assembled.

"This is the Guardian?" asked the squad's leader, rank denoted by blue-tinged tips at the edges of his glittering helmet. "He does look as devastated as you said."

Torny snapped something that Svarde couldn't catch, shrugged Svarde off her shoulder. The barbarian tottered, held his loose balance long enough for the squad leader to go red-faced, order two of his soldiers to grab Svarde.

"The name's Oppan," the leader said, "and it's my job to

get you through to the city's other side. You didn't do us any favors by landing out here, so it'll be a long walk."

Torny, rubbing her shoulders, said, "I have to get back to Eujo. Don't lose that skar. We'll need it back."

Svarde held the stone in his right hand, and he kept holding it as Oppan's squad took the barbarian along side streets and back roads, past sounds of skirmishes, clashing metal, and shouts to surrender, to charge, to slaughter. Smoke rose as buildings caught fire. Mothers, fathers, children fled around them, breaking for the countryside in panic. During the few times Svarde caught a look out to sea, the blue ocean seemed dotted with ships sporting Kance and Noctia flags, swirling around each other in a deadly dance.

The war in earnest, then, on every side.

"The navy doesn't know," Oppan said as they moved closer to the massive port, away from the Sky Palace. "They're fighting Noctia believing a whole Kance stands behind them."

"Can't they see the fires here?"

"Insurgents. Accidents. Or maybe they simply don't care." Oppan's tone carried a certain reverence. "We will fight for the wind isle to the end, Guardian."

"That end might come sooner than you think."

Svarde's rasping speech stuttered, stopped and started, but Oppan gave him time to speak. The squad leader's soldiers shared the man's discipline, keeping sharp eyes out and weapons ready, yet no fight found them during their careful trek.

"Eujo has more loyalty here than in the palace," Oppan said when Svarde wondered at the relative calm. "Gladdring's twisting words don't reach this far. At least, not yet."

"Then he cannot win."

"The Queen thinks Gladdring waits. To bargain with Noctia after Eujo is dead and secure his place as regent." Oppan scowled. "That, to say the least, will not be happening. Not with your help."

Night crept in, a burning twilight, as they reached the northern edges of the city. The same overlook where Svarde had stood with Olgata and plotted his one-man assault. Then, he'd been so certain of his invincible path. Now?

Now he could stand on his own, could lift the blade's tip to his knees, could look up and see the first flares as the firewalkers marched their infernos his way. Svarde held out his left hand towards Oppan, dropped the Vis skar into the man's palm.

"Take this back to your Queen," Svarde said. "If this goes badly, that stone won't save me. But it might still save her."

CHAPTER 41
HERO'S PROMISE

The cave air inside the dome caught Wax as he fell, slid him down into a gentle landing behind the fiend trio and their Whent prey. The two warriors saw Wax, confusion plastering their gritty faces and alerting the fiends the ratio had changed. The middle monster whirled towards Wax, who stood, seemingly defenseless, before the hound-like creature.

Appearances, though, could be deceiving.

Wax started to give the Foti skar its freedom, the day's long drop making relaxing his guard an easy move. The Foti skar's simmering hunger didn't jump to fill Wax's command: a different skar, a stranger one, answered instead.

Noctia cast out her invisible influence, feeling, to Wax, as if he'd sprouted three cold strings from his hands. Those dark lines lanced towards the fiends, encircled their necks and pulled tight. The monsters, choked off, squirmed and coughed. Wax, stunned, watched, felt a new energy rush back into his body, like sleeping a whole night in perfect rest. His muscle aches disappeared, the pressure behind his eyes after so many hours making precise leaps down the Wound faded, and Wax's growling stomach, starved after several days with slim meals, found itself sated.

The fiends withered.

What little fat the monsters had dwindled, their bones pressing tight against their skin. Eyes thinned, mouths shriveled, teeth blackened and dropped. Instead of snarling, biting, the fiends stopped their struggle to collapse, quiet and dead in seconds.

The Noctia skar glimmered a devious satisfaction in Wax's mind, those tendrils fading away and leaving Wax breathing hard, a cool sweat breaking over healthy skin, a sturdy stand.

"What in Whent's name was that?" asked the first warrior as his partner tested the expired fiends with an axe. "And who're you?"

Wax heard the question, but his attention focused inward. Just what had that Noctia skar done? All the other stones sapped Wax's will to power their biggest effects, but here, this . . . Could Wax siphon all the strength he needed from his enemies? Could he keep on going, forever, like an unstoppable—

"Asked you a question, kid," the Whent warrior repeated, standing before Wax, his dual-edged battle-axe held ready. "Don't know where you came from, and I'm happy to thank you for what you did to those damn monsters, but we're in a brawl here. Need to know what side you're on?"

Wax grinned. He felt so good. The best in days, since the first sip of wine with Catya. He had twelve skars and their untold power.

"I'm the new Aegis, and I'm here to end this war."

The war, though, wasn't going all that well. The two

Whent fighters escorted Wax through the place they called the Dead City, though its streets were torn up in continual fighting. Fiends fought Whent warriors and, when different monsters collided, each other. Buildings that'd stood strong days ago were rubble now, with others actively falling apart as Wax and his escorts went past. Stronger quakes continued down here, with Whent lines trying to hold around shifting, sliding rock.

"It's the damn gates," said Jochi, the Whent leader after Wax introduced himself. "The gods, or maybe just Noctia, left doors open to their old homes, and now we're falling in."

Jochi had established a command down a tunnel from the Dead City, past a particularly nasty gate built of bone. The warlord stood over a massive stone table surrounded by a frenzy, with arms and armor racing out to fighters and being replaced with the wounded. Jochi himself had fresh blood—albeit blue and gooey, belonging to a fiend—on his leathers, suggesting time spent swinging two familiar axes on the front lines.

"That pool seemed to keep them in check," Jochi continued, his eyes tracking the table and the figures on it, stone discs showing where Whent scouts thought the swirling motes were. "How, I don't know. Noctia's blood, maybe, but it doesn't matter now. That damned blast, whatever it was, scattered everything."

Wax just listened. Jochi had taken the Vis's appearance in stride, not breaking the evening briefing to several squad leaders, and not giving Wax a moment to talk. That was just fine, as, despite Wax's confidence, all the crazy nonsense he seen over the last few hours was bewildering.

The Wound ended in a pool? One filled with swirling gates that appeared to be portals to the gods' own homes?

Demion and her Guardian had found this place centuries ago and sought to use it to ward off the fiends, an effort that'd gradually failed?

Wax would need several ales after all this, that was certain.

"Those gates are gobbling up everything that falls in them," Jochi continued. "It's a chain, and it's letting all the fiends know where their exit lies. They're pouring in, and I'm not sure how to stop'em." The Whent took a deep breath, gave a look 'round the table. "Or if we even should. Those fiends are fleeing certain death. Doing what's natural."

"It's their world that's dying, not ours," came a voice from across the table, another blood-spattered warrior. "Not our fault. And it's not like they're coming in peace, neither."

Jochi nodded, "True enough, but who knows how many monsters are waiting behind those motes. Thank Whent that Rana gate's clogged with one of those massive sea beasts, and Kance and Vis have themselves so knotted all their fiends just keep fighting each other." Jochi glanced at Wax. "You've not met them yet, but the firewalkers have Foti sealed up for the moment. It's just Whent that's the problem."

"For now," huffed the same warrior from before. "Those gates are spinning all the time. Give'em an hour and we might be dealing with something new."

"Or," came a third, a spindly woman with a map in her hands, one she planted on the table, "we might lose this whole network. Nothing's stable anymore, Jochi. You don't want to lose everything, I say we run."

The warlord seemed to age a decade at those words, but he nodded, returned his eyes to Wax.

"So, Aegis, that's the lay. We run, these gates will keep swallowing our rock. They'll keep spitting fiends until they've emptied. Dozens, maybe thousands of those monsters. Right now, Whent's fighting the battle all alone. Can you help us?"

"I can do more than help," Wax said, feeling the skars rise up with his words, their confidence boosting his own. "Keep me protected, and I can stop all this. Easy."

Jochi raised his eyebrows. "Either you're the hero we've been looking for, or the dumbest Vis I've ever met. I sure hope you're the former." The warlord looked back across the table. "Get him to the most vulnerable spots and let's see what he can do."

"No," Wax said. "I'm not here to kill fiends. Get me to the gates. Like you said, we can't fight every creature that comes through. The gods left those doors open. I'm going to close them."

CHAPTER 42
THE DEFENSE OF MOTTILAN

Go back to his earliest memories, sitting on his father's knee near a crackling fire, and Quik would hear hunters talking about their quarries, about days on end trailing hanoko and other beasts to lairs dark and frightening. The tellers of those tales, though, would reach a point where the serious would become smiles, the thrust of a spear or bow shot signaling victory had, at last, arrived. A toast would rise, wood cups serving peach wine to a laughing, happy city.

Those hunters never spoke of war, because they had never been in one. Vis itself had evaded such disasters for as long as Quik knew, because the rest of the isles wrote Vis off as a curiosity, a trading partner best left to its own quirky devices.

Not any longer, and all because the god that made it, whose fallen body, according to legend, made the very dirt in which Quik now squatted, had given his skars the power of life.

Ferns and other shrubs disguised Quik's chosen spot,

crowded in with other defenders. A few were Mottilan and Kitaye hunters, having made it back from raids or in flight from Vis's other, overtaken city. They held spears, a couple strung bows. Others numbered too old or too young to join the real ranks, called into action nonetheless to protect those still older, younger, or infirm. They held what tools they could use, from blow darts to grass-clearing blades.

Not a one looked as frail as their weapons would suggest, and Quik found courage in their clear eyes, their sturdy frames, thin or wrinkled as they might be.

Across the road, one covered with leaf-shrouded pits and muddy troughs meant to make advancing a treacherous task, waited a stone home. Within its walls and aiming through its square, rough-cut windows, were archers. Lingering behind the building, waiting for Quik's whistle and ready to dash around in ambush, was Deshiva and several more of the best spear-wielders Vis could call its own.

The first line, and just about the only one. A few scattered bands waited lower on the cliff road, and if Deshiva's plan, formed from Quik's suggestion, had its way, the Mottilan forces would strike fast and flee, only to attack again at random intervals all the way down the cliffside.

Would that deter the purple and black Najahn soldiers marching, nearly there, eight across and many deep, shields and voulges at the ready?

No, but it might slow them long enough for Mottilan's evacuation to complete.

The Najahn marched with too much confidence. Their soldiers joked as they walked, their tight formation belying an easy attitude, an assumption of victory. Quik would prove them wrong, and that proof would begin . . . now.

The leftmost Najahn passed by, followed by the second rank. Neither bothered looking hard into the leaves, trying to pierce the inked camouflage hiding Quik and his makeshift warriors.

The third rank didn't get a chance.

Quik whooped. A loud cry carried into the Najahn by his charge, woven shoes biting into the dirt and kicking him, his gauntlets forward in an overhead slash. The Najahn shields, facing forward, didn't provide protection, did nothing to save the soldier's side as Quik's metal-tipped claws rent into the seam at the soldier's neck, an uppercut piercing the gap beneath the Najahn's shoulder. A stab, a tear, a kick, shoving the wounded, possibly dead, Najahn into his own allies.

The hunter did not attack alone. Darts and arrows buzzed in behind and beside him, many clacking off Najahn armor. A few snuck in beneath helmets or into turned faces, though even the misses bought flinches, turned confidence into panic, and gave the four hunters charging with Quik time for a parry-free strike.

But five fighters against forty wasn't a fight that could be won alone.

Quik broke left, swinging those claws to take a turning Najahn in the side, angling the strikes to the weakest parts in the armor. Armor Quik himself had worn, studied in the weeks he'd spent among the Najahn in their home. That knowledge paid off, his gauntlets tearing links and finding flesh beneath. The other four hunters stayed close, their spears stabbing, doing less damage and more delay as the Najahn twisted, broke formation to engage.

And turned their backs on the stone house.

As Quik batted away an offending voulge, back-stepping to see far too many Najahn soldiers staring back at him, he found his voice again. A second whoop, a second volley. Raised Najahn shields and expectations meant the arrows and darts from Quik's back did little, bouncing off into the air. The ones firing would be running in a moment, slipping down through trees and rope lines to the next ambush point.

The ones behind, Deshiva's group, triggered their own surprise. Using bows, with punchier arrows and longer range, the archers in the house let loose a strike into unprotected backs. Najahn plate helped, and Quik saw more than one arrow bounce off a helmet into the air, but Vis trained its archers well, as good shooting was more than just a bragging right: it fed your family, your tribe.

And that skill hit the Najahn at their backs, piercing necks, waists, legs. Soldiers screamed. Quik and his hunter quartet shifted left, down the road, angling less for kills and more for survival. The voulges stabbed in, tentative and confused. Easily defended, and Quik found himself past the Najahn line, his group alone on the dirt path.

Too much success.

The Najahn split, the front ranks following the calls of their captain and breaking for the stone house. Fifteen or more soldiers running at the archers with shields raised. They peeled away, leaving Quik and his band facing undamaged rear lines, some dragging away the wounded, others striding into chakram throws.

"Run!" Quik shouted, then ignored his own advice to backpedal instead, claws up.

Huge, razor discs, the chakram came spinning in arcs. They caught sun as they flew, blinding white lines lancing in at Quik, the hunters. Quik had seen the damage those things could do on Noctia, and lurched to his right, raising the gauntlets to protect his face. One struck, a great throw that sliced through Quik's right gauntlet, biting into his hand beneath and spinning the Vis to the ground.

As his head hit soft dirt, Quik saw another hunter take a chakram to the back, the man's flight too slow to outrun the weapon. The disc drove him to the ground, the spinning, barbed edge digging deep. The hunter twitched once, lay still.

Another soul to avenge.

Quik pushed away the burn on his hand, used his left gauntlet to yank the chakram free, the disc and the blood following it marking the path where Quik found his footing, broke in a run as the Najahn switched to their follow-up: crossbows.

On an open plain, the chakrams would break the defense with their weight and angle, shattering shields and turning the enemy. Crossbows and quarrels would follow, softening what remained for the last step, a voulge charge. A simple strategy rarely questioned for a force who fought only bandits and occasional warlords with too much confidence and not enough smarts.

Quik didn't know whether he had those smarts, but he'd seen enough of the Najahn technique to know a slope put those crossbows out of business. The quarrels couldn't curve so well as normal arrows, so he and the three surviving hunters escaped those darted deaths by dashing down the cliffside road, dancing around covered pits and hoping, hoping the Najahn would follow in victorious rage.

To his right, Quik saw the city's slope all the way down to the piers, the docked fishing boats and few cargo vessels. How lucky this was Mottilan, with ocean-going transport, and not Kitaye, with their curled leaves made for fishing and little else. Escape was possible, though the cargo, the people winding down that dock made it clear more time was needed.

Time Quik and Deshiva would do their best to provide.

The battle for Mottilan had begun.

CHAPTER 43
SALVATION

Salvation was fleeting.

Maena dragged Haggerth, who'd lost conscious-ness with the soul-sucking fiends, with one hand while holding onto a cloud creature with the other. The fluffy fiend's ecstasy kept Maena's pain away, the burns and bruises no match for the unbreakable courage. The golden flowers folded before her footsteps, provided a smooth surface to drag the Whent. The cloud creature didn't object either, drifting along without any opinion at all.

Her object continued to rise before her, ugly and crum-bling even as it grew new chunks with every passing minute. The gateway back home, the only way out of this trap.

What'd been a cleansing, inspiring moment of heroism turned into certain doom as the burnt sky darkened again. As if Maena had lit a beacon, more dark, shrouded fiends drifted in on the horizon. The clouded creatures she'd wiped clean welcomed more, amber lightning crossing their bodies, forewarning an inevitable change.

Ami had said the gods' old worlds were dying, and

Tamas was no different. She'd even said the firewalkers had slowed Foti's destruction with their mighty machines. Maena might've done the same here, but the end would come.

Now that the Rana captain had her body back, her soul whole, she didn't plan to die with this flower-covered world.

The ground slushed at her feet, the pool's remnants squishing with her steps. Ami hadn't mentioned what the gateway back looked like, and there wasn't any reason to suspect the doors would be the same across worlds, so Maena kept looking down, up, and around for the motes. None appeared.

Tamas would not signpost its exit with lights.

Rock and stone, though, would serve.

Maena shifted her pull, stepping in front of Haggerth's hairy skull as they neared the growing mountain. Boulders, dirt, and slick cave rock fell about them now, tumbling past and landing in the flowers with crinkled thuds. The cloud creature didn't try to evade the debris, and Maena couldn't keep herself and Haggerth clear while maneuvering the friendly monster, so the fiend lost chunks of itself as rocks barreled into its puffball body. The ovals it used for legs tore away in a small landslide, scattering through the air behind it like flower seedlings. Its right arm, the one Maena wasn't holding, disappeared when a massive conical slab broke and fell on it.

Yet, for those losses, the cloud creature didn't react. Maena held it closer, kept it aloft, its weight slight, and continued embracing the blissful shield it gave her. Could something like this even feel pain? Understand what was happening?

The cloud creature had no face, no eyes, no expressions. It did not, though, pull away from Maena's grip, and in its cool touch, Maena had a friend. She needed one too, because now that they'd reached the crumbling mountain's edge, Maena realized where the gate lay.

Beneath. Covered in falling rock. The surging stone pile collapsed on itself, expanding outward and offering no options for escape. At least, none that Maena could see from where she stood, side-stepping falling stones and doing her best to keep Haggerth from suffering a smashing fate.

They had no shovels, and Maena didn't have the energy to move so much earth even if they did. Behind them, the sky darkened further as more fiends drifted closer. Beneath them, the golden flowers disappeared as more cloud creatures bobbed their way, apparently following Maena, though she wasn't sure why.

Because she'd helped them?

Maena shook her head. Given them a slight reprieve, maybe, but this world was breaking, and she needed to find a new way out.

Another rock landed near her, splashed in the pool, broke apart at her feet. Water rippled. Trampled flowers lay around them. More cloud creatures closed in, further flattening the golden stalks. A bobbing sea of gray and white, watching her, waiting.

Perhaps.

"Dig," Maena croaked. "Dig together."

She let Haggerth's hand go and dove her damaged arm into the loose, piled rock. Threw what she could grab aside. More sank to fill its place, but Maena didn't stop. That such an act ought to be impossible didn't figure, not when she felt so good, when every motion felt electric, when every whisper about how doomed she was died beneath an ecstatic avalanche.

That same confidence kept Maena digging as the cloud creatures surrounded her, their bulbous limbs scooping rubble out one swipe at a time. Every smooth swing moved small amounts, but the friendly fiends made up for their light weight with numbers. They formed chains, limbs swinging in sync to move rubble further and further from the mountain. When Maena, her left hand bloodied and coated in dirt, stepped back, more cloud creatures took her place, attacking the dirt with silent, simple work.

Still holding the damaged cloud in her right hand, Maena sat next to Haggerth, watched as the cloud creatures broke away the mountain. Rocks and stone fell, small land-slides flattened some of the fiends, but more floated in to take their place. Overhead, the sky continued to darken, the ragged voids watching, waiting.

Not that Maena was worried. She couldn't be. Instead, Maena scooped water from the pool and sipped it, poured some from a cupped hand into Haggerth's mouth. She broke off leaves from the golden flowers and chewed on them, found their in their flavor a pleasant nuttiness. Would either substance kill her, leave Maena ill and ruined?

Never, said the smiling thrill surging through her touch with the cloud creature. Never would Maena feel pain again, so long as she kept holding the fiend.

Time swirled. Maena may have fallen asleep, surrounded by the cloud creatures, but the noise that woke her was one of, as always here, hope. The fiends, stacked upon one another and digging well up the mountain's length, had toppled the loose stone down the far side. They backed away now, tumbling in bopping, head-over-legs fashion, to the wet ground.

Maena stood, found Haggerth's hand again, and trod through the staring, still cloud creatures to witness their victory.

The mountain stood too large to clear, at least thus far, but the fiends had dug out an edge, one marked by those twinkling motes. Just big enough to slip into. The rusty water there appeared a deep blue, and Maena couldn't tell what lay on the other side, but that was a chance she would take.

Would, her sparkling soul said, survive.

"Thank you," Maena said, offering the cloud creatures a slight smile, all her burned and scarred skin could muster.

Then, still holding Haggerth in one hand, the cloud creature and its happiness in the other, Maena stepped through.

The Rana captain alighted in a narrow cavern pool, a place only alien for a moment, until experience told Maena the rock around her was, like the mountain back in Tamas's world, a temporary thing. Tamas motes in their amber glint circled near her waist, vanishing into the rubble wall at Maena's left, the barrier acting as nothing to the god sparks. She regarded this without pain, without concern, because next to her, resting on the water to her right, bobbed the cloud creature.

She smiled at it. The creature had saved her, as had its friends. Maena felt a weight on her left hand and pulled, dragged Haggerth's limp form after her. The water kept the Whent's burden low, and with a few strides, she'd left the makeshift cavern and found herself on the slanted gray slope of the great chamber, the target of Maena's bombs.

Rather than a filled in end, with those gates crushed by endless tons of earth, Maena saw fractured mountains, broken caverns and splashing chaos. The pool had risen with the plunging stones, many still breaking off and falling from above. Fiends splashed free too, arising from the depths in confused frenzy, only to meet each other in sudden combat. The Rana captain looked to the Whent tunnel, the precipice they'd used to talk with the firewalkers, and saw it now sat level with the pool's surface, the cave behind filled in. Saw, too, it was home to a pitched struggle between firewalkers and other fiends. Maena shivered at the violence. She should be terrified, but that wouldn't help Haggerth. The man needed medical attention, and so did Maena.

Another gap in the rock lingered ahead and to her left. She mitght've missed it, except for an odd fiend collection, one with long legs and narrow beaks darting through the hole. An option when no others existed. She took a few steps, felt new ripples strike her legs with gentle laps and turned around.

What she saw made Maena's stretched smile grow. Her new friends were coming, and the happiness they'd bring with them, well, the Whent looked like they could use it.

CHAPTER 44

WAR COUNCIL

The walking inferno behind her matched Ami's hair, if not her face. Svarde had to imagine his friend and fellow Guardian felt the same way, walking down the middle of an abandoned road towards him. Scourged by more than age, that they both still lived was a repeated miracle. Literally so, in Svarde's case, and that bond brought them together in an embrace bent by Svarde's blade and the golden mask covering Ami's cheek.

The firewalkers kept their respectful distance. Over Ami's shoulder, Svarde saw new shading, pieces of Kance roofs lifted aloft by makeshift poles. The day didn't threaten rain, but if a few stray drops could cause permanent damage, Svarde might keep cover up at all times too.

"Like our new tools?" Ami asked, stepping back with a tired smile. "Our Whent friends devised them fast, but it took a few days to build. Not to mention convince these guys."

"But it worked."

"I think they realized they still need a home here. On the isles. It's a powerful motivator."

"Almost as good as a blade to your back."

Ami followed Svarde's look to the black sword. "You're still holding it, but I get the feeling you're not handing us the city?"

Svarde shook his head, "Kance has more problems than the Noctia. Gladdring holds the Sky Palace."

The barbarian laughed when Ami's eyes went wide, laughed again when he told Ami about his deal with Eujo.

"You're striking bargains with a Queen barely old enough to hold her ale," Ami said. "Fassle won't be happy."

"The Circle can suck a voulge, for all I care," Svarde rumbled back. "She's smart, and doesn't have any of those bastard's mindless ambition. We get Gladdring out, she'll do her part."

"So we march the firewalkers to the Sky Palace, let'em scare Gladdring away?"

Svarde again looked past Ami to those standing infernal ranks. What would be left of the city if those monsters walked through?

"I wouldn't be Queen much longer, that's what," Eujo said that night, near the harbor. Svarde and Ami had decided to venture back alone, the firewalkers finding shelter in nearby caves, old sky diamond mines long abandoned. "Who's going to follow a queen that let their home burn down?"

"I would," said the newcomer to the party, a Kance assassin, Livier, who could barely stand. The man leaned on a pole, one lofting a lantern string above tables set out for happier times, ones dusted over as the restaurant they belonged to remained shuttered. "I would follow you, and I would advise you, and I would hope that, together, we could salvage our home after the fires had gone."

The evening had turned silky, a fine mist seeping in and

confirming Ami's decision to keep the firewalkers hidden away north of the city. Svarde had pushed her that way, a delay to Fassle's war to buy Eujo's partnership. A sop, perhaps, to a friendlier notion of the isles than one built on conquest and skar power.

One Svarde could afford to make, as immortal beings could.

Livier was not so immortal and had, so Eujo explained, sustained terrible wounds keeping the Queen out of Najahn hands at sea. The same ocean raid that'd slipped Wax away and damaged the Queen's ship bad enough to force her to Kance. While she could flee on some other vessel, a scurrying rat in the night, Eujo's fates seemed locked to her isle. Livier, now holding clutching Eujo's Vis skar, and explaining why it'd not been easy to part with the thing, kept his free hand near a rapier, despite looking so frail the lightest clash would send him to the other side.

"A nice sentiment, and not one that's going to save your people's lives," Ami said, leaning back in the sturdy metal chair. The whole patio looked built for both the outdoors and the beatings drunken sailors could deliver on anything in their immediate reach. The ice wine, a beverage Svarde sipped without tasting it, clashed with the setting, but when in Kance, one drank as the Queen did. "You've lost your throne to a power-grabbing manipulator, and you'll need it back fast."

"I assume you have a new reason, beyond the obvious?"

"Gladdring's going to realize, if he hasn't already, that there's no winning against you. Either you get enough Kance soldiers willing to throw their lives away, we use my firewalkers, or you simply starve him out up there." Ami folded her arms, smirked. "He's going to die without help, and there's only one place that can help him."

"You think Noctia's going to do it?" Torny, the bandit Guardian, said with a laugh. "Gladdring crossed Fassle. And Yarvick, if you're really true about them working together. No way they'd listen to him."

Svarde, though, caught what Ami was getting at.

"It all comes back to the skars," the barbarian said. "Once they get the stones from Gladdring, what do Fassle and Yarvick care about this isle? And right now, Gladdring has the skars."

"Okay," Eujo said, "let's assume Gladdring comes to the same conclusion. That he has a spy, a glider, or some way we don't know to get messages to and from Noctia. They agree, and then . . . We're right back here? A Noctia fleet that can't get past ours."

"And a whole army of firewalkers that you can't defeat on your doorstep," Ami reminded.

"An army that you command."

"As long as Fassle and Jochi let me. If they order me to march those fiends in here and ruin you, they'll relieve me the moment I don't." Ami's cocky veneer faded into a downward curl. "Much as I'd like to believe the firewalkers would listen to me, they'll fight for the person giving them a home."

"Then we're back to one," Livier said. "Gladdring must go. I'd kill him myself, but, alas."

"Yeah, alas," Torny said. "You didn't need to go all hero on the *Storm's Edge*. I would've had 'em."

"Your little knives didn't even scratch their armor."

"Stop, stop," Eujo cut in. "We've rehashed that fight enough times. Drink some more wine and focus on what matters. Like getting into the Sky Palace." She glanced around, saw no interruptions looming, and brightened. "Now, some of you know, I used to pick a few pockets around here. Nip a treasure or two. That means staying out of sight while getting in and out of where the good things are."

"We all know what a thief does," Ami said.

"Don't interrupt the Queen when she's describing the best profession in the isles," Torny snapped. "I didn't say anything about your big grin when you were talking about those firewalkers."

"Anyway," Eujo said, forestalling Ami's simmering comeback. "I'm saying there's a number of ways we can get into the Sky Palace."

"A number?" Svarde asked. "More than one secret way?"

"Thief's gotta have at least three," Torny said. "Anything less and you're set to get caught."

Eujo smiled, "The bandit's right. If they haven't fixed any, I have four."

"So it's an assassination then," said the assassin. "It always comes back to a knife in the neck."

Torny crinkled her nose, "Always? Geez. What a life you've lived."

"It's worked out quite well for me, quite poorly for many others."

The bandit rolled her eyes. Eujo coughed, drew attention back to her. Behind the Queen, the harbor's waves lapped the stone dockside building as several Kance ships sailed into port to exchange crew, reload supplies. Despite the sort of civil war, Kance at large seemed unperturbed. As if the enemy within ought to be excised without showing the enemy without.

"If we're all in agreement," Eujo said, to nods around the table, "here's how I think we can do this. One day to gather materials, get into position. Tomorrow night, then, we take Gladdring fast. Too fast for any help to arrive, any deals to get struck." She sent her icy eyes around the table, and Svarde again saw Eujo looked the part. "Gladdring cannot escape. At least, not with the skars. Alive and chained, or dead." A second to gather herself, to give what Svarde realized must've been a hard order. "If you have a choice, dead is better. We know what this man can do, and I won't take any chances.

Svarde offered to simply walk up the central stair, plodding with Kivi behind him and slaughtering all comers to draw Gladdring into the open. Eujo refused that offer, on the grounds that the ones Svarde would be slaughtering were all her soldiers, albeit ones twisted by Gladdring's Tamas skars.

Dealing with the stones, though, was Svarde's main job, and why he'd made his way the following morning, early, to the Sky Palace's southern end, not far from the field he'd smashed into. Kance, the wind isle, had heat geysers scattered about, and with a proper glider, one could use those geysers to catch quite a drift. Svarde, with Ami alongside him, would be flying into Gladdring's teeth.

Together, the two Guardians would take as much of Gladdring's focus as they could, draining his energy and—

"Don't worry, Svarde," Ami said as she strapped him into his shielded glider, the clumsy contraption heavy as they stood amid cut grass, near a wide, frothing blow hole. Sulfur smell suffused the air, and several lanky pilots watched their efforts, calling out suggestions here and there. "Gladdring tries to make you jump out a window again, I'll slap your senses right back."

"I think you might do that anyway."

"It has been a while since I've hit something." Ami,

clinching the last cinch into place, patted the blade at her waist, one that'd find its way to her glider's storage compartment in a minute. "Thankfully, where we're going, I imagine there'll be no shortage of blood to spill."

CHAPTER 45
MONSTERS AND DEAD MEN

The hero's bravado stayed with Wax while Jochi gathered an escort. While the Vis had no real idea of what he'd do—Catya suggested letting the skars work together, so that was his plan for now—the clearest path lay to the crumbling pool chamber where all those god gates spun. See them, let the skars guide Wax to close those doors, and walk away with a safe Seven Isles.

Easy.

Except, according to Jochi, a fiend flood waited between here and the cavern Wax needed to visit. His Whent warrior bands were being pressed all day and night with endless fiend incursions, many coming without prelude and with new creatures. Tactics had to be devised on the fly to handle tentacled horrors, packs of dog-like predators, or odd flowing masses of slime. Wax recognized the last from his adventure on Rana, and was about to offer up a fiery solution before Jochi waved it away, declaring they'd battered that one to bits and would the next too.

Until the Whent collapsed from exhaustion.

"Which is why I'm hoping you're right," the warlord

said as they assembled at the Dead City's entry. "I've sent up the call for all the souls we can drag from the surface down here. I'm asking the other warlords to give me every able body from the Pits, offer them an axe and a chance to win their freedom." The man nodded ahead down the broad streets, flush now with military trains hauling arms in and wounded, or worse, warriors out. "If this keeps up, I don't think we'll last long enough for them to arrive."

"They keep coming?" Wax asked as the last of their escorts, a pair carrying bandages and ointments to go with their crossbows and iron cudgels. "You'd think the fiends would run out."

Jochi held up a finger and the march started forward, through those bone gates. Fighters and fixers not in their thirty-strong band flowed around them, ducking into stone alleys or inside homes decorated with Whent war paints. Some raised axes and swords in salutes. Most kept their eyes down, limping with injury or exhaustion.

The fight's third straight day, un-ending and uninter-rupted, was taking its toll.

"I think they're being funneled," Jochi said. "If those worlds are dying, a phrase I never thought I'd say until I came down here, where nothing makes any damn sense, then those monsters are running from certain death. There might be a thousand fiends in every one of those places, maybe ten thousand. A million. All coming right towards us."

A few firewalkers, fiends without mindless destruction as their default mode, might fit on an isle. Millions wouldn't. Even as Wax's Vis heritage, his childhood growing up in harmony with the hanoko, the jungle crea-tures, the life provided by his isle and the respect it earned in turn, pushed the Vis to look for ways to spare the life, he couldn't find an easy answer.

Every map, every distant voyage from the isles found only endless sea until, starving and fearing death amid gray waters, the explorers had turned back. The last big expedition had been decades ago, according to the Vis elders, who used those impossible missions as proof that the isles must be cared for.

There was no other place to go. For human or fiend.

The air swapped forged metal for a different tang: blood's salty sweat. Howls, both of battle cries and mortal wounds, echoed off abandoned buildings. Wax noticed corpses, ones long rotted and barely more than bones, piled up along the street sides. Some had fresh additions now, losses to the fiends without time to move for a burial or funeral burning. Traffic thinned as they passed aid stations, fortifications under hurried construction as engineers piled bricks, overturned carts, and anything else they could grab to hem the streets into choke points.

For all his dire talk, Jochi was making plans to hold the city. Delay fiends long enough to . . .

"You could just run," Wax said as they neared the front line. "The Dark Below is huge. Let the fiends fight one another down here and we clean up what makes it to the surface."

The warlord grunted, "That's what we've been doing for centuries, Wax. The Aegis burns them out, we chop the few who squeeze through, except that's not doing so well anymore right? With all these fiends, we'll be aging out Aegises every couple weeks. Not going to work."

Wax didn't argue; the warlord's blunt assessment, after several more, knocking Wax's confidence a notch. For all the skars buzzing in his head, this here was a real war. Just as dangerous as the attacks on Whent, Foti, and in the seas around Kance, but without his survival as the only goal. Wax was supposed to fight for something bigger, be bolder and braver, but maybe, maybe this was larger than he was meant for.

Ahead, the Whent line loomed. Axes and crossbows, bent helms and battered mail. Furs and ferocity as fighters traded spots with one another, resting and rejoining the line. Jochi had his soldiers in sturdy ranks, the front in stone Whent turtle armor, with more mobile warriors slipping between the cracks to swing an axe, thrust a spear, or fire a crossbow at what lay beyond. The death crossed an avenue, a tight one between several blood-spattered buildings. Crates and bodies stuffed the alleys between, creating a devastating funnel.

"A wave of the dogs now," cracked one commander as Jochi slowed their force a few strides behind the line. "They're easy enough. Their bodies will buy us a breather too."

"Why's that?" Jochi asked.

"Because the next fiends'll eat them, that's why. Take their lunch before taking it to us. Then the wave after that'll attack the chewing fiends. It's a good turn when we see those damn dogs."

Jochi glanced at Wax, "Then that's our opportunity. Once these are down, we push forward. Buy our troops a break and get you a close-up." The Whent commander followed Jochi's look, raised an eyebrow at Wax, only for Jochi to explain. "This kid's our next great hope. He'll either save us all, or prove we can't stay down here."

The commander nodded, "So long as you do one or the other, boy, I'll be happy. Just be quick about it."

"That's the idea," Jochi said, then whistled, the fiend

fray dying down. "We head on now! Fight smart. You have allies, so use them. We work as one, we'll make it back alive."

What Jochi didn't say, what Wax didn't try to add, was whether their mission would be worth any damn thing.

The turtle ranks split with a sigh, the soldiers wearing that heavy armor relieved to find a gap finally given to them. Wax, walking behind Jochi and several Whent warriors in heavy leathers—the stone outfits would be too slow for an incursion like this—saw what lay beyond and felt his stomach heave. His wasn't the only one, and several made clear they couldn't keep their own reactions down.

The Najahn assault on the Foti bandit camp had been the only time Wax had witnessed a true battle's aftermath, and the violence there haunted his dreams for weeks. This trumped those sword-split bodies on the beach in a moment, with steaming, bleeding, broken clumps of bones, skin, and worse left to lie where its owner died. Some fiends still twitched, any mercy killing not coming, as exhausted Whent soldiers tended to their own needs.

Jochi's crew offered those monsters no solace either, with the front six hacking, shoving aside any fiend body too large to step around. For the first few strides beyond the Whent line, the horrors continued, before dwindling fast to bloodstains and splattered memories. The why was clear enough, as Jochi's team found their first fiends feeding on the last remnants of earlier monsters.

Smaller dog-like creatures, with reddish manes and golden eyes. The creatures glanced up from their crimson feast as Jochi's line approached. They turned to run, only for Wax to hear crossbows fire from either side. Quarrels lanced out, drove the fiends to the ground, and Jochi's warriors split off to finish the job before either fiend could find its feet again.

"They were running, why?" Wax asked, Jochi not stopping the march.

Those dealing the killing blow yanked the quarrels free, hustled back into position, the wet ammo returned to the archers.

"Because a fiend might disappear one minute and attack from the shadows the next," Jochi replied. "This is not a mercy mission, Wax. This is a death march, and everything we see will earn an axe or a quarrel." The warlord, without stopping, sent a sharp look back at the Vis. "And when we reach the chamber, I hope you'll put the final knife in their hearts. For all our sakes, Wax."

CHAPTER 46
TORCHES AND TRAPS

Quik rolled into the third break, dirt snarling into the cuts on his left side. That voulge had left its mark, even as its owner had lost his life. Around the hunter, the gray, windy day delivered a matching verdict: chilly and despondent. That only three others joined him from the second break, scampering over traps, around trees, and across prickly lawns ahead of the advancing Najahn added to the oppressive cloak: they were losing. A terrible weight, even if it was expected.

The hunter snatched a look out to sea. The evacuation should've ended by now, the ocean pocked with hope as fisherman's boats and cargo vessels carried Vis's families and elders to the last holdout on Kance. Instead, smoke rose amid the waves. Vis ships clustered in close to the dock, where the shallower draft kept the larger Najahn clippers from cutting in so near, so deadly.

They'd swarmed from around Vis's north side in their rage, black and purple flags flying. The assault predicted in the maps Quik had found, one not countered by a Kance navy somehow too preoccupied with its own waters.

Narro hadn't fulfilled his promised, hadn't come to Vis's aid. The isle stood alone.

His gauntlets, metal tips now a mix of red blood and black dirt, caught the ground and pushed Quik up, though the hunter kept to a crouch as he broke to the cliff road's left side, the narrow, tree-coated break before the steep drop—not so far now—to Mottilan's central square. Amid the ferns and brush he found those few hunters, those old and young, stuffing darts into blow guns with bleeding fingers, cleaning off spears for the next thrust, or staring at nothing, the moment crushing out their sanity.

He needed to say something, needed to wake them up for the next stand. Two more breaks waited after this, trap clusters that'd slow the Najahn with even a soul alone left to man them. Quik gathered his breath, opened his mouth—

"Vis," came the iron tone, as hard as death itself, as Deshiva always was. The hunt master dropped into the copse from above, a wild swing Quik realized must've begun from the cliff wall all the way across the road, through the yard, and the burning house beyond. "The battle continues, but our strategy must change."

Deshiva bore as many wounds as any of them, and her spear only had a single blue-white feather left on its battered body, but she stood as unbreakable as ever. Dropping to the floor as she spoke, Deshiva salved their spirits with a long look across each and every defender's face.

"You've stalled the Najahn as we needed, but only on land. Our enemy comes at us from the sea, and so we must fight them there as well." Deshiva focused now on the archers, their arrows. The most numerous group, the ones who broke first to the next ambush. "All of you that can shoot a bow will come with me. We make for the ships, to delay, destroy, and make the Najahn reconsider their pursuit." She hesitated, found Quik, his gauntlets. "The rest of you, man the breaks. Keep them at bay."

"Without the archers, we're dead," said an older hunter, sitting on the ground and pressing a leafy poultice to a gash along his right leg.

"Then you will die a glorious death," Deshiva said, then brought her spear up to her temple, nodding with both at the hunter. "I salute your bravery, hunter, and Vis sees your sacrifice. Make it worthy of his respect."

Without waiting for any other discontent, Deshiva put two fingers to her mouth and whistled. A high-pitched call, one starting a hunt, and the archers jumped to the summons. As quick as she appeared, Deshiva dashed off the cliff side, leaping to tree and vine, with her followers scrambling after her in ragged lines.

Up the cliffside, the ground shook. Heavy boots approached, even and implacable in their advance.

Ten. Ten hunters left in the copse, and Quik found himself burying a frown at the word. Maybe one other qualified as a hunter here, in the classic Vis sense. Three were fraying and older, called back from groves and lonely lives at one with the jungle to defend their home. The other five would've been lucky to see more than a dozen summers, their courage proven by their standing here.

No longer.

"Leave," Quik said to the younger ones. "Follow Deshiva and break north at the beach. Find Sawi at the cave and go with her group."

When the same one who'd declared Deshiva's order a

death sentence started to speak up again, Quik smashed the argument in the same way.

"Vis is his people, not a place," Quik said, realizing, as he spoke, that the words came from the Najahn histories he'd been forced to learn during his weeks on the island. Originally from a last speech against a fiend assault, Quik figured this was a worthy re-purposing. "Carry Mottilan with you, and go."

The same hunter seemed to realize arguing was both impossible and unhelpful, instead rising to a shaky stand. Another youngster took his friend's arm, and together with the other three, they broke for the long trees and vines offering an escape. Before they leapt, the wounded hunter turned his head to the dull sky and let out a wild whoop.

Quik and his remaining, battered, five echoed the sound.

"And now that you've chased the youth away, how would you have us die?" asked an older woman, one with three blow guns looped around her neck. A dart bandoleer slung across her shoulder, each one dipped in a paralyzing poison. "A glorious charge up against the Najahn? A slow wasting as they cut and stab?"

The Vis hunter didn't answer at first. Instead, Quik turned back to the road. The Najahn had slowed as the attack wound on, both needing to tend to their wounded and navigate the foul traps. They hadn't yet appeared over the next slop, and that space gave Quik time to find a plan.

"There," the hunter said, nodding up the cliff to the black smoke rising from burning homes. Lanterns, torches, either deliberately or in battle's chaos, had found food. "That is our answer."

Quik sent the two most able hunters running down the slope to find torches, while he used his gauntlets to thrash the bushes, the grasses, the ferns and small trees to throw across the road. The brush already covering traps would serve as well. The gauntlets weren't axes, but they scraped and flung well enough, the last two hunters gathering up what Quik threshed and running it along the road.

Would it burn long enough to stall the Najahn for long? On its own, no, but if Quik could start a big enough blaze?

The Najahn crested the slope as the two hunters came running back with their torches. Shields up, voulges out, their ranks reassembled after passing the pit traps, the Najahn moved with deliberate speed, a pace that, with a shout, slowed as they saw Quik standing, alone, in the road's center. Brush covered the ground at his feet, both gauntlets hung off his hands at his waist.

Quik snarled up at the purple and black warriors, even as the older hunter whispered that the torches had arrived.

Now came the show.

"For Mottilan! For Vis!" Quik roared, raising his gauntlets in a two-clawed call to the sky.

As he did, the hunters threw both torches, the flames whirling in the afternoon breeze. They landed near Quik's feet and found a friendly home. Sparks and smoke erupted, the dried brush covering the traps offering enough catch to get the sputtering, green leaves, sticks, and branches a chance.

The Najahn split, several chakram and crossbow wielders stepping before the voulges to take simple shots. Quik did make an easy target, smoke or no, standing there in the road's middle. So he took a single step back, and disappeared.

If he'd not used the gauntlets to catch himself and Sawi on the Great Sana's side, Quik wouldn't have tried dropping into the pitfall trap. Instead, the triumphant gesture let the hunter get the gauntlets where he needed them, where their metal tips dug into the earth and stopped Quik's fall. Quarrels and a single chakram flew overhead, striking up dirt and carving lines into the road. None hit him.

Lying in wait while the smoke grew sparked as an appealing idea, except the Najahn had already seen enough Vis pitfall traps to guess Quik's disappearance wasn't supernatural skill. So Quik pulled himself up near the burning debris, and kicked off after the other hunters. Behind, the Najahn resumed their march.

Quik, almost crawling, hesitated. Glanced back at the armored column and gauged their speed.

Too fast. The fire wouldn't have time to spread. Nor would his hunters have time to light the rest of the blazes, turn Mottilan into the scarring inferno it needed to be to buy enough time.

Deshiva had asked them to give Vis a glorious death. Quik had given an oath to Wax, to buy his brother time. What was it Gladdring had said, that his brother was on his way to Kance? An isle under siege by the Najahn?

Hurt them here, and Quik might yet help Wax. Not as the hunter wanted, perhaps, but as the gods demanded.

"I told you, brother, I would never abandon you," Quik muttered, and turned not left, down the road towards the city, but right, towards a cliffside scarred with brush and stone.

Soon, Vis would welcome another worthy son.

CHAPTER 47

THIEVES OF JOY

As idyllic strolls went, stumbling along a rocky, rough sloping cavern left much to be desired. Maena, though, didn't notice, her mind so happily wrapped in a beautiful aura thanks to her right hand and its unbreakable grip on the squishy, serene fiend next to her.

The cloud creature hadn't maintained its perfect appearance after crossing through the gate, its white and gray fluff earnings slopped mud, dust, and a few missing chunks from falling pieces of cave debris. A look back would confirm the meandering mass trailing them suffered from similar fates, but the mouthless, wordless, bundles of bliss didn't complain. They bobbed after Maena, trailing Haggerth as she pulled the unconscious man after her.

Ahead, the collapsed rock sheltering the Tamas motes and their gateway relaxed via crumbling fragments. Gnarled and glittering with exposed minerals, the long slabs that survived their initial plummet were breaking apart as the ground continued to shake. Some of these pieces would probably fall back through the gate and mash those shrouded terrors waiting inside.

If Maena was especially lucky, the rock and mud might seal the gate all over again and leave those things locked in their dying world.

And, given how good she felt, why not throw luck in the mix?

Not even the sight beyond the sheltered slabs could throw Maena off her high: her chosen path, along the chamber's outer wall, continued with occasional collapsed scars, lines she'd have to work over, but not impossible. No, what would've prompted more concern if Maena was able to feel it, was the sheer chaos waiting near the chamber's southern exit, the one that used to lead back to the caverns and the Whent fortification.

That tunnel had disappeared. Blocked in with fallen rubble and, if Maena was seeing right, patched shut with hasty Whent mortar. A few bits and pieces remained of the firewalker's encampment, their oozing machines and water-diving spheres otherwise crushed to bent and broken bits. Instead, the chamber's exit sat much closer to Maena's own location, a rough oblong entry leading into the dark.

Right, if Maena had her geography in line, to Dead City.

The hole, not much larger than the cavern exit she'd just scrabbled from, wasn't empty and waiting for Maena's crew. It crawled with fiends. Creatures Maena couldn't name, that resembled flailing, bird-like monsters with twitching claws for legs, pressed into the gap and whatever lay beyond. Bodies by the dozens, hundreds lay at the pool's edge beneath the hole, a marker of fiend fighting fiend.

As options went, it seemed like a poor choice, and even

in her euphoric confidence, Maena looked about for a better option. None presented itself: crossing the chamber into darkness—indeed, the chamber's sole light came from the firewalker remnants, holing up near the patched cavern, their glow flickering through the chamber and casting everything in oranges and yellows—gave nothing save a dark drowning or rock crushing as a reward. Behind Maena waited the Tamas gate and a rubble wall.

"So we press on," Maena said, both to Haggerth and the cloud creature.

Neither objected.

The way was neither fast nor pleasant. Maena's hunger and thirst attacked her pleasure, flashes breaking in to declare her devastated body wouldn't be able to stand much longer, but those twinges were like the stumbles and falls along the stones as they walked: temporary, inconvenient, ignored.

Her slow progress had an advantage: by the time they reached the hole, the fiends had all pressed through. None had taken their place, though the frothing waters to Maena's right suggested plenty would be coming. A chance, then, to make it through.

What the Dead City, Jochi, and anyone else would do when Maena walked in at the head of a fiend armada, one beautiful and bringing happiness with every touch, was a problem the Rana captain decided not to worry about.

"Right through here then," Maena said, her cracked voice barely a rasp.

Haggerth, possibly in response, possibly as a result of whatever terrible things were wracking his body, groaned.

The cloud creatures bobbed in silence.

Maena, setting her knees against the rock so she could ascend without breaking grips on either Haggerth or the cloud creature, looked up towards the opening. Not just a hole, large enough to fit big monsters, and broken bigger with rampaging entries, going by the snapped stone chunks, the clawed coughs, and rounded gaps. Yet, for all its size, Maena found her way blocked.

The bird-like fiends were coming back.

Squawking in watery panic, the monsters raced into the gap, barreling down on Maena. The Rana captain pulled herself and the cloud creature back, falling over Haggerth and huddling close. The oncoming fiends poured around them, flooding into the water, until they found contact with the cloud creatures. Despite a few white fluffy bits getting tossed into the air, the frantic noises quieted, simmered to nothing more than dry sighs.

Maena sat up, saw why: the cloud creatures had caught the fiends in their friendly trap. The bird fiends that'd touched the cloud creatures stood still, their eyes half-closed, ragged, stubby wingtips touching the cloud creatures. For their part, the bobbing Tamas creations continued drifting forward from the cavern, floating around the bird-like fiends, wrapping the beasts in the best trap Maena could imagine.

She smiled. Here was a solution. If these cloud creatures could be tamed, why, nobody would need fear a fiend again. Tamas could prove the antidote, the answer to the isles' coming catastrophe.

Because, Maena recognized, bombing out the gates had failed. Fiends were still coming in. But a hero didn't fold just because their ideas didn't pan out. They kept trying until they found success, and Maena wouldn't stop now. Her debts were still outstanding.

She turned back to the gap, began climbing again, only to find the hole filled in with new bodies. Not fiends this time, not unfamiliar limbs or slobbering, fanged mouths. Instead, Maena looked up into a bearded, bloody, angry visage she knew well.

"Rana," Jochi breathed, his axes drawn, eyes narrowed. "Of all the people I would expect to find down here, why am I not surprised it's you?"

Maena flickered a smile, started to reply, when a warrior near Jochi cursed, pointed a blade behind her. The Rana captain, letting Haggerth's hand go, turned, and saw Tamas's other side: those soul-sucking dark spirits flowed from the collapsed side cavern, scooping up the cloud creatures, the bird-like fiends as they went. A grim wave sweeping their way.

This time, the flash breaking Maena's bliss lingered, had heat. She gulped, looked back to Jochi.

"Rockbiter, we have to run."

CHAPTER 48

FLIGHT PLAN

After a lifetime and death filled with harrowing, thrilling moments, Svarde found the breathless seconds after the geyser launched his glider into the sky up near the top of his list. Strapped in, repeating instructions delivered by a teacher who appeared to have just stumbled from her bed, Svarde couldn't resist breaking into a hoarse howl as the landscape receded beneath him. The searing air heated the protective pads beneath his body while billowing out the thin canvas overhead, wanting to turn Svarde vertical and prevented from the same by Svarde's own body weight, by his relentless forward lean.

A dance he had to continue until the glider went high enough to coast Svarde into the dawn ambush.

His target, the Sky Palace spire, lunged upward, climbing in its balcony-bedecked stone. Glass chambers dotted the mountain's sides here and there, odd nodules designed to awe guests by letting them sleep floating in the air. Svarde gave several a startled awakening as he rose, the glider's scalloped triangle interrupting what was otherwise a beautiful sunrise.

Then again, Svarde was doing them a favor: waking up now might give them a chance to flee before the battle.

The geyser's strength petered out after too few moments, letting Kance's ever-present wind take hold. The glider shivered, the canvas snapping as it settled into its new guide. Svarde held onto the bar with his right hand, kept his left on the blade's hilt, though the straps around his legs and chest made grip strength an unnecessary aid. All that protection would make a combat landing tricky, though the teacher suggested a strong yank would undo the clinched ropes.

Something Svarde would put to the test soon. The barbarian turned his glider, leaning per the teacher's fast instruction, to the east. A lazy turn meant to while away a few minutes until Ami could catch the geyser's next eruption, join him up here. The slow wander laid Kance out beneath Svarde, its mountains and their winding passes continuing on to the east. Green fields, bearing spring's first plantings, laid over ridged plateaus. Other gliders already soared out that way too, though not for sight-seeing: Svarde saw the riders emptying bags onto those fields, a faster way to fertilize, to plant, especially for an isle lacking Whent's plowing beasts.

The sight brought with it an odd surge of pride in the isles as a whole, this land that Svarde had dedicated himself, multiple times over, to defending. Not always in the best way, not always with the right methods, but he had tried, and these isles, with their clever people, their wonders left by the gods, deserved to be fought for.

His partner in so much of that fighting soared up with a mild hiss, her glider a yellowed tan to Svarde's soft green. Ami didn't follow Svarde's contemplative loop, instead angling hard north towards the Sky Palace. She had Svarde beat on height, but Ami sacrificed that advantage for speed, screaming in at a balcony she'd decided to target.

They had no maps, no diagrams, no real idea how high the geyser could push them. As strategy went, the pair were to crash into the Sky Palace and fight their way to Gladdring as fast as they could, killing as few Kance soldiers as possible on the way.

The first part would be easy enough. The second?

The balcony came at them kindly, a white stone railing dotted with young potted plants, flower buds just starting to show. A beautiful terrace, and one far too small for their gliders. Svarde thought to yell as much, but then, what was the point?

This wasn't a smooth operation, but a blunt one. Ami reached up as her glider shot in, pulling a rope that tightened the glider for storage, narrowing the canvas wing to a line. She plunged, bounced off the stones, and smashed into the room beyond. The windowed wood doors blew apart, the glider's tempered glass frame shattered into a million sparks, and Svarde saw no more as Ami's landing passed into the room's shadow.

An awful-looking thing, and one Svarde was about to repeat.

The barbarian muttered a Foti prayer, reached up to the same tightening rope Ami had pulled as the balcony came screaming in. He tugged, the wing snapped shut, and Svarde dropped . . . Too quick.

As stone railings went, the balcony's pristine, white-washed barrier numbered among the more beautiful. Little wind gusts had been carved into its length, such that looking at it would send you along an ongoing surf from one end to the next.

Svarde completed that design with a bone-crunching

crash, splitting the railing and sending his glider into a swirling, cracking spin across tiles already coated with Ami's debris. The Guardian's left hand kept its grip, even as the Vis energy in the blade surged forth, leaping at the cuts, bruises, and at least one cracked rib he'd earned in the landing.

Okay, so he'd wrecked the glider, destroyed the railing, and possibly rendered himself useless in a fight, but for a first time flight, that wasn't so bad, was it?

On his back, Svarde took a good look at the room around him. A painted ceiling showcased clouds interlaced with sky diamonds. Scattered furniture, most overturned, and a broken table suggested the place was some sort of sitting room, a place for casual meetings or evening drinks. Either way, at this hour, it was deserted, and no screams echoed down the halls.

Small blessings.

"Well that was a terrible idea," Ami said, and Svarde looked over to see her rising, brushing glass off her flying trousers with her left hand. That done, she reached to her awkward right arm and, with a grimace, yanked hard on her right wrist. Her shoulder snapped back into place, the Guardian snarled a curse, then sighed. "Even the skars don't help with that."

"Just need to get more of'em then," Svarde replied, sitting up, feeling a beat body stretch and stab as he did so.

Vis's power, built into the blade, attacked the pain, almost tickling as his body knit its lifeless self back together. Svarde hadn't yet maxed out their efforts, though he supposed the fall from this same palace must've come close. More than a day lying in the dirt suggested even his blade would slow after a while.

But not yet, not from this fall alone.

They stumbled around for too long, ditching off the glider bits, and buying the skars time to bring their broken parts back from the edge. Svarde kept waiting for Kance soldiers to show, for some ultimatum to appear, but the room's lone entry, a doorless arch into a spire-spanning hallway, remained deserted.

"Either everyone's sleeping in late, or we're getting set up," Svarde said, lifting the blade onto his shoulder and heading towards the entry. His footsteps crunched glass, wood into the tile.

"Knowing Gladdring, the latter." Ami's cuts, unlike Svarde's, still glistened with drying blood. She stood as tall as he did, though, with a large Whent blade in both hands. "I was hoping they'd attack by now, give us a path to follow."

"We'll carve our own, then."

"Just like the old days, right Svarde?"

Svarde grinned, started off. "Remember what happened when anything got in our way back then?"

"We cut'em in half."

That habit found its first target as they rounded the arch into the hallway proper. Decked with paintings and mantels stuffed with glassy treasures, the Sky Palace caught sunlight coming through the terraces and cast it everywhere, rainbow prisms flickering. To the left, the hallway ended fast at the curving spire's edge, another terrace giving a view towards the Kance harbor and the ships beyond. To the right, the smoothed stone tiles continued to the elevators at the spire's center.

Waiting, there, was a greeting.

The man stood, coated in glossy Kance armor. A rapier in each hand, the weapon hilts as gold as anything Svarde had ever seen. A faceguard swept across his helm, leaving only the soldier's eyes visible. He waited as Svarde and Ami approached, making no sound.

"Who're you, then?" Ami asked as they came within a few strides.

The soldier said nothing. Watched.

"Not the talkative type?" Ami asked again, sliding her legs out into a proper stance. "Then let me tell you, right now, that standing where you're standing is a fast way to Noctia. You're not going to win this one, so how about you turn around, scamper down those stairs with those pretty swords of yours, and let us go?"

Again, no reply.

"Either Gladdring's found some loyal mutes," Svarde said, "or he's used the skars to crush this one's mind."

Ami clicked her tongue, "Is my friend right? You have nothing left up there?"

Silence.

"Think he's made his choice, Ami."

"Think he has."

Svarde took two steps to the right, Ami matched him to the left. The soldier and his rapiers stayed still between them. The two Guardians shared a glance, a nod.

The path to Gladdring would be paved in blood. Best get to it.

CHAPTER 49
DEATH'S DESIRES

He'd been doing it all wrong, Wax realized, as Jochi and his warriors took the young Vis beyond the Whent lines. While the Dead City earned, again, its namesake, Wax did little except keep from slipping on the blood-soaked avenue. Whent blades and axes, crossbows and mining picks delivered coordinated death on the fiends foolish enough charge their way. Tentacles, claws, tongues, or teeth, it didn't matter: the monsters met an unceremonious end.

Yet Wax didn't see victorious smiles on the faces around him, the ranks rotating to put fresh arms and legs in front after every skirmish. Songs didn't rise, jokes made no appearance. If Torny had been laying waste like this, she'd have been cracking insults every minute. Bliss would've been signing her staff's kill count. Even Eujo might've put up a grin.

"You celebrate victories," Jochi said, breathing hard after they'd just sent another flock of odd, bird-like fiends scampering in retreat. "In this war, so far, there haven't been any."

"What was that, then?" Wax asked.

"A break. They'll be back, or something else will take their place. The fiends don't stop, Wax, which means we don't sleep. You do your job, and I'll have every Whent down here raising a flagon to your name before nightfall."

That nightfall was an impossible concept down here didn't seem to matter.

As for Wax's job?

The chamber wasn't the shining home Wax had imagined, even with the constant quakes. Jochi had described the place as Noctia's heart, or maybe her soul. Where she kept the homes the gods left behind. If it'd been that way once . . . It never would come close again.

Crumbling stones and dirt waterfalls rained down as far as Wax could see, which, given the dark encroaching from everywhere beyond their torches and the small glow off to the left, where the firewalkers were said to be hunkered down, wasn't far. Splashes echoed off the gouged walls as giant rocks slammed into the pool, the ceiling above so blown apart that Wax would've thought the pool already filled in.

The gods left those gates wide open.

Streaming from one dark corner off to the right, presumably from one of those gates, came an odd, bouncing line of cloud-like fiends. Their silver-gray fluff had grit and grime all over it, and some had chunks missing from their spherical shapes, but they otherwise chained behind a bedraggled woman, one whose skin and clothes were shredded, who looked like she should be dead. The woman limped their way, struggled over rough rubble, and through it all she kept one hand gripping one of those fiends and the other . . . Was that a body?

The bird fiends the Whent had chased away fled back

through the bounding fluffs when something odd happened: the skittish creatures simply stopped here and there, coming to a confused halt amid the bobbing gray spheres. If they were being attacked, eaten, Wax couldn't tell. If he had to guess, by the way the bird fiends slumped their shoulders, closed their eyes, they looked happy?

"Now that is someone I did not expect to see," Jochi said, standing just ahead and to Wax's right, looking out the hole. Warriors flanked him on either side, weapons ready, while the rest of the group fanned out behind, grabbing rest or water. "Stay back, Wax. Maena's dangerous."

Wax didn't have much room to retreat as Jochi knelt, said something to the wounded woman, who'd dragged herself near the hole's entry. Wax kept his eyes on the fiends gathering behind, was the first to call out a warning at the dark, ghostly swarm drifting from the very same cavern the woman—Maena?—had lurched from moments ago. These monsters, which looked like tattered rags covering darker opposites of those white-gray fluff balls, didn't share the placid aura coming off their counterparts.

Instead, the dark fiends landed on the brighter ones, those fluffy white bodies crossing over with jagged amber lightning. Those cracks spread, covering the cloud creatures in crackling lines, only the light didn't fly free, didn't spread out like the thunderstorms of Wax's home. Instead, it curled, fed right into the dark fiends. When the light disappeared beneath those holed, torn black rags, it didn't come back out. As the lightning faded, a shrunken shell remained, the tattered remnants of the cloud creature dark and ruined, but not dead. Instead, it floated up, joining the streaming fiends heading their way.

"Arms up!" Jochi shouted. The warlord turned back to his band and repeated the command, even as the warriors beside him reached down and pulled Maena up into the hole. "We hold here, where the gap's smallest!"

Meana screamed. The woman's eyes went wide, her voice, only a harsh rasp, broke. The warriors pulled her through the hole as the Whent force drew up, crossbows loosing the first shots at the strange fiends. Maena's hands reached back towards the chamber, towards the fluffy fiend floating there, already among the last of its kind as the ragged wave approached. Amber lightning flashed. The darkness grew.

Wax saw his moment. This, this was what the Aegis was meant for. He stepped around the warriors hauling Maena, now twitching, retching, in apparent agony, away from the hole. Jochi stayed at his side, the warlord's eyes going down the slope to another human lying there, unconscious.

"This is a war," Jochi growled as Wax looked at the oncoming fiends, felt the skars surge in his mind. "Your skars ready for it?"

"Are you?"

"Since the damn day I was born," Jochi said, glaring at the fiends, as if his will alone would slow them down. The clacking crossbows certainly had not, the quarrels vanishing into those fiends without much effect. "Looks like this might be your time, Vis."

Wax nodded, sure enough of that. He'd had good food, water, and enough rest to do what Catya demanded. Now was the moment. Bring the skars together, banish the fiends, break the gates, and save the isles.

"Go get your friend," Wax muttered. "I'll handle these."

Jochi took Wax at his word, dropped his axes and slid out the hole. Wax stretched out a hand towards the oncoming, drifting dark wave. They'd devoured the birdlike fiends too, Wax noticed, though those hadn't turned into more floating monsters. Instead, those fiends collapsed, eyes rolled up and limbs still.

The skars raged at the sight, Foti clambering for a fiery blast. Rana demanded Wax grab the pool, wash the monsters away, while Whent found fissures along the trembling rock above: burying the fiends would be easy. And Noctia always waited, hungry and ready to sap the fiends of anything and everything that kept them alive.

Those were all separate acts. Wax needed more, needed to bring them together. He pressed against their urges, like bending a daydream. Collapse the cavern, but use the pool's water to flood the gaps. Melt it together with flame, and—

Jochi cursed. He had both hands on the body, was dragging it up to the hole, when the last clouded fiend, the one Maena had been holding, broke into amber lightning before him. A ragged void swooped in at the warlord, and Noctia took hold. Quit Wax's careful symphony and sent out an invisible bolt, striking the fiend and siphoning its essence back into Wax.

The Vis Renewal felt two things at once, like getting punched in the gut while kissed on the cheek. Happiness and pain, terror and hope. His vision blurred, the skars shouted, and Noctia fed those stones fresh, devoured energy.

Foti spoke first, fiery gouts spraying from Wax's fingertips into the oncoming fiends. Those flimsy rags blazed up, the dark swirls beneath shivering, yet still coming forward. Whent struck next as Jochi pulled himself up next to Wax, the warlord straining to pull his friend up after him, other warriors reaching in to help. The rock around them exploded, cracks racing up the unstable walls and hollowing out chunks far above. Stones crushed the burning fiends, battered them apart, but still more drifted in.

Kance had the answer, summoning up a heavy gust that blew the closest fiends back, where Rana picked up the pool to soak and suck the monsters beneath the churning waters. Wax fell to his knees, his breath going shallow, the skars continuing to spit fire, throw rock, blow and drown the dark wave.

Noctia, again, was ready. Fresh fiends neared, and Wax reached for them, tore their awful energy away and drew it into himself. The skars thundered, ready burn Wax to ash to do the same to the fiends. Behind him, crossbows fired again. Two warriors, either stupid or brave sidled up next to Wax with Whent blades high, stabbing them towards the tattered revenants billowing in.

So many. And beyond them, so many more.

The Tamas skar snuck in behind the raging noise in the Renewal's head, suggesting something else, a reminder, an urge to unite the stones. The gods together, as they'd always meant to be.

"Give me time," Wax said, shuddering as he spoke, and he felt a heavy hand push the Vis back from the gap.

"You will have it," Jochi said, his friend deposited next to the still-screaming Maena behind Wax. "As long as we can give."

Those ragged terrors swooped in, dodging sword thrusts, taking crossbow quarrels to their voids, and feasted on Whent souls.

Beneath the rage, Wax listened for the cadence. The pulse coming from the skars as they shoved his mind towards ruin, destruction, salvation. Foti hammered a steady refrain, constant and crackling. Whent swept in behind, slow and heavy. Rana and Kance skittered in staccato bursts. Tamas and Vis hung to the middle, looping through with smooth melodies. And Noctia?

Noctia blared her demands at random, overtaking the others before disappearing, leaving the echoes of her hunger.

He'd never picked them apart like this, and as he did so, Wax felt them responding to his attention. Their sonorous feeling glowed as Wax turned his focus to each skar in turn, and though Wax wouldn't call himself a musician, Kitaye had been a city of song. Telling Foti to slow its rumble, for Kance and Rana to separate their solos, for Noctia to slam a climax, Wax did these things with his eyes closed, his ears shut to the battle around him.

Whent bodies knocked Wax around, with hands steadying the Renewal if he ever stumbled. Jochi's bellowing orders came through dim, while Maena's high-pitched rasps continued, the woman right at Wax's feet. He pushed that world away. It wasn't important. Not now.

The skars fell in line, an ordered march of power. The synchronicity happened all at once, with no hint, no ramp up. In one moment, Foti fed its energy to Rana, then to Tamas, Kance, Vis, Whent, and, in a tumbling crescendo exploding through Wax's mind, body, like he'd jumped into the coldest sea, the hottest fire, Noctia struck the final chord.

In that moment, sharp doubt dashed in: Catya had suggested the symphony, she'd never told Wax the order.

The skars, unified, released. Wax opened his eyes and saw nothing, but he felt those lines, those invisible Noctia lines launching out from him. Six, stretching ahead and out, searching for the gates. A warrior hacking at a ragged fiend saw her enemy burst alight in purple-black flame, saw the stones behind it dissolve as a line lanced through. The ground quaked. Maena screamed again.

And Wax followed the lines, all of them, all at once, to those swirling motes. The lines swept in, brushing those swirling lights, tracing lines between them, connecting not glimmers, no, but skars. Shimmering skars, stuck holding open the way to their gods' homes. Noctia had bound them, had brought them within herself at the last, and Wax found them, felt them, and heard their songs. They swept back along the Noctia lines, their meters, beats, voices giving Wax a choice.

Leave the gates alone in their eternal chorus, or let Noctia finish the song, let the skar stream along those lines and shatter those swirling gates.

He had only one answer.

Wax gave the skars to Noctia, and the goddess, ever hungry, ate.

CHAPTER 50
CLIFF'S END

The hunter didn't flee. He drew, he enticed, he baited, and flew.

Freed from his fellow hunters, from the chains keeping him to traps and a set, slow path, Quik rediscovered dormant instincts as he leapt, swung, and pulled himself along the cliffs. Mottilan's descending road ran along a rough-edged mountainside, one with a steep slope long hammered out with foot and hoof into a series of switchbacks. Mottilan's defenders had forced the Najahn to grind their way along that winding path with their ambushes, their traps, and now, the burning lines.

Quik would add something more in his last efforts: a tease.

He used shrubs and trees for cover, guessing at handholds, gouging his legs, toes, and palms with frantic jumps as the Najahn flung chakrams, shot quarrels, and shouted at Quik to surrender. That last must've seemed obvious, as Quik wasn't heading towards his allies, but instead cutting back up the cliff, behind the Najahn lines.

Some dim hope lingered between Quik's jumps, his

fakes right to leap left, or to drop along a tree trunk and sprint behind a burning home's shell. If Quik could get far enough, he might outrun the Najahn columns, disappear into the jungle west of Mottilan, then cut north and down the sheer cliffs to the shallows, and from there to Sawi, Annalyse, and the others waiting at the seaside caves.

An unlikely goal and one slipping further and further away with every level Quik climbed: the purple and black didn't end. Sure, their ranks thinned as Quik scampered further from the front, and the shots didn't come so fast, as soldiers unprepared for ambush struggled to raise and fire crossbows, much less the razor discs, before Quik vanished up the wall.

Soon Quik would be at the top, and he'd arrive with his legs and arms burning—his gauntlets, their points so recently sharpened, were already battered to nubs—and yet more Najahn waited for him.

Because this wasn't just a culling, it was an occupation. The Najahn weren't planning to erase Mottilan from the map, but install new leadership. They'd already done that to Kitaye, and the thought threw more fuel into Quik's fire, ever churning on his anger, his oaths, his will to see his isle thrive.

A quarrel slammed off the sun-stained limestone before his right hand, spraying Quik's face with dust, and the hunter dove off the rock wall. Weedy, wet, and short grass greeted him as the hunter rolled onto the last, or first, depending on your perspective, landing leaving Mottilan. Quik stepped fast, curling his back to the building's rear wall, all of two or three strides from the cliffside.

The stone house hadn't been burned, its position as the first ambush point, back when Deshiva and Quik still had more certain hopes, saving it. Above his own hard breathing, Quik heard the shouts marking his position, archers taking up aim along the sides. He could run back to the cliff, but a few more jumps would put him in the open with just a grassy lip to reach for. An easy shot, without brush cover. Going back to the left, swapping to a descent, might buy Quik a few brief moments before the net closed completely. To the right, along the house's rear would bring him to the gentle slope to the road, pass cutting through the mountains.

No cover there either.

A noise drew Quik's eyes up, to a second-story window. Shattered during the fighting, voices came out, one a stern Najahn and the other an exhausted Vis. Quik didn't have to catch more than a sentence to know he heard an interrogation, one offering a chance.

Or, at least, a better death.

Quik spun, jumped, and used what the gauntlets had left to snag a hold on the irregular stone blocks making up the house. The mortar chipped away as he jammed his gauntlets, his claws, into the rock, while Quik kicked himself up with his toes. Mottilan's penchant for plainness —the city saved its creativity for its ships—helped Quik, as no frills or overhangs obstructed his rapid rise, putting him, sweating, tense, and ready, at the broken window in only a few breaths.

Inside, a single thatched chair sat upright in a room otherwise occupied by a straw mat and several baskets. On the chair, wrists already rope-bound, sat a silent, older Mottilan. The man's gaze went to his Najahn interrogators, a pair of soldiers who'd ditched their helmets for more imperious sneers. Their voulges rested against the wall near the lone doorway to Quik's left. One soldier leaned into their prisoner, delivering some spitting verdict Quik didn't catch.

The other, across the room, saw Quik, and pointed.

Getting singled out by a Najahn promised many things, most of them awful, but Quik took the gesture as an invitation. Throwing his left palm flat on the window sill, Quik pulled himself through with a tumble. As his back and butt hit the wood floor, Quik kicked out, catching the interrogating Najahn mid-turn. The plate leggings took the hit, blunting any damage Quik's toenails might cause, but doing little to deflect the pressure: the Najahn's right knee bent inward and the man cursed.

Quik rebounded off the kick, rolling to his left and pushing to a rise, his back to the Najahn for a too-short moment. Their clanking armor gave away their movements, and Quik spun into a hard right jab. The Najahn with the bent knee had turned Quik's way, drawing the back-up blade on his waist, a move that would've made more sense had he left the hunter's reach first. Instead, he turned his unprotected head right into Quik's whirling strike.

A Vis learned to live with a hunt's savagery. Not to relish the strike and what followed, but to accept it as a sign of victory, an opportunity to press on.

Quik did so, drawing back his gauntlet, sliding it down to tug, sever the ropes binding the Mottilan's hands. The other Najahn, seeing a visceral horror no Noctia training, with its assurances about the Najahn's invincibility, would've prepared him for, stood still and screamed.

The Mottilan ended his captor's torment, rising and striking the Najahn square in the throat. The scream became a gargle, became a slow end. Quik didn't pause to witness it.

If the prisoner was smart, he'd wait for the Najahn to come back, declare himself innocent.

Quik himself had no time for allies. Not now.

Beyond the room, the stone house revealed a small second level. A ladder dropped to the first floor from a narrow trap door, with two other bedrooms completing the second story. Neither seemed occupied, though red stains and broken bows suggested more sacrifices from Deshiva's band had met their ends up here. Quik considered the ladder, heard Najahn clustering beneath it. The first metal boots hit the low rung.

Not the way.

Instead, the hunter flung his look across the level and ran. He didn't bother kicking the ladder, going more for speed and uncertainty, angling towards another open, broken, square window on the far side. This bedroom matched the other, empty save the sprawling blood stains. Quik slipped off a prayer to Vis and kept going, tensing his thighs and diving right through the open window.

He flew into too much air, too much space. The yard around the house gave Quik no cover. His only asset was speed, surprise, and, as Quik fell, those two gave him enough, just enough. A chakram lanced where he'd been, cutting the air behind him as Quik struck the grass in a flailing roll. Quarrels whizzed by, one drawing a red line— yet another—along Quik's back. Another embedded itself in Quik's shoulder as he scrambled into the brush, the hunter's Mottilan weave doing just enough to let Quik smack the quarrel free.

Blood welled, another sting joined the litany.

Quik tore through the narrow brush band separating the house's north side from the road, lumbering over sticks and ferns with feet, legs no longer fresh enough to dance like a hunter's ought. He broke through in a stumble, a branch clinging to his hair and a thorny stalk dragging from his left leg.

Distractions.

The hunter held his course, broke across the road. To his left, a Najahn supply train halted, Tamas ponies brought in to haul the carts whinnying as fresh shouts landed in Quik's thundering ears. On his right, running soldiers chased, took aim, fired. Quarrels flew, skittered across the dirt before Quik, behind him, and into his side.

He twisted with the hit, vision flashing red. Instincts took over, keeping Quik on his feet, a whirling dance leaving him on the road's far side. He crashed into undergrowth, ferns, branches, leaves giving Quik cover.

He had no direction now, only to run. The old idea of sacrifice, of an honorable death skittered away there amid the vines, weeds, and green. Quik didn't want spears in his skin, didn't want a quarrel in his chest, to fall into Noctia's cold embrace.

Not yet. Not yet.

So he churned, windmilling his gauntlets to press him through. Behind, Najahn soldiers struggled to follow in their armor. Curses mingled with hard orders to keep after the Vis, to chase him down. To kill on sight.

Yet, Quik was gaining ground. His side was slick with his own blood, but the hunter, for the moment, lived. With life, came chance, came hope, came . . . A cliff.

The foliage gave way to a narrowing precipice, one dominated by grasses, weeds, and an odd machine: a crane with a cage lingering over the cliff's edge. Quik, lungs heaving, stared at the thing like a broken promise. He'd fought, run, dodged all this way only for this?

Stumbling forward, the jungle behind him filling with

Najahn, Quik came up to the crane. Far below, Mottilan burned. The others had done their job, then, and their last remnants streamed onto ships. The hunter picked out Deshiva's archers, returning fire at Najahn vessels. Pesky, but not enough. The purple and black ran across the waves, hunting the fishing boats, the slow cargo ships.

How many of his isles' people would die today?

Quik shook his head, turned back to the forest. The first Najahn were emerging, shaking themselves free from Vis's last grasp. Many Vis would die today, but the isle would live, and with their god, Vis would fight the Najahn forever. His god had defeated Noctia once, and Quik's isle would do so again.

Even if he didn't live to see it.

Thrusting his gauntleted hands up into the air, Quik let out a loud whoop. A hunter's cry, a hero's shout, a Vis call.

CHAPTER 51
DENIED

She didn't choose to scream anymore. It happened, her body wracked with burns, broken bones, cuts, and bruises. Thirst and hunger. Exhaustion should have claimed Maena. Death should have, and she wished for it there on that cavern floor, with the Whent around her falling back. The dark fiends flowed through the hole, siphoning away in their hideous sucking howls, any Whent who stood their ground. Even Jochi, there in the center, swinging his axes as if they mattered a damn, disappeared as the fiends surrounded him.

The only one they avoided, who stood out to Maena's blurred vision, was the strange young man standing just before her. The two fiends who'd come close to him had gone up in purple flames, vanishing to nothing more than a few ash flakes. After that, the fiends had left him alone, and so he'd stood stock still, seemingly oblivious to everything around him.

She'd lost the cloud creatures, and with that, Maena's only chance at sanity. She screamed again, a tremor rising from her leg and spasming through her throat. Another would come in moments, between wheezing breaths. To her right, somehow, lay Haggerth. Still sweaty, cold, and unconscious. A measure of peace in that, at least.

Maena shifted her eyes back to the young man. Another fiend, perhaps overcome with the wild moment, attacked him. Set that dark visage before the man, twisted its shapeless void to match the man's face, only for black and purple flames to rise up from nothing and consume the creature. And in that, Maena found her answer, her escape.

She had done what she promised. Broke the chain. Kept her oaths, as best Maena could.

Would the isles remember her? Would Svarde?

Not all legends needed to be told.

Maena surged up, bones and muscles cracking. She lunged for the young man, diving onto his back, begging for those flames, for that beautiful oblivion.

And bounced off him to the ground, drawing a yelp, an agonized curse from the Rana. She rolled off him, waiting for one of those fiends to take her next, but the ramshackle cavern appeared clean, clear. The orange glow from Whent lanterns met no interruptions, and Maena heard no swinging axes, cutting blades, or clacking crossbows. The sheer surprise dampened the pain, nothing making sense.

"Hey," said the man she'd tackled. "I think I got them." His voice wavered with exhaustion's timbre, something Maena could empathize with. "Here, I think you might need this more than me."

Maena felt her scorched hand pried open, a warm, smooth stone dropped into her palm. A wordless curiosity flushed her mind, and for a terrifying second, Maena thought her split self had returned, until she realized the voice didn't speak in words she knew, or in words at all, really. Instead, the warmth spread throughout her body, quieting the spastic pains and replacing them with itching, with healing's first twinges.

"Never felt that before, huh?" The young man said, crouching over her, a wincing grin on his face. This close, Maena noticed the man's inked lines, sigils Maena had rarely seen but understood. Only, what was a Vis doing here? "It's a skar. A Vis skar, actually. It'll heal you up as best it can, though, uh, you're looking pretty rough."

"Thanks," Maena muttered, closing her eyes.

"I'm saying it'll take a few days. Maybe a week. But we've got the time now," the man stood, rocks shifting, though Maena kept her eyes closed, fell into that warmth. "Jochi, I think I closed them all."

"What?" Jochi's voice, just as tired as her own. "I see you closed this damn hole. Means we don't know where the fiends are going to come next."

"No, I'm saying there's not going to be anymore fiends. It's over. We're safe."

Maena reran that word a few times, marveled that she *could* rerun it. A few moments ago she'd been ready to throw everything away, and now, despite her back lying on hard ground, despite rockbiters all around her, Maena was damn glad she'd failed.

Which left one question. She forced open her eyes, wet her lips, and saw the Whent warriors slapping backs, tending to minor wounds, and, Jochi, kneeling over the last mystery.

"Is Haggerth alive?"

CHAPTER 52
ANIMALS

Gladdring's plan might've worked if he'd been facing normal adversaries. The Kance swordsman, rapiers out, might've been the best fighter on the island. Svarde, though, didn't play by the usual rules.

"Stay back," the barbarian slipped to Ami, before leaning into a lumbering run towards the swordsman, framed in beautiful morning sunlight amid the Sky Palace's glittering halls.

The swordsman bent one knee, not quite to a crouch, and Svarde saw what was coming, did nothing to prevent it. The Foti Guardian closed within a couple strides, and, like a viper, the swordsman struck. He unlimbered into a forward lunge, his right rapier leading to dive deep into Svarde's chest. The left followed with an equally mortal stab into Svarde's gut. Both delivered dull pain, both should've killed the barbarian at a stroke.

Unfortunately for the swordsman, he'd neglected the only thing that might actually kill Svarde: tearing the big blade away.

As the rapiers dove in, Svarde made a choice, and he

acted on it, smashing his sword's black, skar-infused hilt into the Kance soldier's helmeted skull. The hit drove Svarde's attacker to the ground, whereupon Svarde followed up with a hard kick, snapping the Kance fighter's head back, those eyes rolling up and out.

"That's really not fair," Ami said, coming up next to Svarde as the barbarian yanked out the rapiers, bloodless, and tossed them aside. "How was he supposed to know?"

"I left him alive," Svarde replied. "Figure we're square."

Ami laughed, and they looked at the elevators. Neither one was at their level, and even if the pair could get on one, an attentive Gladdring loyalist—or one whose mind had been warped by those Tamas skars—could strand Svarde and Ami between levels.

"We're walking, then," Ami said for both of them, and walk they did.

Common sense suggested Gladdring would put himself on the Sky Palace's upper levels. The geyser-glider method brought the pair close to halfway up, which left plenty of steps to scale. The great slabs ran along the spire's outside, a railing along the length, and some weather protection provided by every level's terraces. A beautiful day meant the climb would be a pleasant one, though not for the people sharing the stairs with Svarde and Ami.

For all their planning, Eujo's sneaky squad hadn't thought about the Sky Palace being, well, a functioning Palace. Even with Kance itself in turmoil, visiting traders, loyal soldiers, politicians, and all the staff needed to care for them still ran around the place, and they passed Svarde and Ami on the stairs with wide eyes, squeaked screams, and at least two separate faintings.

"It's because you look so terrible," Ami said after the second, a willowy man who'd gone paler than anyone

Svarde had ever seen at the sight of his sword. The barbarian had caught the man's fall, set him down on the steps. "Like a petrified, rotten tree, I think."

"At least I'm still all me."

Svarde tapped his face, right where a golden plate wasn't.

"To the misfortune of us all," Ami shot back. "The Dead King had it right, hiding beneath all that armor."

"He smelled awful, Ami. Centuries without a bath, that armor never getting washed."

"It's your future, Svarde."

The barbarian laughed, and the pair picked up their pace. The main mission—retrieving those skars—would be getting underway soon, which meant Gladdring need to be focused on less important things, like keeping his traitorous self alive.

The first step on that self-preservation list was location, and Gladdring hadn't bothered to hide his. Ami and Svarde figured the Tenet would be waiting in Kance's power locus, and, after far too many stairs, with Ami breaking into a sweat despite the cool air—Svarde, among the many bits of life no longer bothering him, didn't perspire—the pair reached the throne room's level. Given up by snapping silver flags in the sunny morning, an overwrought landing bedecked with carved railings and sinewy statues of former queens, the Sky Palace's flagship floor seemed ill-suited to the devastation Ami and Svarde were about to visit upon it.

Not that Svarde cared: if you wanted to keep your pretty things preserved, best not invite battle into your home.

Gladdring offered little resistance. No soldiers barred the pair's path down the hallway, so few that Svarde would've second-guessed their correct choice if the servants bustling about, eyes always drawn to Svarde's black blade, weren't so willing to confirm Gladdring waited down the hall.

Svarde and Ami passed by the elevators, by meeting rooms, toilets, and found most of them full. Kance politicians busied themselves arguing about this and that, as if there wasn't a war going on beneath them, the effect of forced normalcy so off-putting that Svarde, more than once, looked at Ami to confirm this whole thing wasn't some sort of delusion.

Maybe that fall had hit his head harder than he thought.

"Definitely not," Ami said in reply. "Because I'm here and just as confused as you are. With no concussions."

The answer waited in the throne room. A sheet covered the window shattered by Eujo in her escape, the same one Svarde had leapt through. The twin thrones lay empty. The only other furniture was a small table to the entry's right, a glittering silver-and-pearl stone opening. On that table lay breakfast's remnants, several pastries and a coffee carafe left abandoned by the man who, presumably, summoned them.

Gladdring stood near the left throne, all but sagging onto the large chair. His Kance robes were stained with food, rumpled. The Tenet's face was sweatier than Ami's after the climb, hard wrinkles along his eyes. While his elbow lingered on the throne's armrest, Gladdring had both hands in his pockets.

There was no surprise in his stance as the pair walked into the room, their steps echoing on the tile.

"One soldier?" Ami said by way of a greeting. "That's all you sent to stop us? One?"

"Did you kill him?" Gladdring replied, the man's voice as tired as he looked.

"Didn't need to," Svarde answered. He shifted two steps to Ami's right. She had two knives socked away on her person, ready to throw. Not her sharpest skill, but if Gladdring tried to warp their minds, they had an option, and Svarde wanted to give her space to use it. "He'll have a few aches, but he's alive."

"Surprised you care," Ami said, those hands twitching near the knives. "The way you hung us out on Noctia, figured you were a monster."

"On that, I won't argue." Gladdring nodded. "I made mistakes, Ami. We all did. But when you believe you are the Isles' best hope, you must act to keep yourself alive."

"How convenient."

"Convenience has never been my way, nor yours," Gladdring said, then frowned at Svarde. "It seems all my enemies are very hard to kill. Fassle refuses to die, and now, somehow, you stand here after falling far enough to render a normal soul to so much sludge. What have I done to be cursed with such impossible foes?"

"Been an ass, mainly," Ami said. "Your little dalliance with Kance is done, Gladdring. The Queen's struck a bargain, one we'll hold Fassle to. The firewalkers get their home. Fassle gets his skars. You, if you're lucky, get a little farm on Tamas. You can play your games with the pigs."

Gladdring's mouth twitched into a smile, "If the Queen thought I'd go along with that little speech, she wouldn't have sent you."

Svarde narrowed his eyes at that. Gladdring looked so tired, hunched and haggard, that it was hard to imagine him pulling something with the skars, and yet.

"Oh, please say you're planning to fight. That'd just make my day," Ami said, taking a step closer to Gladdring. "Been wanting to stick a knife in your heart since Noctia."

"Ami," Svarde muttered. "Something's not right here."

"I know that's what you want, Ami," Gladdring said, the weight hanging there. "Tamas tells me that. It tells me that you're confident, bloodthirsty, and blind."

Ami didn't bandy another word. The Guardian reached, pulled, and threw the first knife without waiting a breath. The blade struck as Gladdring's line died, burying itself deep into Gladdring's chest. A throw so perfect Svarde glanced Ami's way, surprised.

"I had a lot of time to kill on Noctia," Ami tossed off, her hand drifting to the other knife.

Her target heaved a rattling breath, sank to his knees. His robe reddened. One hand came out from his pocket, reached Ami's way.

"Don't let him—" Svarde started, only for a thin line, a bend in the air, to lance from Gladdring into Ami.

The Guardian twitched, shook, fell. Her skin went pale. Her gold faceplate cracked as it struck the tile.

And Gladdring? Gladdring stood straight, reached towards his chest and pulled the knife free. The former Tenet cast the weapon aside as Svarde angled his black blade for a cutting slash, an attack falling away as footsteps, many footsteps, echoed in the hallway behind.

"You know, her farm analogy wasn't far off," Gladdring said, as Svarde turned and saw those odd politicians, the functionaries, servants, and Palace sculleries running their way. "Only I don't need to go to Tamas, or raise pigs. I have my animals to slaughter, right here."

With ambiguity banished, Svarde went for the obvious. He hollered a Foti battle-cry and charged Gladdring. The man scowled, slipped his hand back inside the blood-stained robe, and Svarde again felt his mind assailed. Ideas slipped in, suggesting Gladdring had too much power to defy, that Eujo was indeed too young to trust, that Fassle would destroy everything.

That the firewalkers didn't deserve a place on the isles.

Svarde might have ceded points to Gladdring on the first few incursions, made at lightning speed as the barbarian crossed the throne room. The last, though, came without Gladdring's usual precision, a blunt lumping of firewalkers in with all other fiends, as terrors to be crushed. Under an assumption so wrong, the Tamas skar's grip slipped, and Svarde regained his fortitude.

Gladdring knew it too. The man cursed, backpedaled. Two strides out, and Svarde swung the blade up, ready to crash it down. Not in some stab or wild cut, but an aim at the only thing that would end this fight.

A schism rattled Svarde's nerves, one sent by Gladdring's left hand, the black stones between his fingers visible now with Svarde so close. The barbarian's muscles shook, his breath vanished as what was left of his lungs curdled, and Svarde knew, if he still had a heart, it would be shriveling.

But one cannot kill a dead man.

Even so, the tremors knocked Svarde's swing off its decapitating course, the blade instead slashing into Gladdring's shoulder, cutting deep and sending the Tenet sprawling to the tiles. Again the robe splashed with red.

This time, the man would have no time to—

Spindly hands grabbed Svarde's left leg. Another body leaped onto the barbarian's shoulders, tripping Svarde forward. A third grabbed his right wrist, holding the black blade, and tried to wrench it free. A fourth skewered Svarde's side with a breakfast fork.

Gladdring's army of addled idiots had arrived.

Svarde caught his fall on his right knee, spinning with

his left hand leading the way. He hit one face after another. Jacked his right elbow back into the chest of the man tugging at that wrist. A snap of Svarde's head broke the nose of the one on his back, driving the wild-eyed woman away, and buying Svarde time to focus on the leg grabber.

Only to find that one twitching, turning gray, and dying. Just like Ami.

Behind the man, rising and looking little worse for wear, was Gladdring.

"My pigs," Gladdring said, as the bloodied ones dove in on Svarde, more bodies burying him beneath their scrabbling hands, biting teeth, kicking feet. "I've come to realize the isles don't want to be saved. The people don't want it. They'd prefer to hold to their petty power, even if it destroys them."

Svarde kept swinging, bashing with the sword, cracking his knees into guts, punching with his fists, and throwing his forehead in one bone-breaking whack after another. Yet the mindless bodies kept coming, and more fingers tugged at the black blade. One lucky pull, one distraction too many, and Svarde's immortal life would disappear.

"But the common man desires less, Svarde. Safety, a chance to raise a family, knowledge that food and water will be there tomorrow?" Gladdring's voice rose. "With these skars, I can give them that, and they will love me for it. What will you give them, Guardian? Death, at your bloody hands?"

Hands Svarde couldn't move much anymore. Too many hands pinned him down, with more pressing his head against the cold tile floor. People sat on his legs, his chest. No longer stabbing him, biting Svarde, just pinning him down. Allowing the ones working Svarde's right hand to pry, little by little, those fingers free from the blade's hilt.

Gladdring loomed over his thralls, staring down at Svarde. "Do you welcome true death, Svarde? Its peace? Or, without this mercy, would you drift forever, a shadow among the living?"

Svarde couldn't answer. Hands clasped his throat, choking off his voice. Instead, he glared, and Gladdring laughed. Gladdring's minions laughed too, their faces all turning to Svarde and mimicking Gladdring's chuckle, down to the last huff.

Two fingers pulled away. Svarde's thumb slipped, hands tugging at it, bending his wrist, biting at his knuckles.

"Goodbye, Svarde," Gladdring said. "I can't say I'm sorry to see you go."

The former Tenet gave Svarde one more curled smile, and lost his head. A clean cut, left to right, and Gladdring crumpled. Behind him, Vis skars in her faceplate shining, stood Ami, slowly bringing her Whent blade back into position. Not that she needed to: Gladdring's horde stopped their clawing, instead blinking, coughing, cursing, and looking lost.

"Sorry, Svarde," Ami said, a thin smile, one Svarde had seen so, so many times on their adventures, lighting on her lips. "Those Noctia skars pack a wallop."

CHAPTER 53
HERO'S DUE

When Maena fell into Wax's back, the Vis didn't feel it. Not like he would've a few moments earlier, before the Noctia skar had taken over the roaring song among the stones, before the skar had reached out to slake its endless thirst by drinking up all those gates, the skars spinning their own songs to keep them open.

The power funneled back into Wax like a thousand well-rested nights, a hundred hot coffees, a dozen smiles from Eujo. He thrummed, inside and out, with what the Noctia skar returned to him, and when Maena smacked Wax from behind, the Vis shrugged off the presence even as he turned all that power to the soul-sucking fiends around him.

His skars still sang in sync, and Wax tilted their attention from those gates to the fiends attacking the Whent warriors. Noctia, again, assumed the lead, snatching out with her bolts to lance every one of the ragged monsters. Foti and Kance came in behind the death goddess this time, at once immolating the fiends from the inside out, and compressing the air around the fiends so the flash fires didn't spread, didn't even last more than a second.

Long enough to kill the fiends, let their remnants flutter to the floor. Whent came next, felling Wax's demand and shoving shut the hole to the pool's chamber. Not just that, though. Wax urged the skar to seal up the broken ground, to fill in the underwater escapes from the pool's chamber. Lock in every possible avenue a fiend might get away, ensuring even those monsters who'd made it through the gates before they slammed shut would be trapped, harmless.

Then, of course, came the wounded.

Wax gave the Vis skar to the injured Rana, bled off enough energy into it—like focusing a thought, or flexing a muscle—to walk Maena back from life's edge. He took the second Vis skar, Catya's, and gave it to the unconscious man. Haggerth, so Jochi called him. Like Maena, the Whent seemed burned and blasted, but still dodging Noctia's final grasp. Now, he'd see tomorrow, and maybe the day, week, year after.

That, at last, earned a hoarse cheer from the warriors around him.

Destiny, as Pan put it, was a burden. At least when it shifted from a life of picking mushrooms and swinging in the jungle to saving the Seven Isles. What Pan never mentioned, though, was how good it felt to fulfill that destiny, to bring that weight off Wax's shoulders, to throw it off with enthusiasm, thrill, delight.

Wax embraced all those and washed each down with more ale. After they'd returned to the Dead City, Jochi had called for a celebration. After, of course, the wounded received their care and the fiend bodies were either burned or butchered. The warlord shuffled Wax away from that, though, and ran him through to a bath and a new set of Whent leathers.

"Heroes must look like heroes," Jochi said as he walked Wax back to the Dead City, to a waiting crowd. "This is the moment you become history, my Vis friend. Own it."

If only Eujo and Bliss had been there to see Wax's grin, the way he raised his hands, one holding the necklace and the skars along with it—Wax kept Catya's hidden beneath his shirt, because how many skars did one hero need?—and soaked in the applause, the clanking ales, the roars from Whent and Noctia who, if Wax had to guess, were cheering their continued survival as much as Wax's part to play in it.

From there, the day, the night, and time itself blended into a roiling party. The reclaimed Vis skars let Wax drink Jochi and most of his friends well under the table, a fact the Vis certainly did not reveal, and as each dipped out, or had to be dragged away, someone else would take their place, wanting to share in the moment, as it came to be called, the Seven Isles was saved.

Routine ended the revelry bit by bit, as repairs, burials, and trade replaced the party. Noctia messages asked for several weeks to fix the ladders spanning the Wound, a timeline too long for Wax, but one he had little control over. The Whent skar was too blunt for precise work, and travel up through the Dark Below to Whent, then a ship south would take almost as long.

Besides, Wax was damn tired. He'd been racing across the isles, gathered the skars, fought fiends and defied a goddess's legacy by shutting those gates. The Dark Below, those caves, weren't where he'd choose to stay, and when Fassle sent a personal message that they'd struck a peace with Kance, that Eujo was alive and in command of her isle, well, the waiting became more bearable.

An idea, a hope, that lasted until an interrupted dinner with Jochi. A Whent scout, declaring visitors were coming, a disheveled group wandering north from Vis. Found barely alive, lost in the tunnels.

Led by none other than Sawi.

CHAPTER 54
THE LAST HUNTER

He stood a shadow before the smoke, the burning city below rising to shroud Quik in a final cloak. The hunter had delivered his war cries, and the Najahn opposing him had the man in their sights, yet they did not fire. No quarrel, no chakram. The lack, his remaining life, brought anger.

Were they humiliating him? Letting Quik stand before an audience to be jeered at?

But no, the Najahn weren't accosting him. Weren't throwing insults his way. Instead, they seemed to be waiting, but for what?

The answer came with armor, without a helmet, with a voulge. Hard eyes and a familiar face. She walked before the soldiers, who parted to let her through without sacrificing their aim. Pavarde, one time bandit hunter and ship captain on Foti, now, somehow, standing here, arms folded and glowering his way.

"Your Lira brought me here," Pavarde said to Quik's stare. "They murdered so many Najahn commanders that I had to leave the seas behind. But even your best need food, rest, a place to sleep. The Third Hand found them, then, and it turns out Lira die like any bandit."

"Why are you telling me this?"

"Because when I saw you last, you wanted to help rid the world of evil. Because when I saw you now, I recognized those claws and their potential." Pavarde tilted her head, as if pointing out the obvious. "You fought for your home and bought their lives with your own. There's more work to be done, Quik. The Najahn need fighters like you for what's coming."

"What's coming?" Quik laughed, waved a gauntlet over the burning city. "What's left?"

"The new order, Quik. The isles ruled, their skars put to better use. There will be resistance, and we will crush it every time it appears," Pavarde's voice fell like iron, buttressed by the hard stares of the Najahn around her. Believers, all. "Your rebellion cost your isle her second city. Kitaye, however, thrives. Not a soul lost to fiends in days. Fresh trade, new opportunities to travel to the other isles. Vis is ready to join the world, will you help?"

Quik measured the distance to Pavarde, figured a certain death would come well before he reached her. A jump off the cliffs lingered as an option, but suicide clamped cold fear on his heart. He wasn't ready for Noctia's oblivion. Not yet.

Which left the offer.

"I don't understand," Quik said. "I fought you. I've killed your soldiers."

"You're a weapon. You did what weapons do." Pavarde smiled, though Quik caught no warmth in it. Like the woman she'd been on Foti, Pavarde had the Najahn spirit through and through. "We have uses for weapons, and rewards."

Quik flashed to the cage. Digging himself out through the sand. Fighting Masayo on the cliffs. He knew all about Najahn rewards, the promises they made and broke without fail. He didn't want to die, but that's what would be waiting for him with Pavarde's poison promise.

Death, though, didn't need to be a waste. Didn't need to come right away.

"If I accept, what do we do now?"

"You come with me, guide us through this city. Show us the traps, any worthwhile treasure. After, we'll discuss in more detail. Over good food and better Tamas ale." Pavarde's smile grew. "Or, if you prefer, some peach wine fresh from Kitaye."

That, after the day he'd had, did sound nice.

And if he was going to slip back inside the Najahn, a coiled spring waiting until he found Fassle's neck within reach . . . Quik would have to play the part.

Vis would have its vengeance, and soon.

CHAPTER 55

HOMEWARD

She rode in the wagon for the first few days, until Maena couldn't stand lying there anymore and forced herself to walk. Her scarred muscle and skin stretched, itched, and told the Rana captain she'd never be one to lead a raid again. Shouldn't go near a battlefield either, if Maena wanted to see the next sunrise.

Not long ago, that thought would've sent her into scoffing bravado, or maybe despair. Now, even without the cloud creature's rosy influence, Maena regarded her present with a healthier view. She lived, she walked, and soon, thanks to Jochi's kindness, she'd go home again. See Rasslebeck, Pennifer. What remained of her old crew.

"Lost in your head again?" came the voice, catching some of its old color now, rising above the rolling cart wheels.

They were still beneath the earth, in tunnels widened and lit by Whent engineers. Would be for another day yet, at least, but with every passing hour Maena swore she could feel a better breeze, smell a fresh flower.

"My head's as empty as it's ever been," Maena replied,

346

looking over to the cart, at the equally battered man within. "And I couldn't be happier about it."

Haggerth sat up, put his chin on the railing. Studied her. Job done, the man was heading home too, given some position by Jochi that wouldn't demand any more dangerous interrogations.

"I still can't believe you're going to get away with it," Haggerth said, the barest hint of a laugh coloring the words. "Kidnapped a scout, nearly destroyed the Dead City by causing a fiend rampage, and yet here you are."

"Thanks to you."

Haggerth blinked. "Say again?"

"Jochi didn't tell you?"

"All the warlord said was he'd forgiven you, that I should forget about the whole thing." Haggerth snorted. "Not a thing I'm capable of doing."

"I saved your life, rockbiter."

Haggerth regarded Maena. The cart rolled on, the oxen pulling it with care through the smoothed stone tunnel. The other Whent around chatted or kept silent, largely avoiding the two burned and odd charges making their way to the surface.

"Odd way of saying you nearly killed me," Haggerth said finally.

"Dragged you out a gate, handed you to Jochi in time to keep that heart of yours beating," Maena said. "Damn heroic of me."

Haggerth shook his head. "I don't believe it."

"Believe what you want. I know the truth."

Again, Haggerth eyed her in that way he had, as if the man were reading her entire soul inside and out. This time, a more genuine smile emerged.

"It's gone, Maena," Haggerth said.

"What is?"

"That look in your eye. That killer's gleam. What's there now, what's there now is someone I'd like to get to know."

Maena laughed, the sound rolling up and down the cave, beautiful and clear.

CHAPTER 56

THE NEXT BATTLE

Given some ale and a straight question, Svarde would admit he had little use for royalty. Of all the isles, Kance was the only one that bothered with it, and so far as Svarde could tell, the idea only brought problems. Yet, as he watched Eujo take her throne—cleansed, quick, of bloody evidence—Svarde couldn't help but get drawn up in the ceremony.

Sure, Eujo was and had been Queen, but here she was a wartime leader. She took her place not in a gilded robe, but in Kance armor sculpted to fit Eujo like a second, shimmering skin. The young Queen looked over soldiers and advisors who took in her first commands without doubt, with good questions, and when the dialogue concluded, Svarde wasn't the first to raise a cheer for Kance, its leader, and a victorious future.

"One you'll never have," Svarde said later, when the throne room had emptied save for a few servants, Eujo's Guardians, Svarde, Ami, and Livier. "You've won the stones, time to make good on your deal."

The big attack on the Sky Palace, the race to capture the

skars, had proved unnecessary. Rendered headless, Gladdring's hold on his various minions dissipated. Eujo said the soldiers barring their way had snapped awake, as if from some dream, and bowed to her. Most of the Sky Palace felt the same, though a few politicians, perhaps feeling their proximity to Gladdring too close to ignore, had delivered swift resignations. Svarde had watched their sniveling flights, making sure to keep his black blade visible to add some speed to their steps.

"I mean to," Eujo said, nodding at Svarde. "But my first speech as sole Queen of Kance can't be a capitulation to Noctia. I need to win their support first."

"At the cost of lives?" Ami asked.

"Najahn lives," Torny muttered, the bandit deploying a neat trick: tossing a knife up and down while chewing an apple.

"It'll be Kance lives if the firewalkers get anxious."

"Why would they?" Eujo said. "Tell them, Ami. I'm going to send an emissary to Noctia today with my terms. If what you've told me is true, he'll accept the deal, and we'll put this war behind us."

"He'll accept," Svarde said. "The man wants his victory, and those skars."

"Then I trust you'll get it done."

The barbarian started, "Say again, your, uh, highness?"

"You, along with Torny and Bliss here, will deliver my terms to Fassle," Eujo said. "Make him agree. End this war."

Torny protested first, saying Eujo would be at risk without the bandit's daggers watching her back. Eujo tossed that off, pointing out Livier and his fellow Vientas assassins were on her side now. Not to mention an isle's worth of loyal soldiers. Bliss didn't offer any objection, save to flash a few fingers, at which Eujo nodded and said nothing. Torny caught the gestures too and stopped her grumbling, narrowing her eyes and matching Bliss's solemn expression.

What was that about?

"Svarde?" Eujo asked. "Will you accept this charge?"

"Of course," Svarde said. "And Ami?"

"I get to keep the firewalkers in line, I expect," the gold-plated Guardian answered. "Which I'm not thrilled about, but I suppose I got to take one head off its shoulders, so I can't complain too much."

"Then it's settled," Eujo said. "Get yourself ready, Svarde, and head to the harbor. The *Storm's Edge* should be ready to sail by tomorrow morning. So many lives ride on you, now."

Svarde laughed, "Your highness, I'm used to it."

CHAPTER 57
SURVIVOR'S QUEST

No Quik.

Sawi and Annalyse said they'd waited as long as they could, until the Najahn landed their ships in Mottilan's harbor and marched their purple and black through its burning streets. Quik never arrived. While most of the Vis city escaped to sea, the rest of their bedraggled band made a harrowing journey north through tunnels long and filled with wandering fiends.

The scientist had used skars, the Vis had used their spears, and they'd still lost several. So many deaths, so much damage, because Fassle and the Najahn had decided to grab power rather than share it.

Wax simmered with Sawi, Annalyse, and Jochi in the Dead City's cathedral. Somehow, discussing what to do next in a changed world came easier with the hulking, dead Guardian looming, the armor's presence bringing weight, focus that Wax found hard to find otherwise.

All he wanted was to drink more ale, talk about his brother, and how Wax had failed him.

Instead, Annalyse and Jochi drove the conversation in a

different way: to the future, not the past, and the thorny reality awaiting the isles in a fiend-free world.

"Fassle's not going to let the Najahn backslide," Jochi said. "He knows all this conquest rests on the fiends and their danger. Once the isles learn the fiends aren't a threat anymore, they'll kick the Najahn out. Or try to."

"You're talking like you're not on his side," Sawi said. "Aren't the Najahn helping you?"

Jochi nodded, "They are, but Fassle isn't the Najahn. There's more reasonable people in their ranks. Tenets not so blind to a more cooperative, better future. We get one of them in the Circle, we might save the isles from erupting into war, or shriveling beneath Fassle's boot."

"You're talking about an assassination," Annalyse said.

"I'm talking about politics," Jochi replied, though the warrior wrapped the words in a feral grin. "Which, on Noctia, do seem to involve a dagger between the ribs more often than not." The warlord turned to Wax. "Fassle's staked his reputation on protecting the isles. There's one person here who can prove him wrong, undercut his claim. That's you."

Wax sniffed, "What, you want me to go up against Fassle?"

"I'm saying you can go up to the Ringed City, find a friend or two among the Najahn, and win their support. You'll have me behind you, and the Aegis's weight too. A true hero for the isles. If Fassle's smart, he'll see his ploy's done and call back his soldiers. If he's not, you brand him an enemy of the peace, and let Yarvick do his thing. The bandit lord won't suffer a liability."

"Can we trust Yarvick?" Annalyse asked.

Jochi shrugged, "He's a thief and a killer, but I've never once heard him talk about taking over the isles. Besides, we don't fight a two-front war. Fassle first. Yarvick, if needed, after." Jochi threw a bearded stare at Wax. "Remember, Vis. Fassle ordered your isle captured. Your brother's death is his doing. Don't let Fassle get away with it."

Oh, Wax wouldn't. The skars, ever whispering, agreed. If Wax had to adopt the hero's mantel to force it, well, he'd already done that. For Quik, for Pan, Wax would finish the journey, bring peace to the isles. And if Fassle didn't agree, well, the Noctia skar, slithering through Wax's soul, was always hungry.

THE FIENDS MIGHT BE GONE, but Wax isn't done yet. With the Najahn attacking Kance and destroying Vis, the one-time Renewal must master the skars and go up against his greatest challenge yet.

Be the first to know when the conclusion to *The Seven Isles* releases, and snag a free story, when you sign up for my author newsletter by clicking the link or scanning the code below:

Acknowledgments

This novel is the product of my family and friends refusing to let a dream die. My wife Nicole, for letting me write in the early mornings and making sure I didn't starve. My brothers and parents for their continual comments, support, and enthusiasm.

And, of course, you, the reader, for giving me a reason to write.

About the Author

A.R. Knight spins stories in a frosty house in Madison, WI, primarily owned by a pair of cats. After getting sucked into the working grind in the economic crash of the 2008, he found himself spending boring meetings soaring through space and going on grand adventures.

Eventually, spending time with podcasting, screenplays, short stories and other novels, he found a story he could fall into and a cast of characters both entertaining and full of heart.

Thanks, as always, for reading!

For more information:
www.adamrknight.com

To Hope and Henry

www.ingramcontent.com/pod-product-compliance
Lightning Source LLC
Chambersburg PA
CBHW022002310726
48972CB00006B/1477